SIGNED
THE
Teammate

BY JESS WRITE JONES

EDUCATED URBANITE
PUBLISHING

Copyright © 2023 by Jess Write Jones
Cover Design by Lamar H./mrsheergenius.com
Images used under license from Shutterstock.com
Model: Danielle R. Armstrong
The text of this book is set in 12-point Garamond
Interior Design by Jessica D. Jones

ISBN: 978-0-9960208-4-8 (trade pbk.) ISBN: 978-0-9960208-7-9 (ebook)

Published by Educated Urbanite Publishing, LLC
P.O. Box 14166, Norfolk, VA 23518

Printed and bound in the United States of America.

I dedicate this book to my aunt, Vanessa K. Robinson, better known as Ms. Write. Through you I got to see what it looks like when someone uses their passion to share their purpose with the world. Thank you for being an inspiration. I love and miss you very much.

I didn't know about you.

That's the first thing you need to read and understand about me.

I ain't know shit about any of you.

But I do now.

Well, I knew about the Wife Bitch, but I thought you all were getting a divorce. We even referred to you as his temporary roommate because you were supposed to move out. We were supposed to be together forever. Imagine my shock when I found out he was seeing four other women. There are five of us; ME, the Roommate Bitch, the White Bitch, the Fake Bitch, and the Dyke Bitch. It hurt to find out about you bitches. For the past couple of months, I have been watching y'all. All of y'all are some using ass bitches. That doesn't excuse Monroe's actions. He is as much to blame for this team as you bitches.How I found out about you is irrelevant. Just know that I know about you. Like, I know the White Bitch is some big-time physical therapist that works out of the gym on 108th and Hilmount. She's only big-time because of her daddy and his reach. Based on her looks, that must be the only reason Monroe messes with her. Ole, basic-ass white bitch. Monroe is only messing with you to get closer to your father. If your father had a pussy, he would have fucked him instead. You're nothing but a means to an opportunity.

Everything about the tall, dark-skinned bitch is fake. Her accent, her hair, her breast, her butt; all that shit is fake. She is just an ignorant hood-ass slut that sells her pussy to lames. It pisses me off that Monroe is throwing all his money away on someone like you. I remember the sacrifices I had to make because Monroe could never do what needed to be done. He treated ME like an obligation and not like the responsibility he created because he was too busy trying to get his dick wet. Excuse after excuse, and then to learn he had the money; he was just using it on you. It's pathetic, and so are you.

All of you bitches disgust me, but The Dyke Bitch takes the whole-fuckin'-cake. You have to be a dyke, because why else would you go out of your way to fuck over a bunch of women who did nothing to you? You have to be a low-ass female to contribute to Monroe's delusion of being some-kind-of franchise owner and for a fantasy-hoe basketball team. You are an enabler and a psychotic bitch. Did you get a kick out of moving us around like pawns? You really out here assisting him with this foolishness all for a fucking check! How do you sleep at night? As a matter of fact, I don't care. FUCK YOU and your whole family.

Collectively, you weak bitches made it easy for Monroe. It is your thirsty, attention-needing, goal-digging actions that resulted in him reducing us to players on some hoe-team:

Point Guard: The Dyke Bitch

Shooting Guard: The Roommate Bitch

Small Forward: ME

Power Forward: The White Bitch

Center: The Fake Bitch

I have always heard that in a relationship, one person always loves the other the most. With everything coming to light, I realized it was me. I loved and trusted him more than he could ever love and trust me. This is how I went blind to his actions. This is how I overlooked the lies, the secrets, and the infidelities. I was too in love and busy to see the truth, but not anymore. I see clearly the arrogance and the mischievousness of Monroe's character. I can't keep allowing his selfishness to affect how he handles his responsibilities when it comes to us. I will hold him accountable. I won't allow him to destroy everything I have created for me and mine.

As for you, bitches, if you ever find out who I am—don't contact me. I only reached out so you could be aware of the fuckery.

Signed,

    The Teammate

CHAPTER ONE

THE MEETING

MARCH 22, 2020

Jamilah swung open the door of her white Lexus and then leaped out with options. She could either act like she never received the letter and then fight like hell to save her marriage, or she could go into this meeting, absorb all the information she could, and then head to her lawyers.

She looked around the parking lot. The strip was packed despite the media urging everyone to stay in their homes. In fact, nothing looked different. Nothing looked suspicious. No one seemed to be looking at her or in her direction. She didn't see anyone but knew someone was watching her. They said so in the letter. They were probably watching her now.

In true Jamilah fashion, she proceeded to give them a show. She smiled and gave her hair a light flip. Her goal was to give off the heir that nothing was bothering her.

But truthfully—Jamilah was bothered.

In fact, she had been bothered for some months. She knew her marriage was going through a rough patch, but it came out of nowhere. She had no inkling that she and her husband had problems. She knew they were sometimes too busy for each other, but that didn't mean they had problems.

You got this girl, she thought to herself. *The show starts now.* She took a deep breath, shut the car door, and then took long, quick strides to the entrance before her mind caught up with her body. She burst through the entrance door like she was being chased. Her actions drew the attention of the dinners. She shot them a *mind-your-business* face and then looked back at the empty parking lot.

Jamilah turned from the entrance and walked further inside the restaurant.

"YOU NEED A MASK!" a little Chinese man yelled at her.

Jamilah frowned her face.

"You have a mask? You can't be here with no mask!"

"Relax," Jamilah replied with an attitude. She opened her purse and fumbled through her things. *I know I put it in here.* She thought of her new life necessity.

"You leave if you have no mask!"

Jamilah pulled out the mask and waved it for the Chinese man to see. "I told you to relax, damn," she snapped.

The Chinese man nodded approvingly. "You must have a mask," he stated, calmer.

Jamilah rolled her eyes. *Got these people all in my damn face*, she thought. She shot a couple of patrons with the *what-the-fuck-you-looking-at*-eyes; that's all they could see now that she had masked up. She turned her attention from their stares to the restaurant's scenery. This was like any Chinese restaurant with its semi-dark ambiance, red accent colors, and dragons. It was weird to see tables marked off. *It ain't even enough people in here for all that,* Jamilah thought. She wasn't impressed with the meeting location. In fact, she was surprised that a white girl would have chosen The White Lion of all the restaurants in Grambleton to meet.

Despite their initial interaction, Jamilah approached the short Chinese man standing behind the podium. She was about to speak, but he cut her off.

"Come this way."

"Hi to you, too," Jamilah replied drily.

The Chinese man said something else, but Jamilah couldn't make it out. Instead of asking him what he said, she stared at him blankly as she tried to decipher his broken dialect.

Realizing that she didn't understand him. He cut his attempt at small talk and repeated his initial request. "Come this way."

"Do you even know me? 'Cause I do not frequent this establishment."

"You here for Ms. Tyler?"

Jamilah frowned. The thought of someone respecting a disrespectful homewrecker ignited something within her. She never respected women who broke up happy homes, and she damn sure didn't appreciate anybody who respected them.

"Come this way," the Chinese man walked away before Jamilah could respond.

Jamilah stood still, but she followed the Chinese man with her eyes. *What if he is like some kind of Willy Wonka Oompa Loompa-type worker for Rebecca? The moment you follow behind him, he gonna start singing about how I fucked up. WAIT A MINUTE! You are Monroe's wife. You ain't fuck up! Them hoes fucked up by fuckin' with me and mine! They crossed the got damn line—not you! Don't let this athletic trainer bitch intimidate you.*

Sensing that Jamilah wasn't behind him, the Chinese man stopped and looked back. He stared at her with an impatient face.

He a mean Oompa Loompa, Jamilah noted. *Do I really want to do this? I can always back out.* Her mind had finally caught up with her body. Even if she did want to follow her mind, her nerves had caught her, and she couldn't move. *I can just be the better woman and walk away. They can have Monroe because hatefulness will get you nowhere. Vengeance is mine, said—*

"You follow?" the Chinese man called from across the restaurant. "You follow," he ordered, waving her in his direction.

Just go. You came this far. Jamilah launched herself forward toward the Chinese man.

"Finally," he commented once she was close enough to him.

Jamilah was about to respond, but she let his slick comment slide. She opted to save her energy if she needed to flip a table on the White Bitch.

"Here," the Chinese man stopped abruptly and pointed at a closed door.

"Here what?" Jamilah questioned. "I'm supposed to go in there?"

The Chinese man nodded.

Jamilah could tell by the slits in his eyes that he was smiling under his mask. This only made the idea of entering a room in the back of the restaurant even more suspicious.

It's a setup, run bitch! Jamilah's feet wouldn't move, though. As a result, she and the Chinese man stood silently by the closed door. He was waiting for her to go inside, and she was waiting to hear about what *was* inside.

"What's behind the door?"

"Oh!" The Chinese man opened the door. "Meeting room."

Jamilah stepped back as the door slowly opened wide.

She felt stupid when she saw that he was right. There was nothing behind the closed door except an empty conference room.

"What would you like to drink?"

Jamilah looked at the Chinese man through squinted eyes. She couldn't shake the idea that he was up to something. "Water," she finally answered. "In a bottle…a sealed bottle."

"Go in," he motioned to her. "Others here shortly."

"Others?"

He nodded his head. He extended his hand, motioning her into the room.

Jamilah didn't move. "Others?" she repeated.

His stance never changed. He simply opened his eyes wider as though that made him friendlier.

The letter told her about *the others*, but she didn't imagine meeting them all. She thought she was there to meet one person—The White Bitch. Jamilah skimmed her mind. Even with it taking The White Bitch forever to confirm their meeting, she never mentioned anyone else being in attendance.

"Please…please," he stated. He added a bowing action to his request.

Jamilah gave in and walked into the room.

Relieved, the Chinese man immediately shut the door behind her and walked away quickly.

The meeting room had a different ambiance than the rest of the restaurant. The meeting room looked like a standard conference room. No sign of the color red, no images of dragons, or anything that would indicate that Jamilah was in a Chinese restaurant. Instead, there was a long, wooden table that could seat up to twelve people, but there were only five place settings. One was at the head of the table, and the other settings were to the right and the left of the table.

Am I meeting all five of them? she pondered to herself. She immediately felt blindsided, but then again, could she really trust a group of bitches, who were fuckin' her husband. As her banter continued in her head, she set her sights on her seat. She walked to the head of the table, feeling confident in her power move. It should be evident to all these hoes that she was the wife.

Jamilah sat down and made herself comfortable at the table when a white woman walked into the room holding two glasses of water.

"I asked for bottled water." Jamilah glanced up at the white woman and then continued rummaging through her purse. *A white girl,* Jamilah thought as she took a second look. It was indeed a white girl. *White women don't work in Chinese restaurants?*

The white woman wore a pair of khaki pants with a blue Nike polo shirt. She had her blonde hair with dark roots pulled into a messy bun on top of her head. A small gold earring sat on her left pointed nostril. She looked like the type of person who would take off running at any moment to keep their heart rate up.

"They don't have bottled water here," she stated, placing a glass before Jamilah.

Jamilah looked at the cup suspiciously. "Do you work here?"

The girl smirked. "Not at all."

Jamilah pushed the glass away from her.

The girl looked down at Jamilah with a smile on her face.

"Don't stand over me," Jamilah requested.

The smile on the white woman's face faded away. She looked over at Jamilah curiously.

Jamilah was pretty with her flawless brown skin and long, bouncy hair that was cut into layers. She was a slim woman, but not tall at all, in fact she was far from what Rebecca had expected. Rebecca had assumed that Monroe would have married someone *beautiful*. Someone who was both pretty on the inside and pretty on the outside. Having just met Jamilah, she instantly *knew* why Monroe was stepping out on her. To Rebecca, Monroe was nice, kind-hearted, and considerate. She couldn't imagine him being with a woman that could look through people the way Jamilah was looking through her.

"You can move anytime now," Jamilah snapped.

The girl sat down in the chair farthest from Jamilah.

Jamilah looked at the cup and pushed it even farther away. "Who are you?" she questioned the girl with her nose turned up.

"I expected you to have ordered something fancy, like a sake or a white wine."

"Excuse me?"

"To look at you, you just seem like the type."

Jamilah was amused by the girl's audacity, "And what type is that?"

"The type to drink alcohol in a fancy glass with your pinky finger raised high."

"Actually, I would expect that from The White Bitch," Jamilah replied.

11

"You are The White Bitch, right?"

"I prefer Rebecca."

"Rebecca," Jamilah frowned. Saying her name left a sour taste in her mouth. Looking at Rebecca confused the hell out of Jamilah. She didn't know whether to be relieved, disgusted, or disappointed. When she first learned about *The White Bitch*, she imagined her to be some kind of Anna Nicole Smith meets Kim Kardashian hybrid. She thought she would be built with plastic parts: fake breasts, ass, and lips. She would be pretty, prissy, and perhaps even delicate. However, the woman in front of her was nothing of her imagination. Rebecca was a regular-ass white girl. She looked to have pale skin that was hiding under a layer of makeup that didn't quite match her complexion. She wasn't shapely and didn't even have a flare for fashion. It was hard to believe that Monroe had stepped out on her for…this.

What the hell are you thinking? Jamilah thought of her husband's actions. *Why her?*

"You're The Roommate Bitch."

"The Wife," Jamilah quickly corrected her. "I am Monroe's wife."

"Potato…Pa-ta-toe."

"No…no…no, there is definitely a big difference. I am Monroe's wife, first and foremost. All the other shit you think you know is just that—shit!" Jamilah stared Rebecca down. "I'm wifey," she stated, pointing at herself. "Remember that." As Jamilah spoke, her words left her sitting taller and confidently in her seat. She crossed her legs and folded her hands over her knee.

Rebecca shrugged her shoulders. "I know you can't be the tall, dark-skinned bitch."

Jamilah frowned. Everything about Rebecca's comment offended Jamilah. "I just told you who I was; were you not listening?"

"It has nothing to do with your skin color, Sweetheart."

"Sweetheart?" Jamilah frowned. "Call me by my name."

Rebecca chuckled. "You're snippy."

"Snippy?" Jamilah repeated. *I can't believe I was nervous about confronting this bitch. I ought to jump across the table and drag the shit out of her.* A smirk crossed Jamilah's face. "You know that I know that you've been fuckin' my husband, right?"

"Monroe and I—"

"Monroe is a married man, Rebecca. He isn't single, so there is no you and Monroe. There's Monroe and me because I am his wife."

Rebecca smirked.

"I'm not making a joke. I am serious. Don't come telling me anything about you and my husband because there is no you and him."

Rebecca put her glass of water on the table. "If you don't want to hear it from me, why come?"

"I need receipts."

"The letter is an itemized receipt," Rebecca stated. "What more do you need? Blood? Do we need to take a lie detector—"

"Sarcasm doesn't help this...so stop it. I deserve much more than sarcasm."

Rebecca had played this encounter out in many ways. It always included Jamilah saying, 'I'm the wife this, and I'm the wife that...blah, blah, blah'. The meeting had just started, and she was already tired of hearing it.

Jamilah burned a hole into Rebecca. She wasn't amused by the approach Rebecca was taking. Her arrogance warranted an ass-whoopin'. She wanted to jump across the table on principle, but Jamilah practiced self-restraint.

"AM I LATE?!"

Rebecca and Jamilah both broke their *stares* and looked to the door.

A tall, dark-skinned woman walked in. She wore a tight-fitting dress that revealed all the curves she had to offer; big breasts, wide hips, narrow waist, thick thighs, and it all seemed to pop out but still stay unified in its movements. Just looking at the dress made Jamilah mad. She could never wear such a dress; it was too revealing and went against her conservative demeanor. Not to mention, she wouldn't be able to fill out this dress like this woman.

Jamilah looked at Rebecca. "Who the fuck is she?"

"OHHHHH!" the tall woman shouted excitedly. "You must be Monroe's wife. Very pretty."

Jamilah took note of her broken dialect. *Typical Monroe to fuck a bitch that can't talk*, she thought. Jamilah held a death stare as the woman strutted through the room.

"I once extended my services to Monroe and you," she stated without missing a breath.

"WHAT THE FUCK DID YOU SAY?" Jamilah jumped up from her seat.

The mocha chocolate woman waved Jamilah's stance away. She was confident that her six-foot frame would be no match for Jamilah. "Oh, sit down! We no animals who fight. We make love and talk." She walked to the right side of Jamilah and sat down directly beside her.

Rebecca watched closely as Jamilah stood for a few seconds and slowly eased her way back into her seat. Watching Jamilah's submission was highly entertaining, considering how Jamilah had been treating her.

Jamilah wasn't paying Rebecca any attention anymore. Her eyes were glued to the Black woman sitting beside her. *This bitch should have sat the fuck away from me like the White Bitch,* Jamilah thought. The longer she stared, the harsher the frown on her face appeared. *This bitch is definitely Monroe's type.*

"I'm Deadria. And you are the wife?" she covered her mouth. "No, you are…" she looked up, trying to recall something. "Oh! The Roommate Bitch!" she laughed loudly.

"No," Jamilah corrected her. "I am the wife. You had it right the first time."

Deadria laughed harder at Jamilah's attempt at correcting her.

Jamilah rolled her eyes at Deadria. Everything about her pissed Jamilah off. Even her accent just sounded like broken English rather than anything exotic.

Deadria pointed at Jamilah and then looked at Rebecca, who sat stone-faced. She couldn't believe Rebecca didn't find this as hilarious as she did.

Rebecca didn't want to laugh, but Deadria's laughter was infectious, and she couldn't help but chuckle, too.

Deadria sighed out the final remains of her laughter. She put her purse down in the empty chair next to her. She looked back at Jamilah and chuckled again. She then looked over at Rebecca, "And you are obviously The White Bitch. How cute are those names? I'm the tall, mocha chocolate authentic woman," she added cat claws for the full effect of her persona.

Jamilah, unamused, replied, "You're actually the tall, dark-skinned fake bitch."

Deadria used her fingers to claw at Jamilah. "You're catty."

"Y'all bitches are fucking my husband. How should I act?"

"Oh, don't be jealous. I think you're gorgeous. Big ample breasts, wide hips. I asked Monroe to join you in bedroom."

"WHAT BITCH?!" Jamilah slammed her hand on the table.

The suddenness of the act startled Rebecca. Initially, she thought that Jamilah was a coward. Why else hadn't she contacted Deadria? However, at this moment, her assumption went out the window.

"I saw a picture of you one day," Deadria continued to speak to Jamilah as though they were long-lost friends.

Jamilah recognized the familiarity that Deadria was using, and it turned her stomach. She stared at Deadria in disgust.

"Let's eat!" Deadria clapped her hands. "CAN WE GET SERVICE?!" she hollered at the top of her lungs, hoping to get someone's attention. It was clear, Deadria was truly unbothered. She reached for the glass of water that was given to Jamilah. "Whose water? May I? I'm so thirsty." She took a long gulp and then came up for air. She looked down at the table at Rebecca. "Why are you sitting so far away?"

Rebecca hunched her shoulders. "From the letter, I imagined you having a heavy accent and mumbling your words."

Deadria laughed. "No, I speak clear."

"Lies," Jamilah mumbled.

Deadria cut her eye at Jamilah. "I can cut it on and cut it off."

"Sounds fake to me," Jamilah spoke up.

Rebecca saw Deadria's glare at Jamilah and smirked. "Good to know," she stated more to herself. Rebecca was feeling confident with an ally in the room, so she moved to the seat closer to Jamilah.

Jamilah looked left at Rebecca as she got comfortable in her new seat. She leaned close to Rebecca. "It's funny that you invited her."

Rebecca smirked. "It's funny that you didn't." She sat back smug in her seat like she had a leg up on Jamilah.

CHAPTER TWO

KNOWING YOUR POSITION
MARCH 22, 2020

"The food was good," Rebecca stated, tossing her napkin on the table.

"It was. What did you order again?" Deadria asked, looking at what was left on Rebecca's plate.

"A veggie lo mein, and I added shrimp." A satisfied smirk rested on her face.

Jamilah frowned at the sight. She played nice and ordered food with everybody, but she wasn't there for friendship and damn sure wasn't there for the food. "We are not here for a reunion. You bitches are sleeping with my husband, and I don't appreciate it."

Deadria made a sad face. "Aww, are you really mad?"

"You don't think I should be?"

"Black men have a hard enough time in this world. Leave him be."

"Leave him be?" Jamilah repeated, offended by the idea of letting Monroe off. "Why are you okay with fuckin' a married man?"

Deadria paused and thought about the question. She shrugged her shoulders. "I'm okay with fuckin' married women, too."

Rebecca laughed.

Jamilah shot Rebecca a look.

The suddenness of the look caused Rebecca to stop laughing.

"What harm has it really caused any of us?" Deadria questioned. "If it wasn't for...what is her name? The one that sent the letter. What is her name again?"

"We don't know," Rebecca answered. "She just kept writing 'ME' in capital letters, like her way of showing importance."

"If not for her, we no know. You mad, you know? Then forget! Everybody is important; let's be important together."

"Monroe is not some single man. He is a whole married man, and you bitches are really nonchalant about our marriage like we didn't take a vow in front of God and our families!"

Deadria stared silently at Jamilah. She then glanced at Rebecca to see if Rebecca was moved by Jamilah's emotions. When she noticed that Rebecca wasn't emotional, she felt obligated to show Jamilah some empathy. "Awww," was all Deadria could think to offer her. She patted Jamilah on the knee. "It's okay," she added.

Rebecca chuckled.

Jamilah knocked Deadria's hand off of her.

Deadria looked at Jamilah, surprised that she didn't accept her act of kindness. "You okay?"

"What do you think?"

"I think it is cute of Monroe to put us on a team. I no been on team, but now I am on team," she clapped excitedly. "I wonder how I made cut. I wish I knew basketball. What is my position?"

"I know a little about basketball," Rebecca replied. She, too, was amused at Monroe's team. "Sitting here with you all. I thought it was kind of interesting knowing the positions and now experiencing your personalities."

Jamilah rolled her eyes.

Rebecca chuckled and asked Jamilah, "You don't see the creativity in this."

"No, I don't."

"Your husband is a basketball player. You never took an interest in his career?"

"I know Monroe's career. I just don't see the amusement."

Rebecca looked at Jamilah skeptically. *No wonder he was stepping out on her. She doesn't take an interest in him.* "Okay, think of it like this," Rebecca reached into her pocket and removed a white paper. It was the letter. It looked like it had been folded, unfolded, read, and re-read about a thousand times. Rebecca tried to smooth it against the table, but her copy was beyond worn.

Jamilah noticed writing on Rebecca's copy beside each of their names.

She leaned forward to get a better view. "What does that say?"

"Just some notes I took," Rebecca stated. Her enthusiasm was showing. "Okay, so for you, Jamilah, we all know you are Monroe's wife," she stated condescendingly. "But according to this paper, he has you listed as a shooting guard."

"Is that a good thing or a bad thing?"

Rebecca looked up at Jamilah. A giant smile appeared. "It depends on how you want to take it."

"She will take it bad," Deadria commented.

"You don't know *how* I will take it."

"You take everything bad. I try to console you; you took that bad."

"Who are *you* to be consoling me?"

"See."

"You don't console shit!" Jamilah snapped.

Deadria held up her *cat* fingers at Jamilah. "What does a shooting guard do?" she simultaneously asked Rebecca.

"Shooting guards are number two on a team of five. Their purpose is to score points. You see them in the paint, driving to the goal."

Jamilah smirked. "I do drive to the goal. I made Monroe successful," she stated boastfully. She was pleased that Monroe appreciated all she had done for him. When they first met, he had a one-track mind. All he wanted was to be a basketball player. With her guidance, Monroe brought and renovated abandoned homes, and then he turned them into low-income family neighborhoods. That was his way of giving back to the community and their way of creating another stream of income. He had even started a nonprofit basketball camp that he named Shooting Goals. It fits that Jamilah was his shooting guard; together, they were shooting goals. With her vision for him, he was now a well-rounded businessman.

Rebecca raised her eyebrows, shocked at Jamilah's audacity. *Can you really make a person?* Rebecca wondered. *And if she can, why would she make a man that would cheat on her?*

"DO ME NEXT!" Deadria enthusiastically shouted.

The moment of love and appreciation that Jamilah was floating in went out the window. Deadria reminded Jamilah that she and Monroe weren't on a team alone. There were four other women in *their* equation.

"He has you listed as the center," Rebecca stated. "They are usually bigger and taller than everybody on the team."

Jamilah laughed. "Humongous."

"Oh! You like fat jokes, eh?" Deadria asked rhetorically. "Have you heard the one about your husband's fat dick deep in my pussy?"

Jamilah jumped up from her seat. "WATCH YOUR FUCKIN' MOUTH!"

Deadria took her time standing up to address Jamilah. "I no watch my mouth. Your husband watches my mouth," Deadria replied seductively. "I can be ugly."

"I see!" Jamilah replied, mocking Deadria.

Rebecca sat in her chair with wide eyes. She liked watching the back-and-forth banter between the two women, but she didn't want to see them fight. "Ladies," Rebecca stated gently as she stood from her seat, too. "Let's keep it cordial."

Deadria, still staring at Jamilah, seductively licked her lips and blew her a kiss.

"You are such a disrespectful bitch!" Jamilah spewed her pent-up venom. "I've tried to talk to you bitches, but I can't. You take this so lightly like I'm supposed to be okay with sharing my husband with you."

Deadria waved Jamilah's speech away. She sat back down—truly—unbothered and picked up her drink. "Sex is sex," she stated after a sip. "Married women put so much in it. Same-married women have no sex with their husbands like they okay with it. I no fuck Monroe to hurt you. I fuck Monroe because he pays me for services. Services he should get from you!" Deadria put her glass back down on the table. "With you excuses… me period, me head, me…me…me…you told Monroe your teeth hurt and you no able to suck dick. You no use teeth for head. I made four hundred dollars that night. I sucked dick with no hands or teeth," Deadria laughed. "Easy money." She waved her hand at Rebecca to get her attention. "Sit," she ordered, "Continue."

Jamilah was standing over Deadria. Her mind was racing. To know that her husband was sleeping with other women and pillow-talking with these hoes about her business, left her disappointed and embarrassed.

Deadria waved her hand at Rebecca again. "Go on!" her tone slightly elevated.

Rebecca looked at Jamilah. "Are you okay?"

"She's fine," Deadria answered for Jamilah. "She no be here if she no want to hear truth. Now, go on," she ordered Rebecca again.

Rebecca looked down at her paper. *Even if Jamilah isn't the perfect wife, that doesn't mean we have to gloat in her face.* Rebecca looked from Jamilah to Deadria and thought to herself, *I wonder if I would subject myself to this type of thing.*

"Go on," Deadria insisted, snapping Rebecca out of her thoughts.

Rebecca glanced over at Jamilah. She didn't want to finish going through the list, but she didn't want to ignore Deadria either.

"Go on," Deadria insisted again.

Rebecca was about to continue when the three women heard a soft knock at the door.

"Here we go," Jamilah huffed and asked Rebecca rhetorically, "You're expecting someone else, aren't you?"

Rebecca looked at Jamilah with sad eyes. "Another teammate," she stated regretfully.

"Which one?" Deadria's eyes lit up.

Before they could determine the identity of the late arrival, the door opened, and a soft feminine voice said, "Hello…hello." It was the type of greeting that alerted people of the appearance of someone who came in peace. Unfortunately, this type of greeting was not welcomed in this room.

"Wait!" Rebecca stated, clearly caught off guard. "Who are you?" Rebecca didn't know Monroe's assistant personally. Still, she knew this tall, slim, light-skinned woman walking into the room was not her. "Are you ME?"

"Am I what?" the pleasantry dropped from her dialogue. The smile she wore was replaced by a look of confusion. "What did you just say to me?"

Jamilah leaned forward in her seat. "Avie?!" She couldn't believe her eyes, "What are you doing here?"

Deadria sat at the table delighted. She picked food from her plate and watched the scene before her as though she was at a movie. She leaned over and tapped Jamilah's arm to get her attention. "How you know her?"

"Of all people," Jamilah said in a whisper. "You're the last person I would have expected to see."

"Hey," Deadria tapped Jamilah's arm again. "Who is she?"

Jamilah didn't respond. She was too in shock to see Avie in front of her. She finally tuned back into the irritating sensation of Deadria tapping her arm. "WHAT?!" she hollered. "What do you want?"

Deadria asked, "You know her?"

Jamilah looked back at Avie. "She's my husband's assistant."

Rebecca shifted her body to look directly at Jamilah. "That's not Monroe's assistant."

Jamilah folded her arms across her chest. Rebecca's audacity was remarkable. "I know my husband, and I know who his assistant is, and Avie is his assistant."

Rebecca turned in her seat to look at the woman beside her. Rebecca was perplexed. She looked across the table at Deadria. Deadria wasn't paying Rebecca any attention, but she held the same look of confusion as Rebecca.

"I'm just going to sit right here," Avie pulled out the seat Rebecca had initially been sitting in. She was about to say something else to Rebecca, but she caught a glance of Jamilah's dagger eyes that had killed the moment.

To say Jamilah was staring was an understatement. She was giving Avie a death glare. She had even sat up in her seat, and the death glare had turned into a snarl.

Avie felt uneasy walking into the room. She tried to convince herself that coming to the meeting was the right thing to do. However, the way everyone stared at her made her feel otherwise.

"BITCH, YOU BEEN IN MY HOUSE!"

Deadria's eyes widened, and then she laughed loudly at Jamilah's outburst.

Rebecca looked between Jamilah and Avie. "How do you all know each other?"

"You friends?" Deadria added to the question. She didn't wait for an answer. She took off with her own assumptions. "You fucked your friend's man?" Deadria seemed to cackle louder than before.

"We're not friends," Avie asserted. "I just know Jamilah as Roe's wife."

Jamilah was offended. "You don't know me, Avie?" Jamilah moved to the edge of her seat. "You ain't been in my house?"

Rebecca noted Jamilah positioning herself to launch. As a result, Rebecca slid her chair ever-so-slightly out of the line of attack.

"I know of you, but I don't really know you, Jamilah," Avie said as though it was common knowledge. "You're Roe's wife. That's all I know. You act like we friends."

Jamilah covered her eyes with her hands. "I CAN'T BELIEVE THIS!" she yelled into her palms. She looked back up at Avie and shook her head.

Rebecca continued to ease her chair out of the way.

Jamilah stared silently at Avie. She had written Avie off as simply a family friend that Monroe had felt obligated to help. It never crossed her mind that Avie could be more; she didn't even seem like the type. Avie seemed like a woman about her business. Although she was familiar with Monroe and his mother, Jamilah remembered Avie arriving at the interview fifteen minutes early with her resume and cover letter. "Hoes don't carry cover letters," Jamilah randomly blurted out.

Everyone looked at Jamilah like *she* had lost her mind.

"Avie, are you fuckin' my husband, too?"

"I read the letter," Avie stated. "I know that's why you invited me," she stated to Rebecca, "But no. Hell no! I ain't—" Avie shook her head, nonverbally pleading her case. She made it a point to look into the eyes of everyone around the table, but she abruptly paused when she looked at Deadria.

Deadria's noted Avie's change of demeanor when the two women made eye contact. "You know me?" Deadria asked. Deadria looked at the other two women in the room. She was trying to determine if they, too, were noting Avie's look at her.

Seeing Deadria had reminded Avie of what she had done the night before. Not that her actions could have been easily overlooked. One would never forget a night like her last night, but to be seated across from Deadria was eerie.

"I know you?" Deadria asked Avie again.

Avie slowly shook her head no, but the two women maintained eye contact.

"Then why are you here, Avie?"

The sudden boisterous sound of Jamilah's anger snatched Avie out of her thoughts. Avie looked at Jamilah. "I came because she invited me," she replied, as she pointed at Rebecca.

"I didn't invite you," Rebecca stated.

"Why lie? I talked to you on the phone. You sent me the letter."

"You said you didn't get it."

"Because I didn't and that's when you emailed the letter to me."

"You did what?" Deadria questioned Rebecca. Deadria noted how Avie was looking at her as she was waiting for Rebecca to reply to her concern.

"No, I invited Monroe's secretary," Rebecca explained.

"If you ain't fuckin' Monroe, then why even come?"

Avie looked at Jamilah. "This is The White Lion. I wasn't about to turn down eating here. They have the best lo mein."

"She just ate the lo mein," Deadria stated, pointing at Rebecca's plate. Deadria knew it was something odd about Avie, by the way she kept looking at her, but Deadria opted to play nice with her.

Avie half-smiled. She, too, decided to play nice despite her initial raction.

"I invited Monroe's assistant to the meeting," Rebecca continued to state her case. "I don't know who you are."

"I work for Roe, but I ain't his assistant."

"Then why accept the invite?" Rebecca questioned.

"Did you not hear what I said about the food? Duh," Avie replied, nonchalantly.

"She is his assistant," Jamilah insisted.

"No," Avie corrected Jamilah. "I am not his assistant. I did earn a scholarship through Shooting Goals, but I—"

Jamilah slammed her hand on the table. "The scholarship was bullshit! It was just a reason for you to be in my damn house, fuckin' my damn husband."

"Scholarship?" Rebecca questioned. "How old are you?"

"SHHH!," Deadria motioned for Rebecca to watch the *show* in front of them.

Avie frowned. "Monroe is just my guy—"

"Your *guy*?" Jamilah interjected.

Avie surrendered with her hands in the air, "It's just a phrase, Jamilah, damn!"

"Monroe is not your *guy*," Jamilah reiterated.

"We grew up together. My momma knew his momma," Avie tried to explain.

"You fucked Monroe, eh?"

Avie looked across the table at Deadria. The sight of her made her queasy. It wasn't that Deadria was ugly. She was just a walking reminder and t turned Avie's stomach.

Rebecca noted the look on Avie's face. "Are you okay?" she asked, as she grabbed a glass of water from the table. "Here," she stated. "Drink this water."

Avie grabbed the glass and took a big gulp. "Suddenly, I'm not feeling too good."

"She's gaslighting," Jamilah observed. "She's been called to the carpet and now she's *so* sick. Ain't nothing wrong with that child."

"WAIT, WAIT WAIT!" Deadria grabbed her letter and skimmed through the page. She looked up at Avie, "You ME?"

"You ME?" Avie frowned. She motioned for Rebecca to pour more water. "What does that even mean?" She looked around the table, waiting for someone to answer her.

"No, no, no, no, you, The Dyke Bitch, eh?" Deadria questioned Avie. "You fuck both boys and girls," the question lingered awkwardly. "You a pretty stud with a hard demeanor."

"She does have a hard face," Jamilah added.

"A hard face, bi—" Avie stopped herself. "She's Roe's wife," Avie reminded herself in an attempt to remain calm.

"You're damn right I'm his wife!"

Rebecca continued to look at Avie confusingly.

"The Dyke Bitch!" Deadria liked the way the name rolled off of her tongue. She repeated it again, "The Dyke Bitch."

Avie grunted. "I'm not a dyke."

"Call a spade a spade."

"Jamilah," Avie called her name warningly. "When Rebecca called and invited me—"

"I didn't call you," Rebecca interjected.

Avie continued, "to this meeting and then I read the letter, did I not try to reach out to you beforehand? I tried to talk to you in your house. I tried to call you and everything."

Rebecca looked up at the ceiling, and she suddenly had an epiphany. She turned to Jamilah, "Is that your MO? Confront and harass me, a white woman."

"White Bitch," Deadria subtly corrected her.

Rebecca looked at Deadria.

Deadria shrugged. "You White Bitch. She didn't call you White Woman."

Rebecca returned her gaze to Jamilah and continued on with her epiphany. "But you don't say nothing to these other bitches."

"Excuse you," Avie stated. "I'm not a bitch!"

"You know what I meant."

"Use your words then," Avie suggested.

"My point is, she damn near harassed me; coming to my job, calling my phone, but when it comes to you...*women*, she either avoided you or didn't even try to address you at all. Why is that?"

Through Rebecca's rant, Jamilah never took her eyes off Avie. Avie's presents hit differently. Jamilah tried to think about all the moments she saw Avie with her husband. She couldn't recall their interactions raising any suspicions. Suddenly Jamilah looked at Rebecca. It had just registered what Rebecca was trying to insinuate. "Excuse me?"

"You never attempted to contact any of these women, but you try to harass me."

"The White Bitch," a smirk rested on Deadria's face after repeating Rebecca's name several time. She shrugged when she noticed everyone looking at her. "Reparations," she offered as an explanation.

Avie chuckled at Deadria's persistence to call Rebecca by *her* name.

"Don't let the tan skin fool you," Rebecca warned Jamilah.

Jamilah sucked her teeth.

Deadria hollered with laughter. "TAN SKIN!" she attempted to coax Jamilah into the joke by hitting her leg. "She said tan skin."

Jamilah was not amused. She sat back with her drink in her hand and took a sip. She peered over the brim of her cup at the bitches in front of her.

"Jamilah," Avie called to her. "I really don't know what this is, but Monroe is family to me, nothing more. If anything, he's like a real-life blood brother, with his mother being my mother type of relationship."

Jamilah clenched her jaw.

"Could be incest."

Everyone looked at Deadria.

Deadria shrugged her shoulders. "Family fuck." She began to make a humping gesture in her seat and grunted loudly. Afterward, she cackled from a deep, hearty place.

"I'm not out here giving my WAP away to everybody," Avie insisted over Deadria's laughter. "And definitely not to no Roe."

Jamilah folded her arms across her chest. "You act like that soothes my mind. According to this letter, you the bitch that knew about all of

Monroe's hoes."

Avie exhaled deeply as she stood up from her chair. "I came for the food, but all of this is too much."

"Uh oh, she out'ha seat," Deadria instigated.

Jamilah stood up. "And what are you about to do?" She put her glass down on the table.

"About to leave," Avie replied. "I didn't know about any of this."

Deadria hummed. "She ain't doing nothing. She scared."

"Of what?" Avie was coached to keep her cool, but these women pushed her buttons. Avie looked back at Jamilah. The two women stared at each other like heavyweight boxers listening to the ref recap the rules.

"Relax, you guys," Rebecca chimed in. "Tell her to stay," Rebecca stated to Jamilah.

"She can go," Jamilah stated dismissively.

"I said I ain't want no smoke with you, Jamilah, and I meant it," Avie stated.

"Then why come?"

"Because—you know what. I know why I came, and it wasn't for any of this."

"You the one that stood up like you were ready for an ass-whoopin'," Jamilah replied as she eased back into her seat.

Avie laughed.

"What's funny?"

"You."

"Me?"

"Yes, you, Jamilah. You out here acting like you are ready to *see* me, but you have been avoiding me." Avie looked between Rebecca and Deadria. "Meanwhile you are in here eating with women who really did fuck your husband."

"And did," Deadria agreed.

Avie shook her head. "How lame is that?" She pushed her chair in and began walking to the door. "You are doing all this over, Roe," she chuckled. "Goofy asses." She walked out before anyone could reply.

CHAPTER THREE

THE WRONG POINT GUARD
MARCH 22, 2020

The room was quiet as they all processed Avie's last words.

"Was she saying Monroe is a goofy ass, or was she calling us goofy ass?" Rebecca questioned.

No one even bothered to explain.

"I've never met her," Rebecca continued talking. "Have y'all met her before? I know you have, Jamilah, but I have never seen her."

"You invited her, eh?"

"She invited everybody else," Jamilah mumbled.

"Yes and no," Rebecca replied.

"What does that mean even?" Deadria shook her head. "You invite, or no?"

"I did, *but* I didn't," she explained. "I had my secretary invite Monroe's secretary to dinner."

"Why does a regular-ass athletic trainer have a secretary?"

Rebecca smiled. "I'm far from a regular-ass athletic trainer, Jamilah. I'm sure you've researched and know about me."

Jamilah frowned. "Research you for what? You ain't shit."

As the two continued to hurl insults at one another, Deadria sat back in her seat and watched quietly. It was funny to her that both women represented a certain societal status quo. Yet, they both sat across from her looking less than. At this moment, Deadria recalled a conversation that she once had with her older brother. He said, 'Wealthy people always looked broke, and broke people always look wealthy.' *My brother was right*, Deadria thought. *Considering who her father is, Rebecca got the nerve to walk around looking like that. She doesn't dress like that when in his presence. That bitch is dressed to the nines.* Deadria grew irritated listening to Jamilah question Rebecca, so she decided to get them back on topic: "What happened to the big-boned assistant?"

Jamilah stopped her taunting of Rebecca, "You met Kelly before?"

"That's who I thought I was inviting. The big one. I didn't know there was a skinny one."

"Big one, no dyke."

Rebecca agreed. "She didn't give off a dyke vibe…at least not to me."

"Avie doesn't give off a dyke vibe either," Jamilah stated matter-of-factly. "She just has those arms."

"She has Angela Bassett's arms. Tight and toned." Deadria looked at her own arms.

"Kind of flabby," Jamilah commented.

Deadria lowered her arms. "Bitch."

Jamilah smirked.

"In my line of work, I always see women with sculpted arms. It doesn't mean they are dykes," Rebecca commented. "Just mean they are heavily involved on arm day."

"They make her look masculine," Jamilah added.

"Monroe like strong women."

Jamilah cut her eye at Deadria. "Anyway, the letter writer wasn't calling Avie a dyke because of her sexual preference per se."

"The letter writer got it wrong," Rebecca concluded.

"Letter writer didn't get it wrong," Jamilah corrected. "Avie is Monroe's secretary. I should know; I am his wife."

Rebecca and Deadria shared a glance and then a giggle.

"You no know about us, *Wife*."

"Fuck you, okay."

"When?" Deadria blew a kiss at Jamilah.

Jamilah rolled her eyes, disgusted at the thought. "That bitch has been all up in my house!" Jamilah raised her voice.

Deadria was still trying to seek clarification. "So, big-boned girl, not his assistant?"

"I've been in your house."

"She was his—" Jamilah paused. She looked at Rebecca, "What did you say?"

"I've been in your house," Rebecca confessed. "And I ain't his secretary."

"I no been in the house. Is it nice?"

Rebecca proceeded to answer Deadria.

Unfortunately, Rebecca never noticed Jamilah's quick movement.

Jamilah had jumped up from her chair and grabbed a handful of Rebecca's hair. She had yanked Rebecca so hard that both she and her chair hit the floor.

Jamilah stood over her and proceeded to punch Rebecca in the face.

Deadria watched with bright eyes. She was impressed by Jamilah's quick reflexes and stance. Nevertheless, Deadria casually pushed herself back from the table. "Aww, poor white bitch," she grumbled as she made her way to the other side of the table. "Jamilah let her go. She know now." Deadria stood next to the fight.

Jamilah, who still held Rebecca's hair, looked at Deadria as she delivered a slow-speed uppercut.

"Let her go," Deadria requested again. She folded her arms across her chest. "She known now. You are not the one to fuck with. She know now. Come on. Let her go."

Jamilah let go of Rebecca. She returned to her turned-over chair, flipped it upright, and sat down.

Rebecca pulled herself off the floor. Her adrenaline was pumping. She bounced from one foot to the other. "I'm ready for you now, bitch," she adjusted her ponytail and then held up her fist. "Come on," she stated to Jamilah.

"Relax," Deadria ordered. She picked up Rebecca's seat and sat down beside Jamilah. "Sit, sit," she pointed to the chair to her left.

"NO, I WANT TO SEE HER!"

"Is this your *tan skin* behavior?" Deadria chuckled.

Rebecca stopped bouncing from one foot to the other, "It's not funny."

"It's not," Deadria lied. To her, this wasn't just funny—it was hilarious. "Sit," she patted the seat. "Come on, sit, sit."

Rebecca kept her eyes glued to Jamilah as she sat down in her seat.

"Don't fuckin' look at me like that, you disrespectful bitch."

Deadria, the mediator, spoke up. "We talk. No fight. We talk like adults."

"Fuck her," Jamilah shot back. "She thinks all of this is a joke. She thinks it's cute having been in and out of my house fuckin' my husband," as Jamilah spoke, her right leg bounced up and down. She was ready to attack again.

"We also did business together, Jamilah. We didn't just fuck."

Jamilah folded her arms across her chest. "What business y'all do?"

"Monroe and my father did business together first."

"Who is your father?"

"Jamilah, stop acting like you don't know. That's probably why you singled me out, because of who he is. What were you trying to get money from me?"

Jamilah didn't respond.

Deadria stared between the two, and then to instigate their silence she said, "Watson Tyler is her father."

Jamilah frowned. "When did they start doing business?"

"I don't know...some years now."

"Doing what?"

"Are you listening to me, Jamilah? I keep telling you I don't know *their* business."

"I believed Avie," Deadria stated. "She no knows us. The big-boned girl should be here. She knows us."

"Her name is Kelly," Jamilah corrected. "Not Big-boned one or whatever the fuck you keep calling her." Jamilah sat back in her chair. "Now her...I can see her being his Point Guard or whatever. They're close."

Close enough to know the dirt, but not the business, Deadria thought to herself. "Call her and invite her."

"She won't," Rebecca answered. "Jamilah just wants to confront and beat up on white women."

"Are you really playing the victim right now?"

Rebecca removed the napkin from her lip. "Are you?"

"Just call her," Deadria instigated. "Call the Big-boned one."

Jamilah pulled her phone from her purse. As the phone rang, she asked the two women, "What am I supposed to say when she answers?"

"Say what you said to me," Rebecca continued to nurse her lip.

"Shh…" Deadria hushed Rebecca. "Just tell her—"

"No need to tell her anything," Jamilah hung up the phone. "It went to voicemail."

"We invite Avie and Big Chops next time."

Jamilah grimaced. "Next time?" she questioned Deadria. "You act like we are friends or some shit."

"I'm still confused—"

"Who gives a fuck," Jamilah coldly responded to Rebecca.

"When did Avie become Monroe's assistant?"

Jamilah refused to answer.

Deadria decided to try something. "When did Avie become Monroe's assistant?"

"I think she started back in October," Jamilah replied.

"Petty bitch," Rebecca mumbled behind the napkin.

Deadria smirked. She was genuinely amused by the two women. "Why she the assistant and not the big-boned girl?"

Jamilah shrugged her shoulders. She knew when and why the change had occurred, but she wasn't about to share her truth with *these* women.

Rebecca spoke through the napkin pressed against her lip. "Who wrote the damn letter?"

"So, is Kelly ME?" Deadria shook her head. "I no get it."

Jamilah smacked her teeth. "That doesn't make sense. Kelly's role doesn't fit the player position of ME."

Rebecca dropped her napkin. "I thought you didn't know player positions, Jamilah?" Rebecca pointed at Jamilah as though she had gathered a major clue.

Jamilah rolled her eyes.

"You are a liar," Rebecca stated.

"Is that a pet peeve for you?" Jamilah asked.

"Yes, because I didn't ask for your lies!"

"Interesting…I didn't ask you to sleep with my husband, but that happened."

"Get over it. We all slept with your husband."

Jamilah stood up. "See, that's what got your ass beat the first time."

Rebecca stood up. "I'm ready for you now!" she tossed the napkin in her hand on the table.

Deadria stood up, prepared to stop the two from fighting.

"Stop using the assumption that I didn't care about my husband to justify your fuckin' my husband, hoe."

"I wasn't justifying anything."

"So, what does it matter if I lied or not?"

"What was the purpose of lying?"

Deadria looked between the two women. "I still no know," Deadria stated. "Finish explaining," she ordered Rebecca. "Explain my position."

"You are probably the letter writer," Rebecca accused Jamilah.

"Me? You're reaching, and for what?"

"You lied about knowing about basketball. Why wouldn't you lie about having written the letter."

"I still no know," Deadria stated. "Finish explaining the positions."

"You think I would bring you bitches together to rub it in *my* face that *you* fucked my husband?"

"It's Not *Bitches*. It Is Just Me!" Rebecca yelled. "You only contacted me! You're manipulative, Jamilah. What were you planning to do? Blackmail me for money?"

Jamilah sat back down in her seat. "I'm manipulative? You are really reaching. You really need a way to justify your actions, huh? You think I want people to know that my husband cheated on me with a hairy-armed, dog face—"

"REAL CLASSY, JAMILAH!" Rebecca yelled back at her.

"I SAY I NO KNOW!" Deadria yelled louder than the both of them.

The room went silent.

"I say it calmly; you ignore. I get loud; you listen. Now, explain the positions."

Rebecca snatched her letter from where she was sitting. "Jamilah is the shooting guard. You are the center." Rebecca looked up from the paper. She didn't want to talk about who she was. She wanted to talk about the lying bitch, Jamilah. She looked back at the paper. "I am a Power Forward and we function like the Center but are smaller. We do a lot of rebounding and low blocks."

Deadria smirked. "Ah, we work together," she clapped her hands.

"Yes...ideally, as a team, we are all supposed to work together."

"And the woman, who wrote the letter?"

"Like you don't already know," Rebecca commented. "I don't know why you're playing dumb."

"Maybe she isn't playing," Deadria commented.

"Are you calling me dumb?"

"Why lie in the first place? If you know about basketball, just say you know it."

Jamilah shook her head. "Stop trying to use that to justify your actions. Whether I know ball or not. You still fucked my husband. That's the problem. That's the real issue, bitch!"

"It's White Bitch!" Deadria yelled. "Say her whole name."

"I don't need to justify anything. I did what I did, and I'd do it again," Rebecca stated boldly. She felt *safe* with Deadria sitting between them.

"I ought to drag the shit out of you."

A smirk rested on Rebecca's face. "Do it then."

"I STILL NO KNOW!"

Rebecca exhaled deeply and turned her attention back to the letter. "The letter writer is the small forward. Small Forwards are like versatile players. They do a little of everything on the team. They score, defend, and rebound. They are like the number three of the team."

"I'm five," Deadria began. "You're four," she pointed at Rebecca, "Letter writer is three, Jamilah is two; so, who's number one?"

Rebecca shrugged her shoulders. "Kelly?"

Deadria clapped. She was amused. She was also exaggerating her excitement to get under Jamilah's skin. It was working like a charm.

"What do point guards do?" Jamilah asked, her voice cracking.

Deadria slid Jamilah's drink closer to her.

Jamilah looked at the glass and then at Deadria.

"Don't be stubborn," Deadria stated, sliding the glass closer to her.

Jamilah picked up the glass and took a sip.

"Point guards are your coach on the court; they would relay the message or the plays to the players from the coach. Monroe is the coach, so he wouldn't be the point guard.

Deadria asked, "The point guard is like the team captain?"

Rebecca nodded.

Deadria shook her head. "Avie, no team captain. Big Chops is the team captain."

Rebecca agreed. "Avie is too young to handle that type of responsibility." Rebecca paused. "And age aside, Avie doesn't look cut-throat enough. Now Kelly…she's cut-throat."

Deadria nodded her head. "She's the captain. She has the style and professionalism."

"She old enough," Rebecca added. "Avie looked like a baby, talking about a scholarship."

Jamilah didn't speak. She stared at the other two women. They all disgusted her, and she wanted them all to pay. They were all hoes using their body for some kind of advancement, whether it be for power, finances, status, or just for the hell of it.

Jamilah's silence caught Rebecca's attention. Rebecca's glare made Deadria look over her shoulder at Jamilah. "Are you okay?" Deadria asked.

Jamilah spoke through clenched teeth. "I want to get even so bad." She balled up her fist. "I sacrificed so much for that man, and y'all are my reward."

Deadria grabbed Jamilah's hand. "Then get even," she gave Jamilah's hand a slight squeeze of support.

Jamilah looked at her hand being covered by Deadria's. *The audacity of this bitch to grab my hand like we are friends,* Jamilah thought to herself. She wanted to snatch her hand back, grab her glass and smash it in Deadria's face, but she thought otherwise.

"We will help," Deadria added.

Jamilah looked at her skeptically, "You will help?"

"We will?" Rebecca asked confused by the gesture.

Deadria let go of Jamilah's hand. She looked at Rebecca with narrow eyes. "Yes, we will."

Rebecca tried to find understanding in Deadria's eyes. She couldn't and instead spoke her truth, "No, I will not help her."

"You say that like I asked you to help me."

"It would be *honorable* to our families," Deadria told Rebecca, placing emphasis on honorable. She wanted Rebecca to read between the lines.

"What does your family have to do with me getting revenge on my husband?"

"It'll be fun to get Monroe, eh?!" Deadria stated, ignoring Jamilah.

34

Deadria looked sternly at Rebecca. "For our families."

Rebecca continued to stare blankly at Deadria. Finally, Rebecca gave in, "Yeah…what she said."

Deadria turned back to Jamilah. "Let's do it," she clapped her hands.

The other two looked at Deadria, who seemed to be the only one excited about the idea.

Deadria held out her hands, wanting both Jamilah and Rebecca to put their hand in hers.

Rebecca looked at Deadria's well-manicured hands. Her long, nude-painted nails were filed to points. The attention to detail on her nail designs let Rebecca know that Deadria spared no expense on them. She looked from Deadria's nail to her face. Everything about Deadria yelled money. To Rebecca, this is how she could tell that Deadria must not have grown up with it around. She wore her money, from her head to her feet, like a badge of honor. Rebecca shifted her gaze from Deadria to Jamilah. In comparison, Jamilah must have grown up with money because she wasn't wearing it. She was presentable but wasn't flashy and covered in other people's names. The most expensive-looking thing on her she wore on her ring finger.

"Come on," Deadria stated, giddy that this alliance was being formed.

Rebecca reluctantly put her hand in Deadria's.

Deadria looked at Jamilah. "Your turn," she told her with her hand still extended.

Jamilah cringed on the inside as she put her hand in Deadria's.

Deadria bubbled over with excitement. She raised her hands, causing the other women's arms to rise in the air, too. "We make Monroe pay!"

Deadria yelled by herself.

MONTHS EARLIER

CHAPTER FOUR

BUILDING THE TEAM
AUGUST 5, 2019

Monroe Whitaker stared at his form in the mirror. His chocolate skin pulled tight over his muscular physique.

He wasn't being vain.

In his mind, he was his only competition, and he was only as good as his last ten reps.

Monroe was a different breed. Doctors told him his knee injury would end his basketball career—but! that was just the motivation he needed.

Those were *their* words.

No one knew about the conversations he had with God. God had told him otherwise, so Monroe maintained his routine. He attended all physical therapy sessions, worked out eight hours daily, and even incorporated yoga into his regime for flexibility.

"Discipline is the ultimate sign of self-love," Monroe stated as he placed the weights on the floor. He turned to look at Zeph. "I know that I love myself. It shows every day with everything that I do. I am disciplined. If success is what you desire, then one must implement discipline into their routine to acquire it," Monroe stared deeply into the eyes of his reflection. He flexed his muscles and stated, "Success doesn't come to lazy mauthafuckas, and it damn sure doesn't come to a nigga with his hand out." He looked from his reflection to that of his gym partner.

The two men had grown up together and were both products of a single-parent household. Between the two of them, they had a mother and a father. Their mother was Monroe's biological mother, Shantell, and their father was Zeph's biological grandfather, Emmanuel. Although they grew up together, their life decisions led them down two different paths. Had it not been for their family, their friendship would not have lasted.

Monroe walked over to Zeph. "My brother, are you awake or are you awake at your own wake?"

Zeph looked at Monroe's reflection. "What?"

"Are you living or are you surviving?"

"Nigga," Zeph warned. When Monroe talked in Hotep metaphors, Zeph knew it was Monroe's way of talking to him like he was better than him.

Monroe repeated his question, "Are you—"

Zeph looked up from his reps to Monroe. "Don't forget who I am."

The smirk that rested on Monroe's face stemmed from him knowing exactly who he was talking to, and he spoke to Zeph in this manner for a reason. Nevertheless, Monroe kept his thoughts to himself, and watched silently as Zeph continued his reps. When Zeph finished, Monroe said, "Nothing comes to sleepers, but dreams and dreams can be forgotten when you wake up."

Zeph nodded his head. It was his way of appeasing Monroe just to shut him up.

"Spot me."

Zeph moved in place as Monroe lay down on the bench. "I took your advice," Monroe lifted the weights from the brace.

"My advice?" Zeph asked. "Two...Four..."

Monroe's strength and energy were focused. He counted ten reps and then signaled Zeph for assistance.

Zeph grabbed the weights and placed them back in the brace. "What advice of mine did you take?"

"I decided to build a team of star players."

"A team of star players?" Zeph repeated.

Monroe nodded his head. "Remember we were watching Katt Williams' standup, and he was talking about having a star player on your franchise team?" Monroe looked around to ensure his wife wasn't lurking nearby. He stepped closer to Zeph and lowered his voice to a whisper, "I'm going to build me a team of star players." He stepped away, nodding his head with a big grin. He stared in Zeph's face, waiting for the lightbulb to go off, but it never did, so Monroe happily repeated himself with even more enthusiasm.

Zeph still wasn't amused. "You're building a team of hoes?" he summarized.

"Watch how you refer to my players. They are not hoes. They are star players who are interested in serving me. I'm not a villain. I'm living every man's fantasy."

"You're building a team of hoes—"

"Star players," Monroe corrected.

"You're building a team…" Zeph's voice trailed off. "Wait," he stated, trying to process everything. "It was a segment from a *comedy* show."

"Be that as it may, it still makes sense to me."

"It was a joke. Actually, it wasn't even a joke. It was advice to take care of your woman. Your woman is your franchise player."

Monroe sat down on the weight bench. He looked through the mirror and continued his conversation with Zeph's reflection. "No listen," Monroe began, "Instead of having one franchise player, why not have a team of franchise players."

"Niggas kill me paraphrasing."

"I'm not paraphrasing."

"You just let the other shit he said to go in one ear and out the other, huh?"

"No, listen. I have a team of thorough-breed women that I won't take for granted."

"Jamilah is your franchise player."

"But imagine having a team of Jamilah's," Monroe whispered, but his facial expression was bright with excitement.

Moments like this reminded Zeph why he and Monroe often bumped heads. They could hear the same message but interpret it differently.

Monroe continued: "Think of it like this; successful, winning teams have experts working in their positions." As he spoke, he noted Zeph's objections through his facial expression, but still continued to plead his case. "Jamilah is…" his voice trailed off. "She's my wife, but she ain't an expert. Jamilah is a jack of all trades but a master of none."

Zeph was half-listening. He had other more pressing matters to concern himself with than listening to a grown man busying himself with trivial activities.

"You hear me?" Monroe questioned.

"I do, but I'm not listening," Zeph admitted. "Jamilah's done a hell of a job with the real estate business. You own like nine rental properties because of her."

"Yeah," Monroe agreed.

"And Shooting Goals," Zeph added. "You about to change the hood through that camp."

"Look, she good," Monroe cut in. "But experts are considered experts because they master their craft. Jamilah has mastered the business, but…" his words trailed off. Monroe found it hard to explain Jamilah. "She could learn to master other things. More important *things*." Monroe didn't even bother to make eye contact with Zeph. His facial expression in the mirror had said enough. Monroe continued to plead his case. "My team will help create structure."

"Nigga, you struggle to be the team captain of a real basketball team, and now—"

"I don't struggle shit!" Monroe replied defensively. "You just mad that I have yet another team. Something you ain't got."

"Mad? Mad at what? The shit is stupid. You can't compartmentalize people—"

"Organization eliminates stress," Monroe repeated his mantra.

Zeph continued: "That's like saying they are only good at one thing. You act like they were put on this Earth just to please you."

"I compartmentalize you."

Zeph dropped the weights to the floor. He stood up from the bench. "What you say to me?" he asked, rhetorically. "You are smelling yourself?"

"You the one taking it personally."

"*You* compartmentalize me—" Zeph repeated Monroe's audacity. "Do you hear yourself?"

"Do you hear yourself?" Monroe questioned. "You're judging me."

"The shit is stupid!" Zeph snapped. "You should be judged. Talkin' 'bout you compartmentalize me, nigga."

"Look, chill," Monroe stated. "I ain't mean no disrespect. I meant you and I do business, but I don't discuss that business with everybody. Like I know everything ain't for everybody. That's what I meant by compartmentalizing people."

Zeph slowly returned to his seat on the bench.

"We good?" Monroe asked.

"We something."

"All I'm saying is I am finding everyone's expertise and capitalizing on their skillset for the betterment of me." Monroe tapped Zeph on the shoulder. "Take Jamilah, for example. That is my baby, my wife."

"She should be your main priority," Zeph mumbled.

"She is, to a certain extent. That's why I'm making her my shooting guard."

"You reduced your rider to nothing more than a player on a *hoe* team."

"It do sound stupid when you say it like that, but that ain't it," Monroe tried to explain. "Jamilah is…" he attempted to explain again, but couldn't find the words.

Zeph shook his head. "You're fucked up."

"You think I'm stupid?"

"Yes," Zeph quickly answered. "We got real shit going on." Zeph turned to look Monroe in the face. "Real shit," he repeated his point. "And you talking about creating a team of hoes."

"I don't have *real shit* going on. That's your thing."

"Until it's time for your cut," Zeph replied.

"What kind of real shit?" Monroe asked.

Zeph was too irritated to respond.

Monroe watched Zeph pick up the weights and begin his reps. "It ain't nothing personal," Monroe offered. "You know that ain't my thing."

Zeph still didn't respond.

"But you know they're not hoes, right?" Monroe stated, attempting to get back on subject.

"You got a good woman and can't even see her."

"Why you on her nuts?"

"I ain't. I'm just telling you the truth. You know how many men would want a real-ass woman on—"

"What other men want ain't my business." Monroe peeped the frown on Zeph's face. He shrugged his shoulders. "Their wants ain't my business," he repeated to ensure Zeph clearly heard him. Monroe lowered his voice, "Now my baby momma…now that's my business." Monroe watched as Zeph's face turned into a question. "Jamilah will know when the time is right," he answered without being asked.

Zeph put the weights down. "Shantell is turning over in her grave."

Monroe grunted. "Not Shantell, but Emmanuel would be turning in his grave." He thought about the only father figure he had ever known. "I think he would understand why I'm moving the way I'm moving?"

"Hell no!" Zeph grunted between reps.

"How would you know?"

"Nigga, that was my grandfather. What do you mean how I would know?" he asked rhetorically. "That man wouldn't approve of this bullshit. He was faithful to my grandmother until the end because my grandmother was a loyal woman. Of all the hoes you brought home, why do you think he approved of Jamilah? He saw qualities in her that my grandmother had."

Monroe waved Zeph's words away. He didn't want to hear what he knew in his heart to be the truth.

"Maria is my small forward. She does everything; balance my books, fuck me good, take care of the kid, cook, and got a good-ass day job."

Zeph finished the last of his reps and then put the weights down. "You made your baby mother a franchise player?"

"Yeah," Monroe paused. "I should have married Maria and kept Jamilah on the side."

"Wow," Zeph called over his shoulder. He grabbed the end of his towel and wiped his face. Zeph had never met Maria, but from what he had heard, she didn't have anything on Jamilah.

"If I had married Maria, then I would've had to hear my mother's mouth. You know, with Maria being Latina and all. She wanted me to marry a—"

"Strong, independent Black woman," Zeph stated, finishing Monroe's sentence. He knew all too well how *their* mother viewed things like that.

"That's how all Black women think," Monroe commented. "I sometimes feel like I married Jamilah out of obligation to the Black community."

"Um."

"I know I'm a Black man living in America."

Zeph half listened to Monroe's delusions.

"I got to be good for the good of the Black community, but not too Black so I won't alarm the white people."

Zeph stared blankly at Monroe.

Monroe wanted people to think he lived a righteous life. He wanted his fans to believe he was a typical all-American basketball star, concerned with bettering his community—but Zeph knew otherwise, and this is why their friendship was strained. Monroe saw himself as much more than he was, and this irritated Zeph.

"Black women too damn demanding," Monroe continued. "They stay with attitudes. Shit, Jamilah, mad now because I went out last night."

"Oh, so you did go see that girl?"

"Deadria?" Monroe's eyes lit up. "Nigga, did I?" Monroe laughed. "That brings me to my Center."

"She made the team?"

"Boy, she sucked my dick so good, I thought I would need to put Icy Hot on."

"On ya dick?!"

"Boy!"

Monroe walked to the door of the gym and peeped out. When he saw that the coast was clear, he returned to Zeph. "She had my whole body tensed up, but when I nutted," Monroe raised his right fist. "I could have knocked down this whole damn city. And when she started doing that thing with her tongue," Monroe shook his head.

"I guess you now know why she is so damn expensive."

"That she is," he replied. "She saw Jamilah's picture come up on my phone. She asked if she could have a threesome with her and me."

"Jamilah ain't doing no damn threesome."

"Might be able to get something going with another one of her team-mates," Monroe smirked at his reflection. "I would let you sample her, but she's off-limits now."

"Community pussy ain't my thing," Zeph informed.

"She thicker than Snicker and flexible as hell. She had that ham hock up here," he held his hand high in the air and began to replay how he was giving it to her.

Zeph didn't want to laugh, but couldn't help it. Monroe was a clown.

Monroe got back into reality. He looked at his physique in the mirror, pleased with himself and his performance last night. "Speaking of flexible. I put Rebecca on the team."

Zeph's facial expression changed. "The trainer?"

"Yep."

"Why?"

"Rebecca is cool as hell," Monroe stated.

"I guess every Black man got to have a white bitch in his pocket."

"It's better than lint," Monroe added. "She's the key to building a better business relationship with her father."

"Our business or yours?"

"Both." Monroe continued to enjoy his reflection.

"Watson Tyler is dirty?"

"The higher I go, all the white people are dirty, and I don't mean trailer trash. They are all into something. Hell, I even heard some of them into that pervert-type shit."

"Yo' ass better not be in that," Zeph warned.

"Nigga, we are talking about me," Monroe pointed at himself. "You know I ain't into that type of bullshit."

"I don't know," Zeph replied, "You out here building teams of—"

"They're not hoes," Monroe corrected before Zeph could get it wrong.

"You know what happens when you play with dirt."

"I play with you," Monroe quickly shot back.

"I ain't dirt, nigga."

"But you have dirty ways," Monroe replied. "Plus, fuckin' with the Watsons don't make my dirt seem so filthy. They are the oldest money in this town. Her father is a huge name around these parts. Google him. He owns everything around here."

"So why she look like she struggling? Bitch drive a Sonata."

Monroe laughed. "Nigga, you drive a Sonata."

"Because I am struggling!" Zeph laughed. "I ain't no bland white woman with a rich ass daddy. That bitch is stupid. I would be stunting on all you motherfuckers if my daddy was as rich as you say he is."

"Rebecca's just...."

"Just what?" Zeph paused, waiting for what he knew would be a bullshit response.

"She's just striving to be a strong, independent, Black woman."

Zeph stared at Monroe's reflection through the mirror, and then the two broke out laughing.

"She wants to be a strong, independent Black woman?" Zeph asked through his laughter.

Monroe nodded. "Why? I will never know. She's so damn prideful. She tries to do things independently, but her father always throws her alley-oops even when she doesn't want it." Monroe acted like he was handling a basketball and then laying it up into the hoop. "I figure if I stand close enough, I might be able to catch a play from her daddy, too."

"He ain't throwing no plays your way." Zeph picked up the weights from the floor and looked at himself in the mirror.

Monroe stood by Zeph, watching him. "Fix your form. You can hurt yourself doing it like that."

Zeph tossed his towel on the bench and then corrected his form.

"He ain't become old money by accident," Monroe stated, turning his attention to his reflection.

"Rebecca knows about our business?"

"No!" Monroe answered. "Hell no, but her father is aware."

"How he know?"

"He asked me about it."

"Wait!" Zeph looked at Monroe. "I hope you ain't out there running your mouth."

"Fuck no."

"Then how does he know?"

"He used to do business with my mother back in the day. He came to me and was like, I wonder if the apple didn't fall far from the tree or some shit like that."

"Shantell ain't—"

"You know she was running the business before you got involved. You don't know who she worked with or didn't work with."

"And you do?"

"I would know more than you."

"Whatever," Zeph put the weights down. "Everybody don't need to know our business."

"Watson is going to be a game changer for us. Plus, we ain't doing anything big. Just moving a trailer or two."

Zeph noted how his comment had gone in one of Monroe's ears and out the other, so he added, "Athletes can go to jail, just like niggas like me," he warned. "We are disposable to people like Watson."

"I got everybody but a point guard," Monroe stated, ignoring Zeph's warning.

"Nigga, you think you're invisible."

"I got to find the right girl because I want her to function like a team captain. Keep all the players in line."

"You want her to be a pimp not a team captain."

"Not a pimp. I just want someone that can keep me organized," Monroe explained.

"A hoe-cretary."

Monroe was now the one with the unamused facial expression.

Zeph paid it no mind and continued: "Like a secretary. Nah, a hoe assistant...a hoe-sistant. I like hoe-cretary better," Zeph added, making up words.

"Seriously?"

Zeph shrugged.

"But you are on to something," Monroe explained. "The Point Guard should be a secretary. She would schedule appointments and meetings, send gifts, and arrange visits and trips. She keeps the team happy while I go out and scout for more potential recruits. And in keeping the team happy, she's keeping me happy."

"And how do you keep her happy?"

"She got a job."

"Ain't no woman gonna stand back and watch you spoil other women in front of her."

"Power?" Monroe replied, uncertain. "Everybody loves power."

"Power ain't gonna be enough."

"It will."

"You already underestimating her, and you ain't even got her yet."

Monroe folded his arms across his chest and stroked his beard. "I could give her this dick," he suggested.

"And add to the number of baby mothers you got?"

"Actually, the secretary's pussy will be off limits."

"Why lie to a nigga that knows you?"

"No lies," Monroe chuckled. He raised his right hand, "I swear I won't fuck her, and I won't even flirt with her. As a matter of fact, she needs to be busted and unwanted by all walks of life. She'll be the MVP of my franchise. She will reap so many perks just for being a diligent expert. All she must do is be loyal, humble, confidential, and appreciative of all I offer. If she does that, I will forever reward her for her efforts. The MVP gets to travel and enjoys the finer things in life."

"Does she need to stay away from water, too? Nigga you sound like you trying to recruit a gremlin and shit."

"I bet I won't want to fuck her."

Zeph shook his head. The older the two men get; the more Zeph realized the importance of limiting his interactions with Monroe.

"I won't fuck her," Monroe tried to convince Zeph and himself. "I *do* have standards. I don't fuck ugly bitches."

"So you about to recruit an ugly bitch and then turn her into a pimp—"

"Point Guard," Monroe corrected.

Zeph continued: "And in return, you will provide her with a life of luxury."

"Last time I'ma tell you. The secretary isn't a pimp, and my players aren't hoes."

"Not all of them," Zeph noted. "So how do you plan to explain this pimp—"

"Secretary."

"Random-ass woman to Jamilah?"

Monroe stroked his beard. He knew his wife well. She wouldn't go for no new woman randomly hanging around. Even if he said, she was a secretary. "I got it!" He stated excitedly. "I'm going to get Jamilah to pick my MVP," Monroe noted the look on Zeph's face. "No, hear me out," he explained. "Jamilah is into controlling situations. So, she can control this situation."

"She gonna pick someone off the wall."

"Oh, I know," Monroe replied shaking his head. "I know, Jamilah. She likes to be in control but also knows how to compromise. Jamilah won't hire a man because she knows I ain't gonna go for having some random nigga in her vicinity all day. She won't pick a dime because—"

"Insecure shit," both men stated in unison.

Zeph thought silently to himself. He hated to admit it, but Monroe's foolishness could work. "She's going to pick your hoe-cretary."

Monroe nodded. He was pleased by Zeph acknowledging his brilliance.

"You're twisted," Zeph replied. "Why are you putting this much energy into this shit? It's stupid."

"But I can do it," Monroe replied, looking at his reflection in the mirror. "So, I'ma do it. I'm going to be a franchise owner."

CHAPTER FIVE

THE NEW RECRUIT

AUGUST 23, 2019

Kelly looked at herself in her full-length mirror. She wore her sexy, laced black panties and matching bra. She ran her hands through her hair. Life was falling into place perfectly. She had successfully advanced her life in a matter of days. In truth, it had taken her two years, but today felt like she was about to reap all she had sowed.

This had been the best week for Kelly; on Monday, the bras she ordered came in the mail. On Tuesday, her cousin, Omari, tightened and curled her sister locks. On Wednesday, she got an email that invited her to interview for a secretary position for THE Monroe Whitaker! On Thursday, she showed up to the interview and showed out. Monroe's wife didn't hesitate and hired her on the spot. Now, it was Friday, and she was getting dressed and ready for her first day on the job. She felt confident in her new gig, but the fact that everything happened quickly did unnerve her a little. It was too good to be true, but it came at the right time.

She once read somewhere that generational curses and shortcomings stop when someone in the family stops them. For the past two years, she had put forth so much effort to change generational curses in her life. The move from DC was just the beginning, then enrolling in school and graduating, and now this job—all her hard work was finally paying off.

"He may not come when you want him, but he'll be there right on time!" Kelly did a combination of singing and yelling at the top of her lungs. She stared at herself in amazement. "Yasssss, bih!" Kelly cheered for herself. She blew a kiss at her own reflection. "I can't get enough of you, baby!"

She grabbed her blue halter-top dress lying on the bed and slipped into it. She grabbed her white blazer and put it on. "And not the icing on the cake," she stated as she slipped her feet into a pair of blue and white splattered heels. She walked back to look at herself in the mirror. "Hard work always pays off."

She turned from the mirror, grabbed her purse, and headed to her new job.

"You found me a secretary?" Monroe questioned Jamilah. He was sitting on his side of the bed, watching her apply her makeup in the bathroom mirror.

"Yeah, babe. She should be here at nine."

Monroe laid back on the bed.

Initially, he thought having Jamilah pick his point guard was a good idea, but he was slightly concerned now. In his opinion, Jamilah could have put more effort into the search. It was just the twelfth of August when he told her he wanted a secretary. Here it was eleven days later, and she had already hired someone. Aside from his main objective for an assistant, he still needed it to be someone proficient and professional. He didn't want anybody in his personal space.

Monroe sat up on the bed. "What are her qualifications? Did she have a resume?"

Jamilah stepped out of the bathroom and looked at Monroe. "You don't trust me?"

"I hope you didn't just pick a busted chick on some insecure shit, and she's not even qualified."

Jamilah stared at her husband. "I'm not insecure. Kelly is—"

"She's white? You hired a white girl?"

"You think Kelly is a white girl's name?"

"Name a Black Kelly."

"Rowland. Kelly Rowland. The only Kelly I care to acknowledge."

Monroe rolled his eyes. "I just hope you took this shit seriously."

Jamilah walked towards Monroe. "Kelly just graduated from college. She has a degree in Mass Communications with a focus in Public Relations. She's new to the area—"

"How new?"

"New," Jamilah confirmed. "New...new," she started, trying to put emphasis on it for her husband. "She's interned with Jordan Moons. Do you remember the Moons? We went to their housewarming party."

Monroe nodded his head. "If she's that good, why didn't the Moons try to hold on to her?"

"Seriously, Monroe? I'm just as particular as you. I am not going to have anybody in our lives."

Monroe looked at Jamilah skeptically.

Jamilah huffed. "They didn't hire her because they didn't have the position available. I called Jordan and had an extensive conversation with him about her." Jamilah straddled Monroe's lap. "Trust me, okay."

Monroe didn't want Jamilah on him. He was irritated at her nonchalant approach to his plan. He wanted her to be as thorough as she was regarding other aspects of their business. "You moved too fast on this," he commented.

"You don't trust me."

"It ain't that I don't trust you, but I need someone proficient, who is organized and pays attention to detail."

"I am just as particular as you are, Monroe."

"Okay…we'll see."

Jamilah tried to kiss Monroe. He turned his head to avoid her attempts.

"Wow," Jamilah stated. "You are really mad right now?"

Monroe pushed Jamilah off his lap.

She moved without hesitation. She hated when Monroe got into one of his moods. "If I moved slowly on this, you would have been mad. I move fast on this; you're mad. Whatever," she moved away from Monroe. "I have meetings all morning."

"What meetings?"

"I'm meeting with the board about changes they want to make to this year's summer camp."

"What changes?"

Jamilah shrugged her shoulders. "You know how they are sometimes," she replied dismissively. "And then I'm meeting with the contractor. I found a house, and he's going to inspect it. I want to see what kind of money we need to renovate it." Jamilah proceeded to find her an outfit from her closet. "I'm waiting for someone to make a fuss about us buying all the property in Fairview County." Jamilah spun around. "We are buying the hood," she smiled broadly. "Then I want to see about creating a community garden that turns into a grocery store."

Monroe stood up from the bed.

"I want to establish key necessities in the neighborhood. A grocery store, hospital, bank, and housing. I met this young man the other day named Jamar. He wants to open a community center. He wants us to be an investor in his project," Jamilah nodded her head. She was impressed by the young man with big dreams.

"You know you don't have to work, right?"

Jamilah stopped dressing and looked at her husband.

"I mean it," Monroe stated. "You don't have to do any of this."

"And do what instead?"

Monroe shrugged. "This takes up a lot of your time."

Jamilah had heard this before from her husband. He didn't understand what working meant to her. She didn't do it for the sake of doing things. She had a dream, an end goal. She wanted to see a Tulsa-like community in her lifetime. Fairview County was the perfect place to create her plan. Still, she had to move slowly to avoid raising *anyone's* suspicions. Even in this day and age, there were still *people* uncomfortable with the idea of a *positive* all-Black community.

"What's so bad about being a stay-at-home wife?"

"Nothing is bad about it. It's just not for me," Jamilah explained. She slipped into a black dress. "Plus, knowing me, I would still work. You definitely wouldn't need Kelly because I would be your secretary."

She couldn't be my secretary, Monroe smirked at his thoughts. He walked closer to Jamilah. "It would be nice to steal kisses throughout the day. Grabbing ass," He grabbed a handful of her butt.

Jamilah giggled.

"Would we even get work done?"

Jamilah stared at Monroe in awe. She could have melted. She wrapped her arms around his magnificent physique and laid her head on his chest.

Monroe wrapped his arms around his wife's shoulders and hugged her tightly. He lightly tugged at her lengthy hair, "I love you."

Jamilah looked up at Monroe. Even though he couldn't see her bigger vision, she still saw everything she ever wanted by being with him. The house, the car, the career—all perks. She had always been there for Monroe and Monroe only. Her friends and even some of her family kept saying that he was out of her league, or they would say things like he was a cheater and would break her heart. They all believed it was impossible for an athlete to love and be faithful to her. Now here she was, living the life, ascertaining her dreams; she was proving all the haters wrong. In the five years they had been married, she hadn't dealt with anything negative aside from the disrespectful bitches that threw themselves at her husband. He didn't take the bait, so she wasn't concerned. They didn't matter. The tall, gorgeous man standing before her was all hers and hers alone.

She smiled broadly at him, "I love you, too."

Zeph was standing in Monroe's kitchen. After Jamilah left, Monroe called him over. The two needed to talk business, but Monroe wanted him to meet his new Point Guard, or as Zeph affectionately referred to her, The Gremassist.

"What time does she get here?" Zeph asked.

Monroe looked at his watch. "Nine."

Zeph shook his head. He couldn't believe that Monroe's twisted plan was working. Secretly, he hated that it worked. Monroe had what every man wanted; a beautiful, educated, supportive, ride-or-die woman by his side, yet it wasn't enough.

Zeph made his phone the center of his attention because he didn't want to be around. His presents only gave Monroe a reason to gloat. Monroe didn't know the first thing about humility. How could one learn the lesson of humility when he always managed to get everything he wanted. Zeph regretted not going to college. He sometimes wondered if Jamilah would have chosen him over Monroe. In his mind, he would have known what to do with a woman of her caliber. Instead, she ended up with a clown who would rather build a team of hoes than focus on business or caring for the treasure he already had by his side.

The doorbell rang.

Zeph looked up from his phone. "The Gremassist can tell time."

Monroe rubbed his hands together with a big smile on his face. "She's here." He jumped up from his seat. "Come meet my Point Guard," he stated, motioning for Zeph to follow him to the door.

Zeph didn't move.

Monroe was down the hallway when he realized Zeph wasn't behind him. He turned back around and walked into the kitchen. Monroe noted the look on Zeph's face. He had seen this look several times. It was a look of jealousy, and this only made Monroe even more pleased about the success of his plan. "Come on, nigga!"

Reluctantly, Zeph got up from his seat and followed behind.

Monroe rushed down the hallway like a kid in a candy store. He opened the door. The woman in front of him was not what he expected. Monroe looked back at Zeph to see if he was seeing what he was seeing.

Zeph stared at Kelly with wide eyes. "That's not a Gremassist," he mumbled. The shocked look on Zeph's face was replaced with one of amusement.

Monroe looked back at the woman standing at the door. He was pissed. Jamilah had done everything that he didn't want her to do. Though this woman in front of them wasn't his typical type, Monroe could not deny the sight of a fly-ass woman.

"Good morning, fellas!" She spoke with a tone of familiarity and a spark of excitement.

"You a morning person," Zeph replied.

She laughed. "Something like that. I guess I'm just excited about my first day."

Monroe didn't respond. He was visibly disappointed.

Kelly could tell. Nevertheless, she smiled broadly, revealing pearly white teeth and dimples. She reached out her hand to Monroe. "I'm Kelly."

Monroe looked down at her hand, but then his attention turned to her coke-bottle shape. She was a big girl but shapely. He liked what he saw, but he was mad. *Why the fuck did she hire her?* he thought. *This ruins my whole-fuckin-plan.*

Zeph nudged him out of his thoughts.

Monroe finally reached out and grabbed Kelly's hand. He noted that her hand was soft and her nails well-manicured. "Monroe," he replied.

"Who doesn't know Monroe Whitaker?" She looked at Zeph, "Who are you?"

"Zeph," he stated, extending his hand.

Kelly noted how attractive Zeph was, with a bad boy demeanor. *Birds of a feather do flock together*, she thought. "You have some pretty eyes," she stated, commenting on his dark, slanted eyes.

As Zeph replied to the compliment, Monroe watched how Kelly seemed more intrigued with Zeph than she was with him. This made him feel some type of way.

"Can I come in?" Kelly asked since no one offered.

Monroe stepped aside as Kelly walked into the house. He watched her closely, waiting for the moment of awe she would have over his home, but it never happened. She didn't seem fazed, like she was used to luxury.

"Who did you use to work for?" Monroe asked. "The Moons?"

Kelly looked back at Monroe. "Yes, I did."

My house looks better than theirs. She should be in awe, Monroe thought.

"Kelly, my office is down the hall on the right. Wait for me in there," Monroe stated.

Between the sway of her voluptuous hips and her heels clicking against the hardwood floors, Kelly seemed to demand attention that she didn't even know she wanted. The two men couldn't keep their eyes off her.

Monroe grabbed the back of his neck.

Zeph smirked. He was watching *the* Monroe Whitaker squirm within his own plan. "It serves you right," Zeph commented when Kelly disappeared into the office.

"What do you think? Why did Jamilah pick her? You think this is a test?" Monroe didn't bother waiting on Zeph to reply. "Did Jamilah outsmart me?" Monroe cupped his hand over his mouth. "Was she listening to us?" His heart was beating fast. "She heard what we said," his eyes shot wide. "She did hear us."

Zeph shrugged his shoulders.

Monroe spun on his heels and darted to the kitchen. Zeph was close behind him. When he entered the kitchen, he grabbed Kelly's resume that Jamilah had left on the counter. He quickly skimmed through the resume and then placed it on the counter.

"What?" Zeph questioned.

Monroe didn't say anything. Having looked over her resume, Monroe knew Kelly was qualified. In fact, she was *overly* qualified. He could understand why Jamilah had chosen her. "I got to get rid of her," he finally spoke.

Zeph looked up from the resume. He nodded his head, impressed by what he had just read. He tossed the resume back on the countertop. "And how are you going to explain that to Jamilah?"

Monroe shook his head. "I'll figure something out 'cause...I think Jamilah outsmarted me."

Zeph smirked. "Good luck with the Point Guard," he taunted.

"Funny," Monroe called after him.

He stood silently in the kitchen. When he heard the front door close, he reached for the resume. He skimmed over it again. *Damn it, Jamilah*, he thought. *Why did you pick her?*

At this moment, he saw his plan going all to hell.

Monroe walked into his office.

Kelly looked at him. "Where's the other guy?"

"He left."

"Oh," she replied and then resumed looking at the plaques and certificates hanging on the walls. "You and Mrs. Whitaker are an impressive couple."

Monroe nodded. "Yeah, Jamilah is...uh...all into succeeding; therefore, we succeed."

Kelly admired the success on the office walls; meanwhile, Monroe admired her curves. His eyes didn't know if he wanted to stare at her hips and thighs or her caramel mountains that tastefully were revealed in her form-fitting blue dress. He was pissed with Jamilah's choice because he found himself attracted to his hoe-cretary, and that was never a part of the plan.

To look at Kelly, he could understand Jamilah's logic for choosing her. Traditionally, she wasn't his typical type of woman. This could be why Jamilah thought her to be a *safe* choice.

Monroe had never dated a big girl or wanted to date one. He always found that the big girls he would slightly be interested in were the self-conscious type. The types to make jokes about themselves before anyone else could. For Monroe, this was a complete turn-off. On the other hand, Kelly stood silently in his office and seemed to ooze with confidence. She smelled expensive, like something Jamilah would wear, and her style of dress was impressive. The curve of her ample backside intrigued him. His eyes rode her never-ending curves, putting him on a lust-filled rollercoaster.

Kelly suddenly spun around. To her, Monroe's face looked like he saw something he didn't like. "Look, I know you were probably expecting some slim, athletic little secretary, but that's not me."

Monroe was silent. He folded his arms across his chest. *Typical self-conscious big girl. Turn me off*, he thought. *It will be the only way my plan works. I can't be attracted to someone who doesn't love themself. Be my Gremassist*, he thought, using Zeph's terminology.

"I'm not that, clearly," Kelly continued. "But I know my shit, and I'm not afraid of hard work. I have my resume with me now if you need to see why I got the job," she stated, opening her red notebook. She attempted to hand him a copy of her resume.

Monroe didn't reach for it.

"Do you want to see it?"

Monroe stared silently at her.

"Well," she stated, tucking the resume into her folder. "I know you saw my resume. You know I could do this job with my eyes closed."

Silence.

"Say something, Mr. Whitaker."

"Call me Monroe."

"Well, say something, Monroe."

"You do know you will be working directly with me?"

"She told me."

Monroe moved to sit behind his desk.

Kelly moved closer to his desk.

Monroe noted how she presented herself. Kelly was pampered, and that was one of his weaknesses. He loved to be around a woman that took care of herself. Monroe believed if a woman took care of herself, she would also take care of her man.

"What else did she tell you?"

Kelly sat down across from her new boss. "She said a lot. I took a lot of notes. I signed a lot of forms. I know for sure one was a confidentiality form."

Monroe didn't respond.

Kelly sat patiently, waiting for him to say something or give her a task. She could feel her face slipping into a frown and her body temperature rising. She had managed to control her nerves. All morning, she had given herself a pep talk until she rang the doorbell. Now, sitting in silence was breaking her confidence down. *Fix your face*, she told herself. *Did you expect anything less than this form of treatment? He is Monroe Whitaker. Remember, he did that one interview. He was a straight asshole. He tries to act humble, but he's not. He's cocky and expects people to kiss his ass. I ain't the one. I've been 'round men with longer money and far more reach.*

"What do you hope to get from this job?"

"Opportunities."

"What kind of opportunities?"

"Business, social…whatever God may bring my way."

"You plan to use me to get a better opportunity?"

"Isn't that the true essence of business? Investing your time and energy into a good or service with the intention of multiplying those investments. This job is to benefit me just as much as it is to benefit you, too, right?"

Monroe smirked.

Kelly continued: "You don't play ball just for the owner's sake. You're getting compensated in a big way, too, right?"

Monroe didn't respond, but Kelly knew she had him where she wanted him. She took this opportunity to look at him as she waited for him to respond. He had a rich chocolate complexion. He had neatly formed waves and a tight edge-up. His dark eyes made her feel inferior. She cleared her throat like it would help to shake her feeling.

"Go do a run for me," he stated, handing her a paper. "Please."

"Yes, sir," she stated, grabbing the paper from him.

"You got a license?"

"Yes."

"Take my BMW."

"The white one in the driveway? Are you serious?"

"Consider it a business opportunity."

Kelly watched Monroe. He never took his eyes off of his computer screen. "You funny," she finally commented.

Monroe smirked.

"At least you listen," she added as she headed towards the door.

Monroe's gaze moved from the screen to Kelly's ass. The click of her heels just added to this lustful moment. *Damn you, Jamilah,* he thought as Kelly exited his office.

CHAPTER SIX

CONFIDENTIALITY
SEPTEMBER 15, 2019

"How is the job coming, Miss Mamas?"

"Zani, it's…ugh," Kelly huffed.

"I wish you would acknowledge me as ya' mova like a normal child."

Kelly sighed deeply into the phone. "We're not normal."

Zani smacked her lips. "You just want to be—"

"Let's not have this conversation tonight. Maybe tomorrow. I might be up for it tomorrow, but not tonight."

"What's wrong tonight?"

A part of her wanted to tell her mother that the job was amazing. Working with Monroe was fun. They talked, laughed, and in his own way, he provided her the opportunities she told him she wanted. She enjoyed herself so much that she didn't mind the long hours and low pay, but like most jobs, there was a downside. In this case, the downside was her *other* supervisor—his wife.

For the past couple of weeks, she had been racking her brain, trying to figure out why Jamilah was acting cruel to her. Kelly couldn't describe it in one word, but she had the perfect phrase for Jamilah's behavior, Nice-Nasty. Jamilah would go out of her way to give Kelly backward-ass compliments or look at her funny when Kelly would try to hold a conversation with her. What was troubling the most, her job didn't have an HR Department. Why mention it to Monroe and run the risk of losing a job she really liked.

"Hello?" Zani called out.

"Yeah, I'm here."

"Is everything okay out there?"

"No," she replied quickly.

"That man isn't messing with you, is he? 'Cause I can get word to your father that you're having—"

"No," Kelly interjected. "That is not my problem. Working for Monroe is an amazing opportunity. I am fine. Just a little emotional today. You know how I can be at times."

Her mother laughed into the phone. "On my soul, I know!"

"Stop it."

"I miss you though. The plan is still the same."

"Y'all still coming out here?"

"Correct," her mother assured her.

"I still don't understand why y'all are moving here."

"To be with you."

Kelly didn't respond.

"Hello?"

"Yeah, I'm still here."

"I promise you. We ain't coming down there on no bama shit."

"I hear you," Kelly finally responded. "Look, I have to go."

Zani sighed into the phone.

"Bye."

"Kelly, I can show you better than I can tell you, baby. Things will be different."

"Okay," Kelly replied. "I have to go. Goodbye."

"Bye, baby."

Kelly hung up the phone. She wanted to be excited about her parent's move to North Carolina. How could she, though? They were prone to bring along with them more of the same. Kelly wanted to call her cousin, Omari, but Omari would try to convince her that she needed to be optimistic about their move. Kelly didn't want to hear that, not even from her favorite cousin.

Kelly was about to make another phone call when Monroe entered his home office.

"What's up, Ms. Kelly."

Kelly smiled. Monroe had a deep voice, and anything he said sounded sexy—even if it was just an innocent greeting. "Hello, Monroe. How are you today?"

"I feel great," he replied. "Got my morning workout in and made a couple of calls," he nodded his head like he was pleased with himself. "It's been a good morning."

Kelly looked at the time on her phone. "Are you ready for your fruit and water snack now?"

Monroe looked up from the papers in his hand. "You think you know me, huh?"

Kelly stood up from her seat. "You are a man of routine."

Monroe smirked. "A man of discipline."

Kelly walked out of the office and headed towards the kitchen. She couldn't help but to be impressed with herself. By learning Monroe's routine, Kelly ultimately learned how to anticipate all his needs before he knew they were needed. During her interview, Jamilah did mention that she would be Monroe's right hand, and she didn't lie. Going into the job, Kelly thought she would focus solely on Monroe's basketball obligations, but she quickly learned that Monroe Whitaker was more than a basketball player. He was a businessman and then a basketball player.

"Kelly Mitchell."

Kelly stopped in her stride when she heard her name. The voices were coming from the kitchen. She knew it was Jamilah and her two snobby friends. She had seen them arrive from the surveillance in Monroe's office. Kelly hadn't met them but hearing their voices and watching how they greeted each other with distant hugs and air kisses on the cheek, she could sense their bougie behavior a mile away.

"Kelly Mitchell? Why does her name sound so familiar?" questioned one of Jamilah's friends.

"She used to work for the Moons," Jamilah replied.

"Oh."

The room was silent.

Although Kelly was in the hallway eavesdropping, she felt uncomfortable. It was the type of silence, like someone in the room, knew something but didn't want to say anything.

Jamilah must have felt it, too because she said, "What do you know?"

The other two women broke up laughing.

Kelly picture Jamilah staring at the other two women with a stone face. Jamilah didn't come off as the type that liked to be the center of a joke.

"What?" curiosity dripped from Jamilah's question.

The other women stopped laughing. They must have realized that Jamilah didn't find any humor in their silence or laughter.

"Oh, Jamilah, it's nothing," one of her girlfriends finally responded. "We were just pulling your leg."

Kelly heard Jamilah's fake chuckle. It was one of those, I-am-laughing-to-keep-the-peace types of laughs.

The two snobby friends must have known it, too. One of them decided to break the silence by approaching the subject of Kelly differently. "You are an amazing woman, Jamilah. I don't know if I would allow a woman to work so closely with my husband."

"Oh, I trust Monroe…with fat women," Jamilah chuckled. "As health and weight conscious as Monroe is, he is not wasting his time on some blubber-butt."

All three women laughed.

Kelly cringed.

Another snobbish friend said, "I never quite understood why women let themselves go. Just go to the gym, for crying out loud."

"Is that why you hired her?" the first friend asked. "Because she's fat?"

"That part," Jamilah replied, "And she is cheap. I pay her two hundred dollars every two weeks. How crazy is that?" Jamilah questioned rhetorically. "She won't be here long anyway. Monroe really doesn't have a use for her. I just went with his request to keep the peace between us."

"Yeah, I do the same thing with my husband when he makes ridiculous requests. Give him what he wants and then move on," replied one of her friends.

"She could be a pretty girl, but she needs to go to the gym and step her wardrobe up," Jamilah commented. "I get so uncomfortable when she tells me she likes my outfits. All I can think is, how can you like my taste in clothes but dress like that?"

Kelly looked down at her attire.

Meanwhile, the three women continued to chuckle at her expense.

"But you know what," Jamilah stated. "She's cheap, so of course, her outfits would be cheap. She must live within her budget, right?"

"How does Monroe like her?"

"Monroe can be very particular sometimes, but he hasn't said anything negative, so I imagine she must be doing a good job."

"Well, kudos to Jamilah. I would lose my mind if my husband wanted to hire a secretary."

"Give him what he wants; just make sure she looks like a dog," Jamilah laughed.

The tears that Kelly wanted to shed earlier had surfaced. She quickly dabbed them away and then walked back to Monroe's office. Once inside, she shut the door behind her and stood silently by the door.

Monroe was on the phone. When he saw Kelly walk back into the office, he got off the phone. "Where's my fruit and water?"

She tried to keep her composure but tears rolled down her face. She didn't want to cry, and she for damn sure didn't want to cry in front of Monroe.

Monroe walked from behind his desk. "Come here."

Kelly walked over to Monroe.

He touched her chin and made her look at him in his eyes. "Why are you crying?"

Kelly tried to shake it off. "Nothing. I'm good."

"Where's my fruit and water then?" Monroe asked with a smile.

"I was going to get it, but your wife and her friends were in the kitchen..." her voice trailed off.

Monroe waited patiently for her to gather her composure.

"They were talking about me, so I preferred not to walk in."

Monroe walked to his desk and sat on the corner. "What did she say?"

Kelly felt vulnerable, like a child tattling on her siblings. "Just talking about my weight, clothes, pay...j-just breaking me down. She made it seem like she only hired me because I wasn't your type."

Monroe nodded his head. "Well, I don't know why my wife hired you, but I do know why I kept you."

Kelly wiped her face. "And why is that?"

Monroe reached out and pulled Kelly to him.

The way they were standing was inappropriate. She was between his legs. Monroe was holding her hands. "Can I trust you, Kelly?"

She nodded her head. "Yeah."

Monroe stared into Kelly's eyes. He was waiting for this moment. He thought it would be sooner, but Kelly was a little tougher than he thought. He watched as she devoured the unnecessary shade that his wife was throwing at her. He never intervened.

He needed it to happen.

Monroe knew Jamilah like the back of his hand. He knew that Jamilah never played nice with other women. It would only be a matter of time before Jamilah would show Kelly her authentic self. Though a strong woman, Jamilah was still a woman, which meant she was still territorial, and Monroe did his part to bring out this side of her.

Kelly was good at her job, but she could have been better. However, Monroe always sang Kelly's praises when speaking about her to Jamilah, like she did marvelous things. He allowed his inner narcissism to subtly devalue Jamilah's ability while love-bombing Kelly's worth in front of her. It was only natural that Jamilah's cattiness would reveal itself. Monroe stood silently aside, waiting for the moment that Kelly would break. Now that she had, Monroe was ready to swoop in like a superhero and build her back up to be his Point Guard equipped with unwavering loyalty. It only took eight days for his plan to work. He was impressed, not with Jamilah's actions, but with his own.

"Forget all that bullshit that my wife was talking about, okay? You work for me, not her."

Kelly nodded her head. Kelly felt safe and secure in her position as Monroe spoke to her. It reminded her of how she felt when talking to her father. Unknowingly, Monroe's words had planted a budding sense of loyalty in Kelly.

"Have a seat," he stated, motioning to the chair in front of his desk. He then moved to sit on the opposite side. He reached into his desk drawer and pulled out a piece of paper. "I want you to read over this," he stated, sliding the paper across his desk to Kelly.

Kelly reached for the paper. She looked at the heading on the form. It said *Confidential* in big, black letters. She looked at Monroe, "Oh, I already signed this."

"No, you haven't. That is a different form."

"What's the difference between this form and the one I already signed?"

"The one my wife gave you is to keep our business confidential from the public. That means you don't talk to anyone about my wife and me or our businesses."

Kelly held up the paper in front of her. "And this form?"

Monroe spoke slowly and clearly. "That one is to keep my business confidential from my wife and the public, with emphasizes on my wife."

Kelly couldn't control her emotions, let alone her facial expression. "You—"

Monroe held up his hand, cutting her off. "Jamilah and I have a happy life, and I want to keep it that way. With you signing this sheet, we ensure that her life…our life stays that way."

"And if I don't sign?"

"You can continue your job, but you'll work for Jamilah—not me—and knowing Jamilah, you won't be here long."

"You don't think she wouldn't find that suspicious?"

Monroe shook his head. "Jamilah knows how particular I can be at times."

Kelly looked back at the form in her hand. Curiosity was getting the best of her. *What could Monroe Whitaker need with a confidentiality form? What kind of privileged information would I find out that his wife doesn't know? Fifty Shades of Grey!* she thought. *Oh no, he is either into some kinky shit or gay. Why are all the gorgeous, well-groomed men gay? Can you imagine a man like him…gay?* She looked across the desk, disappointed but confused. Monroe hadn't done anything inappropriate, but she had caught him a time or two looking at her lustfully.

"What do you say?" Monroe questioned, snatching her from her thoughts.

"You aren't into dominatrix or anything kinky?"

Monroe shrugged. "And if I was?"

Kelly laughed. The mystery of it all was intriguing.

"You want to work for my wife or me?"

"Let you tell it if I work for your wife, then I won't have a job."

"It's the truth."

Kelly looked at the paper in front of her again. *What's another confidential contract? Shit, you need this job, girl. Sign that damn paper.* She looked back up at Monroe. "What kind of secrets could you have? You seem so quiet."

"Sign and find out."

Kelly grabbed a pen. Once she signed, the intense thrill of the mystery had worn off.

Monroe grabbed the paper from the desk. He didn't even wait for the ink to dry. He slipped the contract into a manila folder. "You are officially my Point Guard."

"I'm your what? Point Guard?"

Monroe nodded with a straight face.

"A point guard like in basketball?"

Monroe nodded again.

Kelly frowned. "What do you mean I'm a point guard?"

"Go fix your face and meet me in my car. I want to take you somewhere private so we can talk...honestly to each other."

Kelly sat stiffly in her chair for a moment. She watched as Monroe's eyebrows raised at her lack of action. She took the hint and moved towards the office door as she was told.

"What do you want to ride in today?" Monroe called after her.

Kelly looked back at him. "I don't know."

"Let's take the Tahoe and be low profile."

"Okay," she replied hesitantly.

CHAPTER SEVEN

TRUTH AND BOND

SEPTEMBER 15, 2019

Kelly crawled into the Tahoe.

Monroe called it low-profile because it wasn't one of his most expensive cars. He had heavily invested in this car but was on the lower end.

"You feel better?" Monroe asked.

"Yeah," Kelly replied, fastening her seat belt.

Initially, the music was on, but once they pulled out of the parking lot, Monroe cut the radio off. "You said I can trust you, right?"

"Yeah."

Monroe glanced over at Kelly. "You got your own place?"

"Yes," she replied. It was the half-truth. She felt no need to mention her cousin, Omari, who shared the house with her. She could say it was her house alone; since Omari paid half the rent but was rarely home.

"You like it?"

"It's nice for a two-bedroom apartment."

Monroe nodded.

The car was silent.

Kelly looked over at him. Sometimes she thought he was low-key digging her, but she dismissed it, deeming him just a nice guy. His wife confirmed today that she was not his type. Truthfully, that was why Kelly got in her emotions. Better women had talked about her, which never shook her foundation. However, hearing that she wasn't his type harshly stopped her secret fantasies that played in her mind occasionally. The man she was crushing on would never crush back.

"Where are we going?"

Monroe glanced at Kelly. "Just ride."

They drove silently for thirty minutes, then Monroe entered a gated community.

Kelly sat up straight in her seat. She looked at all the beautiful houses with their well-manicured lawns. "This area is beautiful."

Just as she said it, Monroe pulled into a driveway. "Leave your purse and phone in the truck," he stated as he opened the driver's side door. "Come on."

Kelly looked at him suspiciously but, per usual, did what he said.

They walked to the front door. Kelly was shocked when Monroe produced a key from his pocket.

As soon as Kelly walked in, she was taken back by the grand entrance. The foyer was breathtaking. It had a high ceiling and the most beautiful crown molding she had ever seen. This house's entranceway looked better than the entrance at Monroe's home.

Monroe looked at Kelly. The look on her face made Monroe feel like a big shot. He liked when he was about to shock and awe his audience. "Let me give you the tour," he stated, grabbing her hand. "This is the living room. Through there leads to the dining room," they continued to walk. "It has four bedrooms; two are master rooms, and the others have a Jack and Jill setup that shares a bathroom. I grew up in a house just like this one. I couldn't buy that one, because the owner didn't want to sell it. This one is Zeph's childhood home."

"Really?"

"It wasn't even as close to as nice as it is now. I poured a lot of money into renovating it. It was like my own little personal project. The two of us spent a lot of time in this house with his grandfather. Our grandfather."

"Y'all are related?"

"No, but you might as well say we are," Monroe answered. "His grandfather was the only male role model in my life." The two stood in silence as Monroe had flashes of childhood memories cross his mind. "I fixed everything in here," he looked over the house. "This is how I wish we grew up."

Kelly took in the well-decorated interior. The house was just as luxurious as the house they had just left.

"Growing up here made me want more out of life." He continued to guide Kelly through the house. When they got to the kitchen, he stopped.

"What do you think?"

"Y'all aren't selling this house, are you?"

"There is no y'all," he stated assertively. "Jamilah doesn't know about this house. It's my house. It's in Zeph's name, but it is my house."

Kelly looked at Monroe. "So Zeph lives here?"

Monroe walked close to Kelly. "You live here," he stated, placing the key into her hand.

Kelly laughed. "No way," is all she could muster. "Seriously?" She shook her head in disbelief. "This is really nice, but I...I can't afford this," she stammered.

"You are my Point Guard, remember?"

He pulled out a kitchen chair and sat down.

Kelly stared at the key in her hand. She looked up at Monroe, "What do I have to do for this?" She pulled out a chair and sat down across from him. "What do I have to do for this?" She was now the assertive one.

Monroe moved his chair close to Kelly. "I love Jamilah."

"Okay."

"But she doesn't take care of me the way I want to be taken care of."

Kelly looked at Monroe suspiciously. *This nigga must think I'm some kind of hoe*, she thought. "I have to fuck you for this house?" Although a frown rested on her face, she continued to grip the key tightly in her hand.

Monroe laughed. "No, not at all. You just have to be loyal to me and only me."

"Loyal, how?"

"I have women, four to be exact. They all do certain things for me."

She stared silently at Monroe. *He does think I'ma fuck him for this house*, she concluded.

Monroe continued: "As my Point Guard, it's your job to take care of me and keep my ladies in order for me."

"So what? I'm like some kind of hoe-whisperer."

Monroe laughed. He couldn't wait to tell Zeph this new name, *Hoe-whisperer*.

Kelly didn't find humor in this conversation. She stared at Monroe with narrowed brows. "I'm supposed to wrangler your whores."

"Not whores. My team," Monroe corrected her.

Kelly shook her head. "I don't get it."

"Just help me balance them. Keep track of things. Organization."

"Herd the hoes?"

Monroe laughed again. "Don't think of it like that. All these women contribute to my happiness, but I am a man of discipline and structure. That's how I became the ball player that I am. I want my social life to have that same type of structure."

Kelly looked around the kitchen. "And I get to stay here?"

"No, you won't stay here. You will live here. You once told me you saw working with me as an avenue to other opportunities."

Hoe-whispering is not an opportunity, she thought to herself.

"With my leadership, you will own this house because you will buy this house from Zeph. I won't have anything to do with the transaction from a paperwork perspective. All you must do is say yes to the task, and I will get Zeph to sign the deed to you." Monroe sat back in his chair. His movement was equivalent to dropping a metaphoric mic. "That simple."

Kelly sat back in her seat. "And all I have to do is—"

"Keep me on point. My players are never to meet under any circumstance."

"And I get a house."

"Baby girl, you can get more than a house. This is just the beginning."

"And all I have to do is—"

"Be discreet and be loyal to me and only me."

Kelly sat silently in her thoughts. She looked around the enormous-sized kitchen. Kelly didn't need a place this big. Omari was never in the apartment, but to have her own spot, completely independent of her family, would be a dream come true. *I would be a fool not to*, she thought to herself.

"You gonna do it?"

"I will."

Monroe stared into Kelly's eyes. "Come on," he stated. "Let me finish giving you this tour."

"This is your bedroom," he stated once they reached the second floor.

Kelly immediately fell in love with *her* master bedroom. She opened the closet door and walked in. "A walk-in closet!"

Monroe stood back watching Kelly. Her excitement solidified his decision to trust her. She was appreciative and this was just the type of charcteristic that his Point Guard needed.

"I don't even have enough clothes to fill this closet."

Monroe walked further into the bedroom. "We can change that."

Kelly rushed past him into the master bathroom.

Monroe sat down on the bed. "You like it?"

Kelly leaned against the bathroom door frame. "I always dreamed about living in a place like this."

"My mother did, too."

"I thought you said this was Zeph's childhood home."

"It is. When I couldn't buy my own childhood home, it was my mother who wanted to buy this home."

"She was going to live in this big house by herself."

"At least until Zeph came home."

"From jail?"

Monroe nodded.

"I figured as much. Zeph gives off a roughness about him."

Monroe chuckled. "What do you know about roughness?"

Kelly blushed. She could answer that question in many ways but opted to stay on topic. "I'm in," she agreed. Kelly had sensory overload. She had been in luxury before, but never in luxury, she could call her own. "Count me in."

Monroe nodded his head approvingly.

"Since we are being honest with each other," she began. "I feel like I get mixed signals from you."

Monroe peered at her curiously. "What do you mean?"

"Like..." she paused, hesitant in hopes of not playing herself. "I sometimes feel like you look at me a certain way."

Monroe leaned back on his elbows. He knew what she meant, so he played into it. He looked at her seductively, "And how is that?"

"Like...that," she nodded towards the look on his face.

Monroe smirked. He stood up from the bed. They were less than an arm-length away from each other. "And how does that make you feel?"

Kelly blushed. "I don't know."

Monroe took all of Kelly in. He had to be honest with himself. She was doing something to him, too. How she looked at him with lust and admiration made him feel like an alpha male, like he was unstoppable, both on and off the court.

Jamilah used to have the ability to stroke his ego in this way. He missed her efforts. Now, Jamilah was too busy trying to save the world to notice her own husband. Moments with Kelly often reminded him of how much he missed those moments with his wife.

"Well, when you figure it out. You let me know." Monroe moved to the door. She was off limits to him, but around her, he was weak. He wanted her, and by leaving the room at this moment, he was going to leave her wanting him, too.

And it worked.

Monroe had walked into the second master bedroom at the far end of the hallway. When Kelly walked in, he was sitting on the bed, going through his phone.

"With being your…Point Guard," she was still unsure of her title, "Point Guard," she repeated it, trying to get used to it. It didn't help. "What exactly do I need to do?"

Monroe slipped his phone into his pocket. "First, we need to get you all moved in and settled. I want to do that ASAP because I need you focused."

"You are serious? This is going to be my house?"

Monroe nodded his head.

Kelly stood stunned. Now that she had agreed to everything, it was happening so fast, but not fast enough to outrun her morals. As she listened to Monroe, Kelly's thoughts rambled, *Jamilah is an asshole, but are you really okay with being a part of a nigga's infidelity? That's low. How would you feel if your husband did that shit to you? I wouldn't give my husband the opportunity. Did she, though? She's a bitch. That creates enough opportunity.*

"I want you fully moved in by this Saturday because, on Monday, we will make our rounds so that you can meet everybody, okay?"

"I am supposed to know them. They just won't know each other."

"Correct. They will know you only as my assistant. If they get feisty, catty, whatever the fuck women do, you don't engage. Don't get into no pissing match." He looked Kelly directly in the eye. "This includes Jamilah, too."

Surprisingly, when she heard Jamilah's name, a wave of guilt consumed her. *Why do I take her feelings into consideration? She damn sure doesn't consider me, as she talked shit about me with her bougie friends.*

Monroe laid back on the bed. "Well, now that you are on my team. I can focus on some other shit."

Kelly watched him. She took in his gorgeousness lying on the bed. She spotted his dick print and noted how it lay to the right. "You make it sound like I'm important."

"You are very important to me. You are the key to making sure I'm good."

"Why are you doing this?"

"Structure and order," he summarized his intentions. "It's that simple."

And control, she thought to herself. Kelly walked further into the room and ran her hand across the furniture. "Tell me about your girls."

"You gonna be my therapist."

"Well, I do need to know about them."

"You know my wife."

"Ugh!" Kelly replied, "Some wife."

Monroe exploded from the bed. "What did I just say?" His voice was stern. It stopped Kelly in her tracks. "Don't let that catty, petty shit get to your head. I need you clear-minded and focused. All that other shit is for the birds, and we ain't birds, you hear me?"

Kelly felt like he was yelling at her, but he wasn't. He was blunt and direct, making her feel like a little girl listening to her father's direction. "I hear you," she replied softly. Something about him demanded to be heard, even in the simplest moments. It was that characteristic that turned her on about him.

Monroe resumed his position on the bed. His arms were stretched out like in this *therapy* moment he found relaxation. He continued: "Then there's Deadria. She's a stripper."

"I see Jamilah isn't taking care of business."

"You don't know the half of it," Monroe sighed. "Rebecca is about making connections. We fuck, but mostly we talk business. She's very strategic in her thoughts."

"Jamilah, Deadria, Rebecca," Kelly held up three fingers. "You're missing one."

"Then you got my baby's mother."

Kelly's mouth dropped. "You have a child?" This was more juice than she had anticipated. She listened attentively with wide eyes.

"Monroe Jr."

"How old is he?"

"Two."

"He's not Jamilah's, obviously."

Monroe sat up and looked at Kelly. "Jamilah don't know about him either."

"You have a love child." Kelly could feel her morals being tested. *First, infidelity, and now a child. Where do I draw the line?* she questioned herself.

"I know it's a lot, but…" his voice trailed off. "Shit happened, and I'm dealing with it?"

"By not telling your wife about your two-year-old?"

Monroe's jaw clenched.

"Why didn't you just tell Jamilah when it first happened?"

"You met my wife before, right?" His question dripped with sarcasm. "How do you think she would have taken it?"

"She wouldn't have."

"Exactly."

The two sat quietly, thinking about the consequences if Jamilah ever found out about the child.

Kelly pondered, *Would she be more humiliated by the child or the hoes?*

"His mother is Maria Elliott."

"Where did you meet her at?"

"I met Maria when we were at Anthem University. She was Jamilah's roommate for a year."

"WAIT!" Kelly stated, experiencing juice overload again. "Jamilah knows her?"

"Yeah, they know each other," he paused. "They don't get along. Not because of the baby. They were beefing before the baby."

"So, you fucked your wife's enemy?"

Monroe sighed deeply. Out of all his secrets, this was the worse one. It was the one with moving complexities. His reckless behavior had brought a child into the picture, and he had a lot to lose if it ever came out.

"Why were they even beefing?"

"Women shit. You know how y'all do."

"You were fuckin' Maria in college while you were with Jamilah."

He never denied nor confirmed. He simply replied, "It was childish."

It wasn't childish; you were childish, Kelly concluded to herself.

"And Maria lives in the state?"

"Yeah."

"Does Jamilah know that y'all are in contact?"

"No. We really weren't in contact then. We are now because of MJ, but back then, no. I didn't know she was back in town until I ran into her at a club one night."

Kelly watched as Monroe slipped back into his memory. She walked to the bed and sat down by Monroe.

"That night was wild," he smirked. "We talked all night until the club shut down. The owner was like he was about to roll out and just told me to lock up. I fucked her that night in the VIP section. After that, we kept linking up, and I piped her down every chance I got. Then she was like she was pregnant."

"And what did you do?"

"Shit," Monroe smiled, revealing his only physical flaw—a set of dimples to die for. "I was happy. I have a son! That's the only thing Jamilah could never give me, so I told Maria to keep him. He looks just like me. My little man," Monroe nodded his head proudly.

"When are you going to tell Jamilah?"

The pride drained from his face and was replaced with a look of worry. "I'm a coward when it comes to this situation. Jamilah got her ways, but she's good for me. I don't want to lose her, but I know I need to be around my son more. He's getting older. Seeing him here and there ain't right."

"Is Maria a typical baby momma?"

"What do you mean?"

"Like, does she cause a scene? Is she extra?"

"Hell no! She doesn't want to be in the limelight. She doesn't even want the world to know that MJ exists. Maria is a beautiful person, inside and out. She got her own career. She does her own thing."

Kelly nodded her head.

"When Maria calls, she comes first," Monroe stated sternly.

"After Jamilah?"

"Before Jamilah," he corrected. "That's my child's mother. You understand? Maria doesn't call me; I call her. So, if she calls, it got to be something important. She is to be put through ASAP. No questions asked; just put her through."

"Okay." Kelly sighed. Monroe had dropped so much on her at one time. "I now understand the second confidentiality form."

"This is just the tip of the iceberg," Monroe informed her.

"You have more secrets?"

"You have no idea," Monroe sat up. "Let's see how you manage this aspect of my life, then maybe..."

"Maybe what?"

Monroe didn't reply.

"There's a lot more, huh?"

Kelly was talking to herself. She took the hint. *His secrets ain't got nothing on the shit I have to keep tight-lipped on,* she thought to herself. *He lucked up choosing me as his Point Guard. I have to get used to that title. I'm a Point Guard.* "Thank you for sharing your secrets with me. I kinda feel closer to you."

"It's no kind of...you will be very close to me. You are going to know everything in due time. Just know that you take care of me, and I will take care of you."

Kelly nodded her head.

Monroe looked at his watch. "Come on, let's go get something to eat." He stood up from the bed. He reached back and pulled Kelly up.

"Hugs!" Kelly stated, with her arms reached out.

"Oh, you a hugger, huh?" Monroe wrapped his arms around her waist. "You always smell so damn good."

Kelly giggled.

Their embrace started out innocently, but Monroe squeezed Kelly's waist tightly and buried his head into her neck. She felt his lips lightly brush her neck and felt a quiver from the little man in the boat.

Monroe finally let her go. "Where are you trying to eat at?"

"Anywhere you want," she whispered.

Monroe licked his lips as he looked at her. Their talk had relaxed him. He played it cool in public, but his secrets weighed heavy on him. Kelly had allowed him to share some of his innermost secrets. "Come on," he ordered. He turned to walk out of the room.

Kelly followed him, but then she stopped and looked back into the second bedroom. It wasn't as large as the master bedroom, but it was just as nice and belonged to her. She suddenly felt a surge of responsibility to protect Monroe at all costs. It meant something for him to choose her, and she would show him he had chosen correctly.

If he gives me all this and more, I will show that man the utmost respect and loyalty. "I am his Point Guard."

CHAPTER EIGHT

PROTECTING THE FRANCHISE

OCTOBER 3, 2019

"Do you want me to cut it off?"

Kelly watched Monroe's body language closely. He sat on the edge of her couch with a clenched jaw. He was fuming. His hands were balled into tight fists. He looked as though he was about to explode.

"Huh?" Kelly questioned. "Do you want me to cut it off?"

"No."

Kelly inhaled and exhaled slowly. She didn't expect Monroe, a man with a team of hoes, to have this type of reaction. *What's good for the goose is good for the gander*, she thought as she watched her distraught boss.

"WHY?!"

His outburst caused Kelly to jump.

"Of all the niggas..." he shook his head. His eyes were still glued to the screen. "Of all the niggas, why she had to fuck him?"

Kelly observed that Monroe was mad about the person and not that his wife was cheating. She looked at the screen. If she was in a different setting, she could have easily been aroused by what she was watching. It was sensual and passionate, yet a perfect mixture of dominance and submission that kept Kelly's eyes glued to the screen. The longer she watched, the more she could understand why Monroe was in his feelings. They weren't watching two people fuck. They were watching two people make love—passionately. She looked at Monroe. He was holding the back of his neck like he was forcing himself to continue watching.

Kelly had been working under her second confidentiality form for Monroe for almost four months now. She had learned him like the back of her hand. Indirectly, Kelly had managed to learn Jamilah, too. So much so that she had started noticing things between Jamilah and Zeph. Kelly couldn't explain it exactly, but it was something between them. She needed proof, though. So, Kelly talked Monroe into having cameras installed all over the house. She told him that it would be a nice gesture to Jamilah if he added extra security for her benefit while he was traveling with the team.

Initially, Monroe thought installing the cameras was a great idea, but when he brought the subject to Jamilah—she refused. Jamilah claimed that she didn't want the cameras in the house because she didn't want to feel like she was under surveillance. She said it was one thing to have cameras at the front and back entrances of the house; it was another to have them inside. The couple debated the cameras for weeks, resulting in Jamilah having her way. No cameras would be installed inside their home.

This was unacceptable to Kelly; so, with sneaky paperwork placement; she got Monroe to sign off on installing cameras in the house. When the couple went out of town for a mini vacation, Kelly had the cameras installed in discreet locations. She couldn't let her suspicions go, and this was the way to prove her claims.

When you give a man or woman enough rope, he or she will always manage to hang themselves. Kelly and Monroe were at Kelly's house watching live footage of Jamilah and Zeph hanging themselves, or in other words, having passionate sex in Monroe's mansion, in his kitchen, on his kitchen table.

"I'm not mad," Monroe finally stated, looking away from the television. He stood up from the couch. "I'm not mad at all."

Kelly felt pleased with this moment because her suspicions were confirmed. She hated that it was true because she didn't want to hurt Monroe, but simultaneously, she signed up to protect him at all costs. This was her protecting him.

"What do we do now?" she asked as she looked at Monroe sincerely.

Monroe looked at Kelly and unleashed his rage, "WHY YOU SHOW ME THIS SHIT?!"

Kelly looked at him, shocked by his audacity to yell at her.

"WHAT WAS YOUR FUCKIN' PURPOSE?!"

"Well…" her voice trembled. "I was hired to protect the franchise. I was just protecting the franchise." She had been told that many times; she now believed it and confidently repeated it. She folded her arms across her chest. She wasn't feeling as confident as she spoke. In fact, she was scared. Monroe's six-foot-five-inch frame was intimidating, especially when he was pissed.

"I EAT AT THAT FUCKIN' TABLE!" he launched his glass at the flat screen.

Kelly looked at the broken screen and the liquor slowly rolling down, puddling on her TV stand.

"Zeph...damn nigga. You supposed to be my boy, and you out here fuckin' my wife," Monroe grabbed his head. He sat back on the couch. He watched through the cracked screen as Jamilah did sexual things that she would never do to him. She didn't even sound the same. "This shit is happening right now in my house?"

"Yes," Kelly replied in a whisper. "It is."

"I KNOW IT IS!" he shouted. Monroe got up from the couch and walked to the kitchen.

Kelly followed closely behind him.

He began snatching open cabinets and aggressively slamming them close.

"What are you looking for?"

"I need a glass," Monroe mumbled, still rummaging through the cabinets. "I NEED A FUCKIN' GLASS!" he shouted. He grabbed a cabinet door and proceeded to rip it off the hinges. As the cabinet door fell, it hit Monroe, leaving a gash on his forehead.

Kelly ran to his side. She grabbed the kitchen rag and pressed it against his head.

Monroe knocked her hand away. "I'm alright."

"Stop it," she ordered. "You're bleeding."

Monroe let Kelly doctor him. "Come upstairs," she stated. "My first aid kit is in my bathroom."

"Make me a drink before you come upstairs and bring the bottle," he ordered as he walked out of the kitchen.

Kelly had never seen Monroe so furious. She quickly gathered everything and followed behind him.

Monroe sat on the bed as Kelly stood before him, caring for the wound on his head. Monroe gripped a bottle on Hennessy in his left hand. When Kelly would move, he would take a swig.

"Slow down," she urged.

Monroe put the bottle down on the nightstand. "Maria is about to get married," he mumbled. "And my wife is fucking my childhood friend," Monroe laughed. "I'm surrounded by disloyal mauthafuckas."

Kelly didn't respond. She had overheard a conversation between Monroe and Maria. She couldn't blame Maria. Only a fool would sit around being a baby mother while the man you wanted was already married and playing house. Of course, Kelly didn't let on that she knew about Maria's engagement. She figured Monroe would talk about it when he was ready.

"I told you not to put them damn cameras in my house. Who even approved that shit?"

"You did," Kelly replied.

Monroe knocked her hand away. "No the fuck I didn't. I didn't approve shit."

"You should watch what you sign then," Kelly replied nonchalantly.

Monroe stood up. He already towered over her, but he seemed more prominent, swelled up from so much anger. "You think talking slick to me right now is the right thing to do?"

Kelly was too stiff with fear to move.

Monroe stared at her with a snarl. He wanted to knock her head off, but he didn't need to deal with that extra shit. He walked back to bed.

"I-I…I am sorry," Kelly stammered out. "I just thought you wanted to know," she whispered quietly.

"You thought I wanted to know my wife was fucking my friend?" Monroe grunted. "I specifically told your black-ass not to do it."

"You didn't want to know?"

"WHO SAID I DIDN'T KNOW!" he shouted. He took a swig from the bottle. "I didn't need to see a fuckin' confirmation, Kelly!" Monroe flopped down on the bed.

"I was protecting the franchise."

"Why are you protecting me?"

"BECAUSE YOU TOLD ME TO PROTECT YOU!"

The house was silent, and they could hear the moans from the television.

Kelly attempted to continue to nurse Monroe's injury. "I was trying to protect you."

He knocked her hand away from his head. He was tired of her

standing over him, nursing him. "Tell all them other bitches that." He looked at Kelly with a snarl. She had on a nightshirt that read Love Me. That's all he wanted, too. Somebody to love him. Kelly was proving to be that somebody, although she simply referred to it as *protecting the franchise*.

"I'm staying here tonight," he told her. He stood up and headed for the second bedroom.

Kelly wanted to tell him that he could stay in her room...with her, but he was gone. She didn't have the courage to say it to him anyway. She walked out of her bedroom and followed behind him.

Monroe staggered into the second bedroom and kicked off his shoes.

Kelly stood silently at the door. She watched Monroe remove his jacket, t-shirt, and belt; she finally spoke up, "Hey."

Monroe spun around and looked at her. His pants were unbuttoned and unzipped. They hung from his hips, "What's up?"

"You want to watch a movie?"

Monroe grabbed the bottle and took a sip. "Nah, I watched enough TV for tonight."

"I don't want you to be alone."

Monroe shook his head. It was her fault in the first place that he was left feeling this way. "I can't believe this shit backfired."

"What exactly backfired?"

"Shut the fuck up." Monroe snapped. "You've done enough."

"You can't make people love you, Monroe."

"I made you."

"Did you?"

Monroe frowned. "You don't love me either?" He chuckled. "All you bitches are alike. You use a nigga, and then leave a nigga."

She looked at Monroe with disdain.

"You could have at least faked like you loved me."

"Did I say that I didn't love you?"

"YOU AIN'T SAY YOU DID!" he snapped. His voice lowered, "And that says a-mauthafuckin'-lot."

"What do you think all of this was about?" Kelly questioned. "If I didn't love you, why would I?"

"SHUT THE FUCK UP!" Monroe walked to the bed and sat down.

Monroe was no longer swelled with anger. He looked deflated, like a shell of a man. His head was held low, and he gripped his *bottle* just as a toddler would.

"You look pathetic."

The suddenness of the insult caught Monroe off guard. He looked up to see Kelly's audacity.

She stared at him with a look of disgust. "You heard me. I said you look pathetic, like a little bitch."

Monroe stood up from the bed.

"What you mad?" she taunted. "You look weak and pathetic. Ugh," the sound of her disgust lingered in the room. "I can't believe I thought you were worthy of my loyalty. I thought you were worthy of my love."

Like a beast on a prowl, Monroe moved slowly towards Kelly as she continued to talk recklessly to him. "Bitch, watch how you talk to me."

Kelly folded her arms across her chest. "I'm a bitch?" she laughed. "Your wife is fuckin' your best friend, and Zeph is beating her pussy up. Hard," Kelly moaned, imitating the sounds already playing in Monroe's head. "I bet he would tear my little pussy up, too."

"What? You gonna fuck this nigga, too?"

"She called him Daddy. Did you hear that part?" Kelly laughed because she knew she was getting under his skin. "Your baby's momma is about to marry somebody else because you ain't man enough for her. She thinks you are weak, too." Kelly paused and said, "Oh, Maria told me how you cried and begged her to be with you. The funny part is, she had you on speaker phone, so the new nigga heard the bitch in you, too."

Through clenched teeth, Monroe blew out his frustrations.

"Rebecca is fuckin' a white lawyer because you ain't nothing but her rebellion against her family personified. When you cancel on her, she calls the next nigga to pipe. You just dick to her."

"Watch how you talking to me," Monroe warned Kelly again.

"It doesn't matter what I say to you. The man in front of me doesn't have control. He's emotional. The weak-ass nigga in front of me runs off emotions like a female."

Monroe dropped the bottle of Hennessy on the floor. He had crept so slowly towards her that she hadn't even realized how close he had gotten to her. "Watch your fuckin' mouth, bitch."

"And Deadria fucks everybody. You're just another lame that pays for pussy; just pathetic. Now that's some fragile shit. Your players bring out the bitch-ass in you."

Monroe stood so close, as he spoke, his nose touched hers. "And who you fuckin'?!"

Kelly ran her hand across Monroe's chest. "I'm waiting on you to see me."

Monroe knocked her hand away from him.

"I don't love the franchise, but I love the owner." Kelly moved from between Monroe and the wall. "Well, I used to be," she added as she walked to the bed.

Monroe turned around and watched her, "What you mean you used to?"

Kelly sat on the bed. "I don't have any respect for weak men."

Monroe walked over to the bed and stood in front of her. "I ain't weak," he replied, looking down on her.

"Prove it."

Monroe stared at Kelly. He ran his thumb over her bottom lip. They felt soft to the touch, just as he had imagined.

"Prove it," she ordered. "Prove that you are the strong, dominant man I love."

He slipped his hand into his pants and slowly stroked his dick with one hand as he rubbed his thumb against her lip. Kelly opened her mouth, and Monroe rubbed his thumb against her tongue. The wetness and warmth of her mouth on his thumb turned him on. The fact that she had allowed him to put his thumb in her mouth did something else to him. He slipped his thumb deeper into her mouth.

She didn't stop him. She didn't gag.

This little gesture had turned him on even more. He finally spoke again. "Suck my dick," he ordered.

Kelly turned her head. His thumb slipped from her mouth. "I don't suck off weak, emotional bitches," she spoke with venom.

The denial reignited Monroe's anger. "Suck my dick," he spoke through clenched teeth.

"No," she replied.

Monroe locked eyes with Kelly. His eyes were lit with fire. His look made her moist. She stared at him seductively as he pulled out his dick. She could tell he wasn't fully hard, but the size was already impressive. It was pretty. Wrapped in a chocolate coat, wearing a light brown hat, and standing on top of a well-manicured lawn of jet-black hair. Kelly wanted him, but instead of admitting it, she said, "I. DON'T. FUCK. WEAK. MEN."

With a quick move, Monroe grabbed Kelly by her throat. She never saw it coming nor had a chance to react. Instead, she looked at him, scared and turned on.

"Open your fuckin' mouth."

Defiantly, Kelly forced out a no.

Monroe squeezed her neck tighter.

Kelly gave in to his grip and opened her mouth.

"Ain't shit weak about me," he whispered, guiding his dick into her mouth.

Kelly stared up at him. She watched as he focused on rubbing his dick against her tongue. He let go of his dick. His chocolate muscle stood erect. "Suck my dick."

Kelly submissively obliged his request as she opened her mouth and allowed his dick to feel her wet warmth. She pulled his dick out and spit on it.

Monroe watched as Kelly's spit dripped from the tip of his dick. "Fuck them other bitches," he mumbled to himself. The sight of Kelly using both hands to stroke his dick as she guided it in and out of her mouth, had Monroe stuck. "Love me!" he ordered her.

Kelly removed Monroe's dick from her mouth. "I do love you."

Monroe grabbed the back of Kelly's head and shoved his dick down her throat. "Give me strength," he stated as he rode the curve of her tongue until he reached the back of her throat. The feeling sent electric volts through his body. He guided her head quicker down his shaft.

She gagged.

The sound of her choking, plus the sound of his dick splashing in saliva intensified the sloppy visual of saliva dripping and bubbles forming around her mouth.

"Suck that head," he ordered. He grabbed her hand and made her hold his nuts. Seeing her sucking on his tip and holding his nuts reminded him that he was *that nigga* and these bitches would do anything for him. He just needed to remind them of their places in his world. He pulled his dick away from Kelly's grasp.

She looked at him disappointed that he had stopped her.

Monroe stared back at Kelly. *Look at this bitch*, he thought to himself. He tapped his dick against the side of her face. He grabbed her jaw with his right hand, palmed the back of her head with his left and guided her head back and forth on his dick. "Take this dick," he spoke through clenched teeth. "Put my dick in your mouth," he ordered, holding her head still.

Kelly did as she was told, having no control of her head.

Monroe slowly began to fuck her face. He couldn't seem to get enough of the feeling.

Kelly wasn't gagging, but she was trying to tap out by patting Monroe's leg. She couldn't take it anymore; she needed to breathe.

Monroe wouldn't let up. He continued to thrust his hips, going faster and faster. The sound of her gagging sent a surge of resentment and a need for revenge to course through his body.

He was going to make Zeph and Jamilah pay for their disloyalty to him. He closed his eyes as this newly formed energy of hate had him internally promising that he would make them regret their ways.

Kelly continued patting his leg until it became a sense of urgency on her part. Her patience for him to enjoy himself had left her body, and she was submerged in panic. She couldn't breathe. Her patting his leg turned into fists, punching for release.

Monroe snapped out of his thoughts. He looked down at Kelly.

Her eyes filled with panic.

He waited until the last minute. When he finally pulled his dick out, Kelly gasped for air.

Monroe watched as she tried to catch her breath, but only for a second.

He thrust his dick into her mouth before she could take another breath, continuing at the same pace as before. He gripped her hair tightly and harnessed it as he rode her face. He could feel his nut on the horizon. Between her struggles for air and his thoughts, he could feel his power returning to him. "FUCK THEM!" he yelled. "I WILL MAKE THEM ALL PAY!"

With his mind made up and his eyes closed—he exploded in her mouth!

The sight of his cum dripping from her mouth did something to him. What should have taken his strength did the complete opposite. He felt rejuvenated, powerful even. He felt in control and ready to lead his team again.

Panting, Kelly looked up at him. She didn't bother wiping her mouth.

Instead, she grabbed Monroe's dick and kissed it.

Monroe nodded his head approving of her gesture. He didn't know how, but she managed to break him down and build him back up. She had given him one of the best pep talks he had ever received.

It was at that moment that Monroe decided to rebuild his team.

"We are far beyond those days. I've made connections that have propelled me and—" Monroe stopped talking when he noticed Kelly standing in the doorway. "What's up?" he called to her.

"What's up?" she questioned rhetorically, glancing down at her watch. "I thought the interview started at two." Kelly intended to be thirty minutes early, but she was late by the looks of things. "This isn't the applicant, is it?"

Monroe looked at the young woman and smiled. "Nah, she is more than an applicant."

"I'm damn near family the way Ms. Shantell used to get me, too."

Monroe laughed. "She used to get all of us."

"'Member that time you, Zeph, and Tavi skipped school. Y'all got an ass-whoopin' for skippin' and then I caught an ass-whoopin' because I lied to cover y'all."

"I didn't know she could move that fast. She caught all three of us."

Avie laughed loudly. "I would have been in the clear, but y'all can't skip like regular people. Y'all was all in Terryburg County trying to—"

Monroe cleared his throat.

Avie caught the hint and stopped talking.

"What happened in Terryburg County?"

Avie sat back in her seat. She shook her head.

"Nothing," Monroe replied. He held a smirk on his face. "Nothing happened."

Kelly laughed light-heartedly. She was trying to be a part of the moment, but it was clear that she wasn't privy to *their* secrets. "So if *she* isn't the interviewee, where is she?"

"The name's Avie."

Kelly shot her a fake smile. She could give a damn about her name.

"I canceled her," Monroe replied.

"The two o'clock?"

"I canceled the two o'clock," Monroe repeated.

"Did you reschedule it?"

"Girl, he just said he canceled her. She outta here," Avie inserted herself into the conversation. "I got the job!"

Kelly looked from Avie to Monroe. She expected him to correct Avie's attitude and tone, but he said nothing. Amazed, Kelly looked back at Avie, who sat confidently in her seat. *Nowadays, it's hard to tell who is a stud or not,* Kelly shook her head dismissively. She looked back at Monroe, "So when were you going to let me know?" It was apparent she was irritated. Her hands on her hips help emphasize her frustrations. "I rushed over here for nothing."

"Um," Avie hummed. Her eyes shifted around the room. Avie had known Monroe for years. She knew him well enough to know that he never liked being questioned by anyone, especially not the *help*. Monroe was the type that knew it all and felt as though he could do it all. He never took too kindly to being questioned about his actions.

"I got sidetracked talking to Avie."

Kelly frowned.

"Since you're here, come join us," he motioned for Kelly to sit next to Avie in front of his desk.

Kelly moved to the empty seat and sat down.

The moment that Kelly sat down, Avie could feel the shift in the atmosphere. It was evident to Avie that Kelly didn't like her; so, she added fuel to the fire. "I'm Avie," she stated again. This time she extended her hand to Kelly.

Kelly gave a fake smile. "Kelly," she replied, daintily dropping her hand into Avie's.

Avie looked at Monroe and smiled.

He wasn't amused. He didn't like what he was seeing from Kelly. He thought he had made himself clear when he said don't engage in the feisty, catty behavior. She was now sitting across from him oozing this behavior.

"So, what will you be doing?" Kelly asked.

"I will—"

Monroe interjected. "She will handle what I have her handle."

"She's not handling any of my responsibilities, right?"

Monroe looked at Kelly with a straight face.

Avie knew the look on Monroe's face all too well. "I'll step out," Avie stood up, prepared to exit.

"No," he motioned Avie back to her seat. "I think Kelly needs to leave."

Kelly's jaw dropped. She sat silently, cursing Monroe with her eyes.

A sound wasn't made, but they all heard her loud and clear.

"Can I speak to you alone?" Kelly asked.

Monroe ignored her. He resumed his conversation with Avie as though Kelly hadn't asked him a question. "I can't wait to tell Zeph you're back."

"Oh naw! You should let me tell him."

"He probably won't even recognize you, because..." Monroe shook his head. Avie had grown into herself. Though he considered her like a little sister, he wasn't blind. Avie was no longer the little kid sister that hung around or they had to babysit from time to time. He was now sitting across from a shapely young woman.

"I can't wait to see the look on his face." Avie continued to carry on the conversation like Kelly wasn't there, too. She had seen this side of Monroe on several occasions. She had even been on the receiving end of this behavior a time or two.

Kelly looked at Avie with her nose turned up like she could smell the *bitch* in her. As she looked at her, she thought about how she ended up in this position. It seemed like it was just yesterday when Monroe told her to set up interviews. All she knew was that the position was a summer internship only open to college women with a junior classification. When Kelly asked him why, initially, he told her to just do what he said. Later, Monroe came back and offered an explanation, stating that his basketball camp aimed to empower young men. He wanted to use this opportunity to empower young women. Some of the candidates on paper deserved this type of *empowerment*; however, the more interviews they conducted, Kelly began to realize what was really happening. Monroe was on the prowl; he was recruiting new pussy, and for Kelly, this bothered her, because she knew her loyalty wasn't enough for him.

Kelly continued to take the mental abuse, sitting silently as her supervisor ignored her existence. Instead of directing her frustrations at him, her irritations resided with Avie.

The woman next to her was everything that she was not. Kelly was a confident woman, but sitting beside this woman made her question herself. Not only was she young, with flawless, brown-skin. She was also physically fit, and the worse part of it all, she shared a mutual past with Monroe. Their walk down memory lane left Kelly feeling like the two— three if you include Zeph—had an unbreakable bond. Knowing that she would be *around* pissed Kelly off. Where would this leave her? Was Avie her replacement? It was too much to process for Kelly. She stood up from her seat. "Excuse me," she told no one since they had already dismissed her from the conversation.

Kelly remembered the night she and Monroe had shared as she gathered her things. She loved that Monroe's *power* had returned after taking several personal blows but hated that his loyalty didn't accompany his power.

"See you later," she whispered.

Monroe didn't respond.

Kelly snarled at Avie. *Fuckin' bitch*, she thought as she walked out of the office.

"Hey!" Jamilah called to Kelly as she stepped out of Monroe's office.

Out of the frying pan and into the fire, Kelly thought to herself.

"Hello," Kelly replied as politely as she possibly could. She didn't bother to wait for a response from Jamilah when she said, "I'm going to leave early. I'm not really feeling too well."

"Aw," Jamilah replied. Unfortunately, Jamilah often threw Kelly so much shade; that even her most natural form of caring appeared as pettiness. Monroe had told Kelly to leave the *pettiness* alone, but anything concerning Jamilah bothered Kelly's soul. So much so that Kelly could still recall Jamilah's comments verbatim when talking to her friends. Jamilah's words had created an enemy in her.

"I know you are on your way out, but may I speak with you for a minute." Jamilah didn't wait for Kelly to reply. She turned on her heels and strutted into the kitchen, expecting Kelly to follow.

Kelly sighed deeply. *I am protecting the franchise*, she chanted in her mind. She just wanted to get away from all of Monroe's women. Being the Point

Guard made her interact with all his girls, and it was slowly affecting her. Jamilah was the worse of them all. *She better be easy today because I will level her block with the amount of shit I know. I don't have the time or energy for her bullshit!*

"So," Jamilah stated the moment Kelly walked into the kitchen. "I want to do something special for Monroe." She searched Kelly's face for a reaction to her idea, but Kelly held a poker face.

"What's that look about?"

"What look?"

"The one you're giving me. I told you I wanted to do something for my husband, and you gave me this look. What's that look about?"

Kelly shook her head. "I'm not giving you a look. I just don't feel well."

"Oh, well, when you have an opportunity, give me some dates open in his schedule and draft a list of people we can invite to the party." Jamilah paused. "Matter of fact," she said, after pondering for a few minutes. "I will email you a list of people I think should be in attendance."

Kelly was reaching for her tablet, preparing to take notes. When she finally got it out, she looked up at Jamilah, who peered at her over her wine glass. Kelly cleared her throat. "So, I need to find a date."

"Preferably on the weekend and before All-Star Weekend." Jamilah put her cup down. "Actually, it could be during All-Star Weekend. That way, I know, for the most part, that people would be available and ready to party."

Kelly nodded her head as she continued jotting down notes. "So this party is for next year?"

Jamilah nodded her head. "Obviously."

Kelly frowned.

"There it goes again."

Kelly looked up from her notes. "There what goes again?"

"That face."

"Oh, no, I thought you were talking to me about something happening this year."

"Next year is right around the corner. It wouldn't be wise to procrastinate planning such an important event."

Kelly nodded. She could understand Jamilah's point, but why start today? She had just explained to her that she was feeling bad.

"What should I get him?"

Kelly shrugged. She didn't have an answer, nor did she have the energy to act as though she had an answer.

"Look up some venues as well," Jamilah added. "This is going to be amazing. Maybe we should have a theme."

Kelly closed her tablet. "I will start on the venue and the guest list, but I have to do this later."

"Oh," Jamilah replied with disappointment. "Fine."

"No disrespect, but—"

"No, it's fine, Kelly." Jamilah was now the one with a *look* on her face. "I'll just get Avie to start working on things for me."

Kelly stopped what she was doing and looked at Jamilah as her mind raced, *Oh, so it's official if Jamilah knows. He did hire Avie. Damnit, Monroe!*

"Take some time to feel better," Jamilah stated condescendingly.

Kelly's stare could have killed Jamilah twice. "No, need for that." Kelly opened her tablet.

"Maybe there is."

"No," Kelly insisted. "There's no need for that."

Jamilah smiled. She was pleased with her ability to manipulate Kelly. "What were you thinking as far as a theme?"

Kelly grimaced. *I hate I need this job,* she thought as she looked at Jamilah and forced a smile. *I hate all of Monroe's women.*

Kelly finally made it home after spending her afternoon with Jamilah planning a party that wouldn't occur until February in Chicago.

She was exhausted.

If she wasn't sick before, she was now. The thought of spending so much time with Jamilah turned her stomach. Knowing that Avie was still in her *interview* when Kelly finally got to leave the house two hours later pissed her off, too. She had never had an interview that took two hours. The whole ride home, she kept thinking about their conversation. *What could they have possibly been talking about?* she thought to herself. She couldn't wait to get home and sulk in her solitude.

Kelly walk into her house to find her mother sitting on her couch. "So much for solitude," she grumbled. "Zani, what are you doing here?" she questioned as she placed her things on the opposite end of the couch. The sight of her mother sitting in her living room had irritated her to the high heavens. *Omari, you give your key to any-damn-body,* Kelly thought.

"I decided to drop in on you. You've been distant lately. Both your father and I have noticed it."

Kelly rolled her eyes. She knew a lie when she heard one. Zani may have noticed that she was *distant*, but her father had other important things going on. Nevertheless, Kelly decided to entertain her mother's lies. "I'm surprised he has time to notice anything other than his—"

Zani shook her head. "Watch how you speak about my husband," she interjected. "He isn't perfect, but he is mine, and I will fuck anyone up who dares disrespect him in my presence," she paused and then added, "Even our only daughter."

Kelly sucked her teeth.

"Try me," Zani warned.

Although her mother was always nurturing, Kelly knew that her mother played no games regarding their family and, more specifically, her husband. Kelly didn't necessarily know the details of her parents' relationship, but she had heard stories. Through those stories, she learned valuable lessons of loyalty—be it right or wrong. Naturally, those lessons of loyalty had rubbed off on Kelly, which explained why loyalty meant everything to her. She had seen first-hand what it looked like when a man and woman established this type of relationship with one another. This is the type of relationship Kelly daydreamed about having with Jamilah's husband.

Zani stood up from the couch. She was a short woman with a slender build and was dressed to the nine in heels. At first sight, Zani looked like a fragile, pampered woman. She looked like she could have been one of Jamilah's uppity friends in another lifetime, but her looks were deceiving.

Zani walked towards Kelly with her arms open. Initially, Kelly didn't move, but then she reached out to her mother. Kelly couldn't resist her mother's hugs. Her hugs were always tight and long like she wanted to make sure Kelly could feel her love for her. "My baby," Zani whispered into Kelly's ear as the two embraced. "It's good to see you."

Kelly smiled. "Thank you," she replied. "It's good to see you, too."

Zani stared into Kelly's face. Despite their difference in size, the two women looked identical.

"What's been going on?" Zani grabbed Kelly's hand and led her to the couch.

"Life," Kelly answered shortly.

The two women sat down.

Zani gave Kelly a half smile. She was trying to build a relationship with her only child, but Kelly made things difficult.

"If you are here, does that mean the move is completed?"

"Yes and no. Your father is still handling something in The District, but he'll be this way very soon."

"He's seriously moving to North Carolina?"

"That's the plan."

Kelly shook her head. She couldn't imagine her father, a DC-born and bred man, being okay with moving south. "What things is he handling?"

"I don't care to share details with you," Zani replied. "Just know that your father and I will always be there for you, regardless of our proximity. You understand?"

"Always with the secrets."

"Trust that things are—"

"Always with blind trust."

Zani chuckled. "Remember, everything ain't for everybody."

Kelly pulled her hand away from her mother. "Glad to know that I'm considered everybody."

Zani exhaled deeply. She knew where this conversation was heading. "So what's been going on in your life?" she tried to change the subject.

Kelly didn't have the energy to dig for truths. Her parents have been secretive her entire life. As an adult, she realized that family could be just as toxic and draining as complete strangers. *What's the point of her being here if she isn't honest?* Kelly wondered as she looked over at her mother.

"You still working for that basketball guy?"

"I am."

"Okay, so how is that going?"

Kelly wanted to be as tight-lipped about her personal life as her mother. Still, she could never withhold information from her. Zani could make Kelly feel so comfortable that she couldn't help divulging every aspect of her life—even if it was embarrassing.

"I fell out of love with my boss today."

Zani stared silently at her daughter. Her silence and lack of judgment made it easy for Kelly to talk to her.

The two women didn't have a traditional mother-daughter relationship. Their relationship just worked. Perhaps it was Zani's approach to parenting. She believed in accepting Kelly for where she was in life. No subject was off limits except matters pertaining to her parents' business. That's what prevented them from being *friends*. Their conversations were one-sided, with Kelly sharing and Zani listening.

"I want Monroe. At first, it was sexual; I knew I was lusting for him. I would spend my days daydreaming about having sex with him. Not anything romantic, at least not at first. I just wanted hot, steamy sex. His place, my place, in the bed he shares with his wife..." her voice trailed off. She stared across the room, speaking as though Zani wasn't there. "I find myself wanting to give him the loyalty I see you give Daddy. I want to show him that I am a rider and willing to do anything to see him succeed, but he doesn't see me. He just sees me when he wants to see me. When it is convenient for him to see me. Today, I had to sit through this interview," she shook her head. She still couldn't quite understand what she had experienced.

"You've done that before," Zani chimed in.

"I have..." Kelly hesitated. She wasn't sure if she wanted her mother to know the truth. "It's funny because all of those women whose applications we pulled are intelligent, but the moment they realized that Monroe was looking for more—"

"More?"

"Once they realize what was being said, it's like their brain turned off, and they started answering questions with their pussy." Kelly shook her head. "I couldn't help but wonder, do I ever lose my brain for my pussy when dealing with him?"

"You did."

Kelly cut her eye at her mother.

Zani shrugged.

Kelly continued: "He just doesn't see me."

"You should start dating," Zani suggested. "You have put yourself on hold for someone who is already involved. He's married and clearly still on the prowl. That's not fair to you, because loyalty is a two-way street."

Tears formed in Kelly's eyes. She tried to hold them back, but they rolled uncontrollably down her face. Her feelings were genuinely hurt.

"Plus, Monroe isn't a good guy. He's not the guy I would like to see you with or chase after. I don't want to see you chase after any man, really."

Kelly looked at her mother.

"Just..." Zani hesitated. "You gotta come to your own conclusions about him, but...yeah, no...not him. You can do better."

Kelly was unsure how Zani had formulated her opinion, but she knew there was truth in her words. "As I was driving home, I had come to the same conclusion. I never want to be *that* woman to any man."

"Then don't."

"I won't!" Kelly sat up on the couch. "I will no longer put my brain on pause and talk with my pussy. I will no longer allow myself to let Monroe, or any man, experience my level of loyalty without them devoting themselves to me."

"Good," Zani agreed proudly.

Kelly looked at Zani. "I'ma show Monroe that my level of loyalty is not for free." She nodded her head, confirming her words of conviction. "I'ma give Monroe a taste of his own medicine."

CHAPTER TEN

SHANTELL'S LESSON
NOVEMBER 14, 2019

Jamilah sat at the kitchen island. She was eating a bowl of cereal and looking at Monroe and Kelly on her Lani. They had been there since she had been home. Jamilah watched the two of them closely. She observed how they interacted with one another when they thought no one was around.

Kelly had her head buried in her tablet, probably taking notes as Monroe paced back and forth. If he needed to look at her tablet, he would step close, look, and then move away. He was never too close to her, but he was close enough as though he was moving around in a *safe* zone. They weren't laughing and having a jolly ole time—this scene looked strictly business.

Jamilah squinted her eyes. Finally, she put her spoon down and just stared at them. Something was off about their interactions. It was like the perfect ratio of physical closeness. She went from looking at them to just looking at Kelly. Everything in her demeanor seemed controlled.

Monroe was a chocolate, thick-bodied man, and Kelly acted like she didn't even notice. Even if not on purpose, Monroe was just one of those men fortunate enough to naturally show thick even when he wasn't aroused. But it didn't seem to interest Kelly, not one bit. The fact that she was paying Monroe's physique no mind; set Jamilah's internal alarm off.

She shifted in her seat at the kitchen table. She pushed her bowl of cereal away from her. She laughed at her imagination. *Monroe ain't checkin' for no fat girl. This is the same man that put so much care and concern into his physical well-being. Why would he want someone at the opposite end of the health spectrum? Plus, Monroe wouldn't cheat on me. He damn sure wouldn't cheat on me for that bitch.*

Jamilah pulled her bowl back to her. She picked up her spoon and took a bite. As she chewed her food, she thought about the time Monroe almost lost her. Although she proved triumphant, that was the longest semester of her college career. She never wanted to experience that level of humiliation again.

Jamilah shook herself out of the memory and resumed her bowl of cereal when an epiphany dawned on her. "Kelly is good people," Jamilah stated aloud to no one. She looked around, shocked that those words had escaped her lips. "Kelly *is* good people," she admitted again. "She is reliable, timely, responsible. I really don't have a problem with her." Jamilah watched as Kelly walked towards the house. "But why does her presence bother me so much?"

As Jamiah pondered on her question, she looked Kelly over. Kelly was a plus-size woman, but she had the curves that some women were willing to pay to have and men were lusting after. Even in a simple capri outfit, her shape screamed for attention.

"Is that my problem with her?" Jamilah questioned herself. "Am I jealous?" she looked from Kelly's curvy figure to her husband. He had fallen behind Kelly to take a phone call. She wanted to see if Kelly's shape had the same effect on her husband as she knew it did on other men.

That's when she saw it.

Monroe looked at Kelly's ass. He didn't gawk, but Jamilah saw his eyes watch her ass sway from side to side as she walked away from him.

"Is Kelly his type?" Jamilah's eyes were glued to their interaction. Jamilah watched as her husband called Kelly back to him, and how Kelly so quickly obliged his request and moved expeditiously, pulling out her tablet to answer whatever question he had asked her. Kelly then stood by watching Monroe continue his phone conversation. Something so innocent had reignited Jamilah's insecurities. "Why the fuck is she waiting for my husband?" Jamilah snarled at the sight of them. "Move on, bitch," Jamilah's words came out like a harsh whisper.

Monroe finally got off the phone and began to walk towards the house. This time Kelly was following behind him.

I hope he ain't a gentleman. I hope he let that damn door slam in her face, Jamilah thought. She rolled her eyes as she watched Monroe open the door and motion for Kelly to walk in before him.

"Hey!" Kelly stated. "I didn't know you were home."

Jamilah didn't respond. She just stared at Kelly. All of Jamilah's inner thoughts had manifested on her face, and she didn't even care if Kelly saw it.

Kelly simply smiled to combat the look she was getting from Jamilah. She had already dealt with Jamilah's many moods and expected nothing more from her. In fact, Kelly knew she could do everything that Jamilah would ask of her and still get *faces* like the one she had just received.

Jamilah rolled her eyes and returned to her soggy cereal in front of her. She pushed the bowl away from her. Kelly's pleasantry had disgusted her.

Jamilah looked up as Monroe wrapped his arm around her and kissed her forehead. "What's wrong with you?"

Jamilah shrugged her shoulders. "I don't feel like myself."

Monroe kissed her on the forehead again. "You don't feel warm. Let me check here," he stated, kissing her neck.

Jamilah laughed. "Stop, boy."

Monroe stepped away from her. Jamilah followed him with her eyes as he walked to the refrigerator. When Monroe opened the fridge, Jamilah looked back at Kelly. She wanted to know if she was jealous of the love her husband had shown her. To her surprise, Kelly wasn't paying them any attention. Jamilah continued to stare at her, "Are you wearing makeup?"

Kelly looked up from the tablet at Jamilah. She shook her head. "I'm not wearing makeup. Just put some cocoa butter on this morning after I washed my face."

Jamilah nodded. "I never really noticed how flawless your skin is."

Did she just give me a compliment? Kelly wondered to herself. "Thank you?" she finally replied. Once it left her mouth, she could hear the suspicion in her own voice, so she tried to say it more genuinely. "Thank you, Jamilah!" *Damn, now that shit sounds phony*, Kelly continued to look in Jamilah's direction. She was confused. Jamilah had just said something nice to her, but her facial expression gave off a different vibe, like a fuck-you-vibe. She looked down at her tablet, but she was no longer focused. Kelly shook her head, disappointed in herself. *You just let that bitch mind fuck you.*

Jamilah folded her arms across her chest. Her head was held high, but it was clear that she was looking down her nose at Kelly. "You're glowing," she finally commented.

Kelly looked up at Jamilah curiously. *What is her angle?*

"That ain't a glow; that's sweat. It's hot as shit outside," Monroe stated, finally closing the refrigerator.

"I would rather refer to it as a glow than sweat. Thank you very much," Kelly replied with a chuckle.

Jamilah grunted. "So, Kelly, are you still enjoying your job?"

"This job was a blessing," she replied. "I can't thank you enough for the opportunity."

But you can, Jamilah thought as she gave Kelly a fake smile. "Monroe isn't working you too hard, is he?

Kelly glanced at Monroe and then looked at Jamilah, "No, ma'am."

Jamilah smiled. *Why the hell did he even need you? Or that other little girl, although she is a little more tolerable than Kelly. Monroe doesn't handle shit. I should be the one with the secretaries.* "And you don't have any foundation on?"

Kelly wiped her face and showed Jamilah her hand. "Nothing," she stated with a smile. "But thank you, though. And here I thought I looked thrown together today."

"Oh, really." Jamilah cut her eye at Monroe and then back at Kelly. "Are you being overworked?"

"Oh no, nothing like that."

"Then why are you throwing yourself together?"

"That was just a phrase. It has nothing to do with here, per se. I've just been busy. I haven't gotten used to my new schedule."

"What new schedule?"

"Oh, I am taking some courses at the Tech."

Jamilah looked back at Monroe. "Does this interfere with what you need her to do?"

"No," Kelly answered for Monroe.

Jamilah looked at her. "I was talking to my husband." She looked back at Monroe, "Does it interfere with what you need her to do here?"

Monroe shook his head. "No. We have already worked everything out."

"Um," Jamilah hummed. "I'm glad you could come to some conclusion without my input." She looked at Kelly as she spoke, but her comment was directed to Monroe. "Oh, well, good for you!" she stated, now addressing Kelly.

Kelly smiled. This job was teaching her how to bite her tongue. It was taking everything in her not to jump across the island and slam Jamilah's head into the countertop.

"What are you studying?" Jamilah finally asked.

"Two courses. I'm taking a pre-licensing course to become a Real Estate Broker, and I'm also taking a Quickbooks course. Since I will be handling the books, I need to be proficient with the system that you all use.

"Real estate broker? Books? What books will you be handling?" confusion settled on Jamilah's face. She looked to her husband for answers. "What books will she be handling?"

Monroe looked from the television hanging on the wall to Jamilah. "What did you ask me?"

"I asked what books of yours will *she*," Jamilah pointed at Kelly. "be handling?"

Monroe looked at Kelly. "How about you leave us alone for a minute."

Kelly got up without a word and walked out of the kitchen.

Monroe pulled out a stool and sat down next to his wife. "What's with this attitude you're giving off right now?"

"I don't have an attitude, Monroe," Jamilah snapped.

"Can you hear yourself?"

"You not including me, and that's a problem for me. Like what books will Kelly be handling and why?"

"You know she is my assistant, right?"

"What does that mean?"

"What is really wrong with you right now?"

Jamilah shook her head. "Like—" she cut herself off.

"Talk to me and not at me," Monroe stated calmly.

"I have a problem with her handling books," she paused. "No, actually, being honest, I have a problem with Kelly. I don't want her to work here."

"Why?"

"What do you need her for? And then to give her such a big responsibility. I've seen her resume, Monroe."

Monroe stared at Jamilah like she had lost her mind.

"I handle the books. The Real Estate business is mine." Jamilah picked up her cereal bowl and moved to the kitchen sink. She was about to rinse the bowl when she turned to look back at Monroe, "What does she do for you?"

Monroe got up from his seat and walked over to Jamilah. He attempted to lean in and give her a kiss, but Jamilah moved away.

"Answer me."

"Jamilah, you are my amazing wife," Monroe began. "And I know you want to keep busy, but you're *too* busy. Last night, you were too tired to take care of me. The crazy thing is, last night wasn't the first night I was neglected."

Jamilah rolled her eyes.

"Now, I ain't marry you to be a sex slave, but we are blessed enough to have the time and energy to enjoy each other," he touched Jamilah's chin. "Do you understand?"

Jamilah didn't reply. What Monroe was saying to her wasn't a lie. She oversaw two big projects from the real estate angle and tied up loose ends when it came to the nonprofit. When Jamilah finally got home, she showered and went to bed. When Monroe made an advance on her, she denied him. What she didn't realize was that he was keeping count.

"I think you are working too hard," he continued. "I'm going to kick Kelly a little more money to take over the real estate business."

"So when were you going to tell me about this change?"

"Kelly and I just finished talking about it. I made the decision today."

Although Monroe had a valid point, she still didn't like the idea. The real estate business was her project. She loved doing it. She got to utilize her degree and everything. "So now I'm just responsible for the nonprofit?"

"For now," Monroe replied. "After Kelly establishes a routine, she will take over that, too."

Jamilah's jaw dropped. "You're taking everything from me? You know that I am in the midst of two projects. Who's going to oversee those projects?"

"Kelly."

"Kelly?!" Jamilah stared at Monroe like he had lost his mind. "So that's it? I don't get a say in any of this?"

"No, you don't," he replied. Monroe knew how to handle Jamilah. He spoke direct, calmly, and clearly. Monroe knew his presentation was cutting Jamilah deep, which was the result he sought. He wanted her to feel as lost and as empty as he had felt watching her fuck his friend in the very kitchen where they were standing.

"But those are my damn projects!"

Monroe nodded.

Jamilah chuckled. "How are you going to take something that is mine?"

"If I recall correctly, my mother owns the real estate business and the nonprofit." He paused, giving his statement enough time to *land*. "Am I

103

right?" he added to the gut punch.

Jamilah smirked. Her smirk was packed with so many emotions. "What am I supposed to do? Just step aside?"

"And relax," he added. He attempted to kiss Jamilah's forehead again, but she moved away—again. He accepted her retreat and stepped away from her. "Just relax," he called over his shoulder as he left the kitchen. "You've earned *everything* that is happening."

Jamilah watched him. She wanted to keep this conversation going but knew Kelly was in the house and didn't want to cause a scene. Monroe may have opted to walk away, but this conversation wasn't over for Jamilah.

Fuming inside, Jamilah pulled out her phone and made a call. As soon as the line picked up, she asked, "Can we meet?" she paused, waiting for an answer, and then she said, "Okay, I'm on my way."

Without speaking to Monroe, who was in his office with Kelly, Jamilah grabbed her things and left the house.

Jamilah pulled into the car garage. Once the garage door closed, she exited her car and proceeded to the door that led into the house. This house was nowhere as big as her house, but this house was filled with something that her home was missing. The garage entrance led to the kitchen. Jamilah immediately washed her hands and grabbed a champagne glass from the cabinet.

"You don't think it's too early for that?"

Jamilah looked back at Zeph, and then she looked at her glass.

Zeph stood in the kitchen doorway with his arms folded across his chest.

"You're right." She put the champagne glass back into the cabinet and grabbed a heavy bottom rocks glass. She walked to the refrigerator, dropped some ice cubes in her glass, and then beelined to the liquor cabinet. She poured herself a double shot of D'usse.

"It's too early for that, too," Zeph commented.

"Have one," Jamilah offered.

"I said it's too early for that," he stated as he watched her take a long sip of her drink and then walk to the kitchen table to sit down. He walked over to the table and sat down across from her. "What is going on?"

"Get you one," she ordered him this time. "Don't make me drink alone."

Zeph was hesitant, but he got up and poured himself a drink. He then walked back over to the table. "What's up?" he asked again. "You look beautiful, by the way."

"Thank you." She stared across the table at Zeph. She smiled. "Your presence is comforting to me."

Zeph nodded approvingly. "What's wrong?"

"Monroe fired me today."

Zeph squinted his eyes at Jamilah. "Fired you?"

Jamilah nodded. "Like he really fired me."

"Fired?" Zeph repeated. "How you fire your wife?" Zeph chuckled. "Are y'all just having an argument or something?"

Jamilah went to take another sip of her drink, but it was already gone. She got up from the table and poured herself another. "He's sending Kelly to school so she can take over the real estate business."

"You're still the *all-seeing-eye* of Shooting Goals, right?"

Jamilah grunted. She sipped her drink and then returned to the kitchen table. "I was told that once Kelly gets *settled* in her routine, she, too, would be taking over my position at Shooting Goals."

Zeph's facial expression changed. *Damn, this nigga is playing no games,* he thought to himself. He sat silently, trying to replay his last conversation with Monroe. He didn't remember hearing anything about this. This was new, not just to Jamilah but to him, too. "Wait, aren't you a licensed real estate broker?"

"I AM!" she yelled. "I put so much effort and energy into that fuckin' company. The long nights, the conference calls, the networking, all my got damn time and energy, and he just…" she sighed. "He just dismissed me like I ain't shit!" She slammed her hand down on the kitchen table. Some of her drink splashed the wooden surface. "Sorry," she stated, snatching up her glass and siping. She put her glass back on the table. "He just snatched everything from me."

"Relax."

"DON'T TELL ME TO RELAX!" she snapped. "I won't relax! It's not fair!"

"I was just trying to tell you that there's no need to stress yourself out because Kelly can act like a real estate broker, but if she's not licensed, then—"

"SHE'S IN SCHOOL NOW!" Jamilah yelled. "Did you not hear me?" Jamilah stated, cutting him off. "She said she was getting her license and taking a Quickbooks course because she will be handling the books." Jamilah rolled her eyes. "That bitch," she mumbled.

"That doesn't make sense."

Jamilah looked across the table at Zeph. "None of it makes sense."

"Where is this coming from?"

"Because I wouldn't have sex with him. He said he wanted me to use this time to relax and enjoy our blessings and our marriage together." Jamilah smacked her lips. Her saying it was just as lame as hearing him say it. The bullshit left a bland taste in her mouth.

"That still doesn't make any sense, though."

"What part?"

Zeph knew *what part*, but there were layers to his morals.

He was *virtuously* okay with sleeping with Monroe's wife but not *morally* okay with divulging his secrets. Of all his years of knowing Monroe, he had never known him to be impulsive. Monroe was calculated. He looked at everything from all angles. Even his idea for a franchise team was pondered before it was implemented. Hearing Jamilah talk, Zeph knew immediately that this move presented to Jamilah was part of a well-thought-out plan.

Jamilah continued: "I let him put everything in his momma's name. I thought it was to memorialize her, but it was…" she chuckled to herself. "It was this the whole damn time." She was disappointed that she had been outmaneuvered. "Why the hell didn't I see it?" she said. "Nope!" she continued her conversation with herself. "It ain't me. That bitch got in his head. She fuckin' him, and now he's thinking with his dick." Jamilah went to take another sip from her drink when she suddenly realized something.

Zeph hadn't said a word.

She put her glass down. She tilted her head, waiting for him to say something.

Silence.

"You know something, don't you? He is fuckin' Kelly, isn't he?" She didn't wait for him to respond. "Y'all too close for you not to know nothing."

Zeph shook his head.

"I know you know something, Zeph. Just tell me. I'm a big girl. I can handle it. He stepped out on me for that fat bitch, didn't he?"

Zeph thought about his *morals* again. He would fuck Monroe's wife, but he would never tell his secrets. That wasn't his game. He didn't need to down another nigga to make his bones. "No," he finally replied. "He's not fuckin' her."

Jamilah leaned across the table. She stared him in the eyes. She was hoping to catch a sign of him lying, but she got nothing. Zeph had a stone face. "Are you lying?" she finally asked.

"Why would I?"

Jamilah sat back in her seat. She felt defeated at her own cost. A part of her was still angry that she had been fired, but the other part felt like Karma was coming to her, and she deserved this fate.

Her mother used to tell her that Karma was neither good nor bad; in fact, she would say that Karma solely responded to the energy you put into the universe. Jamilah wanted so badly to say, 'Karma is a bitch,' but if her mother was right, then Karma solely responded to the energy she put into the universe. This would then make her the bitch. She was sleeping with her husband's best friend. The same husband that never cheated on her and always made sure that she was safe and secure.

Jamilah picked up her glass. She downed it all. She needed to feel the burn. It would be the only way to stop her guilt-ridden tears from falling from her eyes. She jumped up from the table and made another drink. She picked up the glass canister and looked back at Zeph. "Why am I not enough?"

Zeph stood up and walked over to Jamilah. He wrapped his arms around her waist. "You have always been enough for me," he whispered in her ear and then kissed her neck.

Jamilah moaned out her pleasure. She put the glass down and then turned and wrapped her arms around Zeph's neck. The two kissed each other passionately. Zeph pulled back. He lifted Jamilah up and sat her on the kitchen island.

Jamilah laughed. She knew where this was leading. "Why are we always in the kitchen?"

Zeph smirked. "I was taught that you are supposed to eat in the kitchen and in the kitchen only."

Jamilah giggled.

Zeph's hands ran up and down her thigh. "I want to make you happy."

Jamilah's lip trembled. The tears she didn't want to fall had formed and dropped from her eyes. "I'm sorry," she stated, wiping her eyes.

"Don't apologize for having feelings, Queen. I just wish those were tears of joy and not tears of sorrow. Monroe doesn't know what he has. I know. That's why I want you."

Jamilah stared at Zeph. He was not traditionally her type. He wasn't an ugly man at all; in fact, he was far from ugly. He stood slightly shorter than Monroe and maintained a physically fit body like her husband. Unlike Monroe, he was covered in tattoos, and some of those tattoos alerted people to the set he claimed. In comparison to Monroe, Zeph was the bad boy. And every girl loved a bad boy—even Jamilah—but for her, it was less about Zeph being a bad boy and more about his masculine energy.

Zeph's alpha male energy overpowered Jamilah's alpha female energy. Around him, she felt her most feminine. She was okay with being fragile and vulnerable because she still felt safe. Being submissive to him was a natural response. She didn't have to force herself to play a submissive role. His aura naturally demanded that from her without a verbal request. Aside from his energy, other things drew her to him. She liked how Zeph lived his life how he wanted to and held his tongue for no one; except Monroe. She didn't quite understand the full extent of their friendship, but she knew that Monroe had bailed Zeph out of trouble a time or two. At one point, Monroe had even enlisted the help of North Carolina's top attorneys to get Zeph out of jail. Jamilah never knew the extent of his legal issues. She didn't ask because she didn't want to let on to her husband that she was slightly curious about his friend. She never asked Zeph about it because his dominance often intimidated her, and she could never find the nerve to ask. In her mind, the air of mystery surrounding Zeph became a part of her fantasies for him.

Monroe and Zeph's friendship should have made Zeph off-limits to Jamilah, but she couldn't help herself. She found herself vibin' with him because he did things her husband didn't. For one, he listened and was willing to provide her with ideas or solutions to problems she would face with competitors. Despite his lack of education, Zeph was well-versed in business tactics. She found a confidant in him, something she had never experienced in her husband.

Monroe would be so consumed with *his* world that she had no choice but to retreat into her *business* world. She found joy in business, and in one split decision, her husband snatched all of that away from her. Zeph was the one thing Monroe couldn't snatch from her. Zeph had a way of physically and mentally reminding Jamilah that she was *that* bitch. Today, she ran to him for that reminder, but it wasn't effective this time. She couldn't shake the power move that Monroe had made.

"Why do you think he's doing this?" she asked. "He hasn't mentioned anything to you?"

Zeph shook his head. "He ain't said nothing."

"I...I just don't get it," Jamilah stated. She laid her head on Zeph's shoulder. "He took everything from me."

Zeph wrapped his arms around her and rubbed her back as she cried. For some reason, Jamilah's last statement, 'He took everything from me', bounced around in his mind and left him with an eerie feeling. It made him think back to his last interaction with Monroe. *It was regular*, he told himself. *I just signed over the houses to him. He said he needed to liquidate his assets. Nothing strange about that. I'm always signing over places.* Zeph shook his head to shake off his suspicions, but they were unshakeable. His suspicions grew louder in his thoughts. *You ain't never sign over all of them simultaneously, though.* Zeph pulled away from Jamilah. "Why would someone liquidate their assets?"

"Random," Jamilah stated. She tried to bring herself out of her feelings by chuckling at his question. She stopped and stared at Zeph suspiciously, "Why would you ask that question?" she paused. "Do you know something? What did Monroe do? If he is trying to divorce me for that fat bitch...." Jamilah continued rambling off a list of vulgar actions she would take if Monroe attempted to leave her.

Zeph walked towards the refrigerator. He opened it and looked inside. He didn't want anything but needed a moment with his thoughts. *We good*, he thought of his relationship with Monroe. *We just ain't been hanging out 'cause we got big shit going on. This deal with Watson Tyler is stressful as hell. And the vultures are on the attack. I'm trying to maintain order; he's playing ball. We are just busy*, he tried to justify their movements. *The last time I saw him, we ate, talked, and I signed over the houses. Everything was normal...*

"Answer me," he stated, sternly. "Why would someone liquidate their assets?"

Jamilah tried to shake off her buzz to provide a clear answer. "Uh... well...I don't know. It could be several reasons."

Zeph looked at her, waiting for her to elaborate.

Jamilah shrugged her shoulders. "I don't know. We once had a client liquidate his business. He wanted to buy the house on Harbor View Road but didn't have enough money."

"So, he sold all his businesses to buy one house?"

"He didn't sell all of them, but he did sell some to buy the house on Harbor View," Jamilah slid down from the island. She continued to ramble on about the House on Harbor View, "That house was worth it, though," she explained. "The location alone—"

Zeph wasn't listening. He had fully tuned into his suspicions. *We need re-up money. Maybe he liquidated the houses to cover the reup. Maybe he realize that we are taking a big hit.*

"Wait!" Jamilah began to panic. "Is Monroe selling something?"

"I don't know."

"Seriously, Zeph, is Monroe liquidating assets?"

"No."

Jamilah leaned against the island. She couldn't allow herself to believe Zeph. "What made you ask about liquidation?"

Zeph shut the refrigerator. "I just asked." He moved through the kitchen, avoiding eye contact with Jamilah.

The kitchen was so silent one could only hear the light drip coming from the faucet, and then Jamilah gasped loudly. "You don't think Monroe knows about us…do you?"

Zeph turned to face Jamilah. "Nah," he quickly answered.

Jamilah grabbed her forehead. The thought of Monroe finding out about the two of them, plus the mix of her quickly consumed drinks, brought on an overwhelming wave of concern and fear. "What if he knows?"

"Relax," Zeph called to her.

"Something just doesn't feel right."

Zeph walked over to the sink. He attempted to stop the drip from the faucet.

"It must be something I did to him specifically. He would have cut you off if he knew about us, too, right?"

Jamilah sighed with relief.

To her, Monroe could be mad about anything, but to be angry about her infidelities meant big trouble. The type of trouble that she wasn't equipped to address—at least not now.

Zeph turned around and leaned against the counter. He watched as Jamilah attempted to comfort herself. It was evident that her several drinks had finally caught up with her. She was swaying side to side like a tune in her head had swept her away. As he watched her, he smiled.

Jamilah thought the smile was for her, so she let loose and began to dance even more. It was her coping mechanism. She could be herself around Zeph with no judgment. Even when it felt like everything was crumbling around her.

But Zeph wasn't smiling at her. Nor was he smiling for her.

He was smiling for Monroe.

After all these years, he thought Monroe wasn't paying attention, but he had. He had learned some of their mother's ways, which made Zeph feel proud of him.

Shantell Whitaker was never one to act irrationally, and she for damn sure never reacted off the cuff. Shantell believed preparation was a key factor on all business fronts, especially when it came to the business of retribution. When crossed, Shantell wanted revenge on all fronts: physically, mentally, spiritually, socially, and most importantly, financially. She tried to leave an impression on her enemies. She wanted them to know that they had crossed her, and she wanted them to fully embrace the consequences of their actions. Monroe's moves were a reminder of Shantell's lesson.

But he wasn't just teaching Jamilah.

He is moving on me, too, Zeph thought, still with a smirk on his face. *Having me sign over the houses—brilliant! But I see you, my boy. I see you coming.*

CHAPTER ELEVEN

THE COMPETITION

NOVEMBER 29, 2019

"I wish every female was like you."

Kelly looked over at Monroe. "Like me, how?"

Monroe smirked. He knew how. He just didn't know if Kelly would be offended if he explained it to her. "You're a good woman," he simplified his answer.

Kelly smirked. The other day her attitude toward her boss was fuck him. These days she was back to wanting to fuck him. He apologized for his behavior and *loved-bomb*ed her with sweet words and gifts. He had hired Avie, but Kelly hadn't seen her around. Therefore, out of sight, out of mind. Kelly was back to being his number-one girl and loved every minute.

Monroe knew he had Kelly where he needed her. The rule of thumb was never to keep the Point Guard mad. She knew too much. He knew he had won her over again when she started back flirting with him. This was doing something to him on several levels. Every time he spoke to her, he would stare at her lips, recalling the night he had the best head of his life. Naturally, his dick would get hard, reminiscing on the feeling of empowerment she had given him. He would constantly move if they had to talk for a long time, hoping she wouldn't notice how aroused she made him. He wanted to go further with her. To fully explore what she had to offer. It had to be something there if she could make him feel like a king off head alone. He could only imagine how her pussy would make him feel.

"You have a meeting with Bishop Carmichael in ten minutes if he is on time." Kelly stood beside Monroe, who sat at his desk. The two were looking at the calendar pulled up on his computer screen. While Kelly looked at the screen, Monroe moved his hand up her thigh. He didn't want to be distracted, but Kelly's physique was distracting. Her curves were sometimes irresistible. The roundness of her ass got his attention every time.

His sudden touch startled Kelly, and she looked over at him. She wanted this man badly, but the conversation with her mother played on her mind. She was forcing herself to not look at Monroe through lust-filled eyes. It was hard work, but she had to manage—sometimes. She was determined not to be his play toy. She even enlisted Zani as her accountability partner, who called daily seeking updates.

Kelly knocked his hand away.

Monroe stood up and towered over Kelly. "I felt your mouth," he stated, brushing his finger across her lips. I want to feel your pussy wrapped around my dick."

Kelly closed her eyes and enjoyed this moment. In fact, she used to fantasize about this moment. "You have a meeting," she reminded him as she stepped back.

Monroe pulled her back to him. "You a good woman to me. Let me show you how much I appreciate you. Let me eat that."

Kelly blushed. Her nipples were erect. *Is this a game?* she thought to herself. "Why now?"

"Why not now?"

"Is it because Avie ain't around?"

Monroe frowned. "Avie has nothing to do with us."

"Then why hire her?"

"Why be jealous of another woman,who is given an opportunity?"

"An opportunity to what?" Kelly questioned. "Fuck?"

"It ain't like that with Avie and me."

"Uh huh. You are different when that *child* is at work."

"She isn't even around when you are around."

"It got to be something to it. You never told me Avie's purpose here. When I do happen to bump into her here, y'all be having secret conversations, and then when I come around, you stop talking. You got her doing things, and you won't answer me when I ask what she is doing."

Monroe smirked. "Don't be jealous, baby. I promise you it ain't what you think." Monroe moved closer. Kelly went to retreat, but he grabbed her by the waist and pulled her close to him.

"Then what do y'all be talking about?"

"It's not impor—"

Kelly knocked Monroe's arms off her and quickly moved out of his reach. She didn't want to hear his bullshit lies. "You have a meeting," she reminded him once she was safely on the other side of the desk.

Monroe smirked. "I like to chase."

Kelly tried to maintain her composure, but the corners of her lips turned up. She liked being chased.

"I will get what I want," he informed her as he sat behind his desk. "We've been working together for a while now. You, of all people, should know I always get what I want."

Kelly avoided eye contact with Monroe. She knew this characteristic about him to be true. *PROVE HIM WRONG, BITCH, PROVE HIM WRONG!* her inner voice yelled at her.

Kelly looked at her watch. "He may be late," she commented, trying to change the subject.

"Bishop is always on time," Monroe replied. "Bishop Carmichael and I used to play ball in college together. I got drafted to one NBA team, and he got drafted to another."

"Is he here visiting?"

"You don't watch ESPN do you?"

"No, why?"

"Bishop just got traded to my team."

"Sooo—" she began to sing out her question. "Is Bishop a good ball player?"

"He aiight," Monroe stated nonchalantly.

His pride wouldn't let him tell the truth. Bishop Carmichael was arguably one of the best basketball players in the industry. Monroe knew it, the world knew it, and worse of all, Bishop, himself, knew it. Monroe was happy to gain a top tier player on his team, but he knew Bishop was going to be a thorn in his side. To combat the imminent battle of their egos, Monroe opted to host a meeting at his home to welcome Bishop to the team. The meeting would also be Monroe's opportunity to subtly remind Bishop that the team was under his leadership and his leadership alone.

"Why don't you keep up with sports?"

Kelly looked at Monroe and shrugged. "I'm not a sports fan."

"But you work for an athlete."

"Actually, I work for a man who is more than an athlete."

Monroe smirked. "That's what I mean when I say I wish every woman was like you."

"I'm just stating facts."

"Most women fake it, especially when they know they will be in the presence of stars. That's their meal ticket."

"I have other ways of acquiring a meal."

Monroe watched Kelly as she jotted something down in her notebook. It was the confidence for him that made her worth the chase. She had her moments of vulnerability and insecurities. Still, he charged that to a characteristic that all women occasionally had. His smirk turned into a full-blown smile. He watched her closely. She dressed to accentuate her curves, and that go-getter attitude added to her swagger.

Kelly looked up from her notebook. "What?"

Monroe shook his head slowly

She knew why he was looking at her like that. She could tell by the seductive look on his face that he wanted her. The thought of being had by him made her body heat rise. *Prove him wrong, bitch! He can't have you*, the little voice inside reminded her.

Monroe sat down in his desk chair. He was about to say something to Kelly when a quick series of knocks interrupted him. Before he could respond, the office door opened, and Jamilah appeared. "Guess who I found outside?"

Monroe instantly switched gears. *It's game time*, he told himself as he moved to the door. "It better be Bishop's ass," he joked as he greeted his guest.

Kelly stood by silently, watching Jamilah, Monroe, and Bishop interact. *Damn, he looks so familiar*, she thought to herself. *Duh! He is a basketball player genius. That's probably why he looks familiar. He is sexy as hell, though!*

Bishop was involved in the conversation with The Whitakers until he spotted Kelly standing off. "Damn, you got all the gorgeous women at your house, huh?" Bishop stated. He smiled at Kelly.

She blushed but then looked away.

Bishop glanced at Monroe. "How did you get so lucky?" he questioned, his eyes still glued to Kelly.

Monroe didn't reply. He knew better not to ignite Jamilah. She was still in her feelings about the transition of power. For Monroe, there was no need to add fuel to *that* fire. "So, how was your flight?" Monroe asked Bishop.

As the two men moved to the sitting area in Monroe's office, Jamilah watched Kelly as she sat behind her husband's desk. Kelly was working on something, and Jamilah wanted to ask her what she was doing, but didn't want to cause a scene, especially not in front of Bishop Carmichael. Instead, she stood silently in the room, trying to make herself small. In doing so, Jamilah noticed something.

No matter how controlled a woman tries to be, attraction cannot be hidden. It is bound to come out in some way, shape, or form, and look'a here, Ms. Kelly blushes. Jamilah folded her arms across her chest as she watched Kelly and Bishop. *Oh, so she isn't attracted to my husband,* Jamilah concluded. Although Zeph had told Jamilah that Monroe wasn't sleeping with Kelly, today, she found inner peace seeing it for herself. *And here I thought Kelly was playing a role, acting like she didn't like my husband for my sake. If she did like Monroe, she wouldn't be able to control her emotions around him. She for damn sure can't control her emotions around Bishop.* Jamilah continued to stare between the two. *I always knew Bishop was a chubby chaser,* she smirked at her thoughts. *And Kelly must really be his type because he ain't paying Monroe a bit of attention. Is Monroe even peeping this flirtation that is occurring between those two? I'ma do something.* Jamilah walked over to Kelly and grabbed her by the wrist. "Come with me," she whispered.

Kelly stood up and followed her. She didn't know what was going on, but the grip on her arm was slightly alarming.

Jamilah pulled Kelly over to the seating area, where Bishop and Monroe were talking. "Excuse my manners," she interrupted.

Monroe looked at his wife with a frown on his face.

"I should have done this before you all started talking, but sometimes I get so caught up in my world; I assume everyone knew each other." Jamilah pulled Kelly to stand beside her. "Kelly," she stated, finally letting go of her wrist. "This is Bishop Carmichael. Bishop, this is Kelly Mitchell. She is Monroe's assistant."

Bishop stood up from his chair and extended his hand to Kelly.

Kelly put her hand in Bishop's hand.

"It's nice to meet you," he stated.

Kelly blushed. "It's nice to meet you as well."

"You all will probably see a lot of each other, as Bishop will be playing ball with Monroe this season," Jamilah stated.

"Yeah, I heard," Kelly replied.

"Kelly's been working for us for about a year now, right?" Jamilah glanced at Kelly as she asked. It was obvious that Jamilah asked rhetorically because she continued talking before Kelly could answer her question.

116

Kelly was speechless anyway. She physically stood a part of this conversation, but her mind was racing. *Is Jamilah really doing this right now? I thought this bitch didn't like me. I know this bitch don't like me.* Kelly ever so slightly cut her eye at Monroe. He had a look about him, but she couldn't tell from her peep in his direction what the look was *saying.*

"I have a great idea!"

Jamilah's sudden burst of excitement snatched Kelly back into this surreal moment. "What?" Kelly asked, trying to masquerade her true feelings with a big smile and a light-hearted chuckle.

"You just got into town, Bishop, so how about all of us go out to dinner tonight?"

Bishop and Kelly shared a glance.

Being phony, Jamilah whispered, "We can make Monroe pay."

Bishop looked back at Monroe, who was sitting back on the couch, watching the scene in front of him. "You hear this?" Bishop asked Monroe.

Monroe's eyebrows were bunched across his forehead, but when Bishop called to him, he quickly fixed his face.

Bishop continued: "I guess you paying tonight, boy," he extended his hand to dap Monroe. In doing so, he pulled him up from the couch.

Monroe replied jokingly, "I guess I can find two nickels to rub together." He looked at Jamilah and smiled.

Jamilah was pleased with her initiative.

Bishop looked at Kelly. "How do you feel about having dinner with me?"

"That's fine," Kelly replied shyly.

Jamilah had a big smile on her face as she watched Kelly blush again. She glanced over at her husband. She was about to joke with him about her match-matching skills, but she saw something. *No matter how controlled a man tries to be, he can't hide his attraction. It is bound to come out in some way, shape, or form,* Jamilah thought to herself. *And for you, Monroe, it's the look of jealousy as your assistant accepts a date with your teammate.*

CHAPTER TWELVE

OFF THE MARKET
NOVEMBER 29, 2019

Jamilah was sitting at her vanity in her room.

She was looking for something in herself. She didn't know what exactly she was looking for, but she was still searching for it. Whatever she was looking for, she knew it was something that Kelly must also possess. That would be the only way to justify why her husband was attracted to her.

As she applied her makeup, she looked over her face. She knew she was a pretty woman, but what else was it that both she and Kelly possessed? Instead of bombarding her thoughts with these questions, she should have asked Monroe, but she was honestly afraid of the answer.

Monroe walked out of the bathroom. He had a towel wrapped around his waist.

Jamilah got up and walked over to him. She stood silently in front of him.

He looked at her suspiciously. "What's wrong?"

Jamilah dropped down to her knees in front of her husband.

Monroe smirked. He missed this version of Jamilah. As soon as they said 'I do,' Jamila threw out the playbook that had gotten her to the marriage level. She stopped being his spontaneous sex mate and traded in her kneepads for notepads and business meetings. She had traded-in random sex acts in random locations for conference rooms and fundraisers.

Jamilah tugged on Monroe's towel while looking up at him.

Monroe looked down at her. He put his hands on his head. He was trying to control himself. He had a habit of grabbing Jamilah's head as she pleased him. Jamilah couldn't understand that he would be caught in the moment. She made it evident that she didn't like when he tried to control her. She once told him it made her feel belittled, like a prostitute. She never considered that sometimes her man wanted her to be his personal hoe.

Monroe licked his lips as Jamilah grabbed hold of his third leg. The moment she got down on her knees, he was instantaneously hard. He was ready to mentally compare his wife to his assistant. Unfortunately, Jamilah just held his dick and looked at it.

"Put it in your mouth," he encouraged her.

Jamilah licked the tip of Monroe's dick.

Monroe could have melted. "I miss this shit," he mumbled as he bit his bottom lip.

Jamilah smiled. "You are a great man, and sometimes I forget that. Not purposefully, but..."

Monroe grabbed his dick and brushed it against Jamilah's lips.

"Ugh," Jamilah got up off her knees.

Monroe looked at her, confused. "What's wrong? Why did you stop?"

"I was trying to talk to you."

Monroe snatched his towel from the floor. "On your knees?" Monroe shook his head. "What kind of shit is that?" he asked with an attitude. He wrapped the towel around himself. "What's your purpose right now?"

Jamilah looked at Monroe, shocked. "What are you asking me?" she questioned, with an attitude of her own.

"I come out the shower, you get on your knees like you about to suck me off, but then you get on some bullshit. What is your damn problem?"

Jamilah flopped down at the foot of their King-size bed. She hated how she had just handled things. She should have never gotten on her knees. Monroe didn't have enough masculine energy to make her consider being submissive. Monroe was no Zeph. She didn't even know what possessed her to do it anyway. She looked at Monroe, who was pouting, as he slipped into his underwear.

It was either now or never; she took in a deep breath and exhaled her nerves. "I saw your face when I introduced Bishop to Kelly."

"WHAT?!" Monroe snapped.

"I saw your face when he asked her to dinner. You were jealous and—"

"Jealous?" he interjected. "Jealous of what exactly?"

"Of Bishop talking to Kelly."

Monroe looked at Jamilah like she had lost her mind.

"I saw your—"

"You got me fucked up!" The venom of his words froze Jamilah mid-sentence. "I was mad because I was supposed to review the playbook with Bishop. Instead, my wife rudely interrupted *my* meeting for some bullshit. Have I ever done anything like that to you?"

"I wasn't trying to—"

"You weren't trying to what? Play matchmaker in the middle of a scheduled meeting? Come on, Jamilah, you know what you were doing."

Jamilah looked away from Monroe.

"That was a scheduled meeting, not just him stopping by to shoot the breeze."

Jamilah sighed, disappointed in herself. Perhaps she had read the moment wrong.

"Ask me again if I was mad. You fuckin' right; I was mad!" Monroe stated sternly. "Bishop coming to the team concerns me because I don't want him to come to my team and try to take over. He did that shit in college, and I'm not about to have that shit happen again. Fuck no!" Monroe sat down on the side of the bed, away from Jamilah. "I bet this nigga thinks taking over the team is easy since I can't maintain control over a damn meeting."

Jamilah's jaw clenched. She didn't even think about it like that. She looked over at Monroe. "I'm so sorry, baby. I just saw how they looked at each other, and then I assumed...I don't know what I assumed. I just...I don't know." She was ashamed that she had brought something so minuscule to him when he had real shit going on.

Monroe held his head down, but a smirk rested on his face. Monroe wasn't concerned about Bishop coming to the team. He knew Bishop could never take over *his* team. The way Bishop was looking at his Point Guard concerned him. Monroe wanted Kelly for himself. Not just to conquer, but she was the MVP of his franchise; to lose her would mean rebuilding everything—again. True, he had positioned Avie to step in if need be, but Kelly was proving to be beyond loyal to him in more ways than one.

Jamilah moved to sit next to Monroe on the side of the bed. She laid her head on his shoulder. "Baby, I am so sorry. Please forgive me."

Monroe sighed as though his wife's actions had really stressed him out. He wrapped his arms around Jamilah's shoulders and kissed her forehead. "It's okay," he replied dryly.

"Really, I am. I've just been so…" Jamilah whispered her truth. "Insecure."

"Though a pretty woman, Kelly's not my type," he stated.

"And what is your type?"

"My type…let's see," he pushed Jamilah from his shoulder and looked at her. "She's got a narrow waistline…kind of like yours. A basketball-sized ass that I can palm."

Jamilah giggled.

"But most importantly," Monroe stated, "She has a beautiful mind," he touched her temple, "and a heart to match," he placed his hand over her chest. "I love you. I don't know where this insecure shit is coming from, but you have nothing to worry about, okay?"

Jamilah smiled. She wrapped her arms around Monroe and kissed his lips. "You know what, let's not go to dinner tonight. Let's stay in and enjoy each other." Monroe pulled Jamilah close to him. "I will still accept the head you were just offering."

Jamilah laughed. "I'll text Kelly and tell her that dinner has been canceled. Maybe we can all do that another day or something," she typed quickly into her phone.

Monroe stood up, grabbed his phone from the dresser, and texted Bishop about the cancellation.

Jamilah's phone vibrated. Kelly had already replied, *Okay*.

Jamilah lay across the bed. Monroe was still on his phone texting. "What are you writing? A paragraph?" she questioned, sarcastically. "Kelly just said, 'Okay'," Jamilah reported.

Monroe nodded, still texting on his phone.

"What did Bishop say?"

"Okay," Monroe stated, placing his phone face down. "All he could say."

Monroe walked over to his wife. He bent over and kissed her lips. "I'm going to shave my face. I'll be right back, okay?"

"Yeah, because your facial hair tickles," Jamilah commented.

Monroe walked into the bathroom and shut the door.

Jamilah was trying to get into a sexy position when Monroe's phone flashed. She crawled off the bed and picked up his phone. It was a text from Bishop that read, *Do you think I can get Kelly's number?* Although she missed her moment to gloat, Jamilah knew she was a good matchmaker.

She grabbed her phone and texted Kelly to see if it was okay to give Bishop her number.

Kelly quickly replied, *Yes!* and even added the emoji with the hearts for eyes.

Jamilah then promptly typed out Kelly's number into a message to Bishop. She returned Monroe's phone where she found it and resumed her sexy pose on the bed while waiting for her husband.

Jamilah found peace of mind knowing that a man was in Kelly's life. That didn't necessarily stop people from cheating—hell, look at her and Zeph—but this did allow Jamilah's insecurities to melt away—even if for a night.

CHAPTER THIRTEEN

GET BEFORE GOT

DECEMBER 14, 2019

Zeph let Monroe *think* he was the man in charge, but he was really the man in charge. Monroe may have been the money of their operation, but Zeph's name and reputation put their empire on the map. Knowing his role, Zeph didn't mind taking a back seat to Monroe's ego.

While Monroe was learning from and idolizing Zeph's grandfather, Emanuel, like a father figure; Zeph appreciated the gem Monroe neglected to see in his mother, Shantell.

To Zeph, she was the mother he had never had since his own was nonexistent. Shantell accepted the title and affectionately referred to Zeph as her fifth child.

Zeph studied Shantell. He admired how she could turn anything into a hustle. Monroe and his family didn't have much, but Shantell ensured that her four kids had what they needed. When Zeph came along, she extended the hustle to include him. It took a lot of work to make ends meet and care for stair-step kids. They were all born a year apart and wanted and needed too much simultaneously. She fell short sometimes, but that was only because of how her cards were dealt. Nevertheless, she played her best hand every time. In fact, nothing was off limits for Shantell regarding survival.

If they were an Italian family, Shantell would have been considered Zeph's Consigliere. To have been a slim, petite woman, Shantell moved like a linebacker on steroids. No situation, no one person ever intimidated her. She would look at things through multiple lenses, from the big picture to the smallest detail. Between Zeph's quick, violent temper and her strategizing ability, the two had built an impressive drug empire in little Grambleton, North Carolina. In fact, their business had surprisingly grown to such magnitude that it had expanded up and down Interstate 95. They didn't have the people needed to make all the runs, so Zeph began to make deliveries. He should have recruited more generals, but he and Shantell believed in keeping their circle small. It was this level of thinking that changed his life forever.

Everything was perfect until it wasn't. Zeph forever regrets having been speeding down 95 through Emporia. What should have been just a traffic stop turned out to be one hell of a drug bust. All the alphabet boys had their hands involved in his case. Newspapers labeled him a Kingpin and tried to wrap him up in a RICO case, but they lacked the ability to put a bow on it. They didn't know, and he never told, that the empire was jointly managed by him and Shantell. He had runners and a couple of generals, but Zeph insulated Shantell. No one knew about her position. In their eyes, she was just his play-mother that happened to be around all the time. Through Shantell, Zeph learned the importance of never being the face of an organization. The alphabet boys never even looked at her when rounding up the empire.

Zeph was given five years in the Feds for posession and intent to distribute heroin.

He ate it like a man.

Monroe knew that Shantell was working with Zeph. He knew Zeph could have easily snitched on his mother and broken up their family, but he didn't. Because of his loyalty, Monroe took the utmost care and concern for Zeph. He made sure Zeph was given the best of lawyers, and when all the dust had settled, Zeph's commissary was always on max. It was the least that Monroe could do.

Zeph was never loyal to Monroe. Monroe only had Zeph's loyalty because of his mother. Just before she died, she sent Zeph a letter. The letter contained three major points: a heartfelt thank you for never snitching, a request to help Monroe through life so he doesn't become a victim, and, most importantly, the letter came with a warning. 'The fame is changing Monroe,' Shantell wrote. 'Beware.' It was a simple, but powerful message from his Consigliere. Zeph never told anyone about the warning, but he kept his eyes wide open.

Until now.

Monroe's power move against his own wife spoke volumes to Zeph. Zeph didn't know for sure what Monroe knew, but he knew Monroe had to know something. It was obvious—now—to Zeph and he knew it was only a matter of time before Monroe would *try* to flex on him like he had Jamilah.

Perhaps Zeph's guest for the evening was a part of the move Monroe was making on him. Although Zeph agreed to meet her, he was still on high alert.

Knock, knock.

Zeph turned from the hotel window and headed to the door. He pulled his gun from his waist as he looked through the peephole.

It was his guest. At least, that is what he thought. He didn't know her from a can of paint. She had just called out of the blue and asked to meet. Initially, Zeph wasn't interested, but his curiosity had sparked the best of him. He set the meeting place, and she agreed without hesitation. This made him even more suspicious of her motive.

Looking through the peephole, the woman was young. He would put her in her early twenties, although she looked like the *off limits*-type of young.

Here we go with the bullshit, he thought to himself. *They ain't about to catch me up on some dumb-ass charge.* Zeph looked down at the gun in his hand. *I should put this up… Nah, I'ma keep it on me,* he second-guessed himself. He returned his weapon to its holster instead of the hotel nightstand and then proceeded to the door. Zeph stood silently with the door partially open. He looked at her from head to toe, searching for any signs of a weapon.

She was dressed in all-black business attire. She could have been about five feet-eight inches without the six-inch heels. She wore her haircut short and it gave her an edgy appeal. Her dark shades framed her face perfectly, but her black lipstick stole Zeph's attention.

"Hello," she greeted.

Zeph watched the words slip through the pink and black of her lips. She shifted from one side to another. Her sudden movement caused Zeph to reach for his gun. "You know me?"

"Yes…well, I used to know you. I don't know you now, but the respect remains."

Zeph frowned. "You know me or not?"

"Okay, you don't recognize me," he stated more to herself. "You knew my brother from the old neighborhood. His name was Octavius."

"Tavi?"

She nodded. "Tavi got time just like you did. He just didn't make it out."

"Octavius Howell? 21st and Hammond."

Her full black lips curled into a smile. "I'm Avie Montgomery, his sister."

"Montgomery?"

"Tavi had his daddy's last name. I got my momma's," she nervously chuckled. "My daddy didn't lay no claim to me."

Zeph stood silently.

"I used to be around all the time," she stated, returning to her point. "I was young then, but it was always y'all and me." Avie nervously laughed.

"I remember now." He relaxed his grip on the butt of his gun.

Avie sighed with relief. She was nervous about meeting Zeph. If he was anything like he was as a kid, then Avie knew Zeph had a quick temper. A true hothead. She knew she was coming to him with good intentions, but she didn't know how it would play out. "Can I come in?"

Zeph hesitated a minute but then moved aside and opened the door wider.

She walked past him, and he caught the scent of a sweet perfume that lingered in with her. She removed her purse from her shoulders and sat on the sofa.

Zeph was leaning against the wall with his right hand behind his back. He was still ready. "What do you want with me?" he questioned. "You here on some revenge shit? You know I ain't have shit to do with your brother's death. That was my guy."

"O-oh, I know," Avie stammered out. "You two were as thick as thieves."

Zeph smiled at the memory. If Zeph ever really had a best friend—it would have been Tavi, especially after Zeph and Monroe took two different paths to success. "Tavi was fast as hell despite his size."

"A big teddy bear."

"To you," Zeph corrected. "Nothing soft about that man. He took that charge and never snitched."

The two gave a moment of silence, reflecting on *their* fallen family member.

"You were in jail when he died, but Shantell cared for us. She paid for the funeral and helped us out from time to time. My mother was her nurse in the end. I used to sit with Ms. Shantell all the time. She would tell us stories about shit y'all used to do." Avie paused. "You know she spoke more about you than her own children. They won't shit in the end, especially EmDee. Jackie came around occasionally. Anytime any of them came around they always had their hands out. That damn stingy ass Monroe kept a tight fist and barely came around to see his own mother. You were different, though. You used to call her every day."

Zeph nodded his head. "My mother kept me alive while I was buried."

Again, the two gave another moment of silence out of respect.

"She would take out anyone if she thought it would protect her *favorite* kid."

Zeph smiled. "I wasn't her favorite."

"You're shittin' me," Avie replied. "You never asked her for a cent while you were inside. You used to send her money."

Zeph nodded his head, recalling the same memory.

"She loved you to death, boy."

Zeph swallowed his emotions. "The feelings were mutual."

Avie nodded. She looked away from Zeph. He had a hard exterior, but Avie could see in his eyes that mentioning Shantell was a sensitive spot for him. She looked away to give him time to regain his composure.

Zeph removed his hand from his gun. Something about mentioning his mother made him relax. He walked further into the room. "You want a drink?"

"What you got?"

"Wait, you ain't even old enough to drink," he stated. "How old are you now? Like eighteen?"

"Funny," she laughed. "I'm old enough to drink."

"I got water for you."

"Nigga please," Avie laughed. "You got brown. I'll take a shot."

"You really old enough to drink?"

Avie smacked her lips. "Yes."

"Damn, I ain't see you in years," he stated. Zeph was hesitant about pouring her a drink. He looked over his shoulder at her.

"Zeph make me drink."

Zeph smirked. He grabbed the bottle of Remy from the hotel fridge and poured a shot. He handed her the cup.

"Thank you."

"Uh-huh," he hummed.

Avie watched as Zeph made him a drink.

When she interacted with him as a seven-year-old child, Zeph was just her brother's dumb friend that shared the responsibility of watching her while her mother was at work. She began to grow fond of him when she started sitting with Shantell and hearing her tell stories about Zeph. He was like the hero of Shantell's hood stories. Now here she was in the same room as him. She used to have dreams about this man. Her dreams reflected her feelings about him; the more she learned about him, the more vivid and intense her dreams became.

Avie looked away when Zeph turned around with a drink in his hand. He sat down in the chair across from her. "You still stay in Terryburg?"

"No, I stay a town over in Collins. I'm enrolled at the university."

"What are you studying?"

"Business Administration with a focus on Human Resources."

"That's what Jackie studied, too, right?"

Avie smiled broadly. "Yep." Although she liked the hood tales as a child, Avie didn't want to live them out. She learned that from Monroe's older sister, Jackie. She went off to college and never looked back. That was Avie's plan, too. "What do you want to do with that?"

Avie shrugged. Suddenly she felt shy. "I don't know what to do with it yet, but I do know I don't want to stay in North Carolina."

"Um," Zeph hummed. He looked Avie over. "I know some things you could do with that."

"Monroe said the same thing."

"What side of the business are you on?"

"Yours."

Zeph stared silently, trying to read beyond Avie's one word answer. "Was that your idea or his?"

"Mutual."

Zeph nodded.

"College isn't free," Avie replied to Zeph's silent judgement.

"All money ain't good money though."

"Regardless, it's a necessity."

Zeph smiled.

Avie did, too. "Tavi used to always say that."

"He did," Zeph confirmed.

Avie looked at her shot, and then quickly gulped it down. "Can I have another?"

"You trying to get drunk?"

Avie chuckled. She sat her cup on the table. "Just trying to settle my nerves."

Zeph never took a sip of his drink. He was hesitant, waiting for the purpose of this meeting. Whatever it was that made her nervous, *it* made him suspicious. "Specifically, what do you do for Monroe?"

"I'm supposed to be like a secretary, but not a secretary because that is Kelly's job." Avie rolled her eyes. "Kelly doesn't like me. I think she is jealous of my relationship with Monroe."

"You fuckin' Monroe?"

"No!" Avie balled her face in disgust. "I don't like men."

Zeph's eyebrows raised across his forehead.

"I mean, I like men. I haven't found one to give myself to…like I'm not sexually active. I'm a virgin." Avie looked away. She was embarrassed that she had shared that information with Zeph.

A look of amusement settled on Zeph's face.

"Anyway," Avie stated, "I'm not fuckin' Monroe, but I think Kelly thinks I'm fuckin' him. She likes him. Not me. She always throwing shade at me."

"You get along with Jamilah?"

Avie shrugged. "She's okay. I'm used to people acting a certain way towards me."

"What do you mean?"

Avie shrugged. "Sneaky people don't like being around people who can read their sneakiness. It hinders them from doing shady shit when someone already suspects them of nefarious activity."

Zeph smirked, noting Avie's word choice. "Who do you think is sneaky?"

"Both Jamilah and Kelly." Avie shrugged. "It's a vibe."

Zeph finally picked up his glass and took a sip. "Why did you want to meet with me?"

"Ms. Shantell taught me a lot. Towards the end, Monroe was acting funny about paying my mother. She had to pick up another job, but the second job prevented her from being a full-time home healthcare worker. We needed both checks so, I stepped in and started taking care of Ms. Shantell."

Zeph's jaw flinched. He recalled conversations with Shantell about her living situation.

"We used to talk about things going on in my world. Shantell used to talk to me like I was a twenty-year-old woman, and I was barely a teen. She taught me a lot though. More than I care to explain at this moment. Just know that I loved everything about Ms. Shantell. I learned to operate just as she did, and in the process, I learned to love who she loved."

"What you saying to me?"

Avie reached into her purse.

"Stop!"

Avie did as she was told. "I ain't trying to hurt you, Zeph. I swear."

"What's in the purse?"

"Just my phone. I recorded a video of a video." Avie's heart was beating out of her chest. "Can I show it to you?"

"Move slow."

She did as she was told and revealed a phone in her hand.

"What's on the phone?"

Avie pulled up a video and then pointed the camera toward Zeph.

Zeph grabbed the phone and looked closely at the video. "What the fuck is this?"

"You…and Monroe's wife."

Zeph moved the phone closer to his face. He was staring at footage of him and Jamilah fuckin' in the kitchen. He looked up from the phone. "Where did you get this?"

"I found the DVD on Monroe's desk."

"Monroe's desk?"

"I think so, but I'm not sure."

"You're not sure where you got it?"

"No, I am. I meant I don't know where Monroe got it."

Zeph put the phone down. "You supposed to be sending me some message from Monroe?"

"No!" Avie stated in a panic. She could hear Zeph's tone change. She had heard about the hot-headed Zephan, as Shantell used to call him, but she had never met him in person. "No, Monroe, don't know I'm here. He doesn't even know that I am showing you this. He doesn't even know I know about this."

"Then why are you showing me this?"

"Ms. Shantell."

"Don't use her name in your bullshit!" Zeph snapped. "What the fuck are you really on?"

"No, she loved you and would do anything for you. Before her own kids, and those were her words. This is me bringing you that," she pointed to her phone. "On the strength of her words."

Zeph continued to look at Avie suspiciously.

"I didn't want you to get got. I know Ms. Shantell wouldn't want that for you, and I don't want that for you either."

Zeph sat back in his chair. His mind was swarming with thoughts. "How did they get this footage?"

"I don't know how they got it, but I know that Kelly brought it to Monroe on a DVD one day. I didn't know what was on the DVD then, but Monroe got mad. He asked her why she felt the need to keep a copy. Then they realized I was still in the room and started discussing it in code. Not like a real code, but…."

"I get what you mean."

Avie continued: "Monroe asked me to leave the office, and I guess that is when he and Kelly really talked it out."

"What made you watch it?"

"I had forgotten that it was even a thing until I came across it days later and remembered their conversation."

Zeph slid Avie's phone across the table to her.

"I know you don't remember me," she chuckled nervously. "You probably find it hard to trust me, but—"

"You're absolutely right," Zeph confirmed. "No buts about it."

Avie swallowed hard. The danger Avie felt like she had voided began to submerge her again. *Please don't let my good deed turn out to be the death of me,* she thought as she looked everywhere but at Zeph.

"I find it hard to believe that a female, who knowing Monroe, is probably getting kicked a lot of money to do absolutely nothing, would sacrifice all that to show me some video of me fuckin' his wife," he paused. "Look at me when I'm talking to you."

Avie forced herself to make eye contact with him.

"What's in it for you?"

Avie was pondering the question when Zeph stood up from his chair. He sat down on the sofa next to Avie. Before she could react to him switching seats, he grabbed her by the neck with his gun pointed at her head. "What's in it for you?"

"LOYALTY!" she yelled out of fear.

Zeph's grip tightened around her neck. She tried to pry Zeph's hand from her throat.

"I knew you as a child; I don't know you now. Why should I expect loyalty from you?" He stared Avie in the eyes. He wasn't in the business of putting his hands on any woman, but she felt like a setup. "I didn't even remember you at first. Why do you want to help me?"

Avie stared Zeph in the eyes as she tried to loosen his grip from around her neck.

Zeph stared back. He let her go when he saw something in her eyes that brought back a familiar memory to him.

Avie doubled over, gasping for air.

Zeph moved from the couch quickly. He paced back and forth.

"I am in love with you," she blurted out.

Zeph stopped in his tracks. "You don't even know me."

"I swear I wouldn't cross you."

"What do you want from me?"

Avie shook her head. "Nothing."

"You really want me to believe that you brought this to my doorstep, and you don't want nothing?"

"Love and loyalty are still a part of some people's DNA. It is definitely a part of mine. It was in Tavi and in my mother's. Ms. Shantell solidified it within me, especially when it comes to you."

Zeph's jaw clenched. Listening to Avie talk, he could hear his mother. She spoke with the same passion that Shantell did regarding subjects like family, loyalty, respect, and the hustle.

"I wrote the last letter you received from Shantell. She could hardly sit up alone, let alone hold a pen." Avie stood up and walked over to Zeph. "I wrote her words, and in her last letter, she clearly told you to beware of Monroe. I know you remember that."

Zeph nodded.

Avie was hesitant, but she touched Zeph's arm to get him to look at her. "I swear I mean you no harm. I didn't want you to underestimate a man who just found out his best friend is fucking his wife."

Avie stepped closer to Zeph. She laid her hand on his chest.

Avie had two motives. She did want to warn him, but she had also watched that video several times. She wanted to experience him like Jamilah got to experience him.

Zeph stepped away from her. "This ain't that."

Avie, feeling embarrassed, turned from Zeph and grabbed her purse. "Look, I just wanted to make you aware," she added as she walked to the door.

Zeph watched. He had so much on his mind. "You really trying to help me?" he called after her. "What do you think I should do?"

Avie turned around to face him. Loyalty wasn't just a word. It wasn't just a song. It was a real-life necessity that she was born and bred to maintain. "Plan and prepare," Avie stated bluntly. "You need to create a path for yourself. A path that can allow you to survive without Monroe."

"You think he out to get me?"

"Wouldn't you be out to get the nigga that fucked your wife?"

Zeph knew consequences would come with his actions, but he didn't expect them to present themselves in this manner.

"I will help you as best as I can."

"What do you want in return?"

"The same thing I am offering you."

"And what is that?"

"Love and loyalty."

Zeph looked into Avie's eye and saw that glimpse of familiarity again. He didn't have the time to decipher his feelings about her presence—yet—but he knew she was right about one thing.

He needed to plan and prepare—quickly.

CHAPTER FOURTEEN

READ THIS

DECEMBER 31, 2019

Dear Jamilah,

~~Ever since we married, I have loved you with all my heart, and it pains me that I have got to be the one to tell you this secret.~~

~~I know this is hard to read, but I got to get it off my chest. Two years ago, I had a son. He's a junior, and he looks just like me. He was conceived by Maria. Maria Elliott from college. The one you hate. I ain't have the baby with her to hurt you. It just happened.~~

~~I have a son that I created outside of our marriage. I know this is hurtful, but I want you to look at the brighter side; we can now be parents since we could never have children. For my own safety, I don't want to disclose my son's mother because I think you would kill me if you ever found out.~~

~~I got a son, and if you can't accept it, then carry yo ass the fuck on because I will not be like my biological father and not take care of my seed. MJ is about to be three, and he needs me more consistently. It ain't your business who the mother is; we are adults and have been co-parenting successfully for the past two years, and we plan to continue doing so.~~

~~Jamilah, I'm sorry, and I hope my taking responsibility for my son as a father doesn't cause me to lose my rib. I fucked up, but I don't want to ruin two lives, yours with this lie of omission and his, by not being a father. I need you both. I fucked up, but I need it to be okay this one time.~~

Monroe looked up from his phone. He had been drafting a letter to Jamilah for two weeks telling her about his son. It was becoming clear to him that he would lose his wife no matter how genuine he was about the situation. Jamilah was a different breed from the women he dated before marriage.

Jamilah wasn't built for drama and because Monroe understood this, he moved differently. It was all to protect Jamilah, who was a sheltered child. Everything Jamilah ever wanted was given to her. She only worked hard to prove to everyone that she could do it without their help or handouts. Life with an invisible safety net is easy when you can try anything regardless of the consequences.

Shantell Whitaker's son didn't have that luxury. As the youngest of four, he grew up in a house where everything was about how to survive. When you grow up with a hustler, some of their skills naturally rub off. That's where Monroe got his hustle.

Monroe looked up from his phone and glanced around the parking lot of the Shauffer Gymnasium. In the distance, he saw a group of boys playing ball on the court. It reminded him of the days he and Zeph would frequent the gym as kids. That's how they stayed out of trouble—for the most part. As kids, they didn't realize that was what they were doing. They just loved the game. At six in the morning—every morning—Emanuel, would drive them there just so he could run drills with them. Emanuel was living vicariously through those boys back then, but Zeph and Monroe didn't know. They just learned to love the game just as Emanual had taught them. Emanuel may have been Zeph's grandfather, but he was a father figure to Monroe, which is why Monroe called him Pop.

Shooting Goals, his nonprofit, was Monroe's way of showing the boys and girls of his camp that the world was bigger than Grambleton, North Carolina. Pop did that for Monroe when his mother's hustling didn't go as planned. The moment Monroe went pro, he showed Emanuel how much he appreciated him and even gave him a job at the camp. Pop proudly worked there until last winter when he passed away.

"Emanuel 'Pop' Greene," Monroe mumbled his name. "I won't disappoint you anymore," he stated with conviction.

Monroe had decided to be an active father on his drive to Shauffer Gymnasium. He wanted to be the father that Pop was to him. Pop did more for Monroe than teach him the game. Pop taught him how to be a man, and he was ready to show the world what he had learned. First, he had to show his wife.

Monroe remembered how disappointed Pop was in him when he told him about Marie being pregnant. He was even more disappointed when he began to understand how Monroe would contribute to parenthood. Pop's exact words, 'I didn't raise you like that.' Those words had always played on Monroe's mind. Drafting letters to Jamilah to tell her the truth was his way of accepting that he was willing to lose everything for his son. That was the man that Pop had raised him to be. Monroe was finally willing to accept responsibilities for his actions and face all consequences.

Maria pulled into the Shauffer Gymnasium. She spotted Monroe sitting on the rear bumper of his car. She pulled up next to him. She was about to grab a manila envelope from the passenger's seat when the driver's side door opened.

It was Monroe being the gentleman that she always knew him to be.

"What's up, baby?"

She immediately melted. Monroe had a way about him that brought her to her knees. She couldn't explain it without risking people calling her crazy.

Monroe reached his hand inside the car to help her out. "You look beautiful."

Maria looked down at her outfit. "Do I really?" she asked, looking down at her black pants suit. Maria grabbed her gun. "Dick is bigger than yours in this suite."

"Your gun is your dick?"

Maria grinned and slowly nodded her head.

Monroe laughed as he pulled Maria to him and gave her a hug. "If you need a dick, you shouldn't marry *that* guy."

"Oh really," she replied after they let go of each other. "Charles is a good man."

"If MJ and you are safe and happy, then I'm happy, I guess."

"And if we aren't?"

Monroe shrugged. "I'll kill the nigga, straight like that."

Maria smirked. "You know you're talking to NCPD's finest, right?"

Monroe looked over Maria. Although Maria wore the most unflattering outfit, he still stared at her lustfully. "Oh, yeah, I know."

Maria blushed. "Stop that," she stated flirtatiously. Maria wasn't a fool. She knew what kind of effect Monroe had on her, so she opted to only meet him in public spaces. True, one night they met in that same parking lot, and the next thing she knew, Monroe had her in the back of his Tahoe fuckin' her brains out.

"I can't help myself."

Maria held up her left hand. "Engaged woman, remember?"

Monroe held up his left hand. "Married man. What's your point?"

"Ummmm," Maria moaned at the thought. "Stop...just stop."

Monroe rubbed his hands together. He knew what kind of affect he had on Maria without trying.

"Whatever."

"Nah, let that nigga know, though. You and MJ are my family. If he do y'all wrong, then he has done me wrong."

Maria looked at him. She was impresed. "What brought the change of heart?"

"You've always bccn my family."

"I know that part," she replied. "I meant you being good with Charles and me getting married."

Monroe shrugged.

Maria smiled. "Charles is a good man."

"Whatever, and I also see it like this," Monroe began. "I can teach you the ropes of marriage."

Maria laughed. "Me, take marriage advice from you?"

"Yeah. I will teach you how to be a good wife, so he won't want to cheat."

Maria stared at Monroe. She sometimes wished she was around so that she could have told Monroe not to marry Jamilah. She never could figure out if she would have been better for Monroe, but she did know that anyone other than Jamilah would have been better. "I guess Jamilah could use those courses, huh?"

"You don't know the half of it."

Maria chuckled. "Seems like you are trying to mature."

Monroe shrugged his shoulders. "I'm trying," he stated. "I-uh...I'm going to tell Jamilah about MJ."

The smile on Maria's face disappeared. "Are you sure about this?"

Monroe nodded. "I was sitting here thinking about Pop and realized how lucky I was to have him. I don't want to be like my father. I don't want to be *that* nigga to my son. I want to be the dad that Pop was to me."

Maria tried to keep her emotions together, but a huge smile appeared. Monroe was a great dad to their son when he was with them. He just missed out on so many moments. Many of MJ's first times, Monroe had to watch a video because his double life prevented him from being there in person. Sometimes Maria wanted to call Monroe so that he could be a part of those moments as they occurred. Still, she reframed because she didn't want any issues for him when it came to Jamilah. She didn't care about Jamilah or her feelings, but she loved Monroe enough not to want to cause him any unnecessary drama.

"What about Jamilah?"

Monroe sighed. He leaned against Maria's car. "I never been one for losing," he began. "I know in this situation that I am going to lose. I keep trying to rack my brain on how to keep everything, but it ain't no way."

"Not with Jamilah."

"But I can't blame her," he quickly added. "Like I have a whole son outside of our marriage, and no matter how I try to communicate the positive in this situation, she won't see it."

"Especially if the son is with me."

"Especially."

"I am grateful for our son, but I sometimes wonder if we should have had him. Don't get me wrong, I love him, but look at all his presence has caused."

Monroe shook his head. "None of which is his fault." He glanced over at Maria. "I don't regret him at all. I wish I had been a man sooner and told Jamilah about him earlier. I should have told her when I found out. Now it's three years later. Three years of lies and secrets. That's my only regret."

"What will you do when she leaves?"

Monroe shrugged his shoulders. "I know the type of woman Jamilah is. I have always believed that one day she would leave."

"Then why get married if you knew it wasn't forever."

"You wouldn't marry me."

"You never asked me to marry you," Maria shot back.

"It's not too late," Monroe replied.

"To ask me? Yes, it is. I am going to marry Charles."

Monroe rolled his eyes. "That nigga is a placeholder, Maria. The moment you understand that the better off you will be."

"You come with a lot, and I don't want to marry *a lot*."

"But you can fuck me *a lot?*"

Maria shook her head. It stressed her out when their conversations would turn into discussions about them as more than co-parents. "We are in two different worlds."

"I'm Monroe in both worlds."

"Detective Maria Elliott shouldn't be affiliated with Monroe, the kingpin."

"You're the mother of my son in both worlds."

"I know that."

"Is that why you regret him?"

Maria shook her head. She never said it, but Monroe's status as a drug dealer was another reason she often regretted having MJ. How would that look in her department if they knew she had a son with one of the biggest drug suppliers in North Carolina? True, Monroe's name never came up in investigations and interrogations, but she knew the truth, and it would only be a matter of time before someone snitched. The empire he and Zeph built would ruin her entire law enforcement career.

Monroe chuckled. "I worked hard to never be the man anyone could be ashamed to know...but here I am."

"Monroe—"

"You're ashamed of me," he concluded.

"I'm not. I just—"

Monroe nodded his head. "You are."

"You are a drug dealer, and I am a detective."

"I'm not a drug dealer. I'm a basketball player and business man."

"You're a basketball player and a drug dealer. Or a basketball player, who sponsors a drug dealer. Either way, Monroe, it ain't right."

"What about all the good I do?"

"Look, I still love you, but—"

"Yeah aiight," Monroe stated, dismissively. "What did you want to talk to me about?"

"Oh, you didn't hear what you wanted to hear, so now you're ready to go."

"What did you want to talk to me about?" he asked, visibly irritated.

Maria stared at Monroe. He was pouting. "I am not Jamilah, Monroe. I won't give you an answer just to stroke your ego. You don't want me because you would have me if you did. You just want to know that you can have me if you wanted me, and I don't work that way."

"You said what you said."

"And am I wrong?"

"You the type to choose your career over love anyway," Monroe commented.

"I would lose so much, and I have MJ to consider."

"And I'm not thinking about him?"

"You are *now*, but…" her voice trailed off.

"Say less."

"So now you're dismissing me?"

"According to you, I'm doing many things *now*, so what's up? Why did you want to meet with me?"

"Fine!" Maria opened the driver's door and grabbed the manila envelope from the passenger seat.

Monroe watched her. When he saw her pull the manila envelope from the car, he quickly stated, "I'm not signing over custody of my child. I don't give a fuck if you're getting married or not."

"Whoa!" Maria stated as she shut the door. "I wouldn't dare ask you to do that." She pushed the envelope into Monroe's hand. "That's not what this is."

Monroe looked down at that envelope. "Then what is it?"

"You need to let that attitude go because it ain't needed."

"I ain't never gonna be good enough for you. No matter what I do or say."

Maria didn't respond. Her silence said more than enough.

"What is this?"

"Something that you need to see. Don't open it around your assistant," she added before she opened her car door.

"Kelly?"

Maria nodded her head. "Whatever her name is. Just don't open it around her. Make sure you read over everything and then give me a call, okay?"

"Is this about Kelly?"

"Just read it."

Monroe looked back at the envelope in his hand.

Maria hopped in her car. "Don't let my response or lack of response strain our communication. We all know what we are and why we can't be." Maria shut the door and rolled the window down. "Thank me later," she added, motioning to the envelope in his hand.

"Yeah, aiight," he replied while watching Maria reverse out of the parking space. He turned his attention back to the envelope in his hand. He opened the envelope and peeped inside as he walked to the car. "Damn," he commented on the amount of paper stuffed inside.

CHAPTER FIFTEEN

DRAFTED
JANUARY 15, 2020

"Tell me, how did you end up working for Monroe?"

Kelly looked across the restaurant table at Bishop Carmichael. *How did I end up with Monroe? The question is, how did I end up with you? God is so good! I can't wait to tell Omari about this.*

"You okay?"

Kelly perked up. "I'm sorry," she stated, embarrassed. *Stay in the moment. Get out of your head*, she told herself.

"Kelly?"

She smiled. "I am. I'm just in awe that I'm having dinner with you."

Bishop shrugged. "I'm a regular guy."

Kelly looked around the Italian restaurant. All of the patrons were looking at their table. "No, you are not a regular guy. Regular guys don't have people gawking at them as they eat dinner."

Bishop looked around at his admirers. He did an acknowledgment wave and then looked back at Kelly. "Somewhat a regular guy," he clarified with a chuckle. Bishop reached across the table for Kelly's hand.

She smiled and put her hand in his.

"Don't pay them any mind. It's just you and me."

Bishop stared across the table at Kelly. He reached across the table and touched one of her hanging locks.

Kelly blushed.

"You look very beautiful," he commented.

Kelly looked down at her simple black dress. She wasn't sure what to wear on a date with *the* Bishop Carmichael. She didn't want to be too sexy and revealing, but she didn't want to look like a school teacher either.

As she looked at him, she wondered if he had stressed about what to wear this evening. He was dressed well, but he had chosen and easy option of a black and white print button up, some black slacks and dress shoes. She liked the fact that he chose to dress subtly, considering he could have worn the most expensive namebrands if he wanted; hell, he could afford to do so.

Kelly inhaled his scent. *A mixture of confidence, manliness, and a light, but probably expensive, cologne*, she thought.

"Tell me," he repeated. "How did you end up working for Monroe?"

Kelly ran her fingers through her hair. "Nothing but God," she stated humbly. "I was working for the Moons doing my internship, but they didn't have a paying position once that was over. Mrs. Moons was a great boss, so she set up an interview with Jamilah because they were looking for an assistant."

"And you went from being an assistant to a real estate broker."

"I'm still Monroe's assistant, but..." she shrugged. "I have more ambition than to just be an assistant."

"I like a woman with ambition," Bishop commented. "What's your next move?"

Kelly smiled. She once read that when a man asks questions about your future, he typically isn't just looking for a one-night stand. He asked questions to determine if the woman was worth investing his time and energy in. She sat up taller in herself. She knew she was worth the investment.

"I want to open my own real estate business," she stated. "Right now, I'm learning everything I can about the business. Monroe recently put me in charge of his Real Estate business."

"Is that smart, considering you just got into it?"

Kelly shrugged. "He still has people in place making the big calls, but he put me in the vicinity of learning from greatness."

Bishop nodded his head.

"There are some things I like about the structure of it and some things I would definitely change."

"What do your parents think about all of this?"

"Supportive."

"Do you see yourself going into business with them?"

Kelly frowned. "With who? My parents?"

Bishop nodded his head.

"They aren't into real estate."

"I can see a man like your father utilizing your legitimacy."

Kelly was taken aback. "What would make you say that?"

Bishop looked curiously at Kelly. "What do you mean?"

Kelly nervously chuckled. "What do *you* mean?" she asked flipping the question. "Utilize my legitimacy? What do you mean?"

Bishop smirked as a reply.

"Are you asking what they do for a living?"

Bishop continued to stare at Kelly curiously, and then he nodded his head.

"You ask questions...awkwardly," she stated.

"Oh," he replied, nonchalantly. He grabbed his drink and took a sip. "Tell me about your parents then. Who are they?"

Kelly was now looking hesitantly at Bishop. She never would have thought someone of his caliber would be awkward. She thought he walked with the same amount of confidence as Monroe. She smiled, amused at her new findings. "Are you nervous?"

"Not at all," he replied confidently. "I'm intrigued, actually. So tell me, who do you tell people your parent are?"

"Okay," Kelly shook her head. "It's just the way you keep sayin' it like that...it's weird, but anyway..." her voice trailed off. She grabbed her drink and took another sip. "My father is well to do on his own. So, he wouldn't need to use my legitimacy or whatever you were saying."

"Oh really?"

"Yeah. He went to law school, where he met my mother. They got married, and two years later, they had me. They live in Norfolk, VA. My mother is a kindergarten teacher despite her law degree, and my father teaches a Criminal Justice course at Old Dominion University."

"ODU, huh?"

"What was that?"

Bishop shrugged.

"I heard condescension in your voice," Kelly noted. "What was that about?"

"Nothing at all," Bishop replied.

Kelly watched him closely. She knew what she heard, and she heard condescension.

"How often do you visit them?"

"My parents?"

"Yeah."

Kelly picked up her glass. She needed time to think. *Why is he asking about them? Oh! This is a relationship interview. I'm on a relationship interview, and family questions are a part of the process. How often do I visit them? Say you don't, and it's an issue. Say you do, then he might question me about specifics. Damn! Why I didn't tell him, they were dead.* "Truthfully," she stated, putting her cup down. "I don't get to see them often."

"And why is that?"

"I just don't." The questions made her uncomfortable, but then again, lying always made her uncomfortable. "We are just a busy family."

Bishop looked suspiciously at Kelly.

"Why are you looking at me like that?"

Bishop didn't respond.

"Oh…you're one of those?" she asked rhetorically. "You ask a person a question and then leave the person to continue the conversation alone while you sit back listening and judging."

Bishop smirked.

"You know, I'm not a bad person because I don't visit my parents. We just live a part. They are all the way in Virginia, and I'm here. We talk, but…." Kelly used her drink as a distraction and took another sip.

"Sounds like you've created quite a backstory for them."

"A backstory?" Kelly questioned. "You think I'm lying?"

Bishop was about to respond when the waiter walked to the table with their food.

Kelly watched as Bishop pleasantly interacted with the waiter. When the waiter left the table, Kelly immediately asked, "Do you think I am lying?"

Bishop reached across the table with his hand palm-side up.

Kelly was hesitant, but she placed her hand in his.

"God, thank you for this meal we are about to eat. Bless the hands that prepared it, and may it provide our bodies with nourishment. In Jesus name, I pray and say Amen."

"Amen," Kelly added at the end. She watched Bishop with mixed emotions. Partly, she was impressed that he was a praying man, but still she was slightly irritated that he had insinuated that she was a liar. "Why do you think I am lying about my parents?"

"I didn't say anything."

Damn, I should have kilt their asses off! she thought as she watched Bishop picked up his utensil and began eating. "Tell me about your parents."

Bishop wiped his mouth. "I can tell you the truth about my parents."

"You say that like I didn't."

"Well, my father—"

"I did tell you the truth."

"You gon'na let me finish?"

"Fine," Kelly picked up her utensils.

"My father ran out on us when we were kids. I haven't seen him since. Wait, I lied. I have seen him. When I was first drafted into the NBA, he reemerged with his hand out, saying he couldn't stay around because he and my mother were like oil and water."

"But he could have still been there for you."

"He could have still been there for all of us."

"How many of y'all are there?"

"Three."

I didn't see that in his bio, Kelly thought. In fact, *I didn't see anything about his family on his Wikipedia page.* "Tell me about your moms."

"She's still living. I don't talk to her much."

"Why is that?"

"She spent our childhood chasing after bum-ass men. She kept putting us in uncomfortable situations because she sought happiness from them at our expense. I learned early on that happiness comes from within, not from others."

Kelly stopped eating. She suddenly felt guilty that she lied about her parents, but her circumstances were different. She couldn't tell him the truth without going into hard details she didn't want to talk about.

"How do you apply that lesson in your life?"

Bishop wiped his mouth and then casually tossed his napkin on the table. "From that, I learned two major lessons. Lesson one, I make me happy first and foremost, and lesson two, I only surround myself with people who know and actively practice lesson one for themselves."

"So, if they are already happy, what do you do for them? Enhance their happiness?"

"Enhance ain't the right word. That would imply that I can take their happiness to another level," Bishop shook his head. "I don't enhance shit. I compliment."

Kelly smirked. "Compliment?"

Bishop nodded. "Say you and I are in a relationship, right. You are a beautiful woman by yourself, and I am handsome as fuck by myself."

Kelly chuckled. "So conceited."

"No, just self-aware," he confidently corrected her. "Together, our looks don't take away or add to how good we look independently. We look good, regardless. That's how I feel about happiness. Your self-happiness isn't added to or taken away by my presents in your life. You should be happy with or without me because I'm happy with or without you."

Kelly nodded her head. "I understand that."

"As my lady, you would receive easy love because you don't have the pressure of being responsible for my happiness."

"An easy kind of love?"

"It is with me. As long as you are honest."

Kelly looked at him inquisitively. "You say that like I'm not being honest with you."

"You say that like you trying to be my lady."

Bishop and Kelly stared each other in the eyes until she could no longer take the connection and grabbed her phone, yet another tool for distraction.

"So, long story short, you don't have a good relationship with your parents," she stated, changing the subject. She put her phone down and looked in Bishop's direction.

"Not at all. Well, not with my biological parents. My mother's brother looked out for us when we were growing up. He and his wife. I would say they were more parents to us than our own parents. And that's crazy to say because Unc was..." Bishop's voice trailed off. "He had the whole family on his back. Our household, his household. He did a lot for us."

"Oh, okay. Tell me about your aunt and uncle."

"Why do you want to know so much about my family?"

"Just a conversation."

"If we are going to have this conversation, then don't you think it should be honesty given from both sides of the table."

"What are you insinuating?"

"Are you telling me the truth about your parents?"

"Why would you assume that I'm not?"

"People don't typically cut off good relationships. They save that behavior for toxic people," he paused. "Or maybe you are the toxic one."

"I'm not toxic," Kelly stated defensively. "They—"

Bishop leaned forward, waiting for Kelly to finish her sentence.

"Nobody is toxic. We are just busy people."

Bishop's silence spoke volumes.

"And where do you get off calling me a liar about my parents?" Kelly grabbed her napkin.

"Because I know your parents."

Kelly slowly lowered her napkin to the table. "What? What do you mean you know my parents?"

"Just like it sounds. I know your parents, and they aren't teachers or whatever the fuck you lied about." Bishop chuckled. He was getting a kick out of the look on Kelly's face. "They don't even live in Norfolk. They live in D.C." Bishop draped his arms over the back of the booth. "I do my research," he answered the question, plastered on Kelly's face.

"And what did your research say?"

"I just sat here and told you." Bishop studied the look on Kelly's face. "Give me some honesty, Aneesa."

Kelly squirmed at the sound of the name Aneesa. She thought she had left that name in D.C., but it seemed to have followed her to North Carolina, just like her parents.

"Just because you know a name; does not mean you know who I am."

"Come on," he stated. "Be real with me."

Kelly stared at Bishop, and then she suddenly grabbed her purse, prepared to dart out the door.

Bishop grabbed her arm. His grip wasn't tight. In fact, it was as gentle as when the two held hands.

To Kelly, it was Bishop's eyes that made her slowly ease back into her seat.

Bishop let Kelly go. "Why lie to me about your parents?"

"How do you even know about my parents?" Kelly questioned back. "Is that why you wanted to have dinner? Are you trying to make connections?"

"Make connections with uh…what, you say, a college professor and his wife?" Bishop laughed. "You don't find that funny?"

Kelly didn't respond.

"Okay, okay, let me be serious." Bishop cleared his throat. "Anessa—"

"Kelly," she corrected him.

"I do not want to nor need to make connections. We are the connections."

"Who are you?"

Bishop looked at Kelly seductively. "You know who I am."

"If you know my father, then I shouldn't be asking, 'who are you?'"

"Then what should you be asking?"

"Not a damn thing because *clearly*, you are someone I don't want to know." Kelly grabbed her purse and stood up from the table.

Bishop hopped up and grabbed Kelly by her waist. He pulled her to him. "Don't leave me, baby," he stated, loud enough to draw attention to them in the restaurant.

"Aww," someone harmonized. "Don't leave him."

Bishop kissed Kelly on the cheek. "Come sit with me," Bishop motioned for her to sit in the booth.

Kelly huffed and reluctantly sat down.

Bishop sat down beside her. "By the way, you smell good." He put his arm around her shoulders and leaned in to smell her neck. He snuck in a kiss on her cheek.

Kelly tried to push Bishop away from her. "Don't put your lips on me."

"I will put my lips anywhere I want to put them," he slid closer to Kelly. He whispered in her ear. "I'd put them on your neck, cheek, thighs, lips…both sets."

Kelly pushed him away. She couldn't deny that Bishop was attractive, but the information he was revealing made her identify him as the opposition. Not because she was in that life but because *he* was in that life.

Bishop laughed. "That was inappropriate, huh?"

"If you have to ask, you already know the answer."

"What's with the change in demeanor?" he asked rhetorically. "You just jumped up, trying to leave in the middle of a conversation." He shook his head. "It's not becoming of you."

"Whatever," Kelly replied.

Bishop looked around the restaurant. "Shit like that, don't phase me, Aneesa. Cause a scene; it won't change anything. You still lied to me."

Kelly folded her arms across her chest.

"Don't worry, my feelings ain't hurt about it."

"What is your purpose?" Bishop asked sarcastically.

"You ask hard questions for this to be a first date."

"This ain't a date!"

"Hmm, what is my purpose?"

"You're not funny," she stated, her irritation plastered on her face. "I'm ready to go."

Bishop looked at Kelly's demeanor. "Why are you pouting?" he questioned as he pulled at her arm. "Uncross your arms. You too beautiful to be sitting here like that."

Kelly side-eyed Bishop. He had set off so many internal alarms that he repulsed her. "Look, if you've done your research, then you should know I don't deal with my parents or anything they do. So, our linking up will not help you make any connections. I don't talk to them."

"I told you," Bishop stated, sternly. "I don't need you to make connections for me."

"I don't give a damn who you made or make connections with because I'm not involved."

"You already in it."

Kelly shook her head. "Go back and review your research."

"You should be an actress."

"What?"

"You acting like you ain't in the life, but you are."

"How you figure?"

"You are Monroe's assistant."

"And what does that have to do with anything?"

"I know you know about his business."

"The basketball team?" Kelly shrugged her shoulders. "I don't know sports. You would know more about the team than I would."

"I ain't talking about the team, Aneesa."

Kelly looked at Bishop confusingly.

"This Kelly Mitchell-shit you got going is a show. I don't want a show. I want Aneesa Wells."

"How do you even know Aneesa Wells?"

"My brother told me."

"Who is your brother?"

"A very important man."

Kelly smirked. "You can't possibly know my father." She opened her purse to look for her confidence. Once she found it at the bottom of her bag, she looked up at Bishop. "Since you know so much, you should know my father handles important people, too."

"Big talk for someone not in the life."

"You're right. I'm not in the life, but my father is, and he doesn't play about his family or his business."

Bishop took a sip of his drink. He found Kelly's big talk amusing. "Your reaction is interesting."

"Whatever," Kelly rolled her eyes. "Who is your brother anyway? I need to make sure my father corrects the right nigga." She watched Bishop closely. She was expecting him to take her threat and be worried about it, but he wasn't. Instead, he was still wearing his cockiness like a badge of honor.

Bishop leaned closer to Kelly and whispered, "Knight."

Just hearing the name Knight sent a chill down her spine. Kelly searched Bishop's face. She was looking for a lie that wasn't there. "Knight is your brother?" she spoke lower than Bishop's whisper.

Bishop nodded his head.

The tough girl act Kelly had put on dripped off her like water. "Look, I don't want shit to do with whatever it is. I'm good. I'm sorry I even mentioned my father." Kelly grabbed her purse.

Bishop grabbed hold of her purse, too. "You can't get out of here that easy. You need to tell me about Monroe's business."

"What do you want to know about? The youth center? The real estate business? What?"

Bishop exhaled deeply. He was enjoying his time with Kelly. After all, she was a beautiful woman, but he was there on actual business. "You know what business I'm talking about."

Kelly looked at Bishop like he was dumb. "Which one do you want to know about?"

Bishop clenched his jaws. He slid away from Kelly. She was pissing him off. "Are you really gonna sit here and act like you don't know?"

"Nigga, I—"

"STOP!"

"What?!" she questioned. "What is your problem?"

"Don't call me a nigga," he stated, staring at her directly. "You can call me anything you want. A motherfucker, a dickhead, Knight's brother... anything, but don't call me a nigga. I work too hard to be reduced to just a nigga."

Kelly laughed in his face.

"Did I say something funny?"

"Do you hear yourself?" she questioned. "As you sit here trying to blackmail me, you have standards on what you need to be called." She laughed. "Nigga, you're full of shit."

Bishop looked around to see if anyone was close enough to hear him. He looked back at her, "Don't fuckin' try me, Aneesa."

The change in Bishop's demeanor slightly scared her. She was grateful when the waiter walked to the table. "Can I get you anything?"

"Double shot of 1942."

The waiter looked at Bishop for confirmation.

He nodded his head.

The waiter turned from the table and walked away.

This nigga ain't my daddy! Oh! Better not call him a nigga. NIGGA NIGGA NIGGA, she smiled at her thoughts.

The waiter returned. He placed the glass on the table, "Anything else?"

Bishop shook his head no.

Kelly watched how fast the waiter moved. *I wonder if he is moving fast because Bishop is a basketball player or because he's Knight's brother.* She pushed the glass away from her. *I don't want that shit.*

Bishop picked up on her protest. "Don't be stubborn," he stated. "You ordered the drink for a reason. Just drink it."

Kelly picked up her glass. She looked into it as though it was telling her how to leave the restaurant without ruffling anybody's feathers. She never met Knight or knew that he had a brother. She had never even seen him, but she most definitely heard of him, and he wasn't one to fuck with or fuck over.

Kelly rushed down her shot and slammed her glass down on the table. She began to speak like liquid courage was a real thing. "I feel like Knight is not the man to lie to, and I have nothing but respect for him," she paused, hoping her sentiment had hit home. "I will tell you anything you want to know about Monroe's businesses."

"Finally."

"So what do you want to know about? The Real Estate business? I really don't know too much about that business, as I just started—"

Bishop raised his hand to silence Kelly. "Anessa, stop fuckin' playin' with me and tell me what I want to know."

"You want to know about his hoes? Fine, he fuck with a white bitch, a foreign bitch, but she's not really foreign—" Kelly flinched when Bishop moved. "Don't hit me," she blurted out.

"That's not the man that I am," he explained. "I don't believe in that shit—at all—okay?"

"But you believe in killing people."

"Only people that don't comply with my requests."

Bishop saw fear overcome Kelly's face again.

"Just listen, okay," he stated to her. "Monroe is moving weight. Major weight. All these businesses that you know about are a part of the show. His real bread and butter is heroin."

Kelly shook her head no.

"Don't shake your head," he ordered. "Monroe is a heron dealer. He has been for years."

"He doesn't. He can't be. He has legal money…legal businesses."

"He does, Aneesa, but not all of it is legal money."

Kelly sat silently, still shaking her head. *Heroin?* she couldn't fathom that as the truth. "Impossible."

"You can move from D.C., change your name and play this new character, but you are not blind. I've physically been in North Carolina since October, and I can tell Monroe is into something far more than real estate and some youth center. I know you see it, too."

Kelly didn't respond.

153

"Okay, then explain this to me. Why does a man like Monroe keep a hitta like Zeph around?" he questioned. "Childhood friends or not, if he's *so* clean, why is he still hanging with a street dude?"

Bishop's words set off an epiphany in Kelly. *Monroe never cut Zeph off. He just put the houses in my name,* Kelly thought. *Why didn't he cut Zeph off? I would have cut Zeph off if he fucked my wife.*

Bishop could tell that his question had sparked a light bulb. "I'm going to run to the restroom. I'll be back."

Kelly thought she had prepped for their date, but as she watched Bishop maneuver through the restaurant, she realized she hadn't. All she knew was the internet-friendly version of Bishop Carmichael. She had even gone as far as remembering his online bio: *6'8, 250 pounds of solid muscle, 32 years old, from Newport News, VA. Graduated third in class from Anthem University in 2007 with a degree in Business Administration. He speaks fluent Spanish and loves to travel. He has no kids and no wife, and the best part is he's the fourth highest-paid player in the league, and that doesn't even include the money from his several endorsement deals.* Kelly snapped out of her thoughts. *I got to get out of here.* Kelly opened her wallet and placed her credit card on the receipt book when she saw Bishop walking back towards the table.

When he sat down, he saw her credit card.

Kelly reacted to the frown on his face and began to explain, "I was just trying to pay. I really need to get out of here."

"Take this," Bishop handed Kelly her credit card.

Kelly grabbed her card without a word.

"You don't pay for anything when you with me. You hear me?"

"I just need to get out of here," she repeated. "I really need to get out of here."

"Where are you going?"

"Home."

Bishop watched as Kelly fumbled with her things. She was trying to return her credit card to her wallet but was having difficulties. He touched her hand.

Kelly looked up at him.

"Are you afraid of me?"

Kelly stopped what she was doing and looked at him. "No," she answered with a straight face. Her heart was beating out of her chest, and her mind yelled, *YES! I'm fuckin' terrified!*

"Aneesa."

"Kelly," she corrected him.

"Aneesa, I need you to make wise decisions from now on," Bishop stated bluntly.

"Wise decisions about what?"

"I need you to get me information on Monroe's business."

Kelly shook her head. "I don't know his business."

"Now that I've told you what to look for, you'll see it without trying."

Bishop stood up from the table. He reached for Kelly's hand.

She was hesitant, but she finally put her hand in his.

When Kelly was out of the booth, Bishop held onto her hand as he led them out of the restaurant.

"I know this wasn't the evening that you expected."

Kelly pulled her hand away from Bishop. She went along with it in the restaurant to not cause a scene, but now in the privacy of the quiet, dim street; she let her true feelings show. "No kidding," she snapped. "You know this is bullshit."

Bishop replied, "Lower your voice."

Kelly looked at him, shocked. His demeanor never changed, but she knew he meant business. She paced back and forth. "If you know me so well, you should know I'm not my parents. I want a different life. I'm striving for a different life."

"And you can have that life, Aneesa."

"How, Bishop? I moved my whole life to escape them and their bullshit. I never agreed with their lifestyle. I never wanted their lifestyle, but…" her words trailed off. "I just want to be free of them. I want a normal life where killing isn't a staple. Like my father is in some shit now. That's why I moved and changed my name legally. I don't want to be tied to that life. That's why I ran and feel like I am still running." Kelly broke down in tears, hearing her reality echo off the night. "I just wanted to be normal," her tears rolled down her face. "Why won't anyone let me be normal?"

Bishop understood Kelly all too well. He sometimes felt that way, too, but it was instilled in him to never turn his back on family. He knew no matter how far a person tried to run, they could never outrun their truth. They would need to just stop and face it. Kelly hadn't learned that lesson yet, and Bishop could tell. He walked to her and wrapped his arms around her shoulders.

Kelly tried to push him away, but she melted into his arms. She needed this embrace, even if it meant getting it from the person that put her in this predicament.

Bishop stroked Kelly's hair as he held her. Over the last few months, Bishop's goal was to discover Monroe's routine. In doing so, he ended up also keeping tabs on Kelly. He had known for months who she was and how she was *acting* like she was someone else. He couldn't understand why she would have gone to such an extent. Initially, he thought her family was working an angle on Monroe, but it was something genuine about Kelly. She didn't move like an individual with a motive. She was an average woman in a not-so-average world. She stayed busy running errands for Monroe and running between classes. She spent most nights alone at her kitchen table studying. He hadn't planned it, but during his observations he had developed a strong interest in her. "You okay?"

Kelly let Bishop go. She wiped her eyes. "Would it even matter at this point?" She turned and began walking up the street to her car.

Bishop wasn't heartless. He wanted to follow behind her, but in doing so, he knew he would have added to her stress. He knew this Kelly *character* that Anessa had created wanted no parts of the world he had been roped into. Hell, he hated that he had been roped into his brother's world, but Knight was the last person he would deny. Bishop didn't fear his brother, his loyalty was out of respect. He didn't have enough fingers to count the sacrifices Knight made for him over the years. What was this one ask? Even if it was to a woman he didn't want to hurt.

CHAPTER SIXTEEN

ACCEPT THE MISSION
JANUARY 15, 2020

"ZANI!" Kelly yelled at the top of her lungs. After leaving the restaurant, Kelly rushed to her mother's apartment. Every time she walked into their apartment; she was reminded they were supposedly changed people now. It could be possible. Back in the day, there would be no way they'd be caught in such a *basic* apartment, but here they were. No longer living a hood-lavish lifestyle.

Zani was curled up under a blanket. To hear Kelly come into the apartment warmed her heart. She tossed her covers to the side and sat on the edge of her couch like an anxious child. Since moving to North Carolina, Zani has had a lot of alone time. These random moments when Kelly showed up at her house meant the world to her. She immediately cut off the TV and looked at Kelly. "Hey baby," she stated, ecstatic. Being close to her only child meant the world to her. She dreamt of the days when her family would be reunited. The only person missing now was her husband, but she knew he would be with them soon enough.

"Why the fuck won't you leave me be?" Kelly hollered at the top of her lungs.

Zani looked around the apartment.

"I'm talking to you."

Zani smirked. Her daughter didn't often have emotional outburst, but when she did, Zani was reminded how much Kelly had in common with her father.

"I deliberately moved here, changed my name, changed my life, so I wouldn't have to deal with y'all's shit! But what do y'all do? You move here and pull me back into your bullshit—why?!"

Zani grabbed her remote control and turned on the TV. A smirk rested on her face. She found Kelly's temper tantrums to be amusing. It made her feel like they were a *normal* family. Although there was nothing normal about The Wells.

Kelly paced back and forth, but it infuriated her even more when she realized she didn't have Zani's attention. "Are you listening to me?!" Kelly shouted. "It's not fair. Y'all niggas are so selfish!"

Zani pulled a cigarette from the pack and threw the box on the table. She looked at Kelly after she lit up. "What the fuck is your problem?" Zani asked. "'Cause you jhi like blowin' me, shorty!"

"You blowin' me!"

Smoke floated with Zani's words. "What did I do to you, Anessa? Kelly, whatever the hell you call yourself these days."

"Unbelievable," Kelly commented. "And just like always, you selfish motherfuckers don't give a shit about me. There are fifty-fuckin'-states; why did you all have to come to North Carolina? Why couldn't you let me have this one thing? Noooo! You got me running into niggas that know my real fuckin' name talking to me about drugs and shit."

Zani stood up from the couch. "WHAT?!"

Kelly continued her rant.

Zani couldn't process fast enough what Kelly was talking about. She returned to her seat. She was irritated that she had allowed Kelly to interrupt her peace.

"You have nothing to say?"

Zani looked at her daughter like she was an out-of-line nigga on the street that she was about to get together—quickly. "I don't know who the hell you think you are talking to, but you doing a lot and you need to relax 'cause I'm your motha. You are not my motha; therefore, you will not talk to me like you are, Elmira Harbell." Zani replied with a calm demeanor. "Let me make that real live for you."

Kelly folded her arms across her chest.

Zani continued: "Now you walk your ass out of my apartment and come back in here like you got some got damn sense."

Kelly stood with her hands on her hips, staring at her mother.

Zani put her cigarette down and stood up.

The two held a staring contest until Kelly turned on her heels and walked out of the living room.

"Coming in here with that bama-ass shit," Zani grumbled as she sat down and picked up her cigarette.

Kelly stood in the foyer, trying to gather her emotions. When she felt she had it together, she walked back into the living room and sat in the recliner across from Zani.

"Don't you ever in your life try me again," Zani warned. "Daughter or not, I will drag you up outtah here, Aneesa. You hear me?"

Although bigger, Kelly wanted to avoid seeing Zani with the hands. Over the years, she had seen her mother in action and no one should ever underestimate Zani's size.

Kelly acknowledged her mother's threat with a non-verbal gesture of submission—she lowered her head.

Zani accepted Kelly's response. "Now, what has got you so tight?" she questioned, wearing her concerned parent hat.

"I met Bishop Carmichael."

"The basketball player?" Zani's face contorted into wonder. "What does your meeting with him have to do with how you just came in here?"

"Don't play dumb."

Zani's face went stone again.

Kelly cleared her throat and rephrased her response. "Zani, you already know."

Zani was getting irritated with Kelly's dramatics. This was one of the things that tended to irritate her about her daughter. "Just say it!" Zani shouted. "All this dramatic shit!" She took a puff of her cigarette, and before she could inhale, she blew the smoke out of her mouth and jumped to her feet. "HE PUT HIS HANDS ON YOU?!" Her eyes seemed to bug out of her head with intensity. "The fuck?"

Kelly was startled by her mother's reaction. "NO!"

"OH!" Zani eased back into her seat. She gave her attention back to the TV. Zani laughed at her reaction. "I was ready! 'Cause if he put his hands on you, it was torched." Zani started throwing punches in the air. She looked at Kelly and shook her head. "Girl, go on with your story."

"Do you know who Knight is?" Kelly responded before Zani could answer, "Bishop Carmichael claims he is Knight's brother."

Zani slowly turned to look at Kelly. There wasn't fear in her eyes, but Kelly definitely saw concern.

"You didn't know?" she asked. Kelly stared at her mother, awaiting a response, but Zani said nothing. "Zani!" Kelly called her.

"Bishop Carmichael is Knight's brother?" Zani asked for clarification.

"You really didn't know they were brothers?"

"I knew Knight had a sister, but I didn't know he had a brother…let alone a famous one." Zani shook her head. "Bishop really said that Knight was his blood-brother."

"He didn't use the term *blood-brother*, but he was serious when he said they were brothers. He was talking about Knight like a sibling he grew up with."

Zani shook her head. She hadn't heard the name Knight since the early nineties. "How this conversation come up?"

"At dinner," Kelly stated. "Bishop asked me about my parents, and I lied, and he called—"

"What'chu mean you lied? You ashamed of us or something?"

"I wasn't about to tell him who y'all really are."

Zani turned her whole body to face Kelly. "Who did you tell him we are?"

"That's not important."

Zani nodded her head. "Message received," she stated. "But'chu quick to run to us when you in a bind."

"You're the reason I end up in binds."

"Um," she hummed loudly.

"Anyway," Kelly continued telling her story like she hadn't heard Zani's remarks. "He told me I was lying and started laying down real facts. He knew Moe and what Moe was into, and then he called me by my government name."

Kelly sat silently, waiting for Zani to speak, but Zani was in her feelings. "Hello?" Kelly called to her. "You not talkin' to me now?"

"You know your father and I did good by you."

Kelly sighed. She didn't want to hear the same ole same from Zani, but simultaneously, she knew her mother. If she antagonized Zani, it would only cause Zani to speak louder with her heavy D.C. accent and mannerisms just to express her point.

Zani continued: "You never wanted for anythang because we made sure you had errythang."

"I don't want to talk about that right now."

"But it deserves a conversation," Zani insisted. Her D.C. accent accentuating the passion in her voice. "We moved here to—"

"Can we focus on the issues at hand?"

"Ungrateful." Zani shook her head. "Ungrateful." She wanted to go in but didn't feel up to the battle. "Just don't let your father hear you talking about how ashamed of us you are."

"I never said I was ashamed."

"Then what'chu lie?"

"What would be the purpose of changing my name to Kelly, just to introduce myself to people as Anessa Wells?"

"You shouldn't have changed your name."

Kelly didn't respond.

Zani looked at Kelly with her lips turned. "You moved out of the city, I get it. The District can weigh heavy on anybody after a while, but that's home. I love it. Your Dad does, too. We accepted that you wanted to leave. Then you went and changed your name. Now this lying bullshit," Zani shook her head. "Your words and actions are hurtful."

"Sorry."

Zani frowned. "It's not what you say, it's how you say it."

"I said sorry, Zani."

"You're not, but okay."

"Ma, I'm sorry."

Zani rolled her eyes at Kelly. She sat back on the couch and propped her leg on the coffee table.

"You mad now? You know that's dumb to change my name, and then introduce people to me using the name I–"

"Don't even finish," Zani warned.

The two sat silently in the living room, until Kelly could take no more. "I wish you would let me talk to you so you can–"

"You know," Zani stated. "Knight is old school."

"Why you say that?"

"By Knight sending his brother, he is letting us know that he knows we are in his town and could touch us if he wanted to. That's why he met with you without our knowledge or consent."

Kelly felt chills down her spine.

Zani stared off into nowhere as she spoke. "Simultaneously, he is letting us know he is coming in peace."

"Where's the peace? Cause I don't see it."

"Why would he make himself vulnerable by exposing a blood brother we didn't even know existed?"

"We don't even know if they are brothers."

Zani shrugged. "I don't know too many niggas out here claiming Knight as a brother. That's a dangerous game to play."

"So, is he telling the truth?"

There was a ong pause, and then Zani said, "I believe him."

"What does Knight look like?"

"I don't know," she replied. "Your father might know."

"Are they in business together?"

Zani shook her head no. "Your father is out of the game, Kelly. That's why we moved down here."

Kelly sat quietly, as though she was allowing Zani's lie to linger in the air. Kelly had heard the *out-the-game* lie several times from her parents. The first time she had believed them. This was now the fourth time she had heard it, and the lie had fallen on deaf ears. "Sooooo y'all are rebuilding the empire—got it," Kelly stated sarcastically.

Zani side-eyed her daughter.

"How did you even meet Bishop?"

"He's on Monroe's basketball team, and they met at his house the other day. It's weird now that I think about it."

"What's weird?"

"Jamilah made it her business to introduce Bishop and me like on some matchmaker-type thing. She even texted me and asked if she could give him my cell phone number."

"I thought she didn't like you."

"I thought she didn't either, but she was adamant about us linking." Kelly replayed the scenario to Zani, "One moment, the four of us are supposed to go out, and then Jamilah tells me she needs to reschedule. I hit her back and say, 'Okay,' like I'm fine with it, but then she texts and asks can she give Bishop my number."

"And you said, okay?"

Kelly nodded. "Hell yeah, Bishop is gorgeous, and I never would have thought he was Candy Man's brother."

"Candy Man's brother," Zani shook her head at the name. "What happened on the date?"

"Everything was good, and then the conversation switched."

"Switched how?"

"He asks me about my job with Monroe, then he asks what's my next plan in life. I tell him, and then he's like, I bet your father would love to use that for legitimacy or some shit like that," Kelly shakes her head. "Then he calls me Aneesa and knows all about me through his associate. I later find out that his associate is Knight."

"What does he want?"

"He got it in his mind that Monroe is some kind of drug dealer," Kelly stated dismissively. She shook her head, still unconvinced, "Monroe, a drug dealer, right."

"Are you asking me, or are you telling me?" Zani stared at Kelly confusingly. She loved the fact that she was able to keep Kelly isolated from the life that she lived. Zani despised being broke but being broke taught her valuable life lessons. Most importantly, being broke instilled in Zani a drive for success and a thirst for the finer things in life. Zani had managed to pass on the latter to her daughter. Kelly was one of the most driven and determined people that Zani had ever met. Unfortunately, looking at her daughter now, the isolation that Zani was grateful she could provide her was turning out to be Kelly's Achille's heel. Kelly was so ignorant and naïve about what people could say and do; it often left her looking stupid. As Zani stared at her daughter, she was also staring at a damn fool.

"I would know if Monroe was a drug dealer."

Zani sat back on the couch and crossed her legs.

"I would know," Kelly explained to her mother's body language. "I schedule all his appointments and travel dates; I have full access to his life. I know that man." Kelly laughed. "I may not know many things, but I know Monroe Whitaker like the back of my hand."

"Right," Zani replied sarcastically. "You cute though, go off."

"I do," Kelly insisted.

"Who are you trying to convince?"

"You!"

"No, Miss Mamas. You are trying to convince yourself."

Kelly bit down on her thumbnail as she contemplated a typical day at work with Monroe. For some reason, she could only focus on the sexual tension between them. A sneaky smirk settled on her face.

Zani looked at her daughter suspiciously, "You slept with him, didn't you?"

"No!"

Zani could hear the defensiveness in her daughter's voice. She knew that Kelly was lying. Her tone always went up an octave when she was lying.

"I was thinking about a typical day with Monroe."

"And?"

Kelly sat back in her seat. "I'm not seeing everything am I?"

Zani shook her head.

"I am a very intelligent woman."

Zani nodded her head in agreement. "That you are."

"It makes me mad because you and Bishop act like this shit is just so obvious. How am I missing it?" she questioned rhetorically. "He doesn't even move like a drug dealer; he is flashy and wants attention. Hell, he is famous. He's the captain of an NBA team. Don't most drug dealers want to be anonymous?"

Zani rolled her eyes. She could name dozens of drug dealers, who wanted to be fly and flashy for the public. "First and foremost, stop using urban movies as a point of reference on how you think drug dealers *supposedly* act. They all don't act alike."

"Monroe's a drug dealer?" She was still very much skeptical. "But why? He's famous. What do you need to sell drugs for when you have multiple businesses—successful businesses at that."

"Stop looking for a person's why and accept who they are." Zani could tell by the look on Kelly's face that the information still wasn't clicking. "It just is what it is," Zani explained in the simplest form.

Kelly shook her head in disbelief. "Okay, a typical day at work. First, I…" she paused. Although she went to work like a typical nine-to-five person, Kelly couldn't describe her job responsibilities. They always changed. She was never focused on one thing as opposed to another.

"Monroe is a drug dealer," Zani confirmed when Kelly couldn't verbalize her duties.

Kelly held her head in her hands. "It's Zeph, isn't it? Bishop called Zeph a hitter."

"Zeph?" Zani repeated. "Why that name sound familiar?"

"Zephaniah Wilkins."

Zani nodded her head. "I know that name. I just don't know from where."

"He is Monroe's bestfriend since childhood."

"Um," Zani hummed. "Bishop called him a hitter?"

"Yeah."

"Zeph might be to Monroe what Che is to your father."

Kelly looked up. Her jaw dropped. "Monroe is a drug dealer," she finally concluded. "How did I miss it?" Kelly's eyes were glued to the floor as though her confirmation would metabolize before her. She looked at Zani, "Does Jamilah know?"

"I don't know what Jamilah knows, and I don't give a damn about what she knows. That shit isn't important to me," Zani stated bluntly. "But listen to me," she sat up on the couch. "Listen," she repeated. "Now that you are over the shock that Monroe is a drug dealer, I need you to understand something else," Zani dramatically paused.

Kelly stared at her with wide eyes. "What do I need to understand?" she whispered.

"Know that Knight is not to be played with."

"I know who Knight is."

"No," Zani replied. "You know about the little nursery tales told around the block. That Candy Man shit. I know the truth. I remember Knight when he used to work for your father. He is ruthless."

"He sold drugs?"

"No," Zani shook her head. "A man with *that* type of audacity isn't a corner boy." Zani zoned out, thinking about the tales her husband used to share with her. The story her daughter knew about was child's play compared to the stories Zani heard.

"What does that even mean?"

"It means," Zani explained, slightly irritated. "Knight is TTG. Trained to go."

"But he used to work for Daddy. That means they're cool."

"Cool?" Zani was disappointed that she had failed to teach her daughter about the streets. "Don't you think the presentation would have been different if they were *cool*? Wouldn't he just go to your father if they were *cool*? Think girl! Why would he involve you if they are *cool*?"

Kelly thought a moment and then said, "But I thought you said they used—"

"USED TO!" Zani hollered out in frustration. "Past tense, baby girl!"

"So, they're enemies."

Zani was about to elaborate, but she stopped herself. *My poor isolated baby. Moe's gonna flip shit if he finds out what Knight did.* "What's funny?" Zani watched her child go through several emotions; anger, fear, confusion, and now this—"Why are you laughing?"

"You talking to me like my Daddy ain't about that life," Kelly stated with a chuckle. "My father is Morris Moe Wells! Who is really stepping to him?"

Zani sighed. "Do you know what happens when two men, who oppose one another, are about *that* life?" she paused, waiting for Kelly's response. "Do you?"

The smirk on Kelly's face disappeared. She shrugged her shoulders, unsure of how to answer.

"People die!" Zani finally answered. "This shit ain't a game. Your father and I have been to war. He lost a lot of good men, and this time around, he almost lost a chunk of time. 88 to life ain't an easy bid. Your father would have died in prison because he is about *that* life."

Kelly swallowed down her arrogance. She and her father didn't always have a good relationship, but his current circumstances made her sad. It was one thing to not see him because of her own views. Having the law *tell* her she couldn't see her father was another story.

"I think you need to look at this situation through a new lens. Start from the beginning; who is Monroe? Who is everyone that he deals with? What are his businesses? Who's a part of those businesses?"

Kelly heard her mother talking, but she wasn't listening. Her thoughts had her in a trance. She was trying to think about everything; the businesses, the people, the meetings, the trips…all the while, her father's sentence and what life would be like if Moe wasn't around kept creeping into her thoughts. She couldn't focus. Nothing stood out except the second confidentiality form.

"Study Monroe," Zani suggested.

Kelly snapped out of her trance. "I got a better idea. Let's tell Daddy—"

"Daddy," she mocked her daughter. "Now he's Daddy. Any other time with you, he's Moe."

"Daddy, Moe, whatever. Let's just let him handle everything."

"You don't want to see your father handle this thing," Zani replied.

"And your father is already handling *other* things. He doesn't need this on his plate."

"He can handle it when he's done."

"No!" Zani snapped. "We will handle it before he even knows about it."

Kelly looked away from Zani's glare. She wanted to cry but didn't want to do it in front of her mother. She didn't want her mother to know the extent of her fear. In fact, she wanted to go home, pack a bag, and run again.

"This was Jamilah's doing," Kelly stated. "Jamilah set all of this in motion."

"How does Jamilah know about you?"

Kelly shrugged. "I never told her. I mean, why else would she be adamant about putting me and Bishop together?"

Zani didn't reply.

Her silence caused Kelly's anxiety to heighten. "See, man!" is all Kelly could come up with.

"I will help you, Aneesa. You just can't be on your selfish shit. You got to be for the family. None of that running shit; for God's sake, be yourself. We named you Aneesa, not Kelly."

Kelly sat quietly. Hearing her mother's *be-yourself*-speech rubbed her the wrong way. Her mother didn't understand that Kelly allowed her to be herself. Being Aneesa came with too many expectations that Kelly wasn't built to fulfill. Kelly's parents, the educators, never would have put her in a life-or-death situation, but Aneesa's parents—that's the only way they knew how to live.

"You really not gonna tell Daddy?"

Zani thought for a minute. She knew that would be right, but then she was hesitant. To tell Moe what was going on would go against the speech that she had just given to Kelly. She knew her husband very well. They had been together for years. She knew he wouldn't take something like this lightly. She knew he would handle this by any means necessary. "Eventually," Zani finally answered. "We are going to give Knight the information he is looking for and be done with it all."

Kelly didn't respond.

"You hear me talking to you, Aneesa?"

"I hear you."

"But are you listening?"

"I am," she responded reluctantly. "I'm listening to you." Kelly sunk low in her chair. Bishop's appearance in her life would be more disruptive than she could have imagined.

CHAPTER SEVENTEEN

SECRET AGENT

JANUARY 20, 2020

"Damn, Kelly! Is this really how you gonna do me?"

Kelly looked up slowly from her phone. Her heart was pounding out of her chest. She had been dreading this moment since she became a *spy*.

"You hear me talking to you?"

She slowly turned her head to face Monroe. He was standing at his desk. He looked from his phone to Kelly. "You hear me?"

"Y-yeah," Kelly stammered.

"Why do you do me like this?" Monroe looked back at his phone.

"I ain't do nothing," her words were defensive.

Monroe looked at Kelly with a frown. "You're actin' weird."

"I'm not acting weird," her tone had gone up an octave. "You the one talking about why I do you like *that*, whatever *that* is, and I ain't do you like nothin'."

"I'm talking about this shit," Monroe stated, holding up his phone.

"What is that?"

"My calendar. You said that I got a meeting with ME tomorrow at noon," Monroe laughed. "I was confused as hell looking at this damn thing. Like, how in the hell am I meeting with myself."

"Oh," Kelly replied drily.

Monroe looked up from his phone. "That's all you got to say?"

Kelly didn't reply.

"What's good with you? You've been acting differently lately."

Silence.

"Do you need a vacation or something?"

Kelly inhaled. *Get your head back in the game*, she told herself. It was hard for her to stay neutral. Listening to negative remarks about Monroe from everybody was starting to impregnate her thoughts. She knew she needed to play it cool. She had been investigating him for a month and still had nothing of value to give Bishop. To make matters worse, Bishop was hitting her up twice a day. He tried to play it cool with small talk, but then he would hit her with the hard questions, 'What did you find out?'

"Hello? I'm talking to you. Do you need a vacation or something?"

"No."

"Then you need to get it together. That attitude shit ain't needed here, okay?"

"Okay." *Get your head in the game*, she thought to herself. Kelly cleared her throat ad then said, "If her mother took the time to give her the initials M-E, then it is only right that we use them."

A smirk appeared on Monroe's face. "There she is," he stated. "That's the woman that I know."

Kelly smiled.

"I need you to call Avie to set up a meeting."

The smile on Kelly's face disappeared. "Why?"

Monroe's facial expression had replied with a question of its own.

Kelly shook her head and turned her attention back to the books. *He probably gonna fuck that funky bitch*, Kelly thought to herself. *Basic-ass resume having ass bitch*. "And what is this meeting concerning?"

Monroe chuckled.

Kelly already knew what his chuckle was about.

"I'm not questioning you."

"Then what are you doing?"

"She works for you…you call her." The words mumbled out of her mouth as though she was back-talking to her parents.

"Excuse me?" Monroe put his phone down. "What did you just say to me?"

"Nothing."

Monroe picked up his phone. He resumed his activity, but he wasn't focused. He couldn't believe Kelly's audacity. "Set up the meeting," he stated, reiterating his point.

"Who is she?"

"The Point Guard on my other team."

The silence in the room made him look up from his phone. The look on Kelly's face brought a smile to his.

"Are you serious right now?"

Monroe was amused. If Kelly was a cartoon character, he would be looking at the steam coming from her ears. "You know I'm playing, right?"

Kelly rolled her eyes.

"I am," Monroe repeated. "She ain't a Point Guard."

"Then who is she?"

"Avie." Monroe shrugged. "Avie is Avie. What? You jealous?"

"Whatever." Kelly went back to working on her tablet. Monroe had brought up mixed feelings in her. She loved him, she even loved being around him, but she hated him, especially in moments like these when he could never give her a direct answer.

"I'm hooking her up with Zeph."

"Then he can get off your wife…hey—"

"Watch yo' mauthafuckin' mouth," Monroe corrected her before she could attempt to clean up her slick comment.

Kelly knew she was out of line. That was a low blow, and she knew it. "I'm sorry."

Monroe didn't reply.

Kelly continued trying to make peace. "When should I set up the meeting?"

"Don't worry about it. I will call her myself."

"I can—"

"No."

"Okay. I'm sorry…I really am. I am just stressed. I got this exam coming up, and I'm dealing with other bullshit from people," she stated, vaguely sharing her truth with Monroe. "I didn't mean any disrespect… seriously."

"I've known Maria for years, and I never thought about her initials spelling M-E."

Kelly smiled. *He must have accepted my apology,* she thought. "You have to find the humor in life."

"What are your initials?"

"K-I-M. Kelly Inez Mitchell," she stated it just as she had rehearsed when first taking the name.

"K-I-M, as in Keep It Moist," Monroe commented.

"No, K-I-M, as in Keep It Moving," she stated, getting out of her seat.

Monroe watched Kelly move to the couch. He played hard, but he could never stay mad at her. It was something about her personality that drew him to her. Monroe moved across the room to sit beside her. "What am I meeting with Maria for anyway?"

"She didn't tell me."

Monroe folded his hands behind his head. "Aren't you supposed to find that out for me?"

"It's hard getting anything out of that woman; she is so secretive. She could work for law enforcement as tight-lipped as she acts." Kelly laughed. She stopped short when she realized that she was laughing by herself. "Does she work in law enforcement?"

Monroe got up from the couch. He made his way back to his desk.

"Here you are trying to act secretive, too."

"Does that mean I work in law enforcement?"

Kelly smacked her lips.

Monroe laughed. He liked it when Kelly got feisty with him. He missed their friendly back-and-forth banter. What they had been experiencing lately was intense. It almost reminded him of the tension he was feeling in his marriage.

Kelly rolled her eyes and continued working on her tablet. As she sat there, she created a new note and wrote, 'Does ME work in LE?' She quickly changed screens and returned to her task in case Monroe was to make his way next to her again.

"Maria is just tight-lipped because she wants to protect MJ," he explained. "He's our main priority."

"That's understandable, but if I had your child, I would want the whole world to know."

"For what reason?"

"Oh no, not for any underhanded purposes, but I wouldn't want my child to know you like you are some phantom at night."

"I don't just see MJ at night."

"I know that, but you're like a phantom, though. He knows you are his father, but you only appear occasionally. You're like an invisible daddy."

"Invisible daddy?" Monroe repeated the verbal gut punch. "I see MJ every day."

Kelly shot a look at Monroe.

"I'm not lying."

"I didn't say you were."

"That face you made did." Monroe repeated himself again, "I do see MJ every day."

Kelly put her tablet down. "You do know that I make your schedule, right?"

"And what does that mean?"

"You don't have to lie to me."

His eyebrows were balled up across his face. "You sayin' I'm lyin'?"

Kelly didn't respond.

"I see MJ every day...for the most part."

Kelly returned to her work.

"I DO!" he raised his voice. "What the fuck do you even know?"

"What do I know?" Kelly chuckled. "I know you so busy running after these hoes—"

"What, you think I'm some kind of lame driven by pussy?"

Kelly sat back and folded her arms across her chest.

"Well, I'm not Kelly!"

"Says the man with a basketball team of hoes."

"You on the team."

Kelly nodded her head. It was now her turn to digest a verbal gut punch. "Are you calling me a hoe right now?"

Monroe stood up. "I'm just reminding you."

"Reminding me of what exactly?"

"You sucked my dick, so you tell me."

Kelly jumped up from the couch. She dramatically gathered her things from the sofa.

Monroe watched Kelly's performance. "Where are you going?"

Kelly didn't say anything. She continued with her storm out. She walked to Monroe's desk and snatched her purse. Papers flew off the desk. "Shit," she stated. She threw her bag on the chair and picked up the papers.

Monroe grabbed her arm and snatched her up from the floor.

"Get your damn hands off of me," she snatched her arm away from his grasp.

"I ain't trying to argue with you. I ain't even trying to disrespect your ass."

"But you did!" Kelly pushed Monroe away from her. "You are just a disrespectful asshole."

Monroe pulled Kelly to him and kissed her.

She tried to pull away from his grasp but wasn't putting forth much effort. She wanted Monroe. And in this moment of passion, she could tell he wanted her, too. Monroe held her tightly, his hands roaming her backside.

Monroe turned Kelly around and bent her over the desk. He pulled her dress up and her panties down. Monroe moved so fast that if Kelly had intended to protest, there would not have been enough time. She couldn't process everything happening until he slipped his dick into her and stole her breath. She went from being palms flat on the desk to lying on her elbows. They stood still, enjoying the suddenness of each other. Perhaps all the tension they had felt for the past month was purely sexual.

Monroe's head was laid back, and his eyes were closed. For him, the initial penetration had sent a shiver down his spine. He could have let his dick sit in her warmth and wetness without moving.

For Kelly, she was stuck in surprise. Monroe had filled her beyond her wildest dreams. Her moans filled the quietness of the office. She slowly moved back and forth on his shaft.

Her sudden movement pulled Monroe out of his thoughts. He was fine sitting in her warmth, but watching how she knew to arch her back without direction making her hips the perfect handlebars was a sight. Every time he hit; Kelly's ass moved like a tidal wave. The sight of her squirming under him, reaching for something that wasn't there, cause him to experience sensory overload. He closed his eyes. He knew he wouldn't be able to last long looking at everything, but closing his eyes didn't help. He gripped Kelly's shoulders, using them as leverage to pull himself in deeper. He then moved his hands down her back and along her waistline, to her hips and then he firmly gripped and spread her cheeks. The softness of her booty in the palm of his hands, plus Kelly's ability to grip and release his dick with every stroke had Monroe stuck. He let go and allowed his body to float and enjoy this moment he had fantasized about for months. He moaned out in pleasure. Hearing himself moan, startled him and he pulled out his dick trying to give himself time to regroup.

Kelly looked back at Monroe.

"Don't rush me," he replied.

"I want it," she whined.

Monroe slipped himself back in and Kelly took off.

"Get yours," Monroe ordered, as he watched the waves.

Kelly's moans were loud and hypnotizing.

She threw her ass back, and he caught it forward; their timing and rhythmic vibe had them climaxing at the same time.

"This my pussy," he told her. He gripped Kelly's ass tightly in his palm as he nutted in her.

This only made Kelly continue to throw it back and milk Monroe until he was dry.

Too sensitive to handle anymore, Monroe pulled out and watched his essence drip from Kelly. In a matter of moments, Monroe went from feeling pleasure overload to instant regret. He silently pulled up his clothes and began to redress.

Simultaneously, Kelly sensed that things were different. She felt vulnerable as she pulled up her panties that were bunched around her ankles. Once dressed, she stood by the desk, trying to regain her composure. She couldn't look at him. She bent down to gather the papers off the floor. In doing so, she didn't notice that he couldn't take his eyes off of her.

"Your meeting is at one," she suddenly stated.

"Uh," Monroe cleared his throat. He was stuck. He wanted to say something to her, but he didn't know what to say. "Right," he mumbled. "Yeah, okay."

"I have my broker's exam tomorrow." Kelly was still stooped low, avoiding eye contact. "Is it okay to take the rest of the day off?"

"Yeah," Monroe replied. "Take the rest of the day off."

"Okay."

Monroe walked towards his office door. Kelly finally looked up just as he turned around to look back at her. The two locked eyes and instantly knew that they felt different about each other.

"Are you going straight home?"

Kelly nodded.

"I'll be over there," he said before walking out.

Kelly watched as the door closed behind him. She kept a poker face while he was in the office, but the moment the door closed she was as giddy as a schoolgirl. Her confidence had replaced her vulnerability instantly.

"He want some more of this wet-wet," she told herself. A sneaky smirk resting on her face. "It was so good," she admitted. The thought of their act sent a shiver up her spine. "Um," she hummed out. She continued to gather the papers from the floor when she was suddenly frozen by an epiphany. *He nutted in me*, she thought. *I need to get a Plan*—her thoughts were interrupted by a sheet of paper that caught her eye. "Well, I'll be damn," she said as she stared at the paper in disbelief. "And here I thought Avie was just a piece of ass to him."

CHAPTER EIGHTEEN

TAINTED

JANUARY 25, 2020

So much was running through Monroe's mind. Usually, sitting alone, silently in his car, was the perfect remedy to cure moments when his mind was overwhelmed. However, he had a hard time sitting in silence. These days, silent moments gave way to graphic flashes of he and Kelly.

Kelly was fulfilling his sexual appetite so much so that he hadn't called Deadria. He couldn't seem to get enough of Kelly. He tried to reprimand himself for messing with her. Kelly was supposed to be off limits, but he couldn't stop thinking about her. Unfortunately, as he thought about Kelly and the things they would do, he found himself trying to combat his guilty conscious by remembering the things his wife and Zeph were doing.

Monroe had retaliated passively against Zeph and Jamilah, but he wanted them to know that he knew. He just needed the right time, and he needed to have an end strategy. He couldn't just let them know that he knew. There had to be consequences for their actions.

For Jamilah, the consequence would be divorce. He didn't imagine her being distraught at losing him, but she would be distraught at losing access to the life she was accustomed to living. Removing her from crucial positions and putting another woman in her place was just the beginning. He saw how this simple move was tormenting her, and he loved every moment, but it wasn't enough. Her disloyalty needed to be punished in other ways.

Zeph was built differently, which meant it would take another course of action to deliver his consequences. With Zeph, Monroe had to be strategic and strike at the right time, and it had to be fatal. If Monroe failed to execute a plan, it could mean the difference between confinement and freedom for him. Hell, it could even mean the difference between life and death.

"DAMN!" Monroe slammed his hands on his steering wheel. He hated that he had willingly gone into business with Zeph, but who would think twice about the loyalty of a man who went to jail for another man's mother.

How do you get a nigga like Zeph back? he thought. When the answer crept into his mind, he slammed his fist against the steering wheel again. He hated the silence because with silence came the truth.

Monroe needed a distraction. He cut on his interior light and grabbed the envelope Maria gave him. Between Kelly having access to his files and his wife being naturally nosey, Monroe had decided that keeping the envelope in his truck would be best. He had tried to go through it a few times, but Maria seemed to have stuffed the envelope with every piece of paper she could find. Initially, he didn't have the time or energy to shuffle through it, but tonight this stack of paper was the perfect distraction from his thoughts.

He tucked the envelope under his arm and got out of his truck. Just standing outside of his favorite restaurant, After Five, brought a level of peace that was indescribable. It was something humbling about being surrounded by sports memorabilia of legends he had yet earned the pleasure of being mentioned alongside.

"The conference room is ready, Sir," the bar manager informed Monroe when he walked in. "If you need anything else, let us know."

"Thanks, man," Monroe replied. He appreciated the owner for letting him get away from the gawking eyes of hometown fans. Monroe moved quickly, never stopping his stride, hoping to get to his location before anyone could ask him for anything.

He walked through the conference door and shut it behind him.

The big room was silent, but you could hear the hums from an electric heater resembling a fireplace. A custom, reclaimed wood conference table surrounded by six high-back, leather armchairs sat in the middle of the room. Monroe's order was in the middle of the table: chicken tenders and fries, a fifth of D'usse, a bucket of ice, and four glasses. A wooden box was also in the middle of the table with the bar's name engraved on the lid that housed cigars for his pleasure.

Monroe walked to the head of the table and placed the manila folder in front of his intended seat. He poured himself a glass, sat down, and took a sip.

He grabbed the envelope and pulled out portions of the documents. "What the fuck is the point of this, Maria?" he questioned aloud. He put down the papers he pulled out. The envelope was still stuffed. "Damn, this shit feels like homework," he mumbled, shuffling through the stack. He paused when he realized the entire stack in his hands were copies of police reports. He skimmed through each police report. No names or situations seemed familiar. In fact, the reports had all taken place in Washington, D.C. He put down the stack and reached back into the envelope. He was now pulling out newspaper clippings from a D.C. newspaper. The clippings ranged in topics but were all about a wave of murders. He noted that some of the articles also contained the names of those he saw in the police report.

He stood up and laid out each police report, and then he began to match the names mentioned in the newspaper clippings to those on the police reports. When he finished sorting, he noted that one police report had a significant amount of newspaper clippings on top compared to the others. "Let's see..." he pushed the newspaper clippings off the report. "This is Morris Wells." Monroe sat on the table and began to read. He grabbed a handful of fries and popped them in his mouth.

The name Morris Wells meant nothing to him. He couldn't figure out how these men out of D.C. had anything to do with him in North Carolina. He had never heard about them or their criminal empire.

"I don't get it," he said to no one. It didn't make sense with everything on the table why it should be his concern. Monroe was in the life, but he wasn't *really* in the life. He was just the money. All that street shit was Zeph. Monroe reached for his phone. He was about to call Zeph, but then he remembered feeling some way about him.

He picked up another report and read the name "Quan'Che Jenkins." Monroe began to read over the report. Quan'Che's file wasn't as thick as Moe Wells'; but he had almost as many newspaper articles. He put down the police report and looked at an article that had sat on top. The headline read *HUMILIATION STRIKES D.C. POLICE AGAIN.* "I'm not reading this," Monroe tossed the long article on the table.

He grabbed another handful of fries and stood back, taking in the sight of the papers. He grabbed the envelope and peeped inside, thinking, *Did she leave me a note explaining this shit?* There wasn't a note, but there was a single folded sheet of paper. It was a copy of an application for a name change filed in Virginia.

"Aneesa Mo'Zani Wells," Monroe read the name on the application. "Wells...I just saw that last name." He picked up the report he had in his hand. "Wells...Wells," he stated, comparing the names.

Monroe put the sheets down and then turned his attention to the articles that once sat on the Morris Wells police report.

"Morris 'Moe' Wells is one-third drug kingpin of a gang out of the Barry Farms area in Southeast, Washington, D.C." He set the article aside and continued to look through the rest. He stopped when he found an article with the heading that read, *FREE AT LAST: WELLS AVOIDS 88-YEARS TO LIFE SENTENCE.* "That man dodged a bullet," Monroe chuckled as he tossed the article aside.

Monroe picked up another article and began to read it out loud, "Wells was named as a large-scale cocaine distributor and the chief enforcer of the gang. He was charged with conspiracy to commit murder, felony murder while armed and premeditated murder while armed."

Monroe picked up the name change application. He looked over the front of the application, flipped the sheet over, and began to read: "The undersigned applicant further certifies under oath...blah, blah, blah...the applicant requests that the Court order a change of name from..." Monroe grabbed his cognac and took a sip as he read. When he saw the name change, he damn near choked on his drink. He slammed his glass on the table, "What the fuck?!"

The door to the conference room opened slowly.

After reading the information in the envelope, Monroe was on alert. His gun sat on the table for easy access. He reached for it as he stared at the door cautiously.

He stood up from his seat with his gun gripped tight in his hand.

And then Maria appeared.

Monroe removed his hand from his gun.

Maria looked up from her phone. She stopped short when she saw Monroe's gun on his hip. She reached for the gun on her hip, "What's the problem?"

"What's your damn problem?" he snapped. "You come sneaking in the room."

Maria dropped her stance. She walked further into the room and shut the door behind her. She knew from the moment she walked into the room that Monroe was irritated. She could tell by the tone of his voice when he called and demanded that she get to the bar.

"Kelly is the daughter of a fuckin' kingpin?!"

"Oh! I see someone finally decided to read what was in the envelope."

"You think this shit is funny?"

Maria walked around the table. "And he laid everything out, too," she added sarcastically. "Look at you, being all organized."

"This shit is not funny."

"It isn't," Maria replied with a straight face. "But if you would have taken this shit seriously when I first gave it to you, you wouldn't—"

He slammed his fist down on the table. "I wouldn't what?"

Hearing his tone on the phone and physically seeing his irritation were two different experiences for Maria. "Don't shoot the messenger."

Monroe sat down in his seat. He grabbed his drink and took a sip.

Maria made her a drink and sat down next to Monroe.

Monroe stared at Maria. His jaw was clenched. He put his glass down and then leaned close to Maria. "Why did you put together this folder instead of telling me from the jump? How long did it take you to compile this bullshit?"

Maria sat back in her chair and crossed her legs. "Am I hearing you right?" she questioned. The original smirk she had on her face had returned. "It sounds like you're trying to make this my fault."

"Did I say that I was?"

"Then—"

Monroe held up his index finger, immediately silencing Maria. "My question to you was, why put together a motherfuckin' file folder when you could have told me this shit over the phone and saved time. You know how many soldiers we have lost—"

"Soldiers," Maria grunted. "I see Zeph is rubbing off on you."

"What the fuck does that mean?"

"I'm just the money guy, Maria," she stated, mocking Monroe. "You don't sound like *just* the money guy."

Monroe looked at Maria like she was scum. "Do you know how many people died?"

"The audacity," Maria stared blankly at Monroe.

"Don't fuckin' look at me like that. You the one acting heartless."

"Heartless? No Monroe, you're the only heartless one in here. You out here selling the shit that destroys families. You know how many times I've had to go to people's homes and tell them their—"

"Get off your soap box," Monroe interjected.

"loved one is dead because they out here fighting over territory that—"

"I DON'T GIVE A FUCK ABOUT THAT SHIT!" Monroe yelled. "I don't give a fuck about what you have to do," he shouted. "You got time to make fuckin' file folders when your ass should have just picked up the got-damn phone."

Maria sat quietly as Monroe continued with his temper tantrum. She heard him yelling, but she wasn't listening. She knew the real reason for his reaction.

Monroe slammed his hand on the desk when Maria didn't explain her actions. "I KNOW YOU HEAR ME TALKING TO YOU!"

"I do," she replied calmly.

Monroe sat down. "Then answer me," he stated. He was trying to calm down, but his tone was still elevated.

"You need to address the real issue here," Maria replied. "Stop focusing on trivial shit."

"Why didn't you just tell me what was going on instead of—"

"That's not the real issue," Maria interjected. "I know you, Roe."

"Since you know so much, tell me the real issue."

"Kelly," Maria quickly replied. "Kelly is the real issue. Or whatever the hell she calls herself."

"Yeah, 'cause she's the daughter of a fuckin' maniac."

Maria shook her head. "It's more than that. You like her, and now you don't know if it was mutual or just an act."

Monroe laid his head back and closed his eyes.

"Am I right?"

His silence was her confirmation.

"I requested the file from D.C. when I became suspicious of Kelly."

Monroe abruptly sat up. "See, that's my fuckin' point right there," he began. "Are you listening to yourself?"

"What?"

"That's why I'm mad."

Maria smacked her lips.

"Why wasn't I put on alert when you first had your suspicions? That's my got damn point!"

"I know you, Monroe. For something like this, you needed proof. Now that I have provided you with the proof, you finding issues with everything but the facts."

Monroe grabbed his glass. "I'm disappointed in you."

Maria smirked. "In me?"

Monroe nodded his head. "This bitch been working for me a whole fuckin' year, and then here you come with this bullshit, talking about you suspected something."

"That's how it happened."

"You should have just fuckin' said something."

"No…no…no…no…you will take responsibility for your shit. This is your fault."

"My fault?" Monroe shook his head. "This shit ain't my fault."

"If you would have done what you were supposed to do; you would have—"

Monroe put his drink down. "And what the fuck was I supposed to do," he stated, interrupting her. "Tell me, Maria."

"A background check, for starters! You are not a regular-ass Joe out here anymore, Monroe."

"I was never a regular-ass nigga!"

"You need to start checking out the people—"

"Remember that shit first and foremost."

"What?" Maria questioned. "What do I need to remember?"

"I never was and never will be a regular-ass nigga."

"Is that all you heard me say?"

"I don't give a damn what you have to say. I said what I said. I was never a regular-ass nigga."

"My point is, had you done a background check, it would have at least alerted you to the fact that she changed her name. But you didn't do that. You 'round here hiring any-damn-body!"

"I didn't hire her!"

"Then who did?"

Monroe sat back in his seat. "Jamilah."

"Why is Jamilah hiring your secretary? Did she hire the new girl, too?"

"Who? Avie?" Monroe shook his head. "I know Avie from back in the day. I hired her."

"Can you trust her?"

"Yeah," Monroe vouched.

"Did you do a background check?"

"On Avie?"

"Yeah, Avie. Who else are we talking about right now?"

"Nah, like I really know her and her family. Avie wouldn't cross me."

"But you didn't do one on Kelly?" Maria shook her head. "You need to be wiser than that, Monroe."

"I told you, I didn't hire Kelly."

"Okay, so did Jamilah do a background check on Kelly?"

"I don't know."

Maria continued to shake her head. She was now going to rub Monroe's nose in it. "So, both of y'all 'round here hiring any-damn-body? Nobody thought to get a background check done? Where the hell did she find Kelly?"

"I don't know."

"What do you know, Monroe?"

Monroe cut his eye at Maria. He knew what she was doing and he wasn't amused by it.

The two sat silently until Monroe said, "You think Jamilah is setting me up?"

Maria quizzically asked Monroe, "Do you?"

"She's been having an affair with Zeph."

Maria's eyes shot wide. She wanted so bad to shout, 'I TOLD YOU SO!' but judging by the look on Monroe's face, Maria knew he had been beating himself up. Monroe played like a tough guy, but he was nothing more than a fragile boy looking for love.

"How you know?"

"I got a video of it."

"Of them fuckin'?"

Monroe nodded.

"How did you get it?"

"Kelly—"

"Kelly?!"

184

"She had put cameras in the house when Jamilah and I were out of town."

"When?"

"Sometime last year."

"Wooow," Maria sang out her surprise. "And she still works for you?" Maria asked rhetorically. "So wait, did you tell her to do that?"

"No."

Maria chuckled at Monroe's stupidity.

He cut his eye at Maria again.

"Don't look at me like that. I mean, come on. You don't think that was suspect right there. Did you approve it?"

"Fuck no!"

"Why were the cameras even put in your house?"

"I don't know."

"Did she have suspicions about them or something?" Maria questioned rhetorically. "Like, I don't understand what would possess someone to get cameras installed in another person's house unless they are looking for something."

"You think she was looking for something?"

"And while she was looking, came across that shit—yes!" Maria paused. She couldn't believe what Monroe was telling her. Nor could she believe that he would be so naïve.

"What?" Monroe questioned her silence. "Say what you got to say."

"I am baffled."

"Baffled?"

"Flabbergasted."

"Flabber-what?"

"Perplexed."

Monroe looked at Maria, confused. "What are you saying?"

"I am shocked. No...no...I'm more confused about why you haven't let her go."

Monroe didn't reply.

Maria continued, "I thought it was something about her, but maybe it's something weird about you. Do you like drama?"

"Hell no!" Monroe snapped. "I don't like no damn drama."

"I don't know because I can't think of why else you would keep her around."

"She's loyal."

"What is she, a dog?"

"You wouldn't understand."

Maria was waiting for him to make her understand.

Monroe was feeling judged. "You wouldn't understand loyalty."

"Oh, I wouldn't, huh?"

"No. You're the same woman about to run off and marry another man."

Maria nodded her head sarcastically, like she was intrigued by Monroe's insight. She wasn't though. "It was hard for me to express my suspicions about her without coming off as…."

Monroe finally turned to face Maria. "Jealous?" he smirked.

"No…I don't know. I just know that it was something about Kelly that I didn't trust." Maria shook her head as she thought back on her suspicions. "I won't lie. I did feel some type of way about having to go through another woman to get in contact with you. Still, my suspicions went into overdrive when I ran into her one day at Crabtree Mall."

"In Raleigh?"

Maria nodded. "She was walking to her car to leave when I pulled up."

"What, you followed her there?"

"Everything was a coincidence. Even me parking near her."

"And what happened?"

"I waited for her to leave because I didn't want to play nice. As I wait for her to go, a flashy car pulls up. A matte black, Fleetwood on rims with tinted windows."

"Who was driving?"

"Some tall, brown-skinned man."

Monroe was scanning his thoughts, trying to see if it could have been anyone he knew.

Maria continued describing the man: "He was well dressed, handsome, with a full beard. Initially, I thought it was a sugar daddy because he was definitely older than her."

"How old?"

"Early to mid-fifties. Truthfully, the guy didn't even look that old. He had a youthfulness about him."

"What? The old nigga, was sagging?"

Maria laughed. "No, but...he still seemed in the know. I can't describe it. It was like he carried himself like he was relevant...in tune with today's society." Maria tried to explain. "Initially, I thought he could be her father."

"How were they acting?"

Maria shrugged. "I mean, they were acting normal. They hugged, spoke about twenty minutes or so, and then he handed her a white envelope."

"What was in the envelope?"

"I don't know. Let's call Kelly now and see what she tells us."

"I don't have time for your sarcasm."

Maria smirked. "Before he pulled off, I wrote down his tag number."

"What made you get his tag number?"

Maria shrugged her shoulders. "Honestly, just being nosey."

"What came back from the tags?"

"The car was registered to a Quan'Che Jenkins."

Monroe looked at the table. Maria knew what he was looking for. "Yep," she stated before he could locate the report. "Moe Wells' right-hand man, but I didn't know that then."

"What is he doing here?"

Maria shrugged. "That's why I called my contact and asked him to run the name. He didn't even need to run the name because...." Maria pointed at the papers on the table. "Obviously, they are a big fuckin' deal. My contact and I concluded that with everything going on in D.C., they must be coming down here to start over." Maria sat back in her seat. "What better way than to take over a preexisting empire."

Monroe huffed. Between the stress and the liquor, he was tired of this conversation. "I'm good. I don't do anything around Kelly."

"You must do enough to make her want to put cameras in your house."

"I ain't out here. Zeph is out here. He's the face. I just provide the finance."

"Umm," Maria hummed. She picked up her drink. "You shouldn't even be in the game."

Monroe ignored her criticism. He looked around the room at the sports memorabilia. "Say Jamilah knows about this aspect of my life."

"Say?" Maria mocked. "You say that like she doesn't know."

"Not from my mouth," he informed her. "I wasn't supposed to be in it long." Monroe shifted in his seat. "I didn't expect Zeph to grow as big as he did."

"Why did you doubt him? He did it before."

"But with my mother's help," Monroe corrected.

"Then she must be with him in spirit."

Monroe cut his eye at Maria.

"You and Zeph have a funny relationship," Maria paused. She studied his demeanor and said, "You thought he was weak."

"Stop talking to me about that nigga."

"Okay." Maria had never been in the same room with Zeph; in fact, they had never spoken to one another. His jacket wasn't as intense and cut-throat as Morris Wells', but Zeph wasn't anyone to fuck with. If Monroe hadn't aligned with Zeph, busting him would have made Maria's whole career. Zeph was a big fish that was responsible for a lot of drugs coming into Grambleton. However, he was off the radar. She only knew this much about Zeph because Monroe had put the pieces together for her. She often thought about busting Zeph, but she knew it would come with devastating consequences that her family didn't need. "Zeph isn't a weak man," Maria stated.

"I said I don't want to talk about that nigga."

"He has built a fuckin' empire…twice! That's not something that a weak man could do."

"Yeah, with my mother's help."

"No disrespect, but she's not here this time…so how do you explain his success?"

"Fuck him and his success!" Monroe snapped.

"If you thought he would fail, why even get involved."

"Because of him, she didn't have to live her last days behind bars. Looking out for him when he got out was only right," Monroe explained.

Monroe would talk to Maria about anything, except for his mother. The little she had learned about Shantell was from him dropping pieces of information here and there. When Maria pulled Zeph's file, she noted how she never saw Monroe's mother's name mentioned on any report. Maria wouldn't have known his mother was involved if it wasn't for Monroe telling her. Maria disagreed with Zeph's decision to be a drug dealer, but she could appreciate that he wasn't a paper rat. Maria was used to seeing the biggest, toughest guys break down when long sentences were mentioned. It was obvious to her that Zeph was not one of those guys.

"What would Jamilah have to gain by setting me up? She ain't getting no money. Everything was in my momma's name when we first got married. I'm in the process of putting it in MJ's name."

"Then why hire Kelly?"

Monroe's jaw clenched. He stood up and began shoving papers into the envelope. He looked at the name change document one last time and then slid it into the folder, too. "Here," he stated, handing her the envelope.

"Aren't you going to need this to talk to Zeph?" she placed the envelope back on the table.

Monroe picked it up and handed it to her again. "I don't need this."

"You are going to tell him about Kelly, right?"

"I will tell him what I want him to know."

Maria looked at Monroe suspiciously. "And what is that?" she stood to her feet.

"Why are you worried about it?" Monroe paused. "You always talkin' about keep you separated from the shit, but you talkin' to me like you—"

"Like I'm concerned about my son's father," she stated. "Your life is no longer your own. My life, Monroe, is no longer my own. Our son is about to be three. We must keep that in mind when making our decisions because it doesn't just affect us. It affects him, too."

"How does the way I share *that* information affect MJ?"

"This is not the time to allow pussy to cloud your judgment."

"Man, go 'head and get out of here."

Maria snatched the manila folder from the table. "Fuck it." She walked towards the door. "Your life is no longer your own, Monroe," she reminded him before slamming the door behind her.

Monroe returned to his seat and propped his legs up on the table. He knew what Maria meant. He even agreed with her, but he wanted to play this thing his way.

CHAPTER NINETEEN

SPARRING SESSION
FEBRUARY 5, 2020

Zeph rolled over in his bed and grabbed his phone, "Yo."

"We need to meet."

The voice on the other line had pulled him out of the little bit of sleep he was still in when he answered the phone. "Monroe?" he questioned, sitting up on his elbow.

"Yeah…meet me at the bar."

"Who you—" Zeph's question was cut short by the dial tone. He looked at the phone in his hand. To be called in the middle of the night was usual for Zeph; especially, with his team fighting a *blind* war, but to get a call from Monroe in the middle of the night was unusual. Zeph was instantly on alert. He sat up on the side of the bed. His phone still gripped tightly in his hand. He looked at the phone as though he could see himself on his last call.

Zeph stood up from the bed. He stretched his arms high and then began shadowboxing. *Bob and weave, punch from the waist, block…block.* He bounced from one foot to another. Feeling confident in his moves, Zeph made his way to the bathroom. He looked over his reflection. He took note of his physique. Monroe may be taller, but he couldn't see Zeph with his hands. Monroe was a coward at heart. He was the type to floss a gun but never use it. Zeph needed a game plan for Monroe. He needed to go into this meeting prepared for anything.

"Just let him do all the talking," he told his reflection, "You just listen. Then you'll know how to respond. Don't go in there showing your hand. Nigga, this *Spades* and that mauthafucka ain't your partner." Zeph nodded his head, a gesture of accepting his own advice. "Kill or be killed."

He walked out of the bathroom and grabbed his jeans from the foot of the bed. He was partially in them when his phone rang. It was Jamilah. He decided not to answer and let the call go to voicemail. He then listened to the voice message: "It's me. Call me…we need to talk." *Make sense for her to call now, 'Roe ain't home*, he thought. He wanted to call her back, but he needed a clear mind.

He continued to get dressed. Although he didn't want to call Jamilah back now. Her voice message played on repeat in his mind. She didn't sound good. *Did this nigga put his hands on her? I'll call her after this meeting*, he told himself. *Is this the night he calls himself confronting me about sleeping with his wife? Why did she really call? She didn't say anything, but then again, Jamilah is discreet. She wouldn't put that shit on a message. I got the element of surprise, though. Monroe may know about his wife and me, but he doesn't know that I know that he knows.*

Zeph grabbed his Desert Eagle off the dresser. "Nigga won't catch me slipping," he confirmed a full clip and one in the chamber. "Head on a swivel," he told himself as he grabbed his jacket and left his house.

It was a typical night—early morning—at the bar. People were out, but nothing that would put Zeph on edge about going inside. Zeph got out of his car and surveyed the land. Nothing seemed strange. He saw no familiar cars, just Monroe's truck parked towards the back like always. Zeph would usually park there, too, but instead, he parked on the street. When Zeph walked in, he made eye contact with the bartender, who subtly confirmed that Monroe was in the conference room.

Zeph opened the door slowly. He took in his surroundings, noting that Monroe was alone in the room. He also noted there were two used glasses on the table. Zeph's eyes went from the table to looking around the room again.

"Nigga, get your hyper-vigilant ass in here," Monroe motioned for Zeph to enter the room.

Zeph looked around the room once more, and then closed the door behind him. As he made his way to the table, he noted the half-empty bottle on the table. *This nigga drunk*, Zeph concluded. *He ain't moving on me. This nigga is fucked up*, Zeph thought to himself. *Stay alert, though. He could want you to believe he bent.* "What's up."

Monroe stood up, and the two dapped each other up. "How have you been?" Monroe motioned for Zeph to sit to his left.

"I've been aiight." Zeph purposely ignored the gesture and sat in the chair to the right of Monroe. He wouldn't dare leave himself vulnerable by sitting with his back to the door.

Monroe looked at him with a frown on his face.

"You know I can't sit with my back to the door."

"Understandable. That's why I sat here. I wanted to make sure I could see everything."

"And how's that working for you?"

"I can see clearly now," Monroe sang and then lightly chuckled. "It's working," Monroe confirmed.

"Um-hm," Zeph hummed. "How long you been here drinking?"

"You get any answers from the guy you kidnapped?"

Zeph looked over at Monroe. The fact that he was speaking so freely made Zeph feel uneasy. He looked around the room again. The first look-over was for a person. Now he was checking for bugs. He acted like he needed to adjust the hems of his jeans over his sneakers and peeped under the table. Zeph couldn't see anything, but to look put him at ease. He then sat up straight in his chair.

Monroe looked at him, waiting for a response.

Zeph didn't answer. He didn't even bother to nod his head or open his mouth.

Monroe accepted Zeph's silence and pushed the bottle close to him. "Pour up," he ordered. "Grab that glass right there," he stated, pointing at a glass in the center of the table.

"Nah," Zeph pushed the bottle away from him. "I'm good."

"You seem like you're on edge."

Zeph shifted in his seat.

Monroe chuckled. "You always about your business. Relax, boy."

"Business over everything."

"Who taught you that?"

"Your mother."

Monroe cut his eye at Zeph. "Shantell taught you that?"

Zeph nodded his head. "Yeah. She taught me to always be about my business. She said everything else would fall into place. She taught you that, too, but I guess you ain't listen."

Monroe grunted. "I was too busy learning beneficial shit. Shit she taught you can't be beneficial. Hell, you dependent on me now."

"Depend?"

"Yeah, you depend on me," Monroe stated confidently. "And it's pathetic," he added. He was about to take another sip of his drink when he noticed the look on Zeph's face. "I know you don't see yourself doing this shit forever, do you?"

"I'm doing my own thing on my own time."

"On my dime," Monroe laughed. "That shit that my mother taught you is just that—shit. It's more to life than business. It's family." He took a sip of his drink. "Pops taught me that."

Zeph shook his head. "You of all people talking to me about family. I see how you treat your family."

"Nah, family is important. You just need to know who your family is 'cause everybody ain't family."

Zeph smirked. He always believed in the saying; drunk minds speak sober thoughts. He heard Monroe loud and clear. So much so that he slipped his hands into his coat pocket and let his fingertips brush against the cold steel. He assumed that Monroe was drunk, but now that he knew, he was listening and was ready to light him up if he heard something he didn't like. He cautiously watched Monroe's movements closely. He could hear Shantell's warning about her son dance through his mind, 'Beware,' and in this moment he was being very aware.

"Who were you meeting with earlier?" Zeph asked.

Monroe looked shocked by Zeph's question. "How did you know somebody was here? You psychic?"

Without a word, Zeph pushed the glass in front of him toward the middle of the table.

Monroe laughed. "Oh shit! Nigga…man I thought you were on some sixth-sensed type of shit." Monroe tapped the glass in his hand against the empty glass that Zeph pushed. The sound of the glasses clinging together echoed in the silent room. "You got me," Monroe stated, still very much amused.

Zeph wasn't though. "Who was here?" he asked again.

Monroe sighed out the last of his laughter. He took another sip. "Maria was here."

"Um."

"She ain't what you think," Monroe stated. "I know how you feel about law enforcement, but she's different." Monroe chuckled to himself. "Maria's law enforcement, but she ain't law enforcement. She's family. She's like our one-man…well, in this case, like our one-woman security team."

Zeph sat silent.

"She watches out even when we don't know we need her to watch out," Monroe stated, trying to sale Zeph on Maria. It wasn't working though. Monroe could tell by Zeph's body language.

Zeph ignored Monroe's ramblings about Maria. He began to look around the room again. Knowing that the *law* had just been in this room didn't sit right with him. In fact, it had caused a sheet a paranoia to settle on top of Zeph. *What if she planted a bug in the room before she left? What if Maria was Monroe's way of getting out? What if he made some kind of deal with her?*

"You good?"

Zeph nodded his head. *Don't say shit*, Zeph told himself. *Room might be bugged.*

Monroe put his glass down on the table. "Family is so fuckin' important!" Monroe looked Zeph directly in the eyes. "You should never cross family."

Zeph gripped the gun in his jacket pocket. His thumb rested against the safety. He was prepared to shoot through his jacket, depending on where this conversation went.

"Family is every man's vulnerable spot." Monroe poured himself another drink. "Family can be your strength or your weakness. Every motherfucker in the world knows that every other motherfucker wants a family. We need that shit to survive." Monroe put the top on the bottle. "We all yearn for that shit!" he stated, talking with his hand. "And that's scary cause there are some niggas in the world that will exploit a person's thirst for a family just to get what the fuck they want." He cut his eye at Zeph and continued with his rant. "It's hard to be me," Monroe stated. "Niggas don't take into consideration that I ain't always strong. They can't process that shit. She can, though, and she loves me even at my weakest. That's why she's important to me. I can't let her go."

"Who? Jamilah?"

"Nah…nah," Monroe whispered into his glass.

I hate wanna-be deep, philosophical drunks, Zeph thought. He was now visibly irritated. "Who are you talking about?"

"Nothing…nobody." Monroe snapped out of his feelings. "Fuck that shit."

"So where is this convo coming from?"

Monroe put his cup on the table. "They say family will cross you before a stranger. You heard that shit before?"

"I have."

"This convo ain't coming from nowhere. I'm good. Just over here thinking about some shit."

"You're doing more than thinking, nigga. If you got some shit on your chest, just say it and stop beating around the bush."

Monroe pushed the bottle towards Zeph. "Get you some," he offered again, wanting to change the subject.

"I told you I'm good."

"Shit, I'm good, too, because I chose to choose my family. Fuck that blood shit. Blood doesn't mean shit!"

Zeph's jaw clenched.

Monroe continued: "Niggas you share biological blood with are only there by God's design. That don't make them special to me. Half of them niggas in the family are there only because niggas got weak pullout games. They're not special. Just because they are there by God's design don't mean they won't hurt you. Them the motherfuckas that will be the first to hurt you." Monroe paused. "The family I chose…I chose them niggas. I decided to put them near me. That's what makes them so special to me because I put them there by *my* design." He shook his head. "But when them niggas cross me, it hurts even more, because I put them in the position to do so. Everyone around me has crossed me. I never thought she would though. I thought we were different. I thought she was different, but she just like the rest of you motherfuckas. All of you, motherfuckas, are disloyal."

Zeph questioned, "Who are you talking about?"

"Nah," Monroe shook his head. "I ain't talking about nobody. I ain't saying nothing. Just talking."

"Something going on with you and Jamilah?"

Monroe shook his head.

The room was silent.

Monroe's random rant didn't sit well with Zeph. It made him even more suspicious as to why he was there. "What you call me for?"

Ignoring Zeph's question, Monroe said: "The family I chose is small. I don't need a lot of niggas around me." He extended his hand to dap up Zeph.

Zeph was hesitant but slipped his hand out of his jacket and dapped

Monroe.

"What? You cold, nigga?"

"Nah."

"Nigga got his hands in his pocket." Monroe laughed. He got up from his seat and walked to the thermostat on the wall. He turned back to Zeph. "When I refer to you as my brother. Feel special because I chose you to be my brother. You feel me? I know I got siblings, but I didn't choose them. My mother made them my family." Monroe began to move back towards his chair. "Can you believe there are really niggas in this world that would sit at the table with you knowing damn well they ain't family…they ain't loyal?"

A smirk rested on Zeph's face as he listened to Monroe pussyfoot around the real issue.

"I was willing to share everything with that girl. I put her on that level."

The smirk on Zeph's face disappeared. Initially, he thought Monroe's rant about family and loyalty was directed at him, then he thought it was Jamilah, but it finally made sense. Monroe was ranting about Kelly. *This nigga done fucked Kelly and now he emotional and shit,* Zeph concluded. *What the hell did Kelly do?*

"And now I got to cut niggas off because everybody crossing me like I'm some weak-ass nigga. I ain't a weak-ass nigga."

Zeph took his hands out of his pockets. "Who you got to cut off?"

Monroe shook his head. "Maaaaaan," Monroe harmonized. "You wouldn't believe it if I told you, but…fuck it. It ain't important."

"You sure you don't want to talk about it?"

Monroe slowly staggered back to his seat. "I cut niggas off," Monroe mumbled as he flopped back into his chair. He laid his head back and closed his eyes. "I must've stood up, too fast," he mumbled. "My head is spinning."

"How are you getting home?"

Monroe waved Zeph's concern away.

"You want me to call Jamilah?"

Monroe peeped at Zeph through one eye. "I have zero fucks to give at this point."

"Oh, okay."

Monroe attempted to open his other eye, but it was too heavy, so he continued to look at Zeph with one eye open. "You say that like you don't believe me or some shit." With his open eye, Monroe looked at the cup on the table and reached for it.

"Do you really need more?"

"I hate disloyal motherfuckers that smile in your face. I'ma show all y'all disloyal niggas who Monroe really is."

"Who is yall?"

"Oh, I'ma show you."

"You know what I hate?" Zeph asked rhetorically. "I hate the niggas, who are loyal by proxy."

Monroe frowned. "What?"

"That shit is just as fake as acting like you're loyal. When you're really not."

"What the fuck is loyalty by proxy?"

"It's when someone displays loyalty out of obligation. They're not really loyal to you, but they are only loyal on the strength of their loyalty to someone else."

Monroe squinted at Zeph. "Loyalty by proxy?" he mumbled. "Loyal by proxy? What you say?

"It's when a nigga *acts* loyal versus *being* loyal."

"Is that us?" Monroe asked before both eyes closed.

"What you think?"

Monroe opened his eyes. He held his head up to get a better look at Zeph. "I feel like you need to get something off your chest."

"This ain't the time," Zeph replied.

"Yeah, aiight then."

"What did you want to talk to me about?"

"I found out who's been hitting our blocks."

"Who?"

"Some niggas out of D.C."

"Washington D.C.?" The confusion in Zeph's tone rode the wave of his question.

"His name is Morris Wells."

"Who?" Zeph questioned. "How you know?"

"Huh?" Monroe grunted.

"'Roe, wake up!" Zeph slapped his hand on the table. "Aye, yo' Roe!"

Monroe still didn't budge.

"WAKE UP AND TALK TO ME, DAMNIT!"

Monroe opened one eye and looked over at Zeph. "Why are you yellin'?" he asked Zeph. It was obvious by his facial expression that he was offended.

"Who is this nigga?"

Monroe grunted. He had closed his eyes but being snatched by his shirt collar had caused his eyes to open wide. "NIGGA?!" he yelled at Zeph. "Fuck off me," he stated, knocking Zeph's hand from his shirt.

"Who is this nigga?" Zeph asked again.

Monroe shook his head. "I don't know."

"Do they have a central location?"

"Maria ain't say."

"Maria told you this?" Zeph returned to his seat. "Maria told you a young nigga from D.C. is moving in on me?"

"He ain't young."

"What?"

"Yeah."

"Yeah what?" Zeph looked at Roe. "Yeah what, nigga? What you mean he ain't young? Is he old? Maria told you an old head is coming for me. How she know?"

"She just does."

"You're giving me these half-ass responses like we ain't losing niggas every day."

"LOOK!" Monroe snapped. He was irritated by Zeph yelling and pulling on him. "All I know is what Maria told me. The new nigga is Morris Wells. She doesn't know shit about him. I don't know shit about him. We just know he ain't nobody to fuck with."

"I ain't nobody to fuck with," Zeph replied coldly. "The nigga want war, then that's what the nigga will get!"

Monroe laid his head back and closed his eyes. His world was spinning, literally and figuratively. Closing his eyes didn't help, so he cracked them open and peeked out. He looked around the room. He could see Zeph's silhouette and could tell that he was on the phone.

"Nah, we need to meet," Zeph spoke into the phone. "I got a name."

Hearing those words come out of Zeph's mouth made Monroe feel queasy. He wanted to ask Zeph what his plan would be, but even in his drunken state, he knew the answer. The thought of war didn't sit right with him. He had more to lose than Zeph. He wanted to express his objections, but vomit had reached his mouth before his words. He tried to make a move to the bathroom or even a trashcan, but it was too late. Monroe had projectile vomited on the table.

"Ugh!"

Monroe could hear the disgust in Zeph's voice along with his quick movement like he had jumped up from his chair. "I'ma call you back..." he grumbled, "This nigga here. Aye yo' 'Roe, how you gettin' home?"

"I'ma sleep here." Monroe slid out of his seat. He crawled away from his puke.

"How you gettin' home?" Zeph was beyond irritated. He had other shit to worry about than a grown man that couldn't hold his liquor.

"I said, I'ma sleep here, damn!" Monroe crawled far enough away from his puke. He lay on the ground with his arms folded across his chest.

Zeph shook his head. "Roe!"

"Yeah."

"You hear me?"

"Yeah."

"We need all the information we can get on Morris Wells. You got to stay on, Maria."

"Or you gonna fuck her, too."

"What?"

Monroe didn't reply.

Zeph moved closer to him to look at him. "What did you say?" he kicked the bottom of his shoes.

Monroe didn't budge. He was sound asleep.

Zeph shook his head. He pulled his phone out. "One of you niggas come get Roe and take him home," Zeph ordered. He didn't even wait for a response. He slipped his phone into his pocket and headed for the door. He had real shit to handle. Real shit like Morris Wells.

It was almost one in the morning, but Zeph was making calls to his generals like it was two in the afternoon. Zeph knew it was time to retaliate. Just this week alone, they had buried three of his homies. He wanted to meet with his guys to set a plan. He wanted them to find as much information as possible on Morris Wells. Zeph even had it in his mind to take a couple of his boys and go to D.C. He needed to find out who he was up against. Monroe was useless. He may have provided a name, but what was a name without a location?

Zeph grabbed his cell phone off the seat. He was about to make another call when he noticed a car tailing him. They were being discreet, but not discreet enough for Zeph. He was overly observant, especially since he was losing men left and right. He didn't disclose to Monroe the severity of the attacks they had taken. Monroe was the money guy. Zeph knew Monroe didn't care about the product or the people pushing the product.

The attacks had kept Zeph up at night, though. The last attack was gruesome. They found his man on a playground. He was chained to the top of a slide, slumped. They had poked so many holes into Zeph's man that his blood had puddled at the bottom of the slide. The sight was stomach-turning, but it wasn't the worst part. They had cut out his eyes and shoved them in his mouth and then pinned a note to him by stabbing him between the eyes with a knife. The message read: Talk Sees Action.

Zeph maintained his speed, but he needed a change in direction. Following traffic guidelines to a tee, Zeph prepared to make a U-turn and head back toward the bar. He wasn't about to lead them to his meet-up. When he pulled over to the left lane, the lights went up.

"Shit!"

Zeph sat straight up in his seat. He hit the button to automatically lower his window. He put his hands on the stirring wheel at ten and two and waited for the officer to approach him. He tried to look in his rearview mirror, but they had strategically kept their high beams on. He couldn't see out of his left-side view mirror either. Even if he could, they had purposefully walked into his blind spot to avoid being seen.

"The great Zephaniah Wilkins. We finally meet."

Zeph was looking straight ahead, but when he heard his name, he glanced at the person outside his window. "I know you?"

"Relax," she stated. "I want to give you something."

Before Zeph could ask what, she tossed a manilla folder into his lap.

Zeph looked down at the folder. He was about to touch it but then thought otherwise. He knew it was heavy by the way it felt hitting his lap. The woman moved, and Zeph went from looking at the folder in his lap to looking at her.

She had leaned closer to the car with her hand on her gun. "I gave this same folder to our mutual acquaintance almost a month ago, and tonight he just looked at it."

Zeph had never seen Maria but instantly knew who he was talking to by her conversation. "Why are you bringing this to me?"

"This thing you and he got going on is out of his league, and he doesn't realize it."

Zeph refused to agree or disagree with her statement.

"I don't think he realizes who he is playing with."

"And you think I will?"

"I know you will," she quickly responded. "Read it and then call me," she stated. She stood up straight and then tossed a phone into the car. "A burner," she said, "You know how those work."

Before Zeph could respond, she had disappeared. Just as he couldn't see her walk up on him, he couldn't see her walk away. He only knew she was gone because the lights behind him had gone off while she pulled away.

When she was further down the street, Zeph opened the manilla folder. It was stuffed with paper. He closed the envelope and slid it under his passenger seat. He pulled back into traffic, prepared to head to his intended location.

CHAPTER TWENTY

LEARNING
SOMETHING NEW

FEBRUARY 8, 2020

"Hey baby," Jamilah called to Monroe from the bottom of the staircase.

"What's up."

"Where are you going?"

Monroe was about to respond when his office door opened. "Kelly, aren't you off today?" His attention was no longer on his wife.

And she hated it.

"I am, but I had some things I needed to finish up."

Jamilah stood with her arms folded across her chest, as the two bantered back and forth.

"Work-life balance," Monroe called out to Kelly.

"That is for the weak." Kelly chuckled, quoting one of his favorite sayings.

Jamilah cleared her throat.

Kelly shot Monroe a *your-in-trouble* look as she eased past Jamilah.

"I got a meeting," he finally replied to Jamilah as he continued down the staircase. When he got to Jamilah, he leaned in for a kiss.

Their relationship was drastically different, but Jamilah played along with the show. As she performed, Jamilah cut her eye at Kelly, who wasn't paying them any attention. After the show, Jamilah asked Kelly, "And what are you up to today?"

"She should be enjoying her day off because we're back at work tomorrow," Monroe answered. "We're looking into buying some houses in Collins County."

Jamilah was beyond her breaking point. She tried to play nice, but her disgust covered her face. "Oh, well, good luck with that," Jamilah smugly replied. "Gregory can be a bit much at times."

"Gregory?"

Jamilah looked at her husband. "She doesn't know Gregory?"

"She will learn," Monroe quickly dismissed Jamilah's attempts to shade Kelly.

"I have big shoes to fill," Kelly stated with a smile. She didn't want to get in a pissing match with Jamilah.

"If you have time now, I can give you the scoop on Gregory."

"Oh." The thought of Jamilah wanting to help her caught her by surprise. "I…uh—"

"She ain't got the time," Monroe interjected. "She needs to go and enjoy this day off. "We got a lot going on in the next couple of weeks."

"Well then," Jamilah smirked. "I was just trying to help. I mean, I do know the business."

"I know you do, but you don't need to anymore." Monroe gave Jamilah a side hug like he does his fans.

"We can chat tomorrow," Kelly stated, trying to soften the blow for Jamilah.

"Perhaps."

A bitch will be a bitch, Kelly thought.

"Go ahead and get out of here," Monroe told Kelly. "I'll see you here tomorrow, bright and early."

"Sure thing." Kelly quickly moved to the door. She couldn't wait to get out of there.

"Hey," Jamilah called after Kelly.

Kelly looked back. "Yeah?"

"How was dinner with Bishop the other day?"

Bitch! Kelly thought. She forced herself to smile.

"Oh, you went out with Bishop the other night?" Monroe asked.

"Uh huh," Jamilah answered. "They sure did."

Kelly didn't even bother to look in Monroe's direction. She could feel his glare without a need to confirm it. "It was interesting," she tried to play it down.

"Interesting in a good way?" Jamilah pried. She didn't really care about the date. For Jamilah, she needed to deliver her husband a gut punch. Jamilah cut her eye at Monroe. By the look on his face, she could tell that she had accomplished her goal.

"Yeah, interesting." Now Kelly was the one being fake.

"Good!" Jamilah called back to her. "We'll have a little girl talk tomorrow, too."

"Sounds like a plan," Kelly replied.

Jamilah waved and then sashayed towards the kitchen.

Kelly noted Monroe's eyes narrowed on Jamilah. She wasted no time using this moment to bolt to the door before Monroe could say anything to her.

Monroe looked back at the front door as it closed. He turned on his heels to follow behind Jamilah.

By the time he walked in, Jamilah was facing him. "I thought you were about to go?"

"How you know she went out with Bishop the other night? They went out the night all of us were supposed to go out together?"

"Yep!"

"I thought you canceled it."

"We canceled on them, but they didn't cancel on each other," she replied. "When you went in the bathroom, your phone went off, and it was Bishop asking for her phone number."

"And you gave it to him?"

"Sure did!"

"Why were you on my phone?"

Jamilah looked at Monroe like he had lost his mind. "I can't be on your phone? Ain't like you got anything to hide," she paused. "Do you?"

Monroe could sense Jamilah's bait. He wasn't going to feed into it. "Why didn't you tell me what you did?"

"I didn't think it was a big deal, first of all. Bishop asked for her number. I told her he wanted her number, and she said, 'Okay,' and I texted him the number." Jamilah walked close to Monroe. She tried to touch him, but he stepped away from her. Jamilah took note of her husband's change in demeanor. She put her hands on her hips, "What does it matter if he was given her number?"

Monroe shook his head. "I already told you how I felt about your matchmaking bullshit."

"Interrupting your meeting to play matchmaker was wrong on my part," Jamilah admitted, "But those are two consenting adults. Why can't they have dinner together?"

"I got to get ready to go to this meeting," he stated, heading for the door.

"We are going to finish this conversation tonight, Monroe," she called after him.

He didn't even bother to give a response. He walked out of the house, slamming the door behind him.

From the passenger's seat of her mother's car, Kelly beeped the car horn twice. She glanced between her watch and her mother's front door. Kelly was waiting for Zani to come out. She had only been sitting outside the house for a minute, but it felt like hours.

"The meeting starts in thirty minutes, damn it!" Kelly stated to herself as she laid on the car horn again.

Kelly was off today as Monroe's assistant, but she was on the clock as Bishop's spy. Monroe usually asked Kelly to schedule all his meetings, but the meeting he had scheduled for today, she wasn't privy to any information. Kelly concluded that this was the meeting he had asked her to set up until she started asking questions about Avie's role. Initially, Kelly assumed Avie and Monroe were fuckin'. After finding the form that listed Avie as the contact person for a freight storage unit, she began to think otherwise. The meeting between Monroe and Avie was about more than sex. All week, Kelly looked for details about the meeting but came up with nothing other than the date. That was why she was in his house on her day off. She needed to see the calendar on his computer that mirrored the calendar on his phone.

Zani finally walked out of the house.

Kelly stared at her mother in amazement as she got into the car. "What the hell do you have on?" she asked.

Zani stopped and looked down at her outfit. She wore an all-black, tight-fitting, long-sleeved catsuit, black pencil-heeled boots, a black bubble-vest jacket, a black Fedora, and a pair of dark shades.

"A Fedora, though," Kelly hollered through her laughter. "Who the hell are you supposed to be?"

"Aren't we going on a stakeout?"

"Zani, it's noon. You are wearing all black at noon. You stand out even mo—" Kelly paused. "Are you wearing a wig?"

"What the hell you got on?" Zani pulled at Kelly's pants leg.

Kelly looked down at her casual outfit of blue jeans and a blouse. "Look here, cat woman. I blend in. You, on the other hand."

"Shut the hell up," Zani snapped. "I look good."

"You look like an extra in a 90's R&B video."

Zani looked at herself in the rearview mirror. "I look good, though."

"Oh my God," Kelly mumbled. "He's going to see us."

"He's not going to see us."

"No, I was just thinking about how embarrassing you look."

Zani looked down at her outfit and then back at Kelly, who held a straight face.

Kelly could hold it no longer and burst out laughing. She began to sing, "Said I'm not gon' cry, I'm not gon' cry, I'm not gon' shed no tears."

"You real funny," Zani stated sarcastically.

Kelly sighed out the rest of her laughter. "Take the damn Fedora off, Mary J."

Zani looked in the rearview mirror again. "No," she stated and then blew a kiss at her reflection. "I look good."

Kelly looked at her watch. "The meeting starts soon."

"Where is it?"

"I set your GPS already. Just drive," Kelly stated.

"Ugh, you're bossy today."

"I'm sorry, Kiesha, Kima, and Pam."

Zani put the car in reverse. She paused. "What did you just call me?"

"The entire group of Total. Every last member."

"I like Total, so I'ma take that as a compliment." She pulled out of the driveway and began to follow the GPS.

Kelly sighed loudly. *What do you say if you get caught?* she questioned herself. *And how the hell do I explain Lil' Kim being with me?* Kelly chuckled to herself as she looked at her mother. Zani's choice of attire was a hilarious distraction, but it wasn't enough. Kelly knew what she had to do but didn't know how. She never wanted to call her father as much as she did at this moment. *I disagree with Moe's methods, but he would make for damn sure that I wasn't out here in these streets playing spy with Adina Howard.* Kelly looked over at her mother and chuckled again.

"Why do you keep laughing?" Zani questioned.

"No reason."

"This is taking us downtown," Zani commented. "They're meeting in an office building?"

"I just put in the address that I got."

"This is not about sex. Monroe is supposed to take her in the other direction by the fancy hotels. This is the business district. Unless they're fuckin' in the parking lot."

"I doubt it."

Your destination is on the right, the GPS reported.

"We're here," Zani stated, "Shit ain't nowhere to park."

"Hit a U-turn and park away from the door," Kelly ordered.

"And draw attention to myself," Zani stated. "Nah, I'ma go around the block and just park up the street."

"What if you miss him?"

Kelly's cell phone rang.

"Oh shit," Kelly commented as she looked at her phone.

"Who is it?" Zani questioned, her eyes glued to the busy street.

"Monroe. Do I answer it?"

"Yeah."

"What if he saw us?"

"Driving?" Zani questioned. "We could be going anywhere...what the fuck is down here? Shit, we're going there." Zani glanced over at Kelly, who was staring at her phone ring. "Answer it."

"Hello?"

"Speaker," Zani whispered. "Put it on speaker."

Kelly switched to the speaker. Her heart was beating out of her chest.

"Why you ain't tell me you fuckin' with Bishop?"

"Huh?" Kelly sighed with relief. She could handle Monroe asking her about her interactions with another man. She couldn't take him asking her anything about her location.

"You huh, you can hear."

Zani pulled into a parking space down the street from the meeting location. She cut the car off. She sat silently, listening to her daughter's conversation.

"I ain't fuckin' with Bishop," Kelly explained. "We just went out to dinner."

"You like that nigga now or something?"

"I didn't say that."

Zani began to motion to Kelly, but Kelly didn't understand. Zani touched Kelly's arm and held her finger to her lip, telling her to be quiet.

Kelly nodded, and then Zani spoke: "Where are you?"

"The question is, where are you?"

Kelly was shocked that Monroe hadn't noticed the change in her voice.

"I asked you first."

"You think I got time to play with you."

"You called me, so you must have some time."

There was a long pause.

Zani looked at Kelly and mouthed: "Is he still there?"

Kelly nodded.

"Hello?" Zani questioned.

"You trying to see me," Monroe finally spoke.

"Yes."

Kelly's eyes shot wide as she looked at her mother, who had taken over her phone conversation.

"You home?"

"Why?"

Monroe laughed. "I take that as a no. I'll be at your house after I run some errands."

Kelly saw Zani about to speak and immediately put her hand over her mother's mouth.

"Okay," Kelly replied for herself. "What time?"

"I'll call you when I'm on my way."

"Okay."

Before Zani could say anything else, Kelly hung up the phone.

"Girl, you 'bout knocked my tooth out," Zani stated, checking her teeth in the mirror. "Why you ain't ask him where he was?"

Kelly shook her head. "He doesn't like that nosey shit. He would have become suspicious."

"He's clearly too jealous to be suspicious." Zani looked in the mirror at her daughter. "Are you fuckin' Monroe?"

Kelly was about to lie, but she already knew that Zani knew her truth.

Zani shook her head. "What happened to all that shit you were telling me? He just my boss, we not fuckin'." Zani shook her head in disappointment. "You messy, child."

"I'm messy?"

"Hell yeah," Zani replied. "The fuck. I stand on that, Aneesa. You are messy." Zani shook her head. "Can you separate your pussy from your plans?"

Kelly laughed. "Separate my pussy from my plans," she repeated.

"I'm serious, Aneesa."

Kelly brought her laughter to a chuckle. "I know...I know," she now sat quietly. She glanced over at Zani. "I do know."

"How long have y'all been fuckin'?"

"What?"

"You heard me."

Kelly didn't respond.

Zani shook her head. "Is that how you got the job with him in the first place?"

"Whoa!" Kelly stated. "I'm not a hoe, and I didn't fuck my way to this position. I am intelligent without opening my legs."

"I don't think you taking this shit seriously."

"I am taking this seriously. I mean, I'm out here on a fake ass stakeout! I think that means I am taking it pretty damn seriously."

"You damn well better be taking this shit seriously," Zani snatched off her shades and tossed them into the cupholder. "What time does the meeting start?"

Kelly looked at her watch. "A few minutes."

"Does anybody look familiar?"

Kelly skimmed the mixed crowd of people walking downtown. No one stood out. Every man or woman, black or white, looked as though they belonged downtown in their suits, pencil skirts, and briefcases. "He's smart as hell for holding a meeting here. Every-fuckin'-body blends in," Kelly mumbled. "What's next?"

"You better suck and fuck the truth out of him."

"We leaving?"

"Ain't nothing to see here," Zani stated as she pointed at the sea of people. "You want to continue to sit here on this dummy mission. Get out of my car and do that shit on your own time." Zani slammed her hands against the steering wheel. "You blowin' the hell out of me," she stated while pulling off her wig. "You aren't taken this seriously enough for me."

Kelly tried to embrace the seriousness of the situation, but watching the wig slide off her mother's head made her laugh.

Zani cut her eye at her. "See what I am talking about. It ain't funny, Aneesa."

"Why did you take the wig off?"

"They not gonna wait forever for you to find something."

"You didn't have to throw the wig like that." Kelly was determined to laugh through this moment.

Zani didn't find anything humorous about this moment. "Knight will kill you."

"Moe won't let that happen."

Zani cut her eye at Kelly. It was bad enough that she dared to call her by her first name, but she should put some respect on her father's name. "Fatha," Zani corrected her, "Ya' Fatha won't let anything happen to you. You are his pride and joy."

Kelly grunted.

"I don't know why you despise him so much, but the more you despise him, the more he loves you and would do anything to protect you," she looked at Kelly. "He would kill anyone over you."

"He out the game, but he would kill for me."

"True," Zani confirmed. "I know all parents say that, but real life, Moe will really do *that*."

Kelly sucked her teeth.

"You don't have to believe that, but when my husband gets here, he will be clear and clean. North Carolina is our new beginning."

"I hear you," Kelly mumbled as she looked out the passenger's window.

Kelly had no information to tell Bishop. He had already called her twice for an update. Zani told her to hold out on the freight information until after this meeting, but this meeting turned out to be a bust.

"LET ME OVER, BITCH!" Zani yelled at the traffic.

She was about to merge when Kelly yelled, "Look!"

Zani slammed on break. "What?"

"Look!"

Zani was looking out the window, but it was so many people she didn't even know where to begin to look. "What am I looking at?"

"There's Avie."

"Where?"

"Right there. The one with the black pantsuit and short hair. You see her, the one with the red bottoms on. You see her right there by the sign," Kelly was doing everything but pointing. "You see her. The brown-skinned girl right there."

"I do," Zani stated, finally focusing on the young girl. "Oh, she's pretty."

Kelly rolled her eyes. "She's aiight."

"This meeting ain't about sex," Zani commented. "She looks like they play for the same team."

"I know!" Kelly perked up. "I thought the same thing when I first met her."

"So, she is gay?"

Kelly shook her head. "I think she's just a tomboy because she was damn sure flirting with Monroe during their interview."

"What did she interview for?"

"Monroe said he was looking to give more women opportunities just like he was giving the young men opportunities."

"What kind of opportunities?"

"Shooting Goals is a basketball camp, and they also have like a job core type of curriculum where they learn trades. He started interviewing women with junior classification for a program that gave them the same opportunities."

Zani nodded her head impressed.

"But I believe he was trying to rebuild his team since all of them were doing their own thing."

"Rebuild his team? What team?"

"The hoe-team.'"

"Um," Zani hummed. Her eyes were still glued to Avie. "Rich people got too much time on their hands. I don't know how he can have a big organization and still have time to manage little shit like a whore team."

"Hoe-team."

"That's what I said." Zani paused and looked at Kelly. "Oh, that's right. You are on the team, too." Zani held her hand to her chest. "I'm such a proud mother. To know all of my daughter's talents and skills helped her to get on a whore team."

"I'm on the team, but technically I manage the team."

"Oh!" Zani looked at Kelly, surprised. "My daughter is a whore manager! Please tell me, what do whore managers do?"

"I used to…." Kelly stopped speaking when she finally noticed the sarcasm in her mother's conversation. "Really, a whore manager?"

"You can either be called a pimp or a whore manager. Which do you prefer?"

"I'm not a *whore* manager," Kelly corrected her mother. "Nobody says *whore* anymore. Stop saying *whore*. You sound old."

"Oh, that's right. My daughter is a *hoe* manager because she is on a *hoe* team."

"I'm not arguing with you, Monifah."

"You can call me all the classy, talented musical artists you want. I don't mind," Zani replied. "It's better than being a *hoe* manager."

The car was silent.

After a minute, Zani said, "So, what is your job description?"

Kelly rolled her eyes.

"Seriously," Zani stated. "What do you do?"

"I used to schedule appointments, meetings, and trips. I managed them and kept everything running like a smooth system."

"You said 'used to' as in past tense."

"Listen, you gotta pick a struggle. You're either a '90s female artist or a grammar teacher? You can't be both."

"Funny," Zani stated sarcastically. She put the car in park and then sat back in her seat. "I was referring to the fact that you said you 'used to schedule appointments…'."

"Yeah, I don't do that anymore."

"What do you do now?"

"Uh…I don't do that anymore. I coordinated meetings with him and the players, but I haven't done that in a while. I've never coordinated meetings with him and his baby's mother though. She usually initiates those meetings for the most part. These days, I handle the organizations Jamilah used to handle."

"So, you do his wife's old job?"

"If you want to put it like that, then…yeah, I guess you can say I am doing her old job."

"So does that mean *she* is doing your job?" Zani questioned while pointing at Avie.

"Hell no! She ain't doing my job," Kelly snapped. "I would know. I mean, I would see her around more if she did what I did."

"Would you really?" Zani questioned, looking at her daughter. She could see the hesitation in Kelly. "Okay, humor me. What role would she play if she was on his team?"

Kelly shook her head. "I don't know. I thought he had all his players."

"What's so special about her to be going to meetings and shit?" Zani questioned. "Bishop should be pressing her for information, not you. You don't know what she knows."

Kelly watched Avie closely. She didn't like her when they first met, and she doesn't like her now. Jealousy was a cruel bitch, and it had a grip on Kelly. *Why does she get to go to the meeting, and I don't?* Kelly thought to herself. She snapped out of her thoughts when she heard Zani laughing. She looked over at her mother. "What? Why are you laughing?"

Zani spoke through her laughter, "I'm just so proud. My daughter got a promotion! She's not a *hoe*-manager anymore." Zani clapped her hands. "You got a promotion and didn't even know it. Look at God! Won't he do it!"

"That's not funny."

Zani stopped laughing. "You're right. The shit is pathetic, but I wouldn't mind telling your Aunt Fe what you do for a living now."

"Whatever."

"He ultimately put you in Jamilah's shoes and put this Avie girl in yours."

"There go, Monroe," Kelly stated, changing the subject.

Zani quickly looked out the window. "I didn't realize how tall he was…

213

oh, no, this ain't about sex. Look how they greet each other. They shake hands. Nothing about their body language makes me think they've had sex or are about to have sex."

Kelly looked from Monroe and Avie's interaction to Zani and then back to them. "You don't think they've had sex?"

"No. That girl doesn't seem like she's remotely attracted to him, and it looks like he knows it by how he handles himself."

"They're just performing. That's how they act around Jamilah."

Zani gasped. She looked around her car and even looked in the back seat on the floor.

Her abrupt movement startled Kelly. "What's wrong?"

"Chiiiild," Zani began. "I thought Jamilah was a stow-away."

Kelly sucked her teeth.

"Thought she done made her way into my Bentley." Zani cackled with laughter.

"This a funkin' fresh Ford Focus."

Zani abruptly stopped laughing. "My point is," she began again. "Jamilah ain't here. Hell, technically, we ain't here either. So, who are they acting for?" she asked, pointing toward Avie and Monroe.

Kelly looked from Zani to Monroe and Avie.

"Nah, that ain't sex," Zani confirmed. "She gives off Kisha vibes. You know from New Jack City. Like she would take a nigga out if she had to. That girl doesn't even look like she like dick. She looks like a cute dyke. What do they call the female...a fem? She's definitely a fem."

"How do you know the difference between a fem and a regular female?"

"I know," Zani stated. "Trust me. I know, but her pants suit is cute though. I wonder where she got it. I would look good in that."

"She likes dick."

"You can't tell someone's sexual orientation just from their look," Zani stated, mimicking Kelly's sentiment. "Oh, that's right! You hoe managers would know, huh?"

"I know she likes dick because of her interview."

Zani frowned. "Is that a question you ask during the interview?"

"No, we handle business professionally. We didn't ask Avie about her sexual preference or anything crazy. But still, I remembered her flirting with Monroe the entire time. She didn't care that I was there either."

"Were they really flirting, or were you just feeling some type of way?"

"I know what flirting is and how it is done."

"Umm, umm, umm."

"Just say what you got to say."

"Nope, I don't have anything to say."

"I know what flirting is."

"Okay."

"I was in the interview, Zani. I saw it with my own eyes. I wasn't jealous of her."

"Flirting is not fucking."

"I know the difference, and she is fuckin' him."

Zani looked back over to Monroe and Avie. "Where they go?"

"They just walked into that building."

"What offices are in that building?"

Kelly was irritated. She hated when anyone tried to tell her what she knew to be a fact. "I can't read that sign."

Zani looked at her daughter. "Duh! Google the address."

"Oh."

"And he made you the *hoe* manager."

"It's not funny anymore," Kelly commented as she looked through her phone. A list of lawyer offices popped up when she entered the address. "Watson Tyler is the only name that stands out on this list."

Zani hummed. "Watson Tyler, the big shot white guy?"

"Yeah. He is Rebecca Tyler's father."

"I know that name."

"You should. Watson Tyler owns like half the town."

"No, Rebecca. Who is she to Monroe?"

"One of the teammates. She's the white athletic trainer."

"He's meeting with her or her father?"

Kelly shrugged.

"What does he look like?"

"A white man. I don't know."

"When you return to work, you need to find anything related to

215

Rebecca Tyler or Watson Tyler."

Kelly shook her head. "I can see them doing *business-business* with Walter Tyler, but not… *drug business.*"

"Drugs are a guaranteed business, just like being a doctor or a mortician."

Kelly stared silently at her mother. It was as though Zani was dropping the illusion of being a perfect parent. For once, Kelly was seeing her mother for who she was—the wife of a kingpin.

"When it comes to drugs, everybody wants a part of it; either supplying it or you're using it." She pointed at the building where Monroe and Avie were once standing. "I'd bet all my money that the white man got something to do with Monroe's drug business." Zani sat up. She put the car in drive, "Now all we have to do is prove it."

Kelly sunk in her seat. "Easier said than done," she mumbled under her breath.

CHAPTER TWENTY-ONE

EAT YOUR WORDS

FEBRUARY 14, 2020

Kelly was lying across her bed when she heard her doorbell ring.

She grabbed her cell phone. There were no missed calls. This meant that whoever was at her door was an uninvited guest, and Kelly did not open the door for uninvited guests. She put her phone down and snuggled under her covers.

The doorbell rang again.

Kelly smiled to herself. *They'll get the picture*, she thought.

And then her phone rang.

Shit, they must know me. She looked at her phone. It was Bishop. "Hello?"

"Come open the door."

"Shouldn't you be somewhere getting ready for the All-Star Game?"

"Come open the door," he repeated, and the line went dead.

"Shit!" Kelly stared at the phone in disbelief. "I don't have nothing to give him." She tossed the covers off herself and sat on the edge of the bed. "Maybe he will—"

Bishop banged loudly at the front door.

"He's not going away." Kelly slipped on her robe and slipped her feet into her slippers.

He impatiently banged on the door again.

Kelly walked down the steps. She could see Bishop's tall silhouette from the opposite side of the door. He looked to be holding something. She opened the door. "Yes?"

Bishop grinned. "That's how you greet a man who comes bearing gifts?"

"Gifts for what?"

"Today is Valentine's Day."

"Oh. It's just another day to me," Kelly replied nonchalantly. A smile spread across her face. "But you brought those for me?"

Bishop extended the gifts in his hand to Kelly.

She grabbed them and immediately buried her nose in the flowers.

"Why aren't you dressed? It's a beautiful day outside."

"It's cold. I was laying comfortably in my bed under the covers."

"I came to lay with you."

Kelly looked from the flowers to Bishop. She rolled her eyes and opened the door wider.

"Does that mean I can come in?"

"What do you think?"

Bishop stepped inside the house and closed the door behind him. "Okay," he stated, admiring her décor. "Can I get a full tour?"

Kelly set the flowers and candy on a table in her foyer. "You don't want a tour."

"I wouldn't ask if I didn't."

Kelly folded her arms across her chest. "What are you really here for?"

Bishop walked up close to Kelly.

She pushed him back. "Can I get some space, please?"

"If you have to ask for it, do you really want it?" Bishop stepped closer to Kelly. "The way I see it, if you really wanted space, you would make yourself some space, right?"

Kelly took a step back.

Bishop took a step forward.

Kelly could feel her temperature rising. Bishop was an asshole that had changed her whole life, but her eyes couldn't lie. Bishop was a sexy brown skin man, and the way he looked at her with those bedroom eyes turned her on more—but she didn't want to be turned on by him. She needed space—and so she made herself some.

"Why did you move away?"

"Because I made me some space."

Bishop moved to the couch and sat beside her.

"I just said I wanted space."

"Just because you know what you want doesn't mean I don't know what I want. And I want to be near you."

"Why, though?"

"You didn't explain why you wanted space. I ain't about to explain why I don't want space."

"Go get into one of your chicken-heads' spaces."

"I am."

"Did you just call me a chicken head?"

Bishop shrugged his shoulders.

Kelly hit his arm playfully. "I'm not okay."

"If you say so."

"Why would you call me a chicken-head?"

"I didn't. Those words never came out of my mouth."

"Do you think I'm a chicken-head?"

Bishop had picked up on Kelly's serious tone. The smirk that rested on his face went away. "I don't think you are a chicken-head. I do think you have a weakness for weak men."

"Excuse me?"

"That's why you are so dismissive when it comes to me. You know I ain't a weak man. I think you think I'm out of your league, so you treat me like you ain't even interested in me."

"No, I don't."

"So, you are interested in me?"

"I would find you attractive if the circumstances were different."

"Different, how?"

"You really don't see a problem with what you did?"

"Circumstances are none existing. It isn't like you got me any information."

Kelly sucked her teeth. "Whatever," she stated. "What are you doing here?"

"Two reasons."

"What?"

"Reason one; I need to find out if you've found anything?"

"My point is proven."

"Second, I wanted to apologize for mixing business with pleasure."

"Pleasure."

Bishop smirked. "I genuinely find you attractive, and then when we had dinner…."

Kelly rolled her eyes dismissively. "You're an asshole, though."

Bishop laughed. "You don't really think I'm an asshole." Bishop looked from Kelly's eyes to her cleavage.

"Perv."

Bishop grabbed the bottom of her robe. "What you got on under there?"

"My business," she pulled her robe from his grip.

"Can I see?"

"No."

"Oh, not yet. You want to handle business first."

Kelly moved from the couch.

"I feel like you are running from me," Bishop stated.

Kelly looked back at him and then continued into the kitchen.

Bishop jumped up from the couch. "I think you be forgetting."

"Forgetting what?"

"I am athletic. I will chase you down."

Kelly smirked. "And then what?"

"Are you flirting with me?"

"And if I was."

"I want you, Anessa."

"And if I don't want you?"

"That's what I pay my lawyers for."

"Oh, so you one of those athletes out here taken pussy?"

Bishop laughed. "Nah, I get that thrown at me. I'ma take ya' heart."

Kelly laughed. "What? Are you some kind of cannibal?"

"Yep, and I'ma eat for days with these ham-hocks," he stated, rubbing his hands down her thighs. "And with these," he said, peeking into her robe at her breast.

"Boy, bye," she giggled. "You wouldn't know what to do with a woman like me."

Bishop touched Kelly's chin.

She was instantly in a trance.

"Let me show you."

"Whatever," she whispered back to him.

Bishop kissed Kelly's lips gently.

Kelly pulled back from his kiss.

"Don't run from me," he stated. He walked closer to Kelly, trapping her between his body and the kitchen island. Bishop pulled at the bow in front of her robe. He stood back and watched the wrapping fall off his gift. "You got a date tonight?"

"No."

"Who are you wearing that for?"

Feeling vulnerable, Kelly grabbed the ends of her robe and tried to tie them up, "For me."

"Must be for me, too."

"I ain't even know you were coming over."

"Don't block my view," he pulled at the bow Kelly had tied again.

"Boy," she stated, still trying to close her robe.

Bishop finally let go and just stared silently at Kelly. He watched, intrigued, as she rewrapped her gift. "You just be around the house in sexy-ass lingerie?"

"I dress for me, and I like sexy-ass lingerie." Kelly closed up her robe again.

Bishop continued to look at Kelly. He knew she had swag in her clothes, but to see that she dripped swag all the way to her matching lace panty and bra set aroused him beyond his expectations. He appreciated the view and wanted another glance, so he pulled at Kelly's bow.

"Why?"

"Cause I like sexy-ass lingerie, too."

"It ain't yours."

"If I put my name on it, it's mine."

She was expecting a kiss, but Bishop got down on one knee before her. She looked down at him with wide eyes. "What are you doing?"

Bishop grabbed the top of her panties. He looked up at Kelly. "You know what to do."

She did know what to do. Kelly spread her legs to make space between her thighs. Her heart was beating out of her chest. She couldn't believe she had gorgeous-ass Bishop Carmichael in her kitchen, on his knees, face-to-face with her treats.

When her underwear reached her ankles, she lifted one foot at a time and watched Bishop remove them. She gasped as quivers shimmied up her spine when she felt Bishop's tongue part her lips and insert itself in her pleasure.

Bishop couldn't get it like he wanted it, so he lifted her right leg and propped it on his shoulder as he buried his face deeper in her pussy. Instantly, Kelly's mind and body began to argue within themselves:

Her mind: Bitch, get this nigga out of your pussy. This nigga has fucked up your hustle and pulled you back into the life you moved to North Carolina to escape.

Her body: To the right…to the right…yes, that's is my fuckin' spot.

Her mind: He probably thinks you easy because you fuckin' him. He gonna believe that you fucked Monroe, too. But I did fuck Monroe. I'm a basketball groupie.

Her body: He is suckin' the little man in the boat. Whoa, not too hard. Oh… oh…just like that baby, yes! Nibble, nibble, lick, lick…

Her mind: You're not really enjoying this because you ain't comfortable. This nigga got you in some skinny-girl position in your kitchen. You're gonna catch a cramp like this.

Her body: Shit, get comfortable! Tell that nigga we going to the bedroom.

Her mind: You just pressed 'cause it's Bishop, a famous basketball player every woman wants and probably had. You are just in his numbers. This head ain't even good.

Her body: Squirt in his mouth and let him know it's real.

"H-hey," Kelly stammered out. She tried to control her moans, she didn't want this man to know that he was getting the best of her, but he was. The toes on her right foot curled, and Kelly could feel a leg cramp on the horizon. "Bishop…baby…wait," she finally got it out.

Bishop stopped, but his face was still buried between her legs. "What's wrong?"

As the heat wrapped around his words, left his mouth and hovered over her clit; Kelly began to melt. Bishop knew what he was doing to her. He purposely pronounced each word to let his lips brush against her as he spoke. "What's wrong with you, Aneesa?"

Something said so innocently drove her crazy. She didn't care that

Bishop called her real name. In fact, this was the first time in a long time that she had felt good about hearing her real name. Bishop was making her learn to love her real name by continuously calling it to her. The A gave her pussy warmth in a wet spot. To say Nee lightly allowed his tongue to flick ever so slightly on the man in the boat. The Sa, ending the saying of her name, was like a gentle kiss at the end of a beautiful date. Oh, Bishop knew what he was doing, so he continued to say her name into her—sometimes fast, sometimes slow.

In return, she loudly called out his name as she grabbed the back of his neck to push him deeper—and he let her. He provided her stability as she began to gyrate her hips on his tongue and ride his face. Fuck a leg cramp, Kelly let go and allowed her juices to squirt in his mouth and drip down her leg. Her body slightly convulsing as Bishop continued to work his tongue on her ever so sensitive spot. When he finished, he kissed her lips deeply, then stood up.

Bishop stared into Kelly's eyes. "Take me to your room," he ordered.

Without hesitation, she replied, "Okay."

CHAPTER TWENTY-TWO

PILLOW TALK
FEBRUARY 14, 2020

Kelly lay on Bishop's chest. He held her tight in *his arms. Bishop must really like me*, she thought to herself. *Or maybe he just wants to cuddle.*

Bishop gripped Kelly tighter. He kissed her on her forehead. "You okay?"

Kelly looked up at him and smiled. "I am. I actually feel really good."

"I feel good, too.

"You say that like you are shocked."

"Oh nah, I ain't shocked." Bishop propped his left hand behind his head. "I see why Monroe doesn't want to let you go."

"Ugh," Kelly slapped Bishop's stomach and moved from his grip. She didn't get far as Bishop grabbed her and pulled her back.

"I was playing."

"I'm not some groupie."

"Aneesa—"

Hearing her name made her smile.

Bishop continued: "This wasn't a one-time thing for me."

"What are you saying?"

"I didn't stutter."

"You didn't, but…you have to talk straight with me. What is this?"

"This me and you about to build something, but before we make this shit official, we got to tear something the fuck down."

Kelly rolled her eyes. "It's hard for me to take you seriously when everything seems to lead back to Monroe."

Bishop sat up in bed. "I know you and I just met, but what you will learn about me is family means everything to me. I wouldn't be the man I am without my family. I would do anything for them. Once we get this shit done with Zeph and Monroe."

"You want to take Zeph down, too?"

"Once everything is handled," he stated, avoiding the question. "We can move on."

"You say move on meaning?"

"I know you see me," Bishop began. "I am very handsome."

"Um," Kelly hummed. "You are so conceited."

"Conceited…maybe, but I ain't community dick. Everybody doesn't get this."

Kelly snuggled under Bishop. She didn't know what this was with him, but Kelly didn't want to think too deeply about it. *Just live in the moment*, she told herself. *He could be one of those that gets what he wants, and then he's out.*

"Get out of your head."

"How do you figure I'm in my head."

"All women are in their head."

Kelly sighed. "Don't be one of those men that thinks he knows what a woman wants or is thinking."

"It's true, though. Women don't know how to—"

Kelly made a loud, fake snoring sound.

Bishop laughed. He looked down at Kelly, who laughed on his chest. "I wish I had met you under different circumstances."

Kelly looked up at him.

The two stared silently at one another.

"I don't want you to think that sex is all I am about. 'Cause, it ain't."

"If I didn't know better. I would think that you liked me."

"I do."

Kelly sat up and looked at Bishop.

"You know about a part of me that I must hide from the world. Do you think I would get endorsement deals if people even suspected my brother was a drug dealer and we are closely affiliated? Fuck no!" he answered his question. "I don't even think people know I have siblings. I won't mention them in interviews, and they don't come to my games."

"Does that bother you?"

"It does. Everybody wants people on the sideline cheering them on, but the way our life is set up, my siblings have to support me from afar."

"Siblings?"

"Yeah, I have a brother and a sister," he replied. "And we would do anything for each other. Shit, we do anything for family, period. We are all we have."

Hearing Bishop mention his brother sent an eerie feeling over Kelly. "Your brother scares me."

"You ain't even met, my brother."

"Your brother was an urban legend when I was growing up. Like a real-life Candy Man, who even had grown men scared."

Bishop smirked. Growing up, he liked that people feared Knight. That meant they never fucked with him. "How you hear about the urban legend?" he mocked.

"My mother told me."

"Your mother knows my brother?"

"I guess from back in the day. She made it seem like he and my father used to work together."

"Directly or indirectly?"

"I imagine it was directly. She talked like they all knew each other personally. I know your brother was the talk amongst my folks back in the day." Kelly shrugged. "Whatever it was, it shook up our business."

"Were you ever involved in your father's business?"

"No," she replied. "My father kept me out of business, but you know how kids are; we eavesdrop on adult conversations."

"True," Bishop agreed.

"I remember hearing about your brother killing that guy. They said he walked up on him in the middle of the street and shot him dead. Like some real Frank Lucas type of shit; no one ever snitched on him. Like they knew if they told, they would have the same fate as that dead man." Kelly looked up at Bishop. "Would he?"

"Would he what?"

"Would he have killed them if they snitched on him?"

Bishop shrugged.

"Yeah, I remember my father and…" Kelly continued to talk, but Bishop's thoughts were elsewhere. He could hear the fascination in her voice, but the words were irrelevant. He was more concerned with why his brother failed to mention having known Kelly's father.

"I heard your brother didn't even know the man he killed. He just walked up on him mid-day, in the middle of a crowd, and took him out." Kelly shook her head. "What made him kill a random guy?"

Bishop tuned back in. "If he did do it," Bishop began. "The guy wouldn't have been random because he would have known the guy from him dating our mother back then."

Kelly sat up in bed and looked at Bishop. "You knew him, too."

Bishop shrugged his shoulders like he didn't know the answer to his own truth.

"Why did he kill your mother's boyfriend?"

Bishop was still lying down. He looked at Kelly. She had a look of fascination on her face. "If he did kill him, it was because my mother walked in on him being inappropriate with my kid sister."

"Inappropriate, how?"

"If this story were true, Knight would have killed him for being a pedophile and taking my sister's innocence away before her time. If this story were true, no one would have snitched on him because they knew what the guy had done and would've respected my brother's alleged actions."

"Not even the cops."

"Cops are people with moral compasses, too. At least some of them. If the story were true, perhaps they also understood and respected the move Knight allegedly made."

Kelly sat silently, lost in thought.

"If it were true, my brother killed a pedophile and not some random innocent man."

"What about the other people he killed?"

"If those killings were true, then the lesson we should walk away with is that every action has a reaction, and sometimes people's actions result in deadly consequences."

"Whatever happened to your sister?"

"She's around."

"What's her name?"

"Queen."

Kelly smiled. "Seriously?"

Bishop nodded. "My mother named my brother and me. She then let Knight name my sister. He chose Queen to keep her in theme."

"Your mother birthed Chess pieces."

"I guess you can say that."

"Bishop, Knight, and Queen."

"That's my family."

"What was your mother's name?"

"Monopoly."

Kelly laughed. "You are a fool."

"Nah, her name was Evelyn."

"That's a pretty name."

"You remind me of me...the whole secret life thing. That's why I pick at you and call you Anessa."

"That's you picking at me?"

"Love taps."

"I hate your love taps."

"You were loving them a minute ago," he joked. "Bishop, yes, baby, don't stop."

Kelly nudged Bishop. "Jerk."

The two were silent, and then Kelly said, "Reason One."

"Reason one?"

"Yeah, you had two reasons why you came here today."

"Oh," Bishop nodded. "I did."

"Reason one," Kelly began. "Monroe has several freights that are supposed to move by land."

"Freights like...storage freights? That's what we talking about?"

"Yeah."

"What's in it?"

"That I don't know."

"Where are they going?"

"Raleigh, but I don't have an address or anything. The papers just say Raleigh."

"So they are in the freight yard as we speak."

"They're not supposed to move until later this week, but right now, they are over by the shore."

"Um," Bishop hummed.

"What?"

"I was just wondering what's in them."

"Guns?" Kelly questioned. "Drugs?"

Bishop didn't engage in Kelly's guessing game. "What else did you find out?"

"The contact person was Zeph, but he had started filling out some form to change the person."

"Change it to who?"

"Avie."

"Who is Avie?"

"His assistant."

"I thought you were his assistant."

"I am, but—"

"He's replacing you?"

Kelly sighed. She sat up and turned her body to face Bishop. "To fully answer your question, I must start from the beginning."

"What, you fucked him?"

"No," she quickly lied. "When I say that, I mean I have to put you into Monroe's state of mind."

Bishop now sat up in the bed. "Okay, go."

"Monroe literally has a basketball team of women around him."

"That's a real thing you were talking about the other day?"

"Yeah."

"Like he has a Point Guard, Shoot Guard, Small Forward, Power

Forward, Center. He has a team and each woman plays a role."

"Who are the women?"

Kelly looked up at the ceiling like she was trying to remember everything. "Let's see, it's Maria Elliott, Deadria…I don't know her last name. She's just a hoe."

"Um," Bishop hummed.

"Then you have Rebecca Tyler. She's the daughter of Watson Tyler."

"*The* Watson Tyler?"

Kelly nodded her head. "Yeah."

"What does she do for him?"

"Connections…they may be fuckin'. I don't know. I set up these meetings, but I'm not in the meetings with them. You have Jamilah, Avie… Avie wasn't initially a part of the team, but I guess she is now, and then you have me."

"You?" Bishop stated, surprisingly. "What role do you play?"

"Point Guard. I know about all these women, yet they don't know about each other."

Bishop looked at Kelly, confused. "What is the purpose?"

Kelly shrugged her shoulders. She never entirely understood the purpose of Monroe's team, but she went along with it all the same.

"Maria Elliott…that name sounds familiar. Who is she?"

Kelly looked at Bishop like a deer in headlights. She was hesitant to talk about Maria. To speak about Maria meant to talk about MJ, his son. She wanted to save her own ass, but she knew this would cross the line, so she lied. "I don't know too much about Maria."

Bishop studied Kelly's face. "You're lying."

"How you figure?"

"You paused," he quickly replied. "Who is Maria?"

Kelly sighed. "I just don't want no harm to come to them."

"Them?"

Kelly stared at Bishop with puppy dog eyes.

"Fine," he gave in. "I don't know who *them* are, but I promise to leave *them* out."

"Maria is Monroe's baby's mother."

"Monroe don't have no kids."

"His son is two or three," she responded.

Bishop shook his head. "Does Jamilah know?"

"She has no clue."

"Monroe is hiding his son?"

Kelly nodded her head.

"This nigga is sorry. I ain't hiding no kids. That's bullshit."

"Supposedly, Maria was Jamilah's old roommate from college."

Bishop covered his mouth, shocked. "I do know Maria."

Now Kelly was the one with a frown on her face. "How do you know her?"

"We all went to school together," Bishop shook his head. "Maria Elliott is his baby's mother?"

Kelly nodded her head.

"Wow," he stated, shaking his head. Bishop was silent, and then a smile crept up on his face. "Oh, wow, that makes a lot of sense now."

"What does?"

"Monroe's operation."

Kelly looked confusingly at Bishop. "I don't understand."

"Maria is a detective."

Kelly's eyebrows jumped across her forehead. "I knew it!" she stated. "I so knew it!"

"What you know?"

"Okay, I didn't know for sure, but I knew she had to be in law enforcement or like some kind of private detective 'cause she was always so damn secretive."

"What do you mean?"

"Just how she would call to set up an appointment with Monroe. For example, she called one day and said, 'Tell Monroe to meet me in the usual location.' She nor he would ever disclose to me the location," Kelly shrugged. "I don't know. I just used to notice things."

Kelly set with a smirk on her face. She kept repeating to herself, "I knew it…I really did know it." Kelly gasped at an epiphany. "That's why he has her on the team."

"Who is Avie?"

"Avie is a new player. My mother and I think that Avie is the new Point Guard."

"But aren't you Point?"

"I was? I guess I'm not anymore."

"So, who are you now?"

"Jamilah, the Shooting Guard."

"So you and Monroe do have a relationship?"

"No!" Kelly answered quickly.

"Then how you replace his wife?"

"I replaced Jamilah in player position. They are still married. He and I are *not* fuckin'," she stated, emphasizing not.

"So, how you replace her?"

"Jamilah is fuckin' Zeph."

Bishop put his hand to his mouth to create a tunnel and yelled, "WHOOOAAA! Jamilah cheating?"

"With Zeph."

"Jamilah is cheating with *his* guy?"

"Yep."

"How you know?"

"Monroe and I saw them fuckin' on camera in his house."

"His house?"

"In the kitchen," Kelly added to the tea. "This is why I think he took Zeph's name off the freights and put Avie's name."

"Is Avie replacing you or Zeph?"

Kelly shrugged. "She was at his meeting with Watson Tyler."

Bishop smirked to himself. When first hearing about this team, he thought Monroe was solely thinking with his dick, but each player was influential in their own way. He couldn't wait to talk to his bother about Monroe's players. "What they meet about?"

"I don't know. I followed Monroe, and that's how I learned about the meeting."

"He didn't tell you about the meeting?"

"No."

"Avie is sounding more and more like the sixth man."

"What is the sixth man?"

"How do you work for a basketball player but don't know basketball?"

Kelly playfully slapped Bishop's leg. "Shut up and answer my question."

"The sixth man is like someone who is almost a starter, but not quite. They get just as much playing time as a starter because they are playmakers...top scorers outside of the starting five."

Kelly stared blankly at Bishop.

"You heard of Jamal Crawford?"

Kelly shook her head.

Bishop sighed. "Um...Lamar Odom?"

"Yeah."

"James Harden?"

"Yep, yep!" Kelly stated, catching on. "He plays for OKC."

"He used to play for OKC," Bishop corrected her. "But yeah...those guys won the NBA Sixth Man of the Year award. They are playmakers but not considered a part of the starting five."

"So, you think Avie is Monroe's, sixth man?"

"If we are thinking on Monroe's level...then maybe Avie is the sixth man. It makes sense since she seems to be doing a little of everything."

"Damn, he didn't even tell me he was getting a sixth man."

"He probably got more than you even know about."

Kelly shrugged. She felt some way about Avie being hired, which put an even bitter taste in her mouth to know there may be others.

"If you got Jamilah's position, what does Jamilah do now?"

Kelly shrugged her shoulders.

"He replaced his wife, but not his boy."

"He doesn't hang out with Zeph like that anymore."

"They were at a bar together a couple days ago."

"They were?"

Bishop nodded.

"How you know?"

"Jamilah will have her job back soon," Bishop stated, ignoring Kelly's question.

She hadn't even noticed. "Why did you say that?"

"Cause, as my lady, you ain't about to be working for this mauthafucka no more. Not in that environment. You got me fucked up."

"I can't just quit."

"Not now, but you most definitely will. He is fucked up, and he got all y'all in his fucked-up web. Not my lady."

Kelly smiled.

"I'm serious. I am only as strong as the woman by my side," Bishop stated. "You understand?"

"I do."

"You ain't about to be a part of this bullshit."

"What next?"

"We got to get Avie?"

"Wait, get her how?"

"I'll figure out something."

Kelly looked closely at Bishop. "You not gonna kill her or anything crazy like that, are you? She's annoying as hell, but she doesn't deserve to die."

Bishop looked at Kelly with a straight face. "Like I said, I will figure something out."

CHAPTER TWENTY-THREE

THE
ROGUE TEAMMATE

FEBRUARY 17, 2020

Jamilah would always hear her family call her an evil ass.

They didn't reference her as evil in the demonic sense but in the sense of being the monstrous combination of both of her parents' worse personality traits. Plus, she wore it on her sleeve, making it easy for people to poke the devil inside.

She had mastered how to keep her evilness at bay. She thought of it as protecting her energy at all costs. She hesitated to let anyone get close to her out of fear of being provoked. She could never explain the anger that resided in her. People wouldn't understand, and she wasn't interested in making them either.

So, she kept to herself.

She made sure that she was always occupied. It was a way to never give herself time to be idle. Being idle gave her time to dwell on negative things, whether about herself, others or something others said to or about her. In response to her truth, Jamilah occupied her time with reading, studying, and trying new things; anything to better herself and to keep being distracted. Through limited interaction, Jamilah made it impossible for other people's actions to bother her. By being busy, she never gave herself any idle time.

And then there was Monroe.

The physical specimen of Monroe was a distraction alone for Jamilah. She couldn't take her eyes off his chocolate physique. It was something about looking at Monroe's broad shoulders, muscular biceps, and chiseled abs. All that magnificence led to a defined V that pointed at her greatest distraction. She was grateful when her husband didn't make ESPN The Magazine's 2014 Body Issue. She didn't want to have to share her husband with the world.

In addition to his physical being, Monroe's drive for success distracted Jamilah. All his gorgeousness housed the mentality of a relentless goal-getter who had the want and ability to be more than what was expected of him. He had a vision, and his vision was Jamilah's distraction. She wasn't a gold digger, but with her husband's wealth and celebrity, she became the successful Black woman she always wanted to be. She was able to accomplish her goals, and she did it without fighting to climb a corporate ladder that was neither designed to accept nor built to hold a woman of her caliber.

By giving Jamilah distractions, Monroe ultimately gave her peace of mind. Not only was she his wife, but she oversaw his most successful business ventures. This took away any anxiety she would have felt being the wife of a highly sought-after man in the athletic industry. In college, Jamilah used to be self-doubting, insecure, jealous, and even furious when women would throw themselves at her boyfriend. Now, she didn't care. For one, she trusted Monroe and felt he had learned his lesson from cheating on her. Two, who the hell had the time to care? Not Jamilah! She was too busy writing business proposals, meeting with money people, and accepting awards that praised her business savvy. She was buying and selling homes, writing motivational speeches—Jamilah was perfectly distracted.

Until the day she wasn't.

In one swift move, Monroe had filled Jamilah with so much insecurity and doubt; simply by giving another woman—a younger woman, a woman of a different body type, a woman of no experience, a woman with limited education—her responsibilities and never even bothering to explain why. The peace that Jamilah once felt had all gone out the window. She was spending her days analyzing herself in the mirror. She was looking for confirmation from her husband, any sign that she was still relevant in his life, but he gave her nothing.

Nothing but idle time.

Initially, she was just being a weak-ass bitch with her idle time. She was sitting around his house, drinking up his wine, thinking about the degrees she earned that he paid for and the multimillion-dollar businesses she had been running, but they were all in the names of other people. To make matters worse, she tried to distract her thoughts by online shopping, but the fact that she was using his money made it impossible for her to enjoy herself. Jamilah finally realized that all her joy and her success were surrounded and controlled by Monroe. Everything was his; nothing was hers. She couldn't believe she had allowed herself to fall into such a trap, but she was there.

He put her there alone and idle. She was drunk with rage, resentment, and spite. The evilness she kept at bay was now alert and ready to react! Nothing that Monroe owned was safe. Jamilah wanted to burn up all his belongings and sabotage his business ventures. She wanted to fuck Monroe up in the worse way possible, but then, she emerged from her drunken abyss.

She decided that she still wanted to be Jamilah Whitaker, the businesswoman. Reacting in that manner would have been pleasing, but she would have lost the most important thing she had worked for— her name. Though she wasn't working for her husband anymore, her name was synonymous with wealth and celebrity, just like his. To pull a stunt like her drunken rage had wanted her to; would have resulted in reducing her character down to some reality TV topic.

Jamilah Whitaker was more than that.

If she was going to leave Monroe, she would do so on her terms. She would leave with her name intact and his money in her pocket. Unfortunately, Jamilah married when she was high on love, so she signed a prenuptial agreement. How foolish was she to sign a document that would bind her to leave the marriage just as she entered it. She didn't have shit when they married, so she couldn't leave with shit if they divorced. But like all good prenuptial agreements, there was a loophole—infidelity. She knew Monroe wouldn't let her walk away with his money. He would lawyer up and play their divorce out tit-for-tat, meaning whatever was done in the dark would come to light. This applied to the two of them. Jamilah was willing to run the risk, though. Staying in a loveless marriage without distractions; was torture. She would die sitting around the house doing nothing and being nothing, so she needed this divorce for survival.

To find proof of his infidelity, Jamilah did the typical rummaging through his belongings, checking his phone, social media, email, clothes, and wallet. She found nothing. Monroe was too smart to be a typical cheater. This called for her to step it up a notch. She decided to use her husband's money to sponsor a private detective.

Dressed in her best business suit, Jamilah sat patiently in the private detectives' office, waiting to be seen. This would mark her second meeting with Jake Bell. Their first meeting consisted of explaining why she thought she needed his services. This meeting was to confirm that she *did* need his services. At least, that is how he made it sound over the phone. She was irritated with his call because he didn't want to talk over the phone, but it was a riddle when he finally decided to answer her questions. Jamilah wanted to holler, 'TELL ME ALREADY!' but she kept calm and simply agreed to meet with him the next day. Now she sat nervously, waiting for him to emerge out of his office.

It was something about sitting in the waiting room alone. Jamilah looked around the bland, beige-colored office with poor lighting. As she waited, she thought about her husband. She scanned her mind to determine what Monroe could be hiding from her. *What am I doing here? Do you really want to know what's going on? Just be blind to whatever it is Monroe has got going on. You can start over.* The thought of starting over brought up an unknown fear. *You're scared,* she finally admitted to herself. *You are afraid to start over.*

"Jamilah."

To hear her name had startled her. Jamilah looked up at a slim man. His close-cropped silver-grey hair gave him a distinguished appearance. The moles that dotted his face added to the look.

"Jamilah," he called to her again. He was looking down at a slip of paper in his right hand. In his left hand, he held a can of Dr. Pepper. He took another swig of soda. "You ready?"

Jamilah finally stood up.

"Come this way," he walked towards his office.

Jamilah took a deep breath and then strutted confidently towards his office. She refused to let anyone—not even the private detective—see her sweat.

In his time as a private detective, Jake Bell had experience with providing heartbroken women with details about their lovers. He saw many reactions, but Jamilah's was his first. As he told her about a white woman named Rebecca and a stripper named Deadria, Jamilah held a blank face, and then she smirked.

Jake noted her response and, in her file, jotted "potential psycho". He considered his own note before he delivered the rest of the information to her. "I found out about another woman."

Jamilah's response, or lack thereof, was intriguing. She didn't even flinch at the mention of another woman. Jake wasn't one to take delight in people's pain, but Jamilah presented a challenge. He was now determined to get a reaction out of her.

This will get her, he thought. "Your husband has a two-year-old son with this other woman." He watched Jamilah's facial expression closely. She looked like she wanted to speak but didn't have the words. *The stone has broken*, Jake thought to himself. "He is a Junior. They call him MJ."

"MJ," Jamilah whispered.

Jake nodded. He watched as a single tear fell from Jamilah's eye.

She quickly wiped it away. Her mind was racing, but she couldn't move. How could she? She was listening to a stranger—a highly qualified, expensive—stranger tell her that her husband was a father.

"Does he know?" she found herself asking. *He can't possibly know*, she thought to herself. *I can't be mad at him if he doesn't know. He can't tell me something that he doesn't know.*

"He knows," Jake answered. "He sees the child. He is definitely supporting the child financially."

Jamilah's heart dropped. She couldn't believe what was being said to her. "We are talking about my husband, Monroe Whitaker, right?"

Jake nodded his head.

Jamilah shook her head in disbelief. "What do you mean he is financially supporting this child? How? I see our accounts."

Jake slid his file over to Jamilah. "He has several accounts that you are not listed on—at all. Not even as a beneficiary."

"So, who is the beneficiary?"

"Majority of the accounts have Zephaniah Wilkins listed as the beneficiary."

"He has a joint account with Zeph?"

"No, not a joint account. Monroe has accounts, and Zeph is listed as the sole beneficiary of those accounts."

"How much is in the account?"

Jake shrugged. "If I had to guess...millions."

"Millions?"

Jake nodded his head.

Jamilah looked back down at the file. She continued to skim through when she encountered a name she knew all too well. "Maria Elliott?" she looked up from the file again. "Maria Elliott is the beneficiary."

"Just on one account," Jake stated. "She's your old college roommate, right?" Jake questioned, trying to flex his knowledge of her life.

"Why is she the benefici—" Jamilah cut herself off. She looked from the file to Jake. "She's the baby's mother, isn't she?"

Jake nodded. He flipped through the pages of the folder in front of Jamilah and slipped out a picture. He placed the photo on top of the page Jamilah was on.

Jamilah could feel her anger coursing through her veins as she looked at the picture. Monroe wouldn't be able to deny this child even if he wanted to; he was the spitting image of her husband, except for his skin complexion. The longer she stared at the picture, she could see Maria in this little boy, too.

Of all the women in the world, she thought. *Why this bitch?* Jamilah tried to keep her tears at bay, but it was impossible to conceal her broken heart. She quickly wiped them away and then flipped the picture over. She couldn't bear to look at the little boy anymore. She skimmed the file to see how much Maria Elliott would benefit from Monroe's demises. She looked up when she saw the figure. "Two million?!"

"That's a lot of money," Jake commented.

Jamilah continued to stare at the figure.

Jake watched as the psychotic smirk he had mentioned in her file reappeared on her face.

Jamilah had seen enough. She slid the file away from her.

Jake reached across the table and retrieved the file. He took a sip of his opened soda. "That's not all," he stated, placing the can back on the desk.

"Do I have to hear it?"

Jake shook his head. "You don't, but wouldn't you like to know everything."

Jamilah shrugged. Really, she didn't want to hear shit else. She could barely digest the information that he had already shared with her.

Jake continued on without Jamilah's answer. "Monroe has real estate throughout the state."

Jamilah snapped. "I know," she sarcastically chuckled. "I bought—"

"No, you didn't," Jake interjected. "You couldn't possibly know about these houses. Your name is nowhere mentioned on any documents or deeds like it is with the other properties."

Jamilah narrowed her eyes.

"Monroe has eight houses," he flipped through the folder until he came across the page he was looking for. "These houses have rotated owners over the years."

"Who were the owners?"

"Shantel, Zephaniah, and Kelly."

"Kelly?"

"She is listed as the current owner of these homes."

"She's listed as the current owner?" Jamilah questioned rhetorically.

"Kelly isn't even her real name," Jake added nonchalantly.

"Wait…wait," Jamilah threw her hands up. "What you mean Kelly isn't her real name?"

"She bought her name; she wasn't born with it."

"So, what is her real name?"

Jake scrolled through his file again. "Aneesa Mo'Zani Wells."

"Why did she change her name?"

"I don't know, but I can find out. Give me some time."

"If Kelly isn't her real name, then he couldn't put the houses in her name, right?"

"If it wasn't legal, he couldn't, but Kelly's name change is legal."

Jamilah sat silently.

Jake Bell continued: "She was Aneesa Wells in D.C., and then she became Kelly Mitchell in North Carolina."

"Does Monroe know?"

"I can neither confirm nor deny."

"Can you confirm if they're fuckin'?"

"I don't have a solid answer on that. Since I have been on this case, I have yet to see them together. Is she still his assistant?"

"It's obvious that I don't know shit about my own husband."

Jake raised his eyebrows. He grabbed his can of soda. He was about to take a sip when Jamilah stated in a salty tone, "What else do you know?"

Jake put his soda down. Jamilah was visibly irritated. He didn't care, though. She paid him for the information, so he would deliver on his end, whether good or bad. Whether she wanted to hear it or not.

Jamilah's mind was racing. She expected Jake to uncover secrets, but she had never imagined secrets of this magnitude. It was too much to process. She didn't know whether to be pissed off about the child, the hoes, the payouts, or her lack of knowledge of it all. "He's buying homes and putting them in other people's names?"

Jake nodded his head.

"Why?"

"If I had to guess, it's so you can't get it."

"Wooow," she sang out.

"Your situation is fascinating," Jake commented. "I've uncovered intricate situations, but this one," he chuckled amusingly. "This one definitely takes the cake."

"How so?"

"Everything is so...questionable. How does Monroe have many accounts filled with more money than he makes in a year? It doesn't add up."

"We have two successful businesses. Monroe has endorsement deals from time to ti—"

"It still doesn't add up."

Jamilah shifted in her seat.

Jake reached into his desk and pulled out a DVD. He slid it across the table. "When you have time..."

Jamilah looked at the disk. "Time for what? What is that?"

Jake cleared his throat. "I found a DVD in Kelly's house."

"Kelly's house?" Jamilah shook her head, confused. "Why were you in Kelly's house?"

"Because she lives in one of the eight homes that she now owns," Jake explained. "I needed to check it out."

Jamilah chuckled to herself. "Kelly is living in one of the houses that she *owns*?" Jamilah used air quotes.

Jake nodded his head.

"Wow Monroe," she stated, as she grabbed the DVD off of the desk. "What's on the DVD?"

"You and Zephaniah having sex in your kitchen."

Life drained out of Jamilah's face. "Zeph made a tape?"

"I don't think he made it."

"Monroe made it?"

"I can neither confirm—"

"Yeah...yeah...yeah," Jamilah cut him off. Her face frowned. "So you can't confirm that Monroe is fuckin' Kelly—"

"But I do know you fucked his business associate."

"I can't believe this," she huffed. "Monroe and Zeph aren't even in business together."

"According to that bank account, they are in something worth millions."

Jamilah stood up from her seat. She snatched the DVD off of the desk.

"I just deliver what I find," Jake stated. He stood up from his seat. "I'm not trying to belittle you, but I am giving you what you paid for."

Jamilah sucked her teeth. She turned to walk towards the door.

"My associate is doing a little more investigating," he called as she rushed to the door. "He's looking into Kelly and these bank accounts. Your husband has a lot of secrets. So much so that he made Kelly sign a non-disclosure."

Jamilah stopped in her tracks. She spun around, "He didn't make her sign a non-disclosure. I made her sign a non-disclosure."

"I don't think you made her sign this," he stated, reaching into the folder. He pulled out a copy of a sheet and slid it across the desk.

Jamilah walked to the desk. She snatched the paper and read over it.

"I don't think you would have made her sign a non-disclosure from yourself."

"From me?" Jamilah quickly skimmed over the paper. She put the paper onto the desk. "Where did you get this?"

"Kelly's house. She is a good file keeper." Jake looked around his office. "I could use her here to be honest."

Jamilah looked at Jake unamused.

He took the hint. "Some of the things we found at Kelly's house, I have my associate looking into."

"What kind of things?"

"Shipments, storage units…" his voice trailed off.

Jamilah shook her head. "You make it sound like Monroe has a double life."

Jake shoved his hands into his pockets.

"What should I do with all of this information?"

"See a lawyer, but…"

"But what?"

"Wait until all information comes back. I got a feeling that your husband is involved in something illegal. If I were you, I wouldn't raise any flags until we determine if you are tied to it."

"But I'm not into anything illegal."

"Just wait to see," Jake recommended.

"Wait to see what? I'm telling you that I am not into anything illegal!"

"I know, but you could have signed something—"

"I DIDN'T!" Jamilah hollered. "I'M STANDING HERE TELLING YOU THAT I DIDN'T!"

"JAMILAH!" Jake hollered back.

Jamilah scoffed. She turned her back to Jake. She was doing anything possible to prevent him from seeing the tears in her eyes.

Jake sat down just as Jamilah turned back to face him.

Jake had reached in his desk and pulled out a box of tissue. He held them out to Jamilah.

She declined the offer with a wave of her hand. "I'll take your advice. I'll wait." She tucked the DVD into her purse.

"Are you okay?" Jake called after her.

"Um-hm," she hummed her response. Jamilah turned and headed for the door. Her pride wouldn't even allow her to say goodbye.

It took everything in Jamilah to not cause a scene in the private detective's office. As soon as she got in the car, Jamilah cut the radio on and adjusted the volume to the loudest decimal. The radio was for show. She didn't care what she was listening to, she just needed it to appear like she was reciting the lyrics. In truth, she was having a whole conversation with herself. Actually, Jamilah referred to these moments as keeping secrets with God. In this case, she wouldn't dare tell her family or friends what she had just heard. She couldn't even believe what she had just heard.

"Like," she started talking. "I don't even know where to start. I'm pissed about the women, but that shit is small compared to..." Jamilah suddenly slammed her hands hard against her steering wheel. "A FUCKIN' BABY!" she shouted at the top of her lungs. "A FUCKIN' BABY AND WITH THAT BITCH!" Jamilah was feeling defeated. She gave up the ruse of singing song lyrics and cut off the radio.

"This nigga cut me off, but he's out here with a whole fuckin' child."

Jamilah buried her head in her hands. "Why Monroe? Why did you do this?" she slouched lower in her seat. "I should have beat that bitch ass when we were in college." She thought about the night her and Maria fought in the college dorm room. "I should have dragged that bitch up and down campus. Starting at Petteway Hall, down the walkway in front of Edgecombe, past the cafeteria and the classrooms, in front of Nash, crossed the street to Collins, and then back in the middle of the street, up to the parking lot in front of Boddie and Centura. I then should have drug her silly ass by the Dunn Center all the way around to the street between the student center and the gym. I should have given this bitch a tour of the campus, but nope I didn't. I let everybody get in my ear. 'She ain't worth it…you better than that Jamilah. Don't get put out of school'. My first fuck up was letting that bitch live and look what the fuck happened." Jamilah shook her head disappointed in her decision as a youth. "Lesson learned," she told herself. "Moving forward, you let no bitch live. If they cross you, you cross the fuck out of them. Starting with Monroe and Maria. I got to get my lick back." She shook her head. "This is what happens when you let bitches that cross you live. They fuck your husband and have a kid. Fuck her and that kid!" Jamilah stared silently at her steering wheel. Her last statement sounded like an alarm in her mind. Suddenly she began to throw haymakers at her steering wheel. Her car horn beeping with every blow. "I HATE YOU BITCH I HATE YOU BITCH I HATE YOU BITCH!" When she finished, she noticed someone in a parked car, looking at her. "WHAT THE FUCK YOU LOOKIN' AT, BITCH?!" she yelled at them. "FUCK OUT MY MAUATHAFUCKIN' FACE!"

Jamilah started her car. She pulled out of the parking lot, screeching tires in the process. "You good, Jamilah. You can't let them see you sweat," she told herself. "Monroe fucked up because he fumbled you. You are a beautiful Black woman. You'a whole fuckin' meal out here in theses streets. FUCK HIM!" she added. "FUCK YOU MONROE!" Her car horn beeped again, as she slammed her hands on the steering wheel. "That's fine. I got something for your ass. I made some major fuckin' plays for you and you fumbled me." She nodded her head. "This nigga fumbled the fuck out of me." She told her reflection. She slammed her hands on the steering wheel. "A FUCKIN' BABY!" Jamilah hollered at the top of her lungs. She was beyond livid. Tears streamed down her face. She was consumed by so many emotions. "I FUCKIN' HATE YOU, MONROE! But I will show you better than I can tell you." Jamilah stated pressing down on the gas petal as she sped home.

Jamilah damn near ran from her car into the house. "MONROE!" she hollered at the top of her lungs. "WHERE THE FUCK ARE YOU?!" She burst into his office.

It was empty.

Quiet.

Clean.

The sight only pissed her off even more. She rushed inside and began ripping down his many accomplishments from the wall. "NONE OF THIS SHIT WAS POSSIBLE WITHOUT ME!" she yelled, attacking the office like a hurricane in a trailer park. She knocked his computer from the desk. She flipped the chairs that sat in front of it. She swiped her hand across his desk, knocking off any papers that she missed in the first wave of her anger. She snatched books from the shelf. She slammed her high heel shoe into the computer screen. "I HATE YOU, MONROE!" Her heel snapped and left a jagged edge at the bottom of the shoe. She then used the jagged edge to scrap into the surface of the desk, and then she used it to dig holes in his leather chair and couch. She snatched open the desk drawers and proceeded to pull, rip and toss the papers throughout the office when something caught her attention. It was a list of female names with basketball positions listed next to them. "These are the names Jake Bell told me about," she mumbled to herself. "YOU FUCKED WITH THE WRONG BITCH!" she shouted at the top of her lungs, as she stuffed the paper in her pocket. She terrorized Monroe's office, until she wore herself out. Standing in the midst of the chaos, she looked around the room. Jamilah was out of breath. Her hair, which was usually laid and styled, was all over her head. She pushed a couple of strands from her face.

"And then you had the nerve to punish me. You punished me, treating me like I'm the bad guy and you out here having a baby with another women," Jamilah broke down in tears. She dropped to her knees and then flopped on the floor. "Your nerve," she forced out. "Your fuckin' nerve. You have a whole kid. A three-year old and you cut me off. You played my face in front of everybody. You…you embarrassed me and…how do… what do I tell my friends? What do I tell my family? How—" her words dried in her throat.

Jamilah was silently laying in the middle of the floor with her anger and tears, and then she crawled to her knees. She looked around at her work. She stood tall to her feet, and then walked to the door, gripping her broke heel tightly in her hand as she limped out. She was about to close the door behind her, but pushed it back open. She walked to the staircase and sat down.

Her mind was racing, and she was slowly regaining control of her labored breathing. That's when fear fell over her. She looked around their lavish house. She had grown accustomed to her lifestyle, but the fear she felt reminded her of all that she would be losing. "Bitch you might go to jail over this nigga," she stated. The chilling words, brought on a feeling of nervousness. "I won't be humiliated and put in jail. No…no…no…. not for him. Not for any-fuckin'-body. Think…think…think…think," she told herself. Her eyes looked from her amazing foyer to her living room to the right of the staircase. She then looked to the left of her. It was just a hallway, but it was a lavish hallway. She remembered the months it took for her and the decorator to choose the right colors.

"This nigga has a double life," she concluded. "Bank accounts. You made sure that bitch is set for life, and you got me out here with nothing like I didn't help you build this shit. You got me…why did I let him get me?" Jamilah shook her head in disbelief. "Maria…you fuckin' bitch." Jamilah's jaw was clenched so tight that she barely got her sentence through her pearly white teeth. "How did I end up like this?" she buried her head in her hands. "He got to explain this shit to me. He got to explain his-fuckin'-self." Jamilah reached for her phone, but it wasn't on her. "Oh no," Jamilah jumped up from the stairs. "You don't get off that easy Monroe Whitaker," she hobbled out of the house and rushed back to her car just as fast as she had rushed into the house. When she got in the car, she grabbed her cell phone. She was about to dial Monroe's number, when her phone rang.

It was Zeph.

"YOU BITCH!" she spat into the phone. She didn't wait for a response. She continued yelling, "YOU KNEW ABOUT EVERYTHING AND YOU SAID NOTHING!" Jamilah sobbed into the phone. She didn't plan to rage out on Zephaniah, but in her heart, she knew he knew. "I confided in you, and you let him play my face."

Still, the other end of the line was silent.

The silence only pissed Jamilah off more. "OF ALL PEOPLE, ZEPHNIAH! I WOULD HAVE NEVER THOUGHT THAT YOU WOULD CROSS ME!" Jamilah took the phone from her ear. She needed to ensure that he hadn't hung up. "I KNOW YOU THERE!" she hollered into the phone.

Silence.

"Hello?" she stated, in a calmer tone.

"Come see me."

Before Jamilah could agree or disagree with the directive, Zeph had hung up the phone.

Jamilah looked at the phone baffled by Zeph's audacity. "Did this nigga just dismiss me?" Jamilah looked from her phone to the rearview mirror at her reflection. "I'ma fix all of them." Jamilah threw her car in drive and peeled out of the driveway like a bat out of hell. "All y'all fucked with the right one."

CHAPTER TWENTY-FOUR

MEETING
OF THE MINDS

MARCH 5, 2020

Deadria wasn't there when her oldest brother walked up on the man, her mother had been dating for a year, and shot him in the head.

But she heard about it.

In fact, she had heard so much about it that she often inserted herself on the corner where it happened when she told *her* version of the story.

But she wasn't there.

She didn't know what was happening until CPS came to their door and dragged her and Bishop out of the house. When alone and submerged in silence, Queen could still hear her mother hollering their names at the top of her lungs.

"QUEEN!"

Deadria snapped out of her thoughts. She looked up at her older brother, Knight, standing over her.

"He's ready. Come on."

Deadria stood up from her seat. She smoothed out her black dress and readjusted her blazer. She grabbed her purse off the chair and immediately followed behind her brother, who was dressed to the nines. Following behind Knight, she slowed her steps to walk in accord with him.

Knight stepped to the side, motioning for his sister to walk into the office first. "Remember what I said," he whispered.

Deadria acknowledged her brother's directive as she walked into the office.

Watson Tyler was on the phone. He held up his pointer finger as he continued his conversation.

Knight and Deadria took a seat across from his desk.

Watson looked at them. Usually, people would linger by the door or sit on the couch and wait until he was ready to speak to them.

Not Knight and Deadria.

"I will call you back," he stated before hanging up. He was intrigued by the people who sat across from him. "Let's sit over here," he motioned to the sitting area, where two couches were positioned. "My daughter will be joining us shortly." Watson walked over to his bar, "Can I make you a drink?"

"I'll just take a bottle of water," Knight replied.

"And for the lady?"

"The same."

Watson nodded his head. He was impressed. Watson had a preconceived notion about drug dealers. He assumed his new associate would fit the stereotype, but Knight and Deadria were not that type. They were far different from Watson's current associates.

Watson returned to them holding four bottles of water. He sat across from Deadria and Knight, who sat beside one another. Watson was issuing out water bottles when his office door opened.

"Hi, Daddy." Rebecca Tyler walked in. She paused in her tracks. She knew her father wanted to meet with her, but she was not expecting to see anyone else.

"Come in," he called to her. He stood up and motioned for her to meet his guest. "Knight, uh…I'm sorry. I don't know your last name."

"It's not necessary," Knight replied.

"Right," Watson replied, moving on. "This is my daughter, Rebecca Tyler."

Rebecca walked over.

Knight stood up from his seat and extended his hands.

Rebecca was taken aback by his height that she completely ignored his extended hand. "Oh!" she grabbed his hand. "I'm sorry. Excuse my manners. How tall are you?"

"6'8," Knight replied. He was used to the question.

"Mr. Six feet eight inches. That is tall," she stated, getting over the initial shock. She continued to look at him curiously. "I know you from somewhere. Have we met before?"

"No," Knight replied.

"I have a feeling we have met before. Do you play ball?"

"No," Knight stated, resuming his seat.

"You have a very familiar face," she commented. "And who might this—" Rebecca swallowed her intended words. The smile that once sat on her face dissolved. Rebecca forced herself to smile again, but she was speechless.

Deadria smirked at the change in Rebecca's demeanor. "Didn't expect to see me today, huh?"

Rebecca tried to play it cool, but she was visibly flustered.

"I see you know my daughter," Watson commented to Deadria, but he was looking at Knight.

Knight didn't notice as he was looking at Deadria. "You know her?"

The two women answered simultaneously. Rebecca opted for a lie, while Deadria staring her in the eye, chose the truth. Hearing Rebecca's response, Deadria smirked. "You no know me," she slipped into her manufactured accent.

Rebecca lightly chuckled. Nothing was humorous to her. Giggling in moments like these was her defense mechanism since childhood.

And her father knew it, too. In fact, he joined in with her chuckling. "Which is it? You either know each other or not."

Rebecca looked at her father. Although the two were chuckling, she read his eyes. He didn't find anything humorous about this moment. "Um…I do know her, but I don't."

Watson looked inquisitively at his daughter. He wanted to know more.

"We just spoke on the phone briefly."

"About?"

"We have a mutual acquaintance," Deadria answered.

Watson continued to pry: "Who?"

Rebecca looked at Deadria with panic in her eyes.

"Someone that frequents my club from time to time," Deadria replied.

"Oh! You're a club owner."

"Not an owner. I'm a stripper at Paper Stacks."

"Oh," Watson looked to Knight. "I never took you as a man who toted his uh...hobbies around."

"Not at all," Knight replied. "She is not a hobby."

Watson chuckled. He pointed at Knight, "This guy. What a gentleman, huh?"

Rebecca looked suspiciously between Deadria and Knight, and then she looked at her father. She wish she knew how to tell him that he had misread the room.

Never judge a book by its cover, Rebecca thought as she sat across from *The Fake Bitch*. Based on the letter she had received, Rebecca expected Deadria to look like a stripper; half dressed, perhaps even ran through. She was shocked that the woman in front of her was the same woman she had spoken to on the phone. The woman across from her had the physique of a stripper, but her appearance read business woman. A professional business woman at that.

Rebecca looked from Deadria to Knight. Nothing about the man in front of her put her in the mind of someone who would align themselves with a stripper. Even if she did clean up well. He looked too professional to recklessly bring a self-proclaimed stripper to a business meeting. It was something about the man in front of her. His clean-shaven balled head and fully grown beard with a distinguishing grey patch made him seem approachable, but the coldness in his eyes made him intimidating. The longer she stared at him, the more she was convinced that they had met before.

"So, tell me," Watson began, "Why did you call this meeting?"

"Initially, I was here about a letter."

"A letter?" Watson unfastened his suit jacket and sat back in his seat. "And here I was thinking we were here to discuss the task I hired you for."

"Watson, I don't work for you," Knight replied.

"Mr. Tyler," he corrected Knight.

"You didn't hire me, Watson," Knight repeated.

"Ah! You're my *new* partner," he stated nonchalantly. "I tend to forget my partnerships sometimes. Tell me, have you retrieved my freight from the trailers yet?"

"I have retrieved *our* freight from the trailers."

Watson smirked. He looked at Knight down his nose. He hated the idea of an *uppity* nigger, but he held his tongue for the sake of business.

"You told me I would find *the usual* kind of merchandise."

"And you didn't?"

Knight smirked. He hated it when people played dumb with him. "You know I did, but I found some other stuff, too."

"Hmm," Watson hummed.

The silence in the office stemmed from the two men having a staring competition.

Watson shifted in his seat. "The extra items will be used in another business venture of mine. It doesn't concern you. Just what we initially discussed. Now do you have that?"

"What kind of business venture?"

Watson smiled. "I never let the right hand know what the left hand is doing."

Knight smirked. He found amusement in Watson Tyler's approach. To Knight, there was a difference between doing business with Corporate America and The Streets. The Streets knew Knight. His reputation proceeded him on many levels, and it was understood by the respect—or fear—he received from them. Corporate America's fearlessness when speaking to Knight indicated their ignorance.

Knight leaned in.

Watson sat up in his seat and met Knight in the middle.

Knight whispered, "I cut off hands," and then he sat back in his chair. He never took his eyes off of Watson.

Watson sat back in his seat, but he never took his eyes off of Knight.

Rebecca didn't hear what was said, but she had concluded that this meeting was about something big.

"Is that a threat?" Watson finally asked.

Maintaining an even tone, Knight replied, "It's a fact."

Watson jumped up from his seat. He walked back to his bar. He spun around with a stiff drink in his hand. "I thought we were here about a letter."

"I said initially," Knight replied. "Now I want to know about the extra freight."

"It does not concern you." Watson resumed his seat with his drink in his hand. "Now, tell me about this letter."

Knight's silence spoke volumes. It was loud enough that Watson was finally compelled to speak. "The business venture is the construction of a correctional facility in Fairview County."

"You're building a jail?" Rebecca questioned her father. "For what?"

"Not now," Watson stated through clenched teeth. He knew his daughter all too well. She took after her mother, who was a *kept* hippie.

Like her mother, Rebecca often took to causes that did not align with Watson's business deals. Yet, both the women in his life loved the perks and benefits of his business dealings.

Watson turned his attention back to Knight. "Does this change our arrangement?"

Knight sat silently.

"Now look here, son—"

"He's not your son," Deadria interjected.

Watson cleared his throat. "It takes a lot to develop a prison. You need state-of-the-art security. You need personnel; guards, doctors, nurses, kitchen staff…it takes a lot to get these businesses started."

Knight shook his head.

"Damnit!" he slammed his glass on the end table. "The money you took was supposed to—"

"You do understand that I walked inside these trailers, right?" Knight questioned, intrjecting Watson's temper tantrum. "Personally, I walked inside every one of them. And there wasn't just money."

Watson cut his eye at his daughter, who had her eyes glued to him. He rubbed his brow. This was his tell when cornered and Rebecca knew the sign.

"I was told by you there was only one freight, but there was more. So, I took all the freight. You never mentioned Campbell & Co pharmaceutical drugs or machine guns, but low-and-behold, they were all there, too."

"You weren't supposed to open the freights. That's not what we agreed upon."

"I know what we agreed upon, and I also know what I did. Now let's move on," Knight stated firmly. "What are you planning?"

Watson looked between Knight and Deadria. "Can we talk alone?"

Knight nodded.

Without a word, both Deadria and Rebecca got up and left the room. Before they left the room, Deadria heard Watson say, "You are the first of your kind—" and then Rebecca shut the office door.

"Follow me," Rebecca stated.

"Where to?"

"The conference room. We need to talk, too."

The two women walked into the conference room. It was located down the hall from Watson's office.

"Your father has a nice office building," Deadria commented as she sat down in one of the plush office chairs in the room. "What did you want to talk to me about?"

"Why are you here?"

Deadria smirked. "You don't sound happy to see me."

"I'm not a child."

"I never insinuate that you were."

"Then why are you here? Are you here to tell on me to my father?"

Deadria laughed.

"I can do what I want to do!" Rebecca was breathing hard, getting her adrenaline worked up. She continued, stating, "You can tell my father about Monroe and me all you want. It doesn't—"

"Honey, relax," Deadria stated dismissively. "We are not here to tell your father about you and Monroe."

Rebecca sighed with relief. "Look, I didn't mean to bother you, but his wife keeps trying to contact me. She's calling my place of business and showing up unannounced."

"And what does that have to do with me?" Deadria asked.

"I was trying to see if she had contacted you."

"And you do this by blowing up *my* phone and coming to *my* job?" Deadria shook her head. "Make it make sense. She harasses you, and in return, you harass me."

"I wasn't harassing you. I just wanted to see if you had the same experience as I did."

Deadria shook her head. "No," she replied. "I didn't."

"I'm not scared of her if that's what you think."

"No, you probably aren't, but I know who you are scared of."

Rebecca raised her voice. "I AM NOT SCARED OF MY FATHER!"

Deadria smirked. "Okay."

"Jamilah can create many issues for my father's different venture deals."

Deadria stared at Rebecca, unamused.

"My father and his business partners built the WJ Enterprise from the ground up. My childhood friend, Sarah, got caught in a scandal, and her family disowned her. I...I just don't want that same fate."

Deadria did as her brother did earlier and sat silently.

This only compelled Rebecca to keep talking. "I didn't plan to sleep with Monroe. It just happened."

Deadria looked at her skeptically. She couldn't even blame Rebecca for sleeping with Monroe. She smirked as she thought about climbing his *pole* a time or two He was fun.

"Seriously!" Rebecca stated. She noted the look on Deadria's face.

Deadria snapped out of her fantasies of Monroe. She tuned back into Rebecca attempting to justify her interactions with Monroe. Rebecca's conversation made it apparent to Deadria who Watson Tyler really was and Deadria didn't flinch as she listened to *his* subtle, racist ideology spewing from his offspring's mouth. *At least I know who I'm working with,* Deadria thought. *Nothing like dealing with people who openly show their hand.*

"Why are you looking at me like that?" Rebecca asked. "I just don't want to be *out*. You can understand that, right? I just don't want you to tell my father about this, please."

"He is already aware of the letter," Deadria began. "They're probably talking about it right now."

"The letter is one thing. Jamilah making a scene is another situation. Has she reached out to you?"

"No."

Rebecca covered her face with her hands.

Deadria looked at the pathetic woman across from her. Suddenly, she felt her *Knight*-like persona drape over her. "What can I do to help the situation?"

"Stop Jamilah before she starts. Like maybe she's harassing me for money."

"What do you propose?"

Rebecca shrugged her shoulders. "Meet with her. I don't know. Just get her off my back." She pressed her lips tightly to distract herself from crying, but that wasn't the case. Her eyes filled with tears. She looked up, trying to keep her tears at bay, but it wasn't working.

The thought of being excommunicated from her family and their fortune turned her stomach. She and her father were never close, but he always supported her dreams. Although Watson's support came from financial contributions, it was better than nothing. She didn't want to end up like Sarah Campbell.

"What exactly does Jamilah want from you?"

Rebecca pulled out her phone. "She left me a voice mail," she stated. Rebecca played the message.

Deadria listened closely. She looked across the table at Rebecca, who was trying to maintain her composure. The message sounded professional, almost like a telemarketer leaving a voice message.

"Have you mentioned the letter to Monroe?"

Rebecca shook her head. "I didn't want to contribute to this shit. Alerting him could cause more problems. He would probably confront her, and then she would still blow this thing out of proportion. I just want this to go away."

"Fine," Deadria began. "Let's meet with her to find out what she wants."

Rebecca stared at Deadria in disbelief. "Meet with her? Did you not just hear me? I don't want this to blow up. Meeting with her will only draw this thing out."

"I heard you and I said what I said.," Deadria paused and then asked, "You do want my help, right?"

Rebecca stared at Deadria skeptically. "Okay," she stated, throwing up her hands. "I will call her back and tell her we will meet with her."

"NO!"

Rebecca looked at Deadria, startled by her objections.

"We will meet with her, but let her think she's just meeting with you. Don't mention me or anyone else coming."

"Anyone else?"

Deadria smirked. "She's going to meet the whole team."

"I don't know them. I don't...no...this isn't a good idea." Rebecca shook her head. "You are not listening to me. I don't want this to get out of hand."

Deadria waved away Rebecca's concern. "Trust me. Call Jamilah and invite her to meet with you at the White Lion Chinese Restaurant. They have a quiet banquet room in the back. She will think she's just meeting with you—"

"But you'll be there, too?"

Deadria nodded. "You, me," Deadria reached into her purse and pulled out her copy of the letter. "His assistant, The Dyke Bitch." Deadria had never met Kelly in person, but the idea of being in the room with her brother's *girlfriend* was a cheap amusement she wanted to experience firsthand.

"I don't know about that."

"Why?" Deadria was offended that Rebecca didn't want to follow her plan.

"I don't want this to get out of hand."

"Too late," Deadria replied coldly. "Jamilah has made her move by trying to reach out to you. It's time for us to make a move."

"Who do you think wrote the—"

"Ladies!" Watson entered the conference room. He was joyful like he and Knight had a productive meeting and everything was okay between them.

Unfortunately, Knight's facial expression told a different story. "Come on," Knight stated to Deadria. Unlike Watson, Knight didn't bother walking into the conference room with them.

Deadria moved on command. She looked at Rebecca. Her eyes read; she'll be in touch.

Rebecca nodded ever so slightly to not attract her father's attention.

Watson walked into the hallway. "You sure I can't convince you two to have dinner with Rebecca and me?"

Knight shook his head. "Gracious for your invite, but we must be going."

"A raincheck then!" Watson called after Knight.

The elevator doors opened, and he and Deadria stepped inside. "Raincheck," Knight called out just before the doors closed.

Watson returned to the conference room with his daughter and shut the door behind him. He quickly spun around and said, "FUCKING A NIGGER, REBECCA JEAN!"

Rebecca's eyes shot wide. "No, Daddy, I swear!"

"What's this about a got damn sex letter?"

Rebecca stood up, prepared to plead her case.

"SIT DOWN!" Watson shouted.

Rebecca quickly sat back down.

"Whatever this shit is, you resolve it, and you resolve it fast!" Watson turned back to the door. "Or else!" he shouted over his shoulder before snatching open the door and storming out.

Rebecca pulled out her cell phone. She searched through her contacts until she came across *The Fake Bitch*. She opened a message and typed, *Let's meet and plan this thing out.*

Knight sat in his truck quietly. His face was balled up. He didn't want his sister to know another man had gotten under his skin—but he had.

Talking to Watson Tyler reminded Knight of when he was a child trying to explain to anyone who would listen that his sister was sexually assaulted. He remembered feeling dismissed, as though his thoughts and concerns weren't valid. But just like now, they were valid.

"Knight? Knight?" Deadria called out. "KNIGHT?!"

Knight stepped out of his thoughts. "All money ain't good money."

"That was random."

Knight sat with a look of disappointment. "I was blinded by greed."

Deadria peered in her phone at a text message she had received from Rebeeca. "Niggas always want to integrate in white spaces like it's some form of validation." Naturally, Deadria was expecting a response, but when she didn't get one, she looked up from her phone.

Knight stared at her with a frown.

"I meant no disrespect," she immediately apologized.

"None taken," he replied. "Keep talking. Explain your statement."

Deadria put her phone down. "You pressed for white opportunities, but then you're shocked that those same opportunities aren't in your favor."

"I see," Knight looked out the window of the truck. "Who taught you that?"

Deadria looked back in her phone. "Negus read."

"That they do."

Deadria concluded her response back to Rebecca's text and then put her phone down again. "So, what did Watson say?"

"He talked in circles. Kissing my ass like I wasn't smart enough to read through his bullshit," Knight replied. "I don't know everything. He wouldn't tell me, but what he did say..." his voice trailed off. "Something big is happening. I just don't know what exactly."

"Are y'all still partners?"

Knight shot her a glare.

"Right…all money ain't good money."

"Somebody has to be the fall guy," Knight added.

"You think he's going to make us the fall guy?"

"There is no *think* about. He is going to make us the fall guy."

"So, what do we need to do?"

"I took what's mine out of the traile. The rest of the shit I put in a U-Haul and sent it to Fairview County. Nobody will look for it there." Knight added, "I don't want Watson to have any of it."

Deadria looked surprised.

"I know," he stated, acknowledging her facial expression. He looked back out of the window. Despite his reputation in the hood, Knight was not a *monster*, per se. He cared about people, it was a lesson that he had learned from his uncle as a little boy.

"I trust your moves," Deadria replied.

"We need to move it. I don't want it in Fairview too long. I don't trust Watson."

"I'll get some of the boys to move it."

Knight nodded. "I also need you to create a distraction. A massive distraction."

"How?"

Knight smirked. "You're creative."

Deadria sat *taller* in her seat. "That I am," she replied proudly. "That I am."

CHAPTER TWENTY-FIVE

BURNER
MARCH 8, 2020

"For a second, I thought you were just as hard-headed as Monroe," Maria told Zeph.

Zeph didn't reply.

Instantly, Maria knew that Zeph didn't like her. "So?" she stated, feeling awkward about carrying on a one-sided conversation. "You read the file?"

Still, silence.

Maria shifted her weight from one foot to the other. She looked around the dimly lit alley he had chosen to meet her in. Maria was confident in her character and job, but standing in the creases between two buildings for a meeting with a known-unknown drug dealer made her feel uneasy. She slowly slipped her hand behind her back and gripped the butt of her gun—just in case.

Maria cleared her throat and spoke again. "Did you read the file?"

Zeph began to move from the opposite end of the alley towards Maria. Unlike her, he felt confident, which was revealed by his demeanor. When he stood close enough to Maria, he held out the file she had given him. "I read it."

"What do you think?"

Zeph reached into his pocket and pulled out a pack of cigarettes. He pulled out one and proceeded to light it up. "You sure Wells is here?"

"He specifically, no. He's still in D.C. A friend says his case should be rapping up soon."

"Is he getting time?"

"It doesn't look to be that way."

Zeph smirked. Wells had become his hero after reading through the reports. Zeph found it inspiring how Wells managed to insulate himself from any shit. Everything he orchestrated and he wasn't going to get any time for it.

"What's the smirk for?"

Zeph blew smoke. He looked Maria over. Other than their early interaction when she gave him the file, Zeph had never laid eyes on her. Now, he could see why Monroe made his drunken comment. Even in her uniform, Zeph could see Maria was thick. She was definitely Monroe's type of woman, from her looks all the way to her usability.

With her intel, I could take over this fuckin' state, Zeph thought to himself. *This bitch here is a gold mine.*

"What?" Maria was feeling uncomfortable by the eerie way Zeph was staring at her.

"Have y'all been able to tie him to the murders of any of my boys?"

"I didn't know I was supposed to be looking into that," Maria replied.

"You can tell a D.C. nigga by their accent, right?"

Maria shrugged her shoulders. "I don't know. Why do you ask?"

Zeph didn't reply.

Maria looked at Zeph suspiciously. "Do you have his boys?"

"I don't have *his* boy," Zeph paused. "But I got somebody's boy. The nigga I got ain't from 'round here, but he damn sure ain't from D.C. either."

Chills scaled up Maria's back. Zeph may not have been a newspaper aficionado like Moe Wells, with lists and links to several people's deaths, but she knew he wasn't innocent either. Her source was the streets. Although no one ever fingered him as a drug dealer, the silence surrounding his name spoke volumes.

"Either these ain't D.C. niggas, or this nigga Moe got the pull to recruit silently and quickly from different states and then plant them here and grow a whole operation without our knowledge." Zeph paused. "You think he got the pull to do all that shit right under our noses?"

Maria rummaged through her thoughts. She finally spoke, "From what I read and heard from my colleagues. I think he has the power and the pull to do just that."

Zeph had never heard of Moe, but he was impressed. Truthfully he knew he didn't have the manpower nor the skillful people to successfully compete with Moe. From the police reports and newspaper articles, Zeph concluded that Moe had loyalty in his numbers and structure. Meanwhile, all Zeph had was a rich little boy that would give him money when his reup was short.

"So, you don't think it's Moe?"

Zeph was about to answer, but then he remembered one important fact—Maria was police. "How do I know I can trust you?"

"Monroe trusts me."

"Monroe trusts Kelly, too."

Maria smirked. "I'm no Kelly."

"You say that like it's worse than what you are."

"What am I?"

"Police."

"I'm a mother first," Maria corrected him. "And I have to protect my son by protecting his father. I am coming to you now to protect my son from his father's stupidity. I hate that he got into business with you. I hate that you even let him—"

"We are talking about a grown man," Zeph reminded her.

"It doesn't matter, Zephaniah! You know he ain't built for that life. He is taking all this shit way too lightly. That's why I'm here now talking to you," Maria stated, her tone filled with concern. "I get that you don't trust me. Let's be clear, I don't trust your drug-dealing ass either."

Zeph laughed. "Ouch. That hurts."

"I know you would know what to do with this information. I need you to help me save Monroe because he is blinded by—"

"Pussy," Zeph interjected.

Maria's jaws flinched.

Zeph knew all too well how police officers operated. Past experiences taught him that they will use any and every one for their benefit. They didn't give a damn how everything would come to pass for the person they decided to use. Maria was no different. Maria may have spoken the loyalty dialect, but who was she exactly loyal to?

"And for the record, I'm a detective, not a police officer."

"What can you tell me about these new niggas?"

"I can confirm that there's a new wave of product called Ice."

"I heard about it." Zeph had done more than heard about it. He had seen firsthand the clear chipped crystals' effects on a person.

Ice was an ectasy-percocet hybrid drug that some college lab rats created. Ice can be ingested in many ways. Some were dipping their cigarettes or sealing their weed with it. Others were shooting it, snorting it; the drug was highly addictive and deadly if done wrong. Naturally, this made it even more enticing for those seeking an escape.

Zeph was uneasy about the arrival of Ice. He could see it had the potential to be more than a trend and have longevity like heroin and weed. He knew that whoever was pushing this product was undoubtedly making significant money.

"Where are they operating?"

"They are moving into your territory," Maria replied. "Aggressively. The bodies are stacking up."

Zeph knew that the new shit had entered his territory. His problem was that his boys were being picked off like they were all selling the same product. He knew the logic behind his opponent's approach; erase all competition in all forms.

"That's why I brought this to Monroe."

"And what did you expect him to do?"

Maria shook her head. "I don't know what I expected him to do. I just need you all to prepare."

"For?"

"At this point, I got dead college kids from the university," she stated. "Dead, white college kids," she placed emphasis on *white*. "And they need a fall guy, you understand? They are looking to put niggas heads on the chopping block."

"You are *they*," Zeph reminded her.

Maria rolled her eyes. "Fine, just know a drug dealer is a drug dealer, and getting one off the streets is just as much a win as catching the nigga actually selling the shit that's killing these kids."

"What you propose I do then?"

"I don't know. You're the fuckin' mastermind. I just need you to make sure you and Monroe are clear from this shit before the shit hits the fan. I tried to talk to Monroe about this, but...." Maria shook her head. "He's fuckin' Kelly, isn't he?"

Zeph shrugged his shoulders. Zeph didn't have a sure answer, but knowing Monroe—he probably was fuckin' her. Monroe was weak over pussy that way.

"You wouldn't tell me anyway."

"She is Moe's daughter?" Zeph questioned, ignoring Maria's inquiry.

Maria rolled her eyes. Off this interaction alone, she knew she didn't like Zeph. He came off as an arrogant asshole and only seemed to entertain this meeting to see how it benefited him. She hated that type of man. She dealt with many of them on the force that felt women weren't good enough to wear a shield like they did. "She's still meeting with them, too," she offered.

"You're watching her."

"I'm watching everyone," Maria replied. "I don't trust that girl. I think Morris has been playing y'all from the very beginning because he got his fuckin' daughter spying from the inside."

Zeph provided no physical reaction to Maria's sentiments. Inside though—he agreed. "Are you watching me, too?"

Maria felt a chill down her spine. Zeph didn't look big in the car, but he was a tall, muscular guy who towered over her like Monroe.

Zeph smirked and flicked his cigarette. "I take that as a yes," he concluded.

Maria stepped forward, trying to gain any ground she could. "I ain't tellin' you about your business. I don't even support your business, but since Monroe decided to foolishly be a part of this shit. Keep him safe," she stated, changing the subject.

"That's a grown man."

"Who has a child!" Maria raised her voice. "Look, just keep him safe because Monroe is over his head."

"You know what I hear listening to you."

Maria tucked the envelope under one arm. "What are you listening to?"

"I hear a woman asking a grown man to care for another man."

"And? That is not an unreasonable request considering wh—"

"What I don't hear," Zeph stated, speaking over Maria. "Is the woman asking the man to babysit getting anything out of this arrangement."

"What do you want?"

"What do you have to offer?"

"I'm not fuck—"

"Don't finish that sentence and play yourself," Zeph quickly shut her down. "You want me to keep that little boy safe? Then give me intel and insight."

Maria held up the envelope in her hand. "What do you think this is?"

"Bullshit about shit that happened years ago," he replied quickly. "Plus, I don't just want intel on other organizations. I want to know what the boys in blue are doing, too. Who are they looking into, why are they looking into them...shit like that. I want to know your job like it was my fuckin' job."

"I want Monroe to win, but—"

"That's how we win," Zeph replied. "Help me, help you."

Maria stared at Zeph.

In all her career, she despised cops that got in bed with criminals. Therefore, she was disappointed when Monroe confessed his involvement with Zeph in the drug world. He had inadvertently made her the type of cop that she despised. What was the point of vowing to serve and protect a city that you were underhandedly polluting and killing out of greed? She hated the drug game because only a few ever benefited from it. Everybody else was a loser in some way, shape, or form. Either they lost their lives, their family, or their time. It wasn't a fair game, yet it was so enticing to so many.

Zeph could tell by the look on Maria's face that she was hesitant about his offer. But she needed to know that Zeph was not a yes man. He wasn't just going to jump and take heed to her requests, threats, and warnings because she was a detective. That title could be bought and sold like anything else in his business.

Zeph slipped the burner phone out of his pocket. "I will keep this on for a few more days and then toss it. I suggest you give me your final answer quickly." He began to walk to his car parked at the far end of the alley.

"What about Kelly?"

Zeph turned around and looked at Maria. "What about her?"

"How are you going to get her out of the way," Maria questioned. She began walking towards Zeph. "Whether I do what you ask or not, it would all be useless if she is still in the picture 'causing us all problems."

"This is true."

"So, what are you going to do about her?"

"What do you want me to do about her?"

The question was so simple, yet so hard for her to answer. She didn't know what she wanted to be done about Kelly. She just knew Kelly was a problem that needed to be solved.

"Huh?" he questioned, after a long pause. "Are you soliciting me for murder, Detective?"

Maria clenched her jaw. She backed away from Zeph. "Just handle it," she stated before rushing off toward her car parked at the other end of the alley. "Remember, she's your problem, too." Maria turned to head back to her car.

"Wait!" Zeph called to her.

Maria turned around. "You see my point, huh?"

Zeph waved away her cockiness. "Find out something for me."

Zeph walked up to Maria. "What do you know about Knight?"

"It comes after day."

"Corny."

Maria still laughed at her joke.

"Seriously," Zeph stated.

"Is that really someone's name?"

"You tell me." Zeph turned to head back to his car.

"Like that?" she called after him. "That's how you end a conversation?"

"You got a task. I got a task," Zeph called over his shoulder as he returned to his car.

CHAPTER TWENTY-SIX

EXPLOIT THE LITTLE

MARCH 18, 2020

"Hey," Avie stated as she got into Zeph's car.

Zeph pulled off without a word.

Avie was okay with his lack of response. It reminded her of her brother, Octavius. Octavius used to justify his silence as the ultimate compliment he could give a person. He would say, 'If I'm silent around you, I can find peace with your presence. I don't have to force unnecessary small talk.' Avie smiled to herself. She thought about her brother often and missed having conversations—or not—with him. She glanced at Zeph. He looked nothing like her brother, but the two were cut from the same cloth.

Although Zeph reminded her of her brother, she didn't view him like a brother. He was a cute teenager, but as a grown man, Zeph was gorgeous. He walk with an heir of dominance that she could no deny. She knew she was attractive, but he didn't acknowledge it. She thought he would want to see her after their meeting in the hotel, but no. He did call to check on her and ask if she needed anything, but that was as far as their interaction went. Avie wanted him even more because he wasn't chasing after her. It was something about the energy around Zeph. Avie knew what Zeph was about and what he was into, but she felt safe around him. Perhaps the scent of weed and Black Ice helped to relax her. She snuggled into her seat and looked out the window.

Zeph glanced over at Avie.

The streetlight allowed him to see her in flashes. Avie had made an impression on him. She carried herself like Shantell and was the sister of his best friend. Zeph was a sucker for nostalgia. Avie was a relic of his past. She was his last connection to everything that was good in his life up until he went to jail.

The two drove down the highway in silence.

All that changed when Zeph turned into a cemetery.

Avie sat up in her seat and looked around. "Why are we here?" She was trying to stay calm, but Zeph could hear the panic in her voice.

He kept his left hand on the steering wheel, and with his right, he reached for Avie and touched her thigh. His intentions were innocent but feeling the smoothness of her thigh against his fingertips had aroused him. "I wasn't trying anything." This was the first thing he had said all ride.

"I know," she assured him.

"I was reaching for your hand," he explained.

Avie replied by grabbing his hand. She interlocked her fingers between his and held his hand.

Zeph replied by closing his grip around hers.

Avie sat back in her seat. She was still alarmed about being in a cemetery at night, but she allowed herself to trust Zeph. "Why are we here?"

"You know where we are?"

"Very much so," she looked at the tombstones she could make out in the moonlight. "Our family is buried out here."

"It's been a long time since I've been called someone's family."

Avie looked in Zeph's direction. "I can show you better than I can tell you."

Zeph lightly squeezed Avie's hand. It was his silent acceptance of her offer.

"My mother had power of attorney over Shantell when she came to her end," Avie unhooked her seatbelt with her free hand when she noted Zeph coming to a stop. "She wanted to put Shantell out here with Tavi. She said she didn't want him to be alone."

"That's funny," Zeph stated, "I come out here to be alone."

"Then why bring me here?"

"Maybe I don't want to be alone tonight."

Avie gently squeezed Zeph's hand. It was her silent acceptance of his sentiment.

"What did you want to talk to me about?"

"I got a call yesterday." She let Zeph's hand go and reached into her purse. She paused. "I'm going to reach in my purse now...is that okay?"

"Yeah, but get out of the car," he ordered, as he opened his door.

Avie suddenly didn't feel so safe, but she pushed her fear aside and opened the car door. Just as Zeph was walking around to her side, she stepped out.

When she was clear of the door, he closed the door behind her and leaned against the car. He placed a cigarette between his lips, "What's in your purse?"

Avie looked around. "Why did we get out of the car?"

"Are you scared?"

"No."

Zeph could tell by her demeanor that she was. "It's peaceful here," he assured her.

"In the daytime," she replied.

Zeph chuckled.

Avie reached into her purse, pulled out the letter, and tried to hand it to Zeph.

He shook his head no. "Read it to me," he blew out his orders in smoke.

"Okay," Avie opened the letter.

"You got this yesterday?" Zeph asked. "Who is it from?"

"Rebecca Tyler sent it to me after she invited me to a meeting at the White Lion restaurant." Although grown, Avie felt awkward reading *those* words to Zeph. She cleared her throat, "I didn't know about you. That's the first thing you need to read and understand about me. I ain't know shit about any of you. But I do now. Well, I knew about the Wife Bitch, but I thought you all were getting a divorce."

Zeph blew out his smoke. Hearing these words made him think about the last time he spoke to Jamilah on the phone. He had been so busy that day that he hadn't realized until this moment she had never come to see him like he had told her. "What the hell are you reading?"

"The letter," Avie replied. "Did you know that Monroe and Jamilah were getting a divorce?"

Zeph ignored Avie's question. "Who wrote it?" he asked instead.

Avie shrugged her shoulders. "I don't know that part. Rebecca doesn't know either, but I know she's fuckin' Monroe." She stepped close to Zeph, "Read that," she pointed at a part in the letter she wanted him to read.

Zeph followed Avie's finger and then started to read aloud: "I first found out about the White Bitch. She's supposed to be some big-time physical therapist that works out at the gym on 108th and Hilmount," Zeph stopped reading and looked at Avie. "How do you even know her real name?" he questioned. "They're calling her The White Bitch."

"I told you she called me," Avie began to explain. "She was like, did you get a letter? And I was like, who is this? She was like The White Bitch. I laughed."

Zeph chuckled. "You laughed at her?"

"She's a white woman calling herself The White Bitch. Can you even imagi—" Avie couldn't even get her explanation out through her laughter. "Who came up with that shit?"

"Yo' you bugging," Zeph continued to laugh.

Avie sighed out the rest of her laughter. "She eventually told me her real name."

"You know who she is?"

"Hell yeah. Roe and I met with her father awhile back. That's what's confusing to me. We were dealing with some real shit, and then she comes at me with this," Avie flicked the paper.

"What were y'all dealing with?"

"A shipment that went missing."

"Oh really?"

"You ain't know?"

Zeph was pissed, but he maintained his composure in front of Avie. "Go on," he stated instead of answering her question.

"Watson Tyler was going on and on about how important the shipment was and how he needed to get it back ASAP."

"What was in the shipment?"

"The old white dude said it was money, but...the way he was going on about it. I think it is more than money."

"What was Roe's response?"

"You know Roe. Acting like he the man and he got everything under control."

"Um," Zeph hummed. "So, who are you supposed to be?" Zeph changed the subject. He looked back down at the letter and then back at Avie. "You do give off a dyke-ish vibe," he joked.

"Funny," Avie pushed him. "They claimed I knew about this team, but I don't know about this hoe coalition." Avie shook her head. "I can't be the point guard."

Zeph stared out into the dark cemetery. *Something bigger is at play here*, he thought. *Why is this shit coming out now?* Zeph pulled another drag from his cigarette. *It's Kelly. She wrote the damn letter. She's the only one that knows about all of them.*

Avie said, "I like to come to the cemetery and talk to my brother. It's like a way for me to feel connected with him."

Zeph didn't reply.

Avie waved her hand in front of his face. "Are you there?"

"Yeah. Just thinking."

"About?"

Zeph looked back at the letter. "This letter wasn't for you."

"Then who was it for?"

"Kelly."

Avie sucked her teeth. "Then why did Rebecca invite me?"

"Now *that*, I don't know."

"She wants to meet with all of us?"

"Jamilah, too?"

Avie nodded. "She made it seem like she was going to get everybody together. We are supposed to meet up at the White Lion."

"I wouldn't go," Zeph stated. "Shit seems childish as fuck. What are y'all meeting for? Everything you need to know is in the letter. He fuckin' all of y'all."

"I ain't fuckin' Monroe!"

"I hear you," Zeph replied nonchalantly.

"No, seriously, I'm not," Avie repeated sternly. "I'm not fuckin' him at all. You yourself said the letter wasn't for me."

Zeph looked at his watch. "I just don't see a purpose of y'all meeting to talk about what exactly?" Zeph abruptly pushed himself off the car. He opened the passenger's side door. "Get in," he stated, holding the letter out for her to grab.

"You believe me, right?"

"Why is it important what I think?"

"Because I want you to trust and believe in me."

"Hurry up and get in," Zeph stated.

"Hurry?" Avie spun around. It was dark, but there was some light along the pathway. She became creeped out by the way Zeph was ushering her into the car. "What you see?"

"Girl, get in," he ordered.

Avie eased into the car. She had one leg hanging out of the vehicle. She took the letter from Zeph. Her eyes pleaded to know what was happening.

Zeph shook his head. "Stop acting scary, Avie. I told you I'm good. We are good. Now put your other foot in the car," he ordered.

"You aren't getting in?" as she spoke, she climbed into the car, grabbed the door handle, and pulled the door closed behind herself. She didn't even wait for an answer. Her heart was beating out of her chest. "Come on!" she yelled through the window to Zeph.

He paid her fear no mind and began to walk away from the car.

"Where are you going, Zeph?" she called to him through the closed window. "Let's go!" she continued to holler, but her fear prevented her from opening the door and following behind him. "Damn, I should have got the keys from him," she stated as she watched Zeph fearlessly enter the dark.

Going to a cemetery in the middle of the night would terrify most, but for Zeph—it was peaceful. He felt like he did some of his best thinking in the land of the dead. Tonight, was different, though.

Tonight, he was summoned to this location. He didn't mention it to Avie, but he, too, had gotten a letter. His letter wasn't childish as hers, but it said enough to make him show up at midnight by Shantell's tombstone. Zeph was looking around, but he couldn't see, not even his hand in front of his face. He heard leaves rustling in the distance and called out, "Who's there?" he reached for his gun on his waist. "Announce yourself."

A light suddenly flashed in his face. Zeph shielded his eyes from the light. He tried to see beyond it, but the light was blinding. "Get that shit out my face!"

The light moved to the ground and illuminated the area like a campfire was lit between the two of them.

Zeph tried to make out the figure across from him but couldn't. All he could tell was that it was a tall, wide-bodied guy. Looking at his shoes, he could tell it was an older guy. Zeph hadn't seen many young dudes wearing Stacy Adams shoes and slacks. It wasn't a doubt in his mind that the guy probably wore a button-up and a suit jacket.

"Who are you?" Zeph asked.

"Who I am is not as important as what I have to tell you."

"What do you have to tell me?"

"It is time for you to sever ties with Monroe," he stated. "I have waited for you to come to this conclusion, but time is running out. You need to sever it now."

"You waited for me? Do I know you?"

"No," he replied. "But I know you very well, Zephan."

Zeph felt a chill. He hadn't been called Zephan since Shantell died. She started calling him that as a joke, but it stuck. That was all she would call him.

"You knew Shantell."

"I know you all."

"How?"

"Would you really believe me if I told you?"

Zeph didn't respond.

"I used to work with you when you were a kid."

Hearing that didn't move Zeph. His unique childhood had him exposed to several different people.

"I am the one who had you put in jail."

Zeph frowned into the darkness. "What did you just say to me?"

"You weren't randomly stopped on I-95. I called you in."

Zeph pulled out his gun. "You got some fuckin' nerve tellin' me some shit like that. You called me in? Who the fuck are you?" Zeph went to point his gun toward the figure, but he felt hard steel pressed against the back of his neck. Without direction, he lowered his weapon.

"You are smart," the person behind him stated. "You should have had that girl be your backup instead of leaving her in the car. What kind of man are you leaving a woman out here in the dark?" the guy chuckled at his rhetorical question. He reached for the gun out of Zeph's hand, and then he moved to stand by his partner.

Zeph noted that he, too, had on dress shoes and slacks. "Put your hands down," the first guy ordered. "We don't want to hurt you, Zephan. We are just here to warn you."

Zeph was heated. *How the fuck did I get myself into this shit? Too fuckin' comfortable*, he told himself. His thoughts slipped to Avie. *Why the fuck did I bring her?* he questioned himself.

The light flashed in his face. "I know that look," the first guy stated. He moved the light away from Zeph's face. "This is why we came to warn you. You are slipping, Zephan. You know that girl shouldn't have been out here."

"Warn me about what?"

"A new alliance that is forming."

"What alliance?"

"One of your business partners has formed an alliance with your competitor."

"Monroe has formed a partnership with Morris Well?"

"Morris Wells is not your competition," the first guy clarified. "He has the potential to be your competition."

"But he ain't your competition," the second guy reiterated. "Wells got bigger fish to fry."

"Then how do you explain Kelly?"

"A coincidence," the second guy chuckled. "A fuckin' coincidence."

"Then who is my competition?"

"Knight is your competition."

"Monroe has formed an alliance with Knight."

"This is who we are gambling on?" the second guy asked the first. "This kid," his tone was that of disappointment.

"Zephan, listen," the first guy stated. "Knight is forming an alliance with Watson Tyler."

"I keep hearing the name, Knight. Who is he?"

The men ignored Zeph's question.

"He and Watson Tyler are planning something. They had a meeting the other day."

Zeph clenched his jaw. *Why the fuck does everybody know about this Watson Tyler bullshit?* he questioned himself. "They just started working together and Watson crossing Monroe already?"

The second guy laughed. "You think fuckin' his daughter made Monroe his family? Monroe is still a nigga. He's just a nigga that dribbles."

"And stop following a man who is leading by his dick!"

"I ain't following Monroe, and I damn sure ain't about to follow you either. I don't even know who you are."

The two men conducted a conversation amongst themselves: "Are we going to be able to work with him? He doesn't listen."

"Don't insult my intelligence," Zeph spoke up. He was irritated by this meeting. "You call me to a cemetery and tell me about a double cross with some character named Knight. I don't know—"

"Hayden Myers' nephew," one of the guys interjected into Zeph's rant.

The name Hayden Myers silenced Zeph.

"Knight is Hayden Myer's oldest nephew," the guy reiterated.

"What Knight want? Retribution?"

The two men could tell by Zeph's question that he was finally picking up what they were lying down.

"There's a new drug. There are new alliances and new money to be made. You need to get away for a while and restructure."

"Without Monroe," the other guy added. "Monroe is not Shantell. The moment shit blows up, he will sell us all down the river."

"Us?"

"Yes," the first guy stated. "Us."

"You're supposed to be my partners? Why should I trust you? I don't even know who you are."

"Clean house, and then we will tell you who we are."

"Clean house?"

"Rebuild without Monroe," the second guy clarified.

"You make me sound like a bitch."

The guy chuckled. His lack of response spoke volumes.

His partner laughed, too.

Zeph grunted. He didn't like these guys, not one bit.

The light began to move away from Zeph. It was the first guy that was moving away. The second stood in place. Zeph looked in the direction that he thought he was standing. He heard his gun being unloaded, and then the sound of two things hitting the ground. "Thanks for my gun," Zeph stated sarcastically.

"Don't reach for it until I walk away," the second guy ordered.

"Like I can see it."

"You can't see a lot these days."

"Funny."

"But true."

"Who are you?"

"Still not important. At least not yet."

"How do I get in contact with you?"

"We will contact you."

The light the first guy was holding turned off. The second guy began moving in a different direction than the first guy. Zeph stood still as he listened to the leaves under the men's feet as they walked further away.

"Think of this like chess, Zephan," one of the two men called back to him. "Exploit the pawns to make way for bigger moves."

When they were far away from him, Zeph patted the ground, trying to find his gun. He located the two items. One was his gun, but the other, he thought was the clip, was actually a phone. *Damn, he kept my shells*, he thought as he stood back up. He slipped the gun on his hip and the phone into his pocket. In doing so, he felt the phone that Maria had given him.

As Zeph walked back to his car, he thought about Hayden Myers. That name triggered so many memories for him, and as those memories flooded his mind, Zeph had a clear idea of Knight's motives.

"Where you go?" Avie called to Zeph when he emerged from the darkness.

"Went to talk to my mother."

"You could have left the keys," Avie *lightly* snapped.

"Were you scared?"

Avie sucked her teeth.

"I was thinking," Zeph began. "You need to go to that meeting."

"What?"

"The meeting Rebecca called. Go to that meeting," he repeated.

"Why the change of heart?" she questioned. "Now that we've talked about it. It is dumb and childish. I don't need to be in a room of women that would likely snap because they think I'm some dyke that orchestrated a team of hoes." Avie shook her head, "No, thank you."

"It's more than that," Zeph stated.

Avie sat up in her seat. She looked Zeph in the face. She was looking for something in him and when she found it, she said, "Fine. I'll go."

Zeph nodded his head approvingly.

Avie sat back in her seat. As she buckled her seatbelt she stated, "I don't understand your change of heart."

Zeph put the car into drive. "You'll understand soon enough."

CHAPTER TWENTY-SEVEN

HE STARTED IT

MARCH 21, 2020

Monroe paced back and forth in front of the locker room. He didn't know what he was about to do. He just knew that he needed to do or say something. Lately, everything seemed as though it was out of his control.

His realty business was experiencing a massive shift in income. As fast as Jamilah purchased a house, she would flip two more in its place. She had a system that yielded more income than debt. Kelly still needed to learn this system and was now liable for two houses that needed to be renovated and flipped. He was beginning to rethink his idea of putting Kelly in the position. Monroe handled his wife's infidelity like a wounded man. All of his moves were based on emotion, and for that, he was hurting financially. He was also taking a financial hit regarding his business with Zeph.

Zeph told him that war was bad for business. Now that it was time to re-up, Monroe understood just how bad. Ideally, Zeph would re-up using the money he had earned from sales. However, the deaths of their foot soldiers meant a shortage of incoming funds, resulting in a deficiency with the re-up money. Monroe moved the capital from his legitimate businesses to cover the deficits. He was nervous about this move. He didn't want his accountants to ask questions that he didn't want to answer, even though he paid them to ask those exact questions.

And now, here he was about to defend the last thing he had control over—his basketball team. Since Bishop Carmichael participated in All-Star Weekend, the team's vibe had changed. He went from being just another player on the team to being stamped as official since he got to play with all the other official basketball greats. Meanwhile, their team captain, Monroe Whitaker, was on the sideline with them watching.

Monroe's response to his team's change in idolization didn't help the tension between him and Bishop. If he hadn't boxed Jamilah out of his life, Jamilah would have been with him during All-Star Weekend. He called himself punishing her by telling her she couldn't go with him, but his decision had bit him in the ass. If she had been there, Jamilah would have devised a strategy that would have helped Monroe maintain his leadership both on and off the court. His stubbornness had got the best of him, and now only his humility could salvage his poor judgment.

Monroe paced back and forth in front of the locker room doors. He was waiting on Bishop to walk out. Initially, he wanted to invite Bishop to dinner so the two could talk about everything, but he felt that would be weak. This whole coming to Bishop about his concerns already made him feel vulnerable.

Monroe stopped pacing. He looked at the locker room door. *What the fuck am I even doing?* He was about to turn and walk away when the locker room door opened. *Now or never*, he thought as he watched Bishop walk out.

"Bishop!" Monroe called to him.

Bishop glanced up from his phone. "What's up?"

"We need to talk."

"Oh, okay," Bishop replied. His eyes never left his phone. "Just text my girl and get her to set something up for us."

"Your girl?"

For the first time since the conversation began, Bishop looked at Monroe. "Kelly," Bishop replied. "Just set something up with her."

"Kelly's your girl?"

Bishop noted a particular look on Monroe' face. The sight amused him. "Oh, you ain't know?" he asked, and then resumed his gaze back into his phone.

"My assistant?"

"Yeah."

Monroe's jaw flinched. The suddenness of Bishop's bomb had caught him off guard, but what pissed him off the most was Bishop not making eye contact, like his phone was more important than respecting the man in front of him.

"Look at me when I'm talking to you," Monroe snapped.

Bishop looked up from his phone. A smirk slowly spread across his face. "What did you just say?"

"I'm trying to talk to you, and you're being disrespectful."

Bishop could hardly contain his laughter.

"Nig—"

Bishop immediately stopped laughing. "If you about to call me a nigga, then you damn sure ain't talking to me." Bishop slipped his phone into his pocket.

"Now that I got your attention."

"You sure do, Captain," Bishop replied, sarcastically.

Monroe flinched. Sarcasm was like a thorn in his side. He hated it from anyone, especially someone he viewed as beneath him. "As the captain of this team, when I am talking to you, you should respect me by giving me your undivided attention."

Bishop stared blankly at Monroe.

"On and off the court," Monroe added.

Bishop chuckled. "On and off the court, huh?" he questioned rhetorically. "Well, you have to earn my respect. I don't just give it, because somebody gave you a title."

"I've earned my dues. I have been with this team since going pro."

"What else have you done other than *being* with the team?" Bishop questioned. "You still ain't won a championship ring."

"I grind when I come in here," Monroe stated defensively. "There are a lot of factors that contribute to why we haven't gotten a championship."

"If you say so."

"I ain't trying to have a pissing match with you."

Bishop chuckled.

Monroe wanted to knock the shit out of Bishop, but that wasn't the purpose of pulling him to the side. Monroe wanted to set boundaries for Bishop to follow because he was getting out of line. "Listen," Monroe tried another approach. "I'm just trying to make some things clear to you."

"And what are those things?"

Bishop's arrogance had pushed Monroe over the top. "THIS IS MY TEAM!" Monroe shouted.

Bishop smirked.

Bishop's smirk only set off Monroe even more. "I opened my home to you to welcome you to the team. Did I not?"

Bishop appeared bored listening to Monroe continue on his rant.

"I wanted us to work together," Monroe stated. "That's why I did that, but you are—"

"I'm what?" Bishop dropped his bag to the floor.

"This right here," Monroe stated, pointing between the two of them. "You're creating a hostile environment, because you feel the need to attack my authority."

"Attack your authority?" Bishop repeated. "You're calling bullshit ass plays!"

"Plays that coach is telling me to call," Monroe shot back. "Are you saying I should go against coach?"

"It's a way to do things," Bishop replied. "If you are this team's captain, you have a voice. You can tell that man that running college plays in the NBA is stupid. You need to utilize players that have openings. Every play depends on you, and guess what? Four other men are on the court, and they're good."

"I do what's best for every—"

"Don't lie to me. I'm on the court with your ass, and the truth is—you don't. You're a selfish ball hog."

"I call the plays that coach sees fit!"

Bishop didn't even bother to reply.

Monroe looked around. He noted that their sudden outburst had grabbed the attention of some of the players near them, and this was not his intentions. "Look, I'm glad you're here," Monroe began. He was trying to ease the tension for the sake of *their* audience.

Bishop grunted. "Glad I'm on your team, right?"

Monroe cleared his throat and started his thought again, "I'm glad you're here. Your contribution to the team is proving to be valuable."

"But..."

"But you need to remember your place."

"Remember my place?" Bishop nodded his head like he was amused by Monroe's choice of words. "And tell me, what's my place?"

"You know your place. You're not stupid," Monroe stated. "You're doing the same shit you did in college, but I'm here to tell you that this ain't college."

"I can't tell by the plays."

"I'm not gonna let you come in and take over my team."

"Your team?"

"I didn't stutter."

Bishop nodded his head. "Is that it?"

"Is it your mission to make this a disrespectful conversation?"

"I asked you a simple question; is that it? Did you make your point?"

It took everything in Monroe not to steal Bishop in the face. Instead, he readjusted his bag on his shoulder and replied through clenched jaws, "Yeah...that's it."

Bishop picked up his bag. He turned his back and began to walk away. He glanced over his shoulder, "Good talk...Captain," he called to Monroe and then laughed.

The laughter triggered something in Monroe, who dropped his bag and began to follow behind Bishop. "What's funny?" he called to him.

"You," Bishop called over his shoulder as he continued walking away.

"What the fuck you say, nigga?"

Bishop stopped in his tracks. Something about the word *nigga*. Bishop turned around. "Did you just call me a nigga?" Bishop dropped his bag again and walked up to Monroe.

"You damn right. You laughin' and shit like a bitch."

"I was laughin' at yo' weak ass."

"What the fuck is your problem?" Monroe asked.

"My problem. I have no problems until you call yourself trying to check me."

"I ain't try to check shit," Monroe snapped. "All I said was, this my motherfuckin' team, and you need to fall in line."

Bishop chuckled again. "Or what?"

Monroe and Bishop stood face to face.

"HEY...FELLAS!" The head coach called out to Bishop and Monroe. He didn't know what was happening in this moment, but it didn't look good from his perspective. The coach knew the conversations around the locker room instigated tension between his two starting players. It had even created a great divide amongst the team. He tried to control it, but it was bound to come to something. "GUYS!" he called out to them again. "What's going on?"

Bishop threw his hands in the air. "I'm good, coach. I ain't got no problems with the team's mascot." Bishop laughed.

"Fuck you nigga!"

There goes that word again...Bishop stopped laughing and looked sternly at Monroe.

"You don't like being called a nigga, then stop acting like a nigga."

A smirk rested on Bishop's face. "I know what the problem is...you are losing control of everything, but I ain't to blame. You're just a weak bitch. This ain't your team. It's mine! And if I had a tolerance for loose pussy bitches that fuck her man's friend, then your wife would be mine, too."

Monroe couldn't believe his ears, but he heard what he heard, and it ignited something in him.

Monroe pushed Bishop and immediately followed with a right punch that landed and knocked Bishop back. Monroe wouldn't let up, though. Seeing Bishop stumble pumped his adrenaline. He needed to get all of his rage out. Monroe tackled Bishop and knocked him to the ground. He held Bishop down with one hand and proceeded to land punch after punch until somebody pulled Monroe off of Bishop.

Bishop wasn't out, though. He immediately jumped to his feet and stormed towards Monroe. With everyone holding Monroe back, Bishop used the opportunity to land several shots. He made Monroe his human punching bag, hitting him with all his might while simultaneously taunting him about his wife's infidelity.

The coach yelled, "GRAB BISHOP!"

Monroe's adrenaline had allowed him to eat Bishop's punches. He pressed forward through the crowd, trying to get at Bishop.

Finally, someone grabbed Bishop by the wrist, and the momentum shifted as the outsiders began to push Bishop away from Monroe.

"I'ma beat your ass!" Monroe yelled over the commotion.

"With Zeph beatin' ya wife, I guess you gotta try to beat something."

Monroe was furious. "You ain't shit but talk!"

"I can show you better than I can tell you," Bishop taunted.

"YOU TWO CUT IT OUT!" the silver-headed coach yelled. He was winded. Holding Monroe back reminded him of doing two a day in the gym.

Monroe and Bishop stared at each other silently. They were both fuming.

The coach exhaled loudly. "ALL OF YOU HEAR ME AND HEAR

ME GOOD!" he stated after finally catching his breath.

The brawl between Monroe and Bishop had provoked an impromptu team meeting in front of the locker room.

"We are all on the same damn team! Fuck what the networks are saying, fuck what your social media is saying. Fuck what you all are saying amongst yourselves," he paused to let his words sink in. "This is my got damn team! You hear me!" he hollered. "I call the got damn shots. I decide who plays, I decide who shoots, and I decide who sits! If you have a problem with that, you have a problem with me because this is my team. Not Monroe's and not Bishop's. You hear me?!"

Everyone in the crowd responded but Bishop and Monroe. The two men stared silently at each other, as they were being held apart by their teammates.

"You two!" the coach stated. "You fuckin' hear me."

Bishop nodded his head. "Yes sir," he replied, but his eyes were still glued to his opposition.

"I hear you," Monroe mumbled reluctantly.

"Monroe with me!" the coach stated as he pulled Monroe back towards his office. "You get out of here," he directed Bishop.

Monroe and Bishop never took their eyes off each other as the crowd began to push the two men in different directions. The coach may have ended their verbal conversation, but the two men were still talking, and they had come to one agreement.

This was far from over.

CHAPTER TWENTY-EIGHT

WORTH THE WAIT

MARCH 21, 2020

Zeph stood outside of his first home.

It was initially a house purchased by Shantell. She had brought the house right before Zeph was sent to jail. Shantell and Zeph had used her last residence as their headquarters, but this house would be different. This house would be their home. It was big enough for them to have their own space from each other. Zeph found it necessary, especially when Shantell's health became a concern. This house had enough room for them and a home-health nurse. They were close to closing on the house when Zeph was picked up on I-95. Shantell still moved into the house. She wrote Zeph and told him the house would be his safe haven when he returned home, but she died before he got out. In her last letter, she told him the house was his to keep. Of course, her Power of Attorney, Monroe, had a different plan in mind. In fact, this house was the first sign to Zeph that Monroe was loyal by proxy to him.

It was about time to put his plan into motion. He was just waiting on Avie to come through. She was supposed to meet with him by midnight. It was already eleven thirty at night and she still wasn't there. Truth be told, he didn't want her to come. He had learned his lesson at the cemetery, but Avie was adamant about being involved.

Zeph continued to look around when he saw a figure coming down the street. He could tell it was a woman, but he didn't know if it was *his* woman. He pulled up his hoodie, slipped his hands into his pocket, and gripped his pistol.

"Hey," they whispered when they got close to him.

It was Avie.

She was dressed in all black, too. She wore oversized clothes but still walked with a sway in her hips.

When she got closer, Zeph said, "You ready?"

She looked at him like a scared little girl, but she was ready for whatever.

"You know what you got to do, right?"

Avie nodded her head.

The two were about to start walking towards the beige house with white shutters and the well-manicured yard, but then Zeph grabbed Avie's arm and snatched her behind a car.

"What?!" she questioned, alarmed.

"Car coming," Zeph replied.

The two peered over the hood of a random park car and watched as bright halogen lights zoomed in their direction. As fast as it was going, one would have thought they would continue, but it didn't. It slowed up directly in front of their target—the beige house with the white shutters.

"I thought you said she was home?" Avie whispered.

"She is," Zeph replied. His eyes were still glued to the scene in front of him.

"Then who is that?"

Zeph didn't answer. He looked back at the scene that was unfolding in front of him.

Is it Monroe? he questioned himself. The bright halogen lights were attached to a big, black SUV with tinted windows. "It is," he mumbled to himself.

"It is what?"

"Monroe," he finally answered her.

Avie looked back at the scene in time to see a big, light-skinned guy get out of the truck. He, too, was dressed in all black. And noticeably carried a gun on his waist. "That's not Roe," Avie stated the obvious.

They watched as the driver walked to the rear passenger side back door. When he opened it, a tall, black woman got out. She wore a long ponytail, a short black dress, and thigh-high lime green and black stiletto boots.

As the girl walked to the front door, someone else exited the black truck, but Zeph didn't recognize him. The man walked to the door, following behind the girl. Another man then left the truck, and if he didn't know better, he would assume that the second guy had gotten out of the vehicle twice. The second guy had the same stature and complexion as the first, but Zeph couldn't determine who he was. He looked professional; maybe he was a lawyer or business guy.

"You know them?" Avie questioned.

"No."

"What do we need to do now?"

Zeph looked down at his watch. He looked back at the front door in time to see Kelly open it for her guests. From the look on her face, he felt like they were a surprise to her, just as they were a surprise to him. Zeph continued to watch closely. He noted how Kelly was hesitant about letting them into the house. Eventually, she opened her door wide enough for them to walk inside.

Zeph finally answered Avie. "We wait."

Zeph and Avie stayed sitting behind the parked car for an hour. Zeph moved from sitting to stooping on one knee when the front door opened.

"What the fuck?" he grumbled. He stared at the scene with a frown on his face.

"What's wrong?" Avie questioned. "Why do you look like that?"

"Nothing," Zeph quickly dismissed her.

"No," Avie grabbed his arm. "If I'm about to do this. I want to know what your facial expression is about."

Zeph looked between Avie and monitoring the three people leaving Kelly's house.

"Now," she stated.

"Look," he motioned with his head. "The girl is Deadria. She a jump Monroe be fuckin' around with. You're going to meet with her tomorrow."

"I am?"

"The meeting is tomorrow Avie, remember? With Rebecca?"

Avie nodded her head. "Right right right," she quickly stated as she looked at her watch. "Well, technically today I'm supposed to be meeting with them."

"It's midnight already?"

"Yeah."

Zeph looked down at his watch. "They're holding me up," he mumbled.

"Is that Bishop Carmichael?" Avie asked.

Zeph looked up from his watch to Bishop. "Yeah, that's him."

"I knew it!" she stated, excitedly.

Zeph looked at her.

"I don't know him like *that*."

"Um," Zeph hummed. He looked back at the trio, who had finally made their way into the black truck.

"I saw Jamilah in the house the other day."

Zeph looked at Avie. "You saw Jamilah?"

She nodded.

"At Roe house?"

Avie nodded again. "Yeah."

"Monroe was there?"

"Nope. She had a bag. I tried to speak to her, but she ignored the fuck out of me."

"Why were you there?"

"I have been there all week setting up meetings and taking calls. He about to barricade the whole damn house."

"Why he ain't got Kelly doing the shit?"

"I think they beefin'."

"Um," Zeph hummed.

"He doing all this because Jamilah fucked up his office. He don't think it was her though. I know it was her," Avie stated. "She ain't been staying there. Shit, after fuckin' that office up like that, I wouldn't stay there either." Avie shook her head. "Awards, furniture, computers…destroyed. Papers were everywhere."

Zeph hummed. He had had intentions of reaching out to Jamilah, but with everything going on, it slipped his mind. He took a mental note to call her after they handled tonight's business.

"I wonder where she's staying," Avie cut her eye at Zeph. "She ain't at the house," she reiterated.

Avie didn't know the extent of Zeph and Jamilah's relationship, but she could still recall images from the DVD she had watched of them. Jamilah and Zeph weren't just fuckin' around; they were making love. She wanted so bad to ask him about Jamilah and their relationship, but figured this wasn't the time.

Zeph wasn't paying her any attention anyway. His eyes were glued to the black truck that had just pulled up.

"I said, I wonder where she's staying," Avie couldn't resist and decided to ask again.

"Not with me," Zeph finally replied. "I haven't talked to her."

Avie wasn't paying attention to the scene in front of them. Zeph had her attention. "So, if she isn't with you, then where is she staying?"

"I don't have time to think about that."

"Well, I've been thinking…"

Zeph could hear Avie talking, but he wasn't listening. Her ramblings did remind him of the call he had gotten from Monroe the day his office was vandalized. Zeph chuckled to himself, thinking back on their phone call. "When Monroe found the office fucked up he called me on the phone in a panic." What started as a chuckle turned into a full laugh. "He thought the ops had broken in. The nigga think he is that damn important and shit."

"Wait, hear me out," Avie spoke over Zeph as he talked. "I think—"

"Monroe actin' like he Nino Brown and shit—"

"Jamilah wrote the letter."

"Talkin' 'bout he wanted the boys to guard his…" Zeph looked from the black truck to Avie. "What?!" he had finally processed what she had said to him.

Avie nodded. "Think about it. It makes sense. Why else would she randomly fuck up his office? 'Cause she found out about his hoe coalition."

"How do you know she did it?"

"Come on," Avie frowned. "Nobody running up in Roe office. You said yourself he thinks he important, but nobody even know Roe is affiliated. It has to be her."

Zeph shook his head. "Kelly wrote the letter."

"You say Kelly, I say Jamilah."

"If it was Jamilah that means she would know every—" Zeph's voice trailed off. *Does she know everything?* he questioned himself. *Why was she mad the other day?*

"What?" Avie stared at Zeph waiting for him to reply. His silence had set off her internal alarm again. "What?" she questioned, anxiously. "Stop doing that shit. You are scaring me. Just talk."

"Jamilah may know."

Avie's eyes shot wide. "So, she did write the letter then?" she stated, excitedly. Avie had become low-key obsessed with the letter. Everything about it had intrigued her. "What would be her point though?"

Zeph shook his head. "We just assuming."

"Seems like a pretty good-ass assumption to me."

Zeph cut his eyes at Avie. He thought back to the last time he was on the phone with Jamilah. She was yelling at the top of her lungs when he called. Naturally, he hung up, refusing to entertaain her tantrum. In this moment, he wished he would have listened to her.

"That means she wrote that shit about herself?" Avie smiled broadly. "That bitch is crazy. You got to be a lunatic to write about yourself. Wait, do I still go to the meeting?"

Zeph exhaled. Avie's question was a valid one. He just didn't have the right answer at the moment. "One thing at a time," he replied. "Look," he stated, turning their attention back to the task at hand. He and Avie watched as the driver looked around one last time, before entering the truck.

"You think they are coming back?" Avie questioned.

"I don't know, but they already got me an hour behind our plan," he stated, looking at his watch.

Avie suddenly tapped Zeph's arm excitedly. "She on the move."

They both watched as Kelly appeared to run to her car with a bag on her shoulder. She tossed the bag into the truck. She was about to hop into the driver's seat when she must have realized that she had forgotten something. Zeph and Avie watched Kelly rush back to the front door and let herself in.

"Come on." Zeph abruptly jumped from behind the car and jogged towards the front door.

Avie scrambled to her feet and closely followed behind him.

"Cover your face," he told her as he slipped on a black ski mask. He continued to the front door. Just as he arrived, the door opened.

Kelly wasn't paying attention. She was looking down at the bag in her hand. It was too late for her to react when she noticed the two ski mask figures.

Zeph hit her across the face and knocked her back into the house.

Kelly was out cold.

Zeph stepped over her body that lay sprawled out in the foyer.

Winded from their brief jog, Avie said, "So, who's picking her big ass up now?"

CHAPTER TWENTY-NINE

HE FINISHED IT
MARCH 22, 2020

Zeph stood at the entrance of the master bedroom door. He had used Kelly's facial recognition to gain access to her phone. He had scanned her pictures, her call log, her text messages, and all of her social media.

He was never a fan of smartphones. He thought they were too smart for their own good. At this moment, he was right. Zeph had learned everything about Kelly in less than thirty minutes by going through her phone. Still, it wasn't enough. Zeph wanted to know more. He wanted to know about tonight.

He walked over to the bed where Kelly was tied. He had gagged her mouth, just in case she came to and started screaming.

"What are we going to do with her?" Avie asked. She stood at the bedside, looking down at Kelly.

"Wake her up."

"I can't believe we got her big ass up here," Avie commented as she examined Kelly's body from head to toe. "Why didn't we tie her to the refrigerator?"

"Wake her up," Zeph ordered again.

"You hit her so hard."

"Aye," he called to Avie.

She stopped talking and looked at him.

Zeph took her rambling as a sign that she was nervous. "Breathe," he directed. "Stay focused and do what I said, please."

Avie nodded. She reached back and slapped Kelly across the face as hard as possible.

"Damn, you mad?"

"No, I just figured it took a hard hit to knock her big ass down, so it must take a hard hit to wake her big ass up."

Zeph shook his head.

"She deserved that hit anyway. This bitch was always rolling her eyes at me or making noises when I would talk to Monroe."

"They were fuckin'."

Avie gasped.

"You shocked?"

"I assumed, but…" her voice trailed off. "They were fuckin'?" Avie shook her head. "Monroe puts his dick in anything." A frown crossed her face. "She ugly." A few seconds later, Avie said, "She ain't really ugly," Avie glanced up at Zeph. "She got an ugly-ass attitude." Avie looked down at Kelly's body. "She got a bomb shape, but…that attitude, ugh…that's what makes her an ugly bitch to me."

Zeph stood by quietly, watching Avie go back and forth with herself about Kelly. As she spoke, he looked down at Kelly. He remembered the very first time he met her at Monroe's house. He didn't think Kelly was ugly. She had other characteristics that made him hesitant of her even before he found out her truth.

"You think she ugly?" Avie asked Zeph.

"No."

"You like big girls?"

Zeph nodded. "I like intelligent, go-getting women, and they come in all types."

"So, you date white girls?"

"No."

"But you would fuck a white girl."

"No, I wouldn't and I haven't."

Avie looked back down at Kelly. "Have you fucked Kelly?"

Zeph shook his head no.

"But you would, though."

Zeph silently stared at Avie. Even with a mask on she could tell that he wasn't about to entertain her line of questioning anymore.

"Hit her again," he stated.

"My pleasure," Avie replied.

She had started to reach for the heavens when Zeph said, "Not so hard."

Avie readjusted her stance and lightly tapped Kelly on the cheek.

Kelly looked at the two mask figures standing over her, and panic settled in her spirit. She tried to jump up, but then she realized that she was tied to the bed in a crucified position. Her hands were tied to each side of the headboard, and her feet were bound together and then secured to the footboard. Every time Kelly moved, she could feel the plastic ties cut into her flesh.

"It will only get worse, so just stop struggling," one of the masked individuals told her. She couldn't see her face, but she could tell it was a female talking to her.

Kelly attempted to yell, but her screaming was muffled by the cloth in her mouth.

"You done yet?" The other masked individual asked her. She looked over at the figure. She recognized the voice.

Zeph sat down on the bed beside Kelly. "Nod your head if you know who I am."

Kelly stared at him. If the voice didn't give him away, his eyes definitely did. Zeph had those dark, slanted eyes that were unforgettable.

Zeph pulled out the gun on his hip and sat it on his lap. He repeated his request, "Nod your head if you know who I am."

Kelly slowly nodded her head.

"I'm going to ask you a couple of questions, and you will answer me."

Kelly didn't respond.

"Nod your head if you understand."

Kelly gave herself a reminder and looked down at the gun on Zeph's lap. She looked back up at his eyes and slowly nodded her head again.

Zeph stood up from the bed and returned the gun to its holster.

Kelly watched him closely. As she was looking at him, she saw a flicker out of the corner of her eye. She looked around her room. She noticed that the candles she had strategically placed in her room for a romantic evening with Bishop were lit. There were two Champaign glasses, one on the nightstand to her left and the other on the nightstand to her right. She looked down at herself. She was no longer wearing the black sweatpants and white T-shirt she had on earlier. She was now dressed in one of her sexy, pink night robes. As she looked at her new attire, she noted how she was tied up. She couldn't see the details of the knots, but however they had her, she couldn't move, and when she did, the knot tightened.

"Take it out?" The other masked individual asked.

Kelly looked between the two figures. *Take what out?* she thought. *Why is Zeph doing this to me?*

"Yeah," Zeph replied.

Kelly cut her eye to the right side of the bed. *Zeph, you motherfucker!* she thought. She then looked from Zeph to the masked individual on the right. *If that is Zeph, then she has got to be Jamilah. They are paying me back for telling Monroe about them.*

As the individual on the right moved closer to her, Kelly slammed her eyes shut; she didn't want to see what would happen to her.

Her eyes shot open when the gag in her mouth was forcibly ripped out of her mouth. The aggressive act left Kelly's mouth throbbing. She groaned in pain.

"You get loud, and you will regret it," Zeph warned.

Kelly clenched her jaw and narrowed her eyes. *Moe gon'na kill this nigga,* she thought. *He picked the right one today.*

"I know who you are. I know who your daddy is. I just want to know why."

"Why what?"

"Why did you write the letter?" Avie interjected.

"The letter is child's play," Zeph stated. "I don't give a shit about a letter."

"I just wanted to test my theory," Avie stated.

Kelly sighed. "I'm tired of hearing about a fuckin' letter. I ain't write no damn letter."

"And that means I was right!"

"Fuck all that," Zeph stated, dismissively. "I want to know what your father has planned."

"What my father has planned?" Kelly repeated. "My father doesn't have anything planned right now. Doing this type of shit will have him planning something."

"I like threats."

"Look what your doing," Kelly tried to snatch her arm, but the stinging in her wrist immediately stopped her attempt.

"Tell me everything."

Seeing the gun, now, gripped in Zeph's hand inspired Kelly to talk. "My name is Aneesa Wells. I am the daughter of Morris Wells. About a year ago, I left D.C. and moved to N.C. because I didn't want anything to do with my father and his legacy. I changed my name, I moved here—"

"You already said that."

Kelly looked over at the other masked individual. *That's not Jamilah. This girl sounds too young and immature to be Jamilah.*

"Why is he here?"

"He's not here, but he's coming here to build a relationship with me."

"Why are you lying?" Zeph asked.

"I'm not. Moe is still in D.C. in court."

"You call your daddy Moe?" Avie asked.

"That's his name," Kelly snapped.

"Bitch—"

"Chill," Zeph stated, silencing the bickering. "Why are you working for Monroe? What's your angle?"

Kelly frowned. "It's a good opportunity. He is a famous basketball player with connections."

Avie sucked her teeth. "So, you'a gold digger?"

Kelly looked over at the female. "Who are you?" Kelly looked at Zeph, "Who the fuck is this irrelevant person?"

"You're talking a lot of shit to be tied up," Avie replied.

"Then un-fuckin'-tie me and see how much shit I talk then," Kelly snapped back.

"CHILL!" Zeph yelled over them again.

"I'm not a gold digger," Kelly reasserted her truth. "I am so tired of people saying that to me."

"If many people say it, maybe it's true," Avie stated matter-of-factly.

"Look, I'm not bragging because I didn't want that lifestyle, but let's be ever-so-clear; I don't have to be a gold digger. My father is an over-provider, honey. I didn't have to ask for anything. Everything I have acquired since I left home, I have earned. I went back to school, and I studied for those tests. Monroe didn't just put me in charge of his business for shits and giggles. I am really qualified because I put in the work."

"Are you really giving speeches at a time like this?" Avie questioned.

"Whatever bitch, I'm not a gold digger."

"We both know you got hush money," Zeph interjected.

Kelly tried to snatch out of her restraints again. "Y'all are irritating," she stated. "Let me go."

"Cut it out," Avie shook her head. "You are pathetic. Ever since the first day I met you."

Kelly stopped struggling. She looked at the figure to her left. "Avie," she stated with a laugh. "You are fuckin' childish-ass, Avie. I should have known. What's your fuckin' angle, bitch?"

"I don't have an angle, bitch. That's you. You sneaky cunt."

"Sneaky?"

"CHILL!"

Both Avie and Kelly looked at Zeph.

"Why were Bishop and Deadria here?"

Kelly sighed.

Zeph took the safety off the gun.

Kelly shook her head. "I don't want to die, but they scare me more than you and a gun."

Zeph didn't respond. He expected Kelly to cry, plead, and holler, but she silently shook her head from side to side.

"You really are that scared of them?" Zeph concluded. "Why? She a hoe, and he a basketball player." Zeph laughed. He pulled the hammer back on his gun. "You afraid of them, but not this mauthafuckin' lead I'm 'bout to pump you with." Zeph looked across the bed at Avie. "You believe this shit?" he asked her rhetorically. He looked down at Kelly. "I will kill you," he stated calmly.

Avie laughed. "Do it," she stated, playing along with Zeph's performance. "This bitch stupid, anyway."

"It's not them per se I am scared of," Kelly admitted. "It's their brother."

"Their brother?" Zeph repeated. "Deadria and Bishop are siblings?"

"Yes," Kelly replied. "They are brother and sister."

Zeph moved the hammer forward and took his finger off of the trigger.

"Her real name is Queen, not Deadria," Kelly stated.

"Monroe is fucking Bishop's sister?" Zeph shook his head. "What is this? Payback for you and Bishop fuckin'?"

"No, you got it all wrong!" Kelly exclaimed.

Zeph replied, "Then make it make sense."

"That bitch drawing this shit out," Avie commented.

"I'M NOT!" Kelly yelled. "I am telling you the truth. I'm not dating Bishop—"

"But you did fuck him," Zeph held up Kelly's phone.

Kelly laid her head back between her shoulders. She then looked back at Zeph. "I fell in love with my captor," she declared.

"Captor?"

"Bishop is blackmailing me for his brother."

"Who is his brother?"

"Knight."

Had Zeph had his mask off, Kelly would have seen the look of confusion plastered on his face. He thought of the conversation he had with the men in the cemetery. "Moe ain't my competition," he spoke more to himself than the women in the room. "Knight is Bishop Carmichael's brother?"

Kelly nodded her head.

Avie looked at Zeph. She didn't know what the hell was going on, but she felt an eerie feeling fall over her. "We need to get ready to go," she told Zeph.

"And Deadria is their sister." Zeph chuckled. "Was Knight with them tonight?"

Kelly nodded her head. "They were all here tonight."

Zeph's jaw clenched. It pissed him off to see how his empire had been infiltrated on so many levels due to his business partner thinking with his dick.

Avie touched Zeph's arm.

Zeph glanced over at Avie. "I heard you," he acknowledged her. His response was snippy.

Avie stepped back, having read Zeph's disposition.

"I swear to you that the job with Monroe wasn't some well-thought-out plan. It was simply a come-up for my professional life. I was working with the Moons, for Christ's sake. I was a regular-ass person until Bishop came into my life."

"And how did he come into your life?"

"I met him through Monroe."

"Monroe hooked y'all up?"

"No. Jamilah hooked me up with Bishop on some matchmaking shit."

"Jamilah?"

Avie hummed loudly. "Jamilah orchestrated all of this."

Zeph looked at Avie. If she had her mask off, then he would have seen her I-told-you-so face.

"Another sneaky bitch," Avie commented.

"Jamilah knows who Knight is?"

"I don't know. It's possible. They all knew each other in college."

"Bishop went to college with Monroe?"

"And Jamilah," Kelly added.

"Do Monroe know that Deadria and Bishop are siblings?"

"No. Honestly, I just found out tonight. I knew Deadria as one of the teammates, but I didn't know she was undercover and related to Bishop and Knight."

"So, you meet this man and suddenly start snitching to him about their business?" Avie questioned rhetorically. "Loyalty is just as dead as chivalry."

"Bishop blackmailed me! I wasn't disloyal for the hell of it." Kelly explained. "Bishop said that he would expose me."

"Expose you about what?"

Kelly looked at Zeph. "My father is a known drug dealer, currently on trial. Bishop would have told everyone who I was and who I was related to, and you know this community. You know they wouldn't have accepted me knowing that shit."

"What does Knight want with Monroe?"

"He wanted to know about the drug business. I didn't even believe that Monroe was a kingpin."

Avie chuckled. "Monroe ain't no damn kingpin."

"What have you told them?" Zeph asked.

"I told them about the trailers. That's all I knew about."

"Knight took my shipment?"

"I guess. I just brought Bishop the information. I don't know how he used it. I didn't really care. I was just trying to buy my freedom."

"You didn't care," Zeph shook his head. "You know how many people died because you were out here running your mouth, not caring."

"I didn't do it spitefully," Kelly explained. "I just wanted to be left alone. I never wanted to be a part of this life."

"Sins of our fathers," Zeph replied coldly. He stared down at Kelly in disgust. Kelly mentioning the freight like it was something minute pissed him off. He had lost millions off of that power move. "Where are the trailers now?"

"I don't know. They were talking about Fairview County. Maybe that is where they are."

"Why were they here tonight?"

"Because I had been ducking Bishop. He wanted more information, and I didn't have it. I barely had what I gave him."

"So you were going to skip town?"

"Yes," Kelly whispered her truth.

For the first time since they started talking, Kelly showed fear. "I just want out of all this shit."

Avie was over the dramatics. "We definitely know now she ain't write no letter."

"FUCK THAT LETTER!" Kelly shouted.

"SEE BITCH! I WAS ON YOUR SIDE!" Avie yelled back. "I DIDN'T EVEN COME AT YOU LIKE THAT!"

"NO!" Kelly shouted back. "Between you and Deadria. I don't know shit about a fuckin' letter, but y'all keep blaming me like I'm out here starting shit and I'm not. Keep talkin' about a meeting. I DON'T KNOW SHIT ABOUT A MEETING!" Kelly shouted at the top of her lungs. "I hate I took this fuckin' job."

Avie folded her arms across her chest. "All money ain't good money, huh?" she taunted.

"I didn't write no letter!" Kelly cried. "I swear."

"I told you, I don't give a fuck about a letter," Zeph stated.

Zeph had been quiet through Kelly and Avie's back and forth. Kelly never noticed that he had his gun pointed at her again. She was about to react to the sight of the gun, but without hesitation, Zeph pulled the trigger and shot her between the eyes.

The sound of the gun startled Avie and she gasped loudly.

Zeph looked at her. She stood frozen with her mouth open. Her eyes were glued to the scene.

With Kelly's arms still tied to the bed, her head had fallen back between her shoulders. She looked asleep, but the splatter of blood on the headboard proved otherwise.

Avie pulled her glare from the bed. She looked at Zeph. He had a tall stature that never intimidated her, but it did at this moment. She watched how casually he slipped his gun back on his hip as though he didn't just take someone's life. He turned and walked out of the room.

"You just gonna leave her like this?"

"Yes," he replied over his shoulder. He walked out of the room with a *normal* stride. Zeph was clearly unbothered by his actions.

Avie, on the other hand, was frozen. She looked back at Kelly's dead body. She couldn't believe it. She watched the bed absorb her blood. She thought Zeph was just talking, trying to scare Kelly. Avie never thought he would go through with his threat.

"COME ON!" Zeph hollered from downstairs.

Avie moved towards the door. The shell casing on the floor caught her attention. She picked it up and pocketed it. She was about to rush out of the room but stopped to take in another look at the gruesome sight. She pulled out her phone and snapped a photo of the horrific scene.

Just in case, she told herself before walking out.

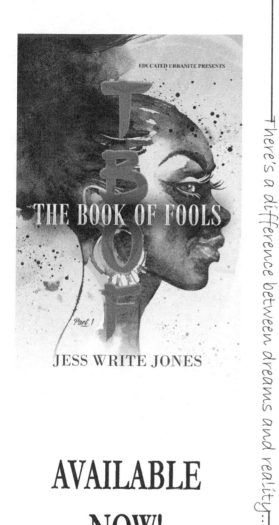

ABOUT THE AUTHOR

Picture it, Jess Write Jones, with a collection of Barbie dolls stored in a pink and white, travel-size trunk. At fourteen (Yes! I was still playing with Barbie dolls at that age), I tried to get my older cousins to play with me. The oldest, nineteen at the time, refused. The second oldest, who was fifteen then, came up with this bright idea to (and I quote) "Let's play Barbies on paper." Honey, when I say that one-liner changed my whole life! I have been writing ever since and truthfully, between me, you, and God when I tell you I'm writing…I'm really playing Barbies on paper.

After receiving a BA in English from NC Wesleyan College, I started my own publishing company, Educated Urbanite. It has always been a goal to publish my writings. This is my third novel and God willing, I plan to publish more!

I currently reside in Virginia—757 to be exact.

<u>ACKNOWLEDGMENTS</u>

GOD.

MY TEAM OF ANCESTORS.

ME.

MY PARENTS.

ME.

MY INNER CIRCLE.

ME.

(In that order.)

STAY CONNECTED!

iJessWrite.com

EDUCATED URBANITE PRESENTS

T
B
O
F

THE BOOK OF FOOLS

Part 1

JESS WRITE JONES

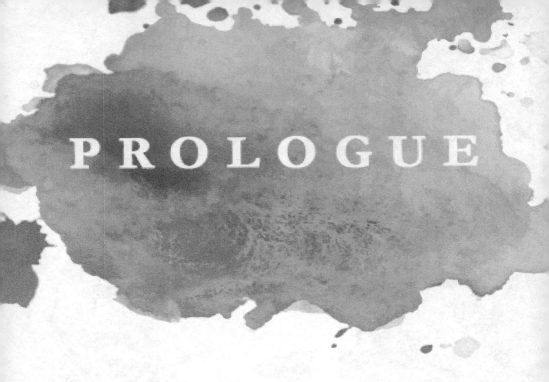

PROLOGUE

Ryan walked into the house and looked at the little boy in the middle of the living room floor. Toys were scattered everywhere, and if it hadn't been for Ryan's keen eyesight, he wouldn't have noticed the boy.

"Hey boy," he called to him, "cut that damn TV down."

The four-year-old boy glanced at Ryan and then turned back to the television.

Ryan watched the little boy pull his arms inside his stripped blue and yellow t-shirt, "Where is your grandmother?"

The little boy quickly slipped his arms out of his shirt, "Her gone." He looked at Ryan and then at the television just in time to see *Spongebob Squarepants* dance across the screen.

Ryan walked into the bedroom across from the living room. It was clean and quiet. In fact, it was too clean and quiet. Almost seemed like it didn't have an occupant, but Ryan knew all too well whose room it was. He immediately walked out. Even with the occupant not in the house, Ryan felt odd standing in her room. Perhaps he could feel her hatred for him even when she wasn't in the room. The eerie feeling made him walk out of the bedroom immediately. He continued down the hallway, passing the family pictures hung neatly on the walls. At the very end of the hallway was a room on the right. Ryan stopped in front of the closed door. He paused for a moment, contemplating whether he should walk in. Before he could change his mind, without knocking, Ryan walked into the room.

The lights were off. The room would have been pitch-black if it wasn't for the sunshine peeking from behind the blinds. The room's occupant attempted to block out the remaining light with black curtains, but it still made its way in. Ryan pushed the door shut, but it didn't close. He glanced back at the cracked door, giving it another push to completely close it. He turned his attention to the body, hibernating under the bedroom covers. Ryan nudged the body, and a slim, brown skin female with long hair emerged from under the covers. A sneaky smirk crept onto her face as she looked at Ryan with lust-filled eyes.

Ryan sat down at the foot of the bed.

The woman was happy to see him. She tossed off the covers and jumped on his back, pressing her body against his back. "Hey baby," she stated, wrapping her arms tightly around his shoulders.

He shrugged out of her grasp and replied sourly, "You cook?"

"I wasn't expecting you this early."

"I told you I was coming."

"And—" she began mumbling her explanation. She regained her confidence in the middle of her speech. "But I remember asking you to call before you came here."

"When ya' mother gonna be home?"

"She at work. You'll be gone by the time she gets home," she stated, rolling her eyes.

The small bedroom went quiet, and they could hear the cartoons blaring from the television in the living room.

Ryan stood to his feet and removed his jacket. He threw it on a chair full of clothes next to a dresser. The zipper from his coat hit the mirror and made a loud noise.

"Don't break my shit nigga," she snapped at him. She wasn't *really* mad, but snapping at him over something so minute leveled the playing field just in case he had an attitude about her not having cooked. Now she had an attitude about him *almost* breaking her shit.

But Ryan wasn't fazed. He knew her too well and dismissed her *attitude* with a simple glare.

"I'm just sayin…" she mumbled. "Be careful."

The two of them fought all of the time. It's how their relationship worked. They fucked hard, and then they fought harder. Despite the circumstances under which they met; she loved spending time with Ryan. Unfortunately, she couldn't openly express her love for him. Too many factors were at play that limited their ability to be together.

Ryan stood by the bed. The previously laid-back, nonchalant male became aggressive. He snatched the girl up to her knees, revealing her wardrobe of old, oversized T-shirt and grey sweatpants. He began tugging and pulling at her clothes, demanding without words that she be naked now! Caught up in the moment, she gave in to his non-verbal aggression and immediately began helping him remove her clothes. Once disrobed, he pulled her naked body to his, holding her tight while tonguing her down. His grip on her ass was hard, and she could tell he wanted her just as much as she wanted him. His anticipation showed through his fingers and tongue that circled clockwise and counterclockwise around her areola. In one swift move, he devoured her nipple into his mouth.

Her body became weak and flooded from his actions.

She grabbed the back of his neck, finally feeling his soft, freshly cut hair. The more she stroked his soft hair, the more aggressive and assertive he became with her nipple—the more turned-on she became. They were night and day lovers. She wanted soft and sensual affection; he just wanted a nut.

She knew this about him. His actions made it obvious where he stood when it came to her, but she was determined to win him over with her pussy. It was a challenge, and her aggression level had risen. She wanted to please him as badly as she wanted to be pleased *by* him on all fronts; physically, mentally, emotionally, and publicly. She kissed his lips while pulling up his white t-shirt. He assisted in taking it off, and she ran her hands across his chest. He pulled her close to him, both chest to chest, her damp nipples staining his skin.

He pulled away from her and admired her body being kissed by the sun that peeked through the bent blinds in her room. She pulled his body to hers. The two were passionately kissing on each other's lips and tongues as she pulled out his manhood. She massaged his shaft as the two stood making out. She took control, showing her experience, and pulled him onto the bed. He repositioned himself on the bed, and she maneuvered his pants and boxers down to his knees. Still on her knees, she bent closer to his manhood, took him in her mouth, and tasted his bittersweet juice on the tip of her tongue. He moaned as though the suddenness of his body being consumed caught him off guard. She licked around the head and down the shaft until being teased became too much for him. He grabbed her head and guided her mouth up and down his dick. He let go of her head once the routine was established, and he, high on enjoyment, let his moans ring out. She was turned on by his heavy breathing and light curse words used to describe his moment.

"Try to take it all," he whispered to her.

She attempted.

He laughed at her failure.

She twisted and sucked his dick until his laughter was replaced with, "Do you have any teeth, shit?"

Nibbling on the head of his dick, his legs tensed up until he finally stopped her. He got off the bed and began to slide out of his shoes. His pants and boxers dropped to the wooden floor beneath his feet.

Ryan positioned her on her hands and knees. He got close to her and guided himself into her wetness. He inserted himself and pulled out, unable to enjoy it all at the first entrance. Afraid he might nut before his roller coaster ride took off, he slapped her damp pussy with his dick and reentered. He grabbed her by the hips to control the situation; however, she was stubborn and refused to let any man control her—not even during sex. He joined in, catching her rhythm and spot simultaneously, resulting in her squirting out her pleasure. Turned on by accomplishing such a feat, he began to speed up their motion on a new beat, breaking her stance into a *lazy* dog, her face smothered in the covers with her behind raised high in the air. He pulled out and flipped her on her back by her ankles. He positioned himself on top of her, asserting his dominance. Aside from other reasons, this is why the two could never be together. She didn't know how to let him lead, but now he was prepared to show her. Staring at her as he forcefully pushed himself inside, he liked watching her squirm under his control.

"Don't stop," she demanded, "I'm about to cum."

"No, you not," he stopped stroking and began teasing her like she had teased him.

He sucked on her breast.

Frustrated, she attempted to push him off of her, but his strength overpowered her, and he held her down by her wrists and continued to play with her nipples in his mouth.

She fought with him, but he held her wrists tighter in place.

"You ain't stronger than me," he told her, "I will beat this pussy up when I'm ready."

She stopped fighting him, and he reentered her moisture. She grabbed his forearms and squeezed them tightly as she squirted out her pleasure again. He continued providing her with his massive manhood, folding her into positions. He pulled out and turned her over by her ankles. She had regained her energy and began controlling the situation, bouncing back at him on her own beat. He took back control and broke her down until he finally squirted out his enjoyment on her butt.

Feeling freaky, she smeared his semen into her skin and licked it off her fingers.

He watched, pleased at his accomplishments. He sat down and then laid back on the bed, attempting to regain his composure. The sunlight began to dance on both of their bodies.

Against the hardwood floor, Ryan's phone, in his pants pocket, vibrated loudly. He sat up and grabbed his jeans from the floor. He looked at his phone and slid it back into his pants pocket. He stared off into the pile of clothes stacked by the wall.

She draped her body over his shoulders like before.

And, like early, he moved away from her grasp. He stood up and began to redress himself.

She sat back on the bed and watched him closely, "You have to leave already?"

"That's what I'm doing, ain't it?"

"Why you can't stay longer?"

No response.

She smacked her mouth, disappointed at how she was used for her pussy *again*.

"Your mother will be home soon anyway," he reminded her.

She rolled her eyes. Her mouth still twisted, showing her frustrations.

In her mind, pussy was supposed to keep him in place. That is why they lasted for so many years. The more she thought about it, the more she realized she was used to the drive-by dick sessions they shared. But just like the other times, this one bothered her.

Ryan grabbed his jacket from the chair and put it on.

He walked to the cracked door and opened it wider. He looked back at the brown skin girl pouting with her legs crossed at the foot of the bed, "Stop acting like that, Rachel," he called to her. "Get dress and cook so that boy can eat."

"Which boy?" she asked, "You or him?"

"Funny," he replied. Ryan walked out of the room. He turned around to pull the door shut when he noticed the boy sitting by the bedroom door.

The boy looked up at him silently.

"Why are you sitting here?" he asked, shutting the bedroom door behind him.

The little boy hunched his shoulders.

"Go back in the living room and watch TV. She's sleep," he lied.

The little boy didn't move.

"Badass," Ryan mumbled as he continued down the hallway. He paused at the front door and readjusted his clothes.

"Bye, Uncle Ryan."

Ryan looked down the hallway at the boy, "Later."

Ryan was about to walk out of the house when he caught a glance of himself in the hall mirror hanging by the front door. He will become a changed, faithful man in a couple of days. Ryan walked closer to the hall mirror and looked at himself. He slipped into thought, and then he shut the front door. He walked back to the bedroom at the end of the hallway.

"Go sit in the living room." His voice boomed in the little boy's direction, causing him to jump and scurry down the hallway. When Ryan saw him disappear into the living room, he opened the door and walked in. He shut the door behind him while looking at the slim, brown-skinned girl standing butt-naked in the middle of the room.

The suddenness of the bedroom door slamming behind Ryan startled her. "What did you leave?"

"Look, Rachel, I'm about to marry your sister, and this shit between me and you gotta stop. It should have never happened then and damn sure not today, but—" Ryan stated, trying not to make the situation hot, "I just got caught up."

Rachel folded her arms across her chest. A smirk resting on her face. "Really?" she called his bluff. "You don't want to end this. You just want to ensure that I don't do or say anything to blow your game."

Ryan frowned at her assumption. "Nah, it ain't even that."

Rachel fanned Ryan's words away, "Whatever nigga. You like all the rest, and if my sister wasn't dumb, stupid, or deaf, she would not even be thinking about walking down no church aisle with your ass. She wouldn't even want to walk down a damn grocery aisle with you."

Ryan clenched his jaws. He wanted badly to tell Rachel she won't shit, but if he pissed her off, she would call and tell her sister everything before he could pull out of the driveway. Instead, he remained calm and said, "Think what you want to think, but I just know I can't do this again," he stated, pointing between them.

"She's that important to you?" Rachel couldn't understand why everyone always seemed to favor her twin sister more than her.

Ryan instantly knew it was time for him to leave, but he continued to stand there listening to Rachel. He didn't want to make her erupt. He could now hear the jealousy that he always knew existed within her.

"You're just going to walk away from me without a second thought?"

"Without a second thought," he stated before leaving the room. He shut the door behind him.

"FUCK YOU, RYAN!" Rachel yelled from the other side of the door, "FUCK EVERYTHING YOU ABOUT, RYAN. YOU AIN'T SHIT AND WILL NEVER BE SHIT!"

Ryan continued down the hallway. He stopped by the mirror on the wall. Although an attractive man, Ryan stared at himself with disgust. He took a deep breath and exhaled slowly. Ryan looked at the opposite wall, where family portraits hung. He focused on a picture of two little girls. He moved away from the mirror and walked closer to the image.

The two little girls looked like twin baby dolls in white and yellow dresses. Ryan gently ran his finger across the image of one of the twin girls. *We are going through bad times right now, but I will get you out of this damn house. We gonna get married, and we gonna live happily ever after*, he thought. *I'm gonna do right by you because you deserve that from me. God, please allow me to get over this dark moment in my life. You gave me a good woman. Please don't let me lose her because I didn't realize what I have; in Jesus' name, I pray, Amen.*

Ryan opened the front door and walked out of the house. He felt like he had been born again, cleansed by the sun that shined on him.

Made in the USA
Monee, IL
14 March 2024

55077220R00174